THE MOST IMPORTANT RULE

ZOMBIE RULES BOOK 9

BY DAVID ACHORD

THE MOST IMPORTANT RULE

WWW.SEVEREDPRESS.COM

ISBN: 978-1-923165-28-1

JOURNAL ENTRY: JULY 4TH, 10 A.Z.

July 4th, a special day for the United States, and a great excuse for the members of Mount Weather to throw a party. It was a family affair until twenty-hundred hours, that's when the younger kids were herded into the theater room to watch movies. The teenagers had their own thing going and the adults commandeered the party room where they could imbibe in homemade wine and other things. I chose to go with the kids. Once the movie started, I found a spot in the back and booted up my laptop.

I'm so busy these days I seldom have time to update my personal journal and there are times I wonder why I work on it anymore. When I first started it, I thought it might possibly one day become a historical document which, years from now, would provide insight to people who wanted to know how their ancestors survived the apocalypse.

Here at Mount Weather, we have a supercomputer located deep within the bowels of the bunker. Reports are written about everything and stored on the computer's hard drive. I know those reports will be the true documents historians will refer to, which I guess would make my personal journal unnecessary. Even so, I cannot and will not give up on it. It's important to me, and I hope it will be something my grandchildren and great grandchildren will revere.

So, let me recap the activities of the past few months –

First and foremost, my family. Kelly, my wife, is still the most wonderful woman I've ever known, and I love her more and more every day. Frederick, Macie, and Hardy are the joys of my life. They're growing like weeds, they're healthy, smart, vibrant, and full of life. Kelly is almost totally responsible for this. We've talked about perhaps having another child and decided to let nature take its course. If it happens, it happens.

Now, on to Mount Weather. After the suicide of President Gilbert VanAllen, I was formally requested to return to Mount Weather. The decision was not an easy one to make. Personally, I loved Oak Ridge, as did my family. The community was tightknit, and the place was run like a well-oiled machine. It was a positive environment, and I learned a lot from the engineers and scientists who lived there.

But duty called, and so, on a freezing cold morning in February, I packed up my family and moved back home. Almost the entire population of Mount Weather was at the front gate awaiting our arrival. Our newly elected president, Robert Clark Duckworth Junior, was leading the cheers. With his arm draped across my shoulders, he announced to the crowd that I was immediately being reinstated as the Director of Operations.

My first task as DO was to help with the President's State of the Union address. We decided on a basic, honest presentation of past events, an assessment of the current state of affairs, and then delineate goals to be achieved in order to preserve our future.

Although all of this information is on record in great detail within the Mount Weather reports, for the sake of my journal I'll summarize the state of affairs and the ongoing activities for the past few months.

1. The winter of year ten was normal, nothing unusual, until February. A powerful cold front, commonly known as an Arctic blast, swept across the northeastern United States and most of Canada. The entire month was beset with freezing temperatures; single digits during the day and below zero at night. We lost a fair number of livestock, which put a strain on our meat and dairy production. Our animal husbandry peeps put in a lot of hours ensuring every female livestock we had was properly impregnated. A lot of jokes were made at their expense, but they've been invaluable to our survival. On a sidenote, a family of eight who lived in a nearby farm died of carbon monoxide poisoning due to a clogged flue in their home.
2. The cold blast also put an enormous strain on our electrical grid. Our power crew was severely overworked. There has been an attempt to recruit apprentices for them, but so far, we've only gotten two.
3. An unintended consequence of the bitter cold February, several of the women are pregnant. Even Kelly. There was a time during this terrible apocalypse when it was risky for a woman to become pregnant. While there are still concerns, the rest of the expectant fathers and I are ecstatic.
4. On the same day the president re-appointed me Director of Operations, he issued an executive order appointing Liam and Logan O'Malley United States Marshals. Now, they officially and legally have jurisdiction over the entire United States.
5. The Marcus Hook trading post officially opened on April 1st. It has been moderately successful, but not without issues. The Fitzgerald family, along with Johnny G and Roscoe,

thought prostitutes and drugs would be an excellent trading commodity. Perhaps it is, but there is a large contingent of Amish and Mennonites in Pennsylvania. Needless to say, they were appalled by this. Also, the attempt to reintroduce the dollar was a dismal failure. People were only interested in barter as a means of exchange. It did not help that Roscoe and Johnny G declined the request to sell diesel for cash. They also chose barter. Even so, it has been agreed by consensus that the trading post will be open year-round. Trade and commerce are important aspects of civilization, and it is hoped that this will pave the way to more business ventures.

6. Trader Joe Fitzgerald agreed to conduct a census of all trading post attendees. The numbers were about what we had expected and closely align with the population models that the late Parvis Anderson created, with the help of the Mount Weather supercomputer. The surprising part of the census was the number of Mennonite survivors. Back before, there were approximately 180,000 Mennonites and Amish living in Pennsylvania. Although their numbers had been decimated, there was still a sizeable number, approximately 5,000.
7. We have agreed to work on route 322, which is the major roadway beside the trading post. This includes the Commodore Barry Bridge, which is showing signs of age and erosion.
8. The late Rochelle and Gilbert VanAllen – it's difficult to measure the amount of damage caused by these two. Their personalities caused strife and divisiveness in the Mount Weather community. Rochelle's assassination may have prevented her from ruining everything, which she most certainly would have, but there was collateral damage; tangential things that will take a long time to repair.
9. Who murdered Rochelle and her entourage? The silent consensus points toward the Fitzgerald family. There is no physical proof, nor any eyewitnesses. Only circumstantial evidence. The question is, why? Why did they do it? We may never know. Also, we may never be able to successfully prosecute them, but this is another aspect of the aforementioned collateral damage. The Fitzgeralds are now regarded with suspicion. And since Johnny G is Riley's

lover, he too is regarded with distrust. How will this all play out? I don't yet know. Personally, I'm conflicted. I like the Fitzgerald family. I like Johnny G. I think the death of Rochelle VanAllen was probably a good thing.

10. Fort Detrick – I've mentioned in a previous journal entry that I'd had recurring dreams of Patient Eve. When the weather cleared, I paid a visit to Fort Detrick and fulfilled the request made by her in the dreams. In short, I took a torch and cut open the doors to the lab that had been sealed off. Since then, there has been no zed attacks and I've had no further dreams involving her. We've conducted surveillance, but there's not much to report. They send out hunting parties, but all they hunt are animals.
11. Along with our own numbers, the birthrate continues to improve. I believe this is due to several factors. One unintended consequence of the apocalypse is the quality of the food. Our food products are no longer contaminated with preservatives, pesticides, steroids, or other additives. We are eating healthier than ever. In addition, with the exception of some hot zones, pollution is significantly lower. Physical exams are mandatory. If someone exhibits an illness of any kind, it is addressed immediately, and that includes quarantine. And finally, there are no abortions being performed. There are, and always will be, instances of a child being born that is not wanted by either parent. Our remedy to that is to let it be known that Mount Weather will take the child, no questions asked. Marcus Hook and Oak Ridge also have this policy. Human lives are so precious these days after all.

We have made progress. We can only pray that there will not be another virus outbreak, or a natural catastrophe. A major earthquake, volcano eruption, hell, even a large meteor strike could finally succeed in killing off the human race. But we must not give up.

CHAPTER 1 - ZACH & THE MCCOYS

I awoke before sunup, as usual, got cleaned up, kissed my sleeping wife and kids, and headed to the cafeteria. Breakfast time was delayed due to last night's July Fourth celebration party, so there wasn't even any kitchen staff working. I found some oranges, grabbed a couple, and headed outside.

It'd been hot for several weeks, but a front moved in late last night, bringing rain and dropping the temperature. As a result, the morning was shrouded in a thick, pea soup fog. Great weather to go on a ride.

I went to the barn and chose a big gentle gelding named Blinky. He was well trained, thanks to Fred, and didn't spook easily. I gave his back a quick brush before saddling him and walked out of the main gate ten minutes later. Zoe, my German Shepherd, spotted me and happily followed along. The lone guard at the main gate came outside as I walked up. His name was Reese. He and his small group of people joined Mount Weather a couple of weeks ago. He was young, maybe around seventeen or eighteen, skinny, with shoulder length brown hair he had tied back. He was clean though, indicating he showered before coming on duty, and he didn't look hungover.

"Good morning," he greeted.

"Back at you. You by yourself?"

"Yeah, but I've got it covered," he replied.

"How about the other guard posts? Are they manned?" I asked.

"They are, but a couple of them might still be feeling the effects of the party."

"Yeah, probably. I'll see you later," I said and nudged Blinky. My first instinct was to check the guard posts and chew out anyone who I caught sleeping but opted against it. No need getting myself in a bad mood before the day had even started.

Fred was waiting for me at the head of his driveway holding an insulated mug, which I'm sure contained hot tea. It went without saying that he had his ever-present pistol strapped to his side.

"Good morning," I said. He replied with a small nod. "How'd you know what time I'd show up?"

"You always get up at five and I know your routine. You're about five minutes later than I expected you though. You see something?"

I shrugged. "There was a new guy manning the main gate who wanted to talk. His name's Reese. Have you met him?"

"Can't say I have," Fred answered.

"He seems okay, although I don't like him manning the gate by himself. Hell, he's only been at Weather a couple of weeks."

Fred gave a small knowing nod but didn't comment. He waved me in and secured the gate behind us.

Rachel met us at the door with little Sarah balanced on her hip. She'd given birth back in March and I swear I've never seen her happier. Fred was too, but I think Rachel is the only one who saw it. Their home was neat as a pin and the aromas of cooking food filled the air. I followed them into the kitchen and sat at the table.

"Have you eaten?" she asked.

"Just a couple of oranges." I inhaled. "I wouldn't turn down one or two of those biscuits I smell cooking."

Rachel grinned and handed off Sarah to Fred. Soon, she had hot biscuits, butter, and molasses on the table.

"I'm supposed to have breakfast with Kelly and the kids in a couple of hours so don't let me eat more than one or two," I said with a grin. Rachel poured a mug of tea for me, and I dug in.

"How're things at Mount Weather?" she asked.

"Not too bad. We have the big powwow scheduled next week."

"What's on the agenda?" she asked.

"The usual. Crop and livestock data. Population and community development. We'll also talk about the asphalt project, but the big item is the tire plant."

"So, it's really going to happen then?"

"Yeah, there are still some issues to be worked out but we're going to try to get things going by August. Fred, you should come."

Fred grunted. "No thanks."

Rachel gave a lighthearted laugh. "You know Fred, he'd rather gouge his eyes out than sit and listen to a bunch of blowhards prattle on. How's the road project going?"

"Once I convinced Norman to become the project manager, we're back on schedule. I'd say it'll be finished by the end of the month."

Project Asphalt was something we started back in March. The goal was to fix the road damage on the interstate from Mount Weather to Oak Ridge, much like we had done to the roadways to Marcus Hook. Some people thought it was unnecessary and unneeded, but those people didn't know the whole story. Norman Marnix was one of the older residents of Mount Weather. The man seemed to know a little bit about everything, including how to properly pave a road.

We sat and chatted for almost an hour before I stood and stretched. "I guess I should get on back. Are you three coming by Weather anytime soon?"

"We'll be there tomorrow," Rachel said. "Sarah and I have a visit with the doctor."

"Good. Oh, where is your protégé at?" I asked Fred, referring to Nikki.

"She's visiting her mother. She should be back tomorrow," he said.

"How's she doing?" I asked.

"Good," Fred answered. "She listens, tries hard, she's a natural with horses, and she's tough."

"Her reading skills have improved immensely," Rachel added.

I nodded. Our education system at Weather was decent, but the same can't be said for the outlying communities. It was nonexistent in some places. Like the Shenandoah community. When Nikki first arrived at Weather, she could barely read and write. Math skills? Forget it. The kids weren't being taught anything other than basic stuff anymore. It was concerning. At Oak Ridge, advanced math and engineering was being taught to the sixth graders. And it was mandatory. We were well behind the curve in that respect, but I was going to fix that.

We talked until I'd finished my second cup of tea and told them I better get back, so I didn't miss eating with the family. Fred secured the gate behind me and gave me a nod before turning and walking back down his drive.

I urged Blinky into a gallop. Zoe enthusiastically ran alongside. After a couple of miles, I slowed him to a walk and eventually stopped under a large oak tree whose limbs have been steadily growing across the roadway. I took in the scenery. It was peaceful. The only noise was from Blinky's heavy breathing and an occasional bird singing.

There was a time when I couldn't go on a morning ride like this. Too many zeds. They were still around, but there weren't many of them anymore. There were still wanderers, but most of them that were still alive were congested in the big cities. With the lack of humans, most of their meals came from the vermin that all big cities had.

No sooner did those thoughts surface in my mind than Zoe alerted. I soon heard sounds like something running. Maybe a deer or a coyote, I thought. I hadn't seen any zeds running in a while. Even so, I instantly had my handgun out and pulled my poncho aside. A few seconds later, Melvin emerged from the fog. He was wearing sneakers, shorts, and nothing else. Oh, and he was carrying his trusty Chinese war sword. When he saw me, he waved with his free hand.

"Top of the morning," he cheerily greeted.

I'm sure Blinky and Zoe were in as much disbelief as I was. Melvin jogged by without a care in the world. I had to smile. There were some unique individuals at Mount Weather, and Melvin was definitely one of them. He was former special forces, and I don't think anything rattled him.

When the sky started turning gray, I knew it was time to head back. Reese was standing outside waiting for me when I rode up. He didn't look happy.

CHAPTER 2 – NIKKI & THE BUCK

At about the same time as Zach had arrived at the McCoy homestead, Nikki was sitting against the base of a large dead tree that bore the telltale streaks of having been struck by lightning. Ten feet in front of her was a rocky creek, probably only two feet at its deepest. The forest was quiet, save for the occasional bird or insect. The rippling waters barely made any sound. Nikki sat like a statue, quiet and unmoving. Waiting. She had found the spot while there was only a hint of daylight in the sky. As time passed and the sun broke the horizon, the darkness changed into a dirty gray, thick with rain clouds.

Nikki hoped the limited visibility would work to her advantage. She'd spotted him yesterday while she was driving to see her mother. It took some good quality recon work, but she found his tracks around the creek and decided that was where she was going to set up and wait for him.

The first indicator was a hint of sound, followed by a ripple in the shadows. After a few seconds he silently emerged from the woods, not more than thirty feet away. He was magnificent looking. He had a large ten-point rack, and the coronets were thick and gnarled, indicating he was old. Probably around ten years or more. He was thick with muscle, and she thought she detected a few old scars, causing her to wonder what kind of life he'd had.

She watched as he paused at the edge of the creek and sniffed the air. She wasn't worried about her scent. She was downwind, and as far as she knew, there wasn't another human around for miles. Still, the buck was cautious. She smiled to herself. He hadn't grown old by being otherwise.

Nikki remained motionless, blending in with the tree. He didn't spot her, perhaps his vision wasn't as good as it once was. Satisfied he was alone, he dipped his mouth into the water and began drinking. She slowly, carefully, brought the compound bow up and waited. When the buck gave her his flank, she loosed the arrow, striking exactly where the heart should be. The buck jolted and sprinted away. Nikki smiled to herself, knowing her aim was true. He wouldn't go far before laying down and bleeding out.

She stood slowly and looked around as she stretched the kinks out. She knew she needed to work quickly. If there were zeds around, the scent of fresh blood would draw them. She'd left her horse in a grove about a hundred yards south of her location, untethered. It was a risk, but she didn't want him to be hindered and helpless if some zeds or wolves found him. To her relief, he had not wandered far and nickered when he spotted her. She responded with a soft click of her tongue. The big roan trotted over to her and nudged her face.

"Hey, Leeroy. I told you I'd be back," she whispered to him and gave his nose a rub before hopping on.

She then guided him back to the spot where she had shot the deer, followed the blood trail, and soon found him. The buck was bleeding out, but still alive. He stared at her with sad brown eyes. Nikki dismounted and slowly approached, crouching when she was a few feet away.

"I'm sorry I killed you, but I want you to know I am thankful for you," she said.

The deer stared. Whether or not he understood, only God could answer. Nikki did not move and watched as his breathing slowed, eventually stopping. She waited a few more minutes to ensure he was dead before pulling out her knife and field dressing him.

Finishing, she attempted to lift him onto Leeroy, but couldn't. Nikki weighed about a hundred and thirty, all of it lean, sinewy muscle. Even though she was stronger than the average woman, she struggled with the heavy, limp deer. She figured he had to weigh at least one-ninety, maybe more. Hoisting him onto Leeroy's back was proving to be a problem.

Looking around, she spotted a fallen hickory tree. It was a little over three feet in diameter, and it gave Nikki an idea. She dragged the deer over to the fallen tree, and after a good deal of wrestling with the carcass, standing on the fallen tree gave her enough height to get the deer across Leeroy's back.

Succeeding in the effort, she paused a moment to catch her breath and look around before lashing him down with some rope. Ensuring the knots were tight, she once again scanned the area as she took off her outer shirt. Her tee shirt was damp with perspiration. She wasn't wearing a bra, and the morning air cooled her damp shirt. She had to admit to herself that it felt good against her breasts. She stood motionless for a minute, eyes closed, her nipples hardening. Her thoughts briefly wandered back to the last time she'd made love. It was with Colton, and it seemed to have been a lifetime ago.

Shaking off those thoughts, she opened her eyes and walked back to the creek. Leeroy dutifully followed. She scanned the area once again before taking off her hat and crouching by the stream. She rinsed the blood off and splashed the cold water on her face before staring at her reflection in the water.

The rubber band she'd been using to keep her hair pulled back had broken and now her thick brown mane was flowing freely. She could see the slight crook in her nose, and when she smiled, she could see the space where a bicuspid was missing.

She didn't like the way she looked. Back when Colton was alive, he'd always teased her. They'd found some old porn magazines in a house they searched one day, and Colton had to look at all of them, oohing and aahing over each nude picture. It still bothered her. She knew she wasn't ugly, and with the exception of her boobs that were smaller than those tarts in the magazines, she had a body that could compete with any of them, but still, the teasing from her first love left lasting emotional scars.

Despite those feelings, she took comfort in knowing she was tough. Tougher than any of those girls in the magazines. She was a survivor and getting better at it every day.

She stood and put her outer shirt back on before wiping the sweatband of her hat before putting it back on. She then stared at Leeroy. "Let's get out of here, okay?"

She gave the lashings another tug. Satisfied the deer wouldn't fall off if she had to spur Leeroy into a full gallop, she pointed him toward the west and led him off at a leisure walk.

The next few miles were going to be tricky. It had nothing to do with the terrain, Nikki was an expert on a horse, it was the blood. She'd rinsed off as much as she could, but the zeds somehow had an amazing sense of smell. She draped her bow across her shoulders and now had her rifle out. Leeroy seemed to sense her unease and snorted. She reached down and patted his neck.

"Be quiet, boy," she admonished.

Technically, Leeroy was Fred's horse, but back when she and Fred had gone on their first scouting mission, Leeroy took an instant liking to her. They bonded the moment she hopped on the saddle for the first time. That was back in November. When she moved in with Fred and Rachel, Leeroy always followed her around whenever she was outside. Rachel joked about it, saying Leeroy was the best kind of boyfriend a woman could have.

Nikki smiled at the thought while she rode but wondered if she'd ever find someone to love again. Colton was her first love and because of her naiveté, she was blinded by his many flaws. He was her first though, and after he died, a period of grief and depression followed. She was better now, but she had to admit she was still lonely for the type of companionship a horse could not provide.

There was only one single man at Shenandoah, and that was Colton's brother, Collin. He was an immature asshole and Nikki despised him. So, there were no romantic prospects at Shenandoah. There were plenty of men close to her age at Mount Weather, but so far, the only ones she found appealing were taken. Same with Marcus Hook. Savannah had suggested she go visit Oak Ridge.

"There are plenty of men there," she said with her trademark mischievous grin.

Nikki scoffed at the thought and readjusted her hat. It was getting a little old, had a little bit of an odor to it, and since Leeroy had stepped on it a few days ago, the fit was off. But she loved the hat, it was a gift from Colton.

She let Leeroy walk at his own pace and although it looked like a rainstorm was imminent, she was in no hurry. Instead, she admired the scenery as she thought. She loved the area. It was beautiful and she knew it like the back of her hand. Sadly, she no longer loved the survivor community she had grown up in.

They called their community Shenandoah due to its proximity to the Shenandoah National Park, although the settlement was closer to a place known as Lewis Mountain. Nikki grew up there with the married couple who saved her, Herman, and Lou Ellen Mullins. They were nice people. When her biological parents became infected, they took her in without hesitation and raised her as their own. If not for them, she probably would not have survived.

Frankly, she didn't much like the rest of them. The men thought of the women as inferior, only good for cleaning, cooking, and bedding. Most of the women were older than her and resented her independent nature. Nikki gave them credit for surviving through the years, but it wasn't until she'd seen Mount Weather firsthand that she knew they could have done much better if they weren't so stubborn and narrow-minded.

She rounded a curve in the road and immediately tugged on the reins. Leeroy obediently stopped and waited. Nikki's attention was drawn to a fallen tree lying partially in the road. It was a pitch pine, a big one, maybe seventy feet long, and it'd been there a while. Nikki had ridden by it on the way out here. But something caught her eye, something was different about it now. There were a couple of small, fresh scrapes on the bark. If she had not ridden by the tree earlier, she would not have given the scrapes a second thought. Even now she guessed it was probably from an animal. Maybe even the deer that was strapped behind her had done it.

She nudged Leeroy forward. She stopped him again when they were a couple of feet away. That is when she saw a thin monofilament line stretched across the road causing the hairs on the back of her neck to begin tingling. She backed Leeroy up several feet and dismounted. This time she tethered him to another tree.

Rifle in hand, her head on a swivel, she carefully walked closer. The line was thin, probably fishing line. It was about three feet off the ground, presumably to keep small game from bumping into it. She followed the line with her eyes across the road where it disappeared into some bushes. She carefully made her way into the bushes. Spotting the line again, she saw it looped around a thick weed and then the line went straight up for another three feet. She followed it to its terminus, and it took a second or two for her to realize what she saw.

Someone had used some rope to tie a hand grenade to a tree and the line was attached to the safety pin. The grenade was about six feet from the ground, high enough so that when it detonated it would hit someone who was on a horse.

Her body was instantly covered in goosebumps when she realized this was a booby trap meant for her. She spun around staring wildly out into the forest, trying to spot the person she believed was out there, lying in wait. After a couple of frantic spins, she remembered Fred's training and stopped. She forced herself to take a couple of slow deep breaths to calm herself and then began a slow, deliberate scan.

It was deadly quiet. And still. Nothing was moving. She didn't even see any birds.

Nikki made her brain reassess the situation. Was the grenade meant for her? It wasn't here yesterday, nobody lived in the area with the exception of the Shenandoah group, and hand grenades were not plentiful; people simply did not have a surplus where they could set up booby traps at random locations.

The only logical answer was yes, it was meant for her. No doubt about it. So, the question was, who did it? Who was trying to kill her and why?

She mentally went through a list of people who didn't like her. There were only a few. Which one of them hated her enough to kill her? And, which one of them had access to hand grenades? They didn't have any back at the Shenandoah settlement. Not that she knew of. She wished Fred was here. She could sure use his input right now.

She made one more scan before setting her rifle down and pulling out her knife. She gently and cautiously cut the monofilament line from the safety pin. Carefully removing the grenade, she inspected it closer. It was olive drab in color, about the size of a baseball, but several ounces heavier.

Her first thought was to put it in her saddlebag, but then she wondered if the jostling around during the ride back may activate it. Besides, once she arrived back at the settlement, who's to say the perpetrator would be there waiting on her and search her for the grenade? Thinking it over a moment, she opted to hide it and come back for it later.

Once she had accomplished this, it was time to do some investigating. She circled around the tree until she spotted boot prints in the ground. She put one of her boots alongside one of them. It was larger, definitely a man's boot.

Rifle at the ready, she followed the tracks. They led her along for fifty yards to an old dirt road. There she found a set of unshod hoof prints in the mud. Nikki frowned in trepidation. The mud was almost dry, indicating this was done sometime yesterday after she'd travelled through here. That meant somebody had followed her and she failed to detect them. The tracks led toward the direction of the settlement.

She heard movement behind her and turned suddenly. It was Leeroy, trotting up the road.

And four zeds were following behind him, arms reaching out, trying to catch up with him.

CHAPTER 3 – ZACH & KATE

The first thing I saw when the main gate emerged from the fog was Reese standing outside of the guardhouse, staring in my direction. As I approached, I could make out his facial expression and he didn't look happy.

"I wonder what this is all about," I muttered. Blinky twitched an ear at me. Reese had the gate already open and waited until I'd stopped before speaking.

"I caught hell because of you," he said.

"Why?"

"Apparently, I was supposed to get clearance to let you out and I was supposed to find out your destination and your estimated return time, but since I didn't do any of that, well, you know the rest," he said.

I eyeballed him a moment before responding. He was a few years younger than me, skinny, long dark hair he kept tied back, and a scruff of a beard. He didn't look like much, but he was alert and appeared to be clean, an indicator he'd bathed before coming on duty. And, most importantly, he had his M4 slung properly to the front and at the low-ready, and the safety was on.

"Reese, we don't know each other too well, but I'll let you in on something. There's only one person alive who's my boss, and that's my wife. Are you married?"

Reese's frown gave way to a bashful grin. "Hell, I haven't even been with a girl in over a year."

I wanted to be mad at him but couldn't help but smile now. "That could be a good thing."

"Easy for you to say," he grumbled. "They had a couple of working girls at the trading post. Between you and me, I thought I might hire one just so's I could remember what being with a woman was like, but good Lord Almighty they were ugly."

I laughed now. "I know the female to male ratio around here is not the best, but I think a few of the visitors from New York are going to relocate here. There were a few young women around your age. Keep your fingers crossed."

He sighed. "I will."

"Okay, so who's giving you hell because I left the compound?" I asked.

"The Officer of the Day," he said. "She's in the TOC and ordered me to direct you to report to her as soon as you returned."

TOC. The Tactical Operations Center. It was the hub of operations for the security of Mount Weather and surrounding area. I was curious who the Officer of the Day was and why they felt the need to act like an asshole to the new guy. I reassured Reese he did nothing wrong, and I would take care of the problem before heading toward the TOC. Walking in, I spotted the OD, Kate Redbank.

I'd first met Kate Redbank almost eight years ago. She and her little sister, Kyra, had come from Oklahoma to Tennessee with Sarah. The sisters were Native American, tall with distinctive facial features and jet-black hair. If not for their personalities, they'd be considered a catch. But, their shit personalities chased away any romantic prospects.

She looked up when I walked in, stared without emotion, and closed her laptop.

"So, Reese informed me I didn't have the proper clearance to leave this morning."

"You didn't," she replied.

"I don't need clearance," I rejoined.

Her jawline tightened. "According to Mount Weather protocol you do, the protocol you wrote, correct?"

"That applies only when we are in lockdown. It's very specific. When we're not in lockdown, people can come and go as they please. All they need to do is sign out."

"I know that," she huffed.

"Then why did you say that to Reese?" I asked.

She didn't answer and instead found something over my shoulder to stare at. I pulled out one of the chairs and sat down. I thought of several responses, a few of them would not have been complimentary, but I chose a more diplomatic approach.

"I have no doubt you know the SOPs. After all, you had to pass the test before you could do this job, but there's something I think needs to be addressed."

"What?" she asked.

"The protocols that you mentioned, one of them is that the front gate be manned by two people at all times."

"The other person who was scheduled called in sick," she said and held up a hand. "I know what you're about to say. It is the duty of the OD to assign another person in this type of situation."

"Why didn't you?" I asked.

Her face darkened now. "Zach, you don't know how it is these days."

"What do you mean?"

"I couldn't find a replacement because nobody here likes me. You don't even like me," she said. I could see her eyes watering up.

"That's not true," I replied. "I admit, we've not been the best of friends, but those of us who came from Tennessee together have a special bond, right?"

She stared at me through her tears. "Oh, yeah? When's the last time you or Kelly invited me to do something together?"

She had me on that one. I don't think we ever invited her to join us to do anything together. My seat suddenly became uncomfortable. I walked in ready to give her an ass chewing but I suddenly found myself on the defensive.

"Alright, point taken. I've got to be honest though, Kate, neither you nor your sister ever gave me any indication you wanted my friendship. Kelly has said the same thing, and you know her, she's friends with everyone."

"Yeah, everyone likes her," she said and now a tear slipped out and dropped on her cheek.

I reached out and held her hand. After a second, she responded and gripped it tightly. I didn't have it in me to hug her, because she was right, I didn't consider her a friend.

"How about I discuss it with Kelly? I believe we're hanging out with the Garcias after dinner this evening, maybe playing some cards or something. You're welcome to join us."

She shook her head. "I appreciate the thought, but I'm not in the mood for kids. No offense."

"None taken. Alright, the next adult only night, you are cordially invited."

"Sure, sounds good." She didn't seem any better.

"Is there something else bothering you?" I asked.

She threw up her arm in exasperation. "I need a change, Zach. This dealing with people and their constant bullshit is getting to me. In answer to your earlier question, Jonesy was the one who was supposed to be on the gate with Reese this morning. He'd tried to get together with me a few days ago, and when I turned him down, he's been a major dick toward me ever since." She threw up her arm again. "And when I told you I couldn't find a replacement, I didn't go into details. The truth is everyone I asked basically told me to go fuck myself. Will you please find me a job where I don't have to deal with people's bullshit?"

I rubbed my chin for a moment in thought, and then I came up with an idea. "Data entry. Is that something you can do?"

She eyed me like I was being sarcastic. "Uh, yeah. Back before, when I worked at the casino in Oklahoma, I started out in the office doing data entry, why?"

"Perfect. I've got a job for you."

"What is it?" she asked.

"You know Mount Weather has a supercomputer, right?"

She nodded. “Yeah, but I have no idea why it’s so super over other computers.”

“Think of the fanciest computer you’ve ever worked with and then put it on a megadose of steroids.”

“Uh, okay.”

“That’s what we have. Ironically, we’re only using about twenty percent of what it’s capable of. Garret and I were fooling around on it a few months ago and we discovered an unused program. A brief explanation is that it compiles and analyzes food production and consumption. It can project models of all kinds that may be useful in the years to come. The problem is, before we discovered it, I’ve been keeping all the data on excel spreadsheets, and I’m a few months behind in the data entry part. The spreadsheets will need to be merged into the program and the backlog will have to be caught up. It’ll be a permanent job and eventually you’ll have to take on additional data entry jobs. What do you think?”

For the first time since I walked into the TOC, Kate looked hopeful. “You’ll tell Lydia to take me off the work roster?”

“Yep, I’ll let her know. You’ll start your new job tomorrow.”

Kate started to say something but was interrupted by the radio.

“Mount Weather, this is South Mountain. We have a SITREP, over!”

Kate grabbed the microphone and responded. “South Mountain, Mount Weather. Go with your SITREP.”

“We’re under attack. Approximately five hundred zeds!”

The voice at the other end sounded like a frightened young girl who was on the verge of panic. As Kate coaxed additional information out of her, I reached over to the big red button mounted on the wall beside the radio and sounded the alarm, alerting both the guard posts and the Quick Reactionary Force.

CHAPTER 4 – SHENANDOAH

The community of Shenandoah was reminiscent of an old frontier stockade settlement. The cornerstone of the compound was a church, of which most of the community's habitants were members of, back before. When it was accepted that Armageddon had arrived, the first thing they did was string the perimeter with an ample amount of barbed wire around the church. This was soon followed by additional fortifications, modifications, and expansions.

As the months and years rolled by, cabins were built and connected together, with the outer wall of each cabin being integrated into the stockade wall. The whole thing was built in haste and with materials at hand. Concrete, boulders, bricks from nearby dismantled houses, a few guardrails from the state highway, you name it. It was not aesthetically pleasing to the eye, but it worked. Other areas were protected with cattle fencing, barbed wire, and anything else they could repurpose. It served as an effective defensive perimeter against zeds and lightly armed marauders.

Of course, if someone were to attack them with explosives or heavy weapons, breaching the fortifications would only be a minor impediment, but you did what you could with what you had and prayed for protection from the good Lord above.

Nikki stopped in front of the main gate and waited a moment. When nobody appeared, she shouted out. "Hello!"

After a moment, an older man approached and peered through an opening. His name was Marvin, a good man who'd been with the group since the beginning.

"Well, hey there, Nikki. How was your trip?"

Asking about her trip was a code phrase that had been put in place a few years ago and had never been updated. The response to the challenge was to mention the weather if everything was okay. If things were not okay, one could talk about anything, but not the weather.

"Good. It's a little muggy out. I think it might rain later," she said.

Marvin nodded in satisfaction and began working the bolts and unlocking the chains. In a few seconds he had the gate open wide enough for Nikki to lead Leeroy inside.

"What happened to manning the gate full time?" Nikki asked as she helped him lock the gate back.

Marvin gave a patient smile at the girl he still viewed as a kid. "Oh, Nikki. The zeds have all but disappeared and we haven't been attacked by marauders in years. You know that."

Nikki was about to tell him of the four zeds she'd killed not more than a mile from their present location, but then thought, why bother? This was a perfect example of why she'd made the decision to move out. They lived in their own little world and to tell them that there were still zeds around would only be met with arguments and denial. And there was the oft repeated refrain, the good Lord will protect them.

Marvin walked over to Leeroy, spotted the deer, and whistled in admiration. "That there is a fine looking buck. Where'd you find him at?"

"Over by the creek," she replied.

He eyed her. "Rifle or bow?"

"Bow," she answered.

Marvin chuckled. "I remember when you first started learning how to shoot. Now you're as good as anybody, looks like."

Nikki thanked him for the compliment and changed the subject. "Say, has anyone else been outside the gate today?"

Marvin scrunched up his face in thought for a moment before responding. "BC and his smartassed son went out to cut some firewood. They said they'd be back before sundown. Oh, and there's Drill Bit. He left yesterday on his weekly fishing trip."

Nikki nodded to herself. Once a week, Drill Bit would ride over to the Shenandoah River and fish for a day or two. When he'd return, he usually had a cooler full of fish that were fileted and ready to cook. Only rarely would he invite anyone to go with him, which seemed odd to Nikki. To her, the man seemed to want attention from other people.

"Did anybody go with him this time?" she asked, to which Marvin shook his head. "When's he supposed to come back?"

"Today," Marvin answered and squinted at the sun. "If he left at sunrise, he should be traipsing back in an hour or two." He suddenly grinned. "Hey, do you know why he's called Drill Bit?"

"Because he has a small boring tool," Nikki murmured.

"Because he's got a small boring tool!" Marvin exclaimed and erupted into a belly shaking laugh.

Nikki refrained from shaking her head in irritation. Marvin and a couple of the other older men had a habit of telling the same jokes over and over again. Yet another character trait about Fred that she admired; he didn't tell stupid jokes. Hell, he didn't tell jokes at all. A dry quip once in a while, but a regular joke? Forget about it. She wondered if he was always like that.

"Alright, I guess I'd best get this deer butchered. I'll see you later."

"Okay, Nikki," Marvin replied, still grinning.

Nikki returned his smile before leading Leeroy toward the back of the compound. Marvin could be annoying, but she still remembered a time back when she was a scared ten-year-old kid. She and some other kids were in a bus, driven by Marvin. It broke down in the middle of Culpepper, Virginia. The zeds appeared as the sun was setting. They'd surrounded the bus and were trying desperately to get in. Marvin was the only adult on the bus. He kept the kids calm and prevented them from getting hurt.

And he never wavered from going out of his way to help the kids, her included. So, with that event and others like it forever etched in her memory, she gritted her teeth and listened without complaint to his corny jokes and long-winded stories.

Nikki found her mother in one of the gardens. She and a woman named Rori were hoeing the fresh rows of dirt, getting rid of the incessant weeds. Both women stopped when Nikki walked up.

"Hi, sweetheart, what 'cha got there?" Lou Ellen asked.

"A big ole buck," Nikki answered. "Lots of meat on his bones."

"Oh, that sounds wonderful," Lou Ellen said.

"I'm heading over to the butchering station now. Do you want to give me a hand?"

"I would, but I'm in the middle of helping Rori. We're going to plant some okra and summer squash."

"I've got this, Lou Ellen," Rori said. "You go help Nikki dress that deer. I'll be expecting a backstrap for dinner though."

"It's a promise," Lou Ellen said with a pained grin. Nikki noticed and also noticed her mother's crooked posture as the two of them walked.

"How's your back?" Nikki asked.

"Oh, about the same," Lou Ellen replied. "No need complaining about it."

"Bending over a garden hoe didn't help it any," Nikki remarked.

"I'm not going to have people going around calling me a malingerer," Lou Ellen retorted.

"The only person saying that is Drill Bit. What is it with him anyway?"

"Ssh, lower your voice, you don't want Rori hearing you," Lou Ellen admonished.

Nikki frowned. Rori was a plain-looking woman in her fifties. She was a friendly, caring person who would rather be working in one of the gardens than killing zeds, but she could do that too, if required. She was an original inhabitant of the group, and somewhere along the way, she and Drill Bit became an item, even though she was several years older than him.

The butchering station was nothing more than a couple of plank tables and drying racks located in a spot that was separated from the rest of the compound because the scent of freshly butchered meat tended to attract zeds, flies, and scavenger animals.

As Nikki approached, she noted the pungent smell was worse than usual and the numerous flies were an indicator nobody had cleaned it up in a while. Leeroy gave a snort of agreement. She looked it over with a curled nose.

"I see nobody has been bothering with keeping this place clean," she remarked.

"You know how it is," Lou Ellen replied. "If you'll go fetch some buckets of water, we can scrub it down before getting started."

Nikki didn't argue. She handed over the reins to Lou Ellen and then hustled over to the other side of the compound where there was a well that was accessed by a handpump. Filling two buckets, she hustled back, only to find Lou Ellen had gotten the deer off of Leeroy and was struggling to lift it onto one of the tables. Nikki hurried over and set the buckets down.

"Mom, you're in no shape to do any heavy lifting and you know it."

"Leeroy looked tired, and he doesn't need that big heavy deer on his back any longer than necessary," Lou Ellen said.

Nikki scoffed. "It could have waited until I got back, and you know it."

Nikki had a few more gruff remarks before letting Leeroy drink out of one of the buckets while the two of them scrubbed down the tables with homemade lye soap. Once they were satisfied the table was relatively free of bacteria, Nikki hoisted the deer on it and the two women began the butchering process. They'd done this many times before and worked well together.

"How long are you staying?" Lou Ellen asked.

"I'm leaving this evening," Nikki replied.

Lou Ellen glanced at the young woman she'd considered her daughter. "You only came here to kill a deer?"

"You know why I came," Nikki replied.

Lou Ellen let out a soft sigh. Her bad back had limited her from helping out as much as some people believed she should have. Notably, Drill Bit. At dinner the night before last, he'd called her a malingerer in front of everyone and went on to say she hadn't earned the privilege of eating with them. As if to emphasize the severity of her pain, she suddenly flinched and winced. Nikki put a hand over hers.

"Mom, go over there and sit down. I'll finish this."

Lou Ellen was a stubborn woman and Nikki expected her to reject the directive, but when she walked over to the chair and sat without arguing, Nikki knew her mother was in a lot of pain.

"You need to come back to Mount Weather with me," she suggested. It was an oft repeated suggestion, and Nikki already knew what her mother's response was going to be.

"This is my home, Nikki. My friends live here, friends I've had for ten years or more. I don't have any friends at Mount Weather."

"Your friends aren't treating you very well," Nikki said.

"Oh, that's only Drill Bit mouthing off."

"Yeah, but who came to your defense? Nobody, right?"

Lou Ellen didn't respond. She didn't need to. The look on her face was enough. Nikki sighed.

"I'm going to take care of Leeroy and then finish all this. Why don't you go lay down and give your back a rest?"

Lou Ellen stood awkwardly. "You need help. You don't even have the hide cleaned."

"No, Mom. I'll take care of it. You go rest your back. I'm not going to argue with you." Nikki pointed a finger. "Go."

Nikki watched her walk toward her cabin and felt awful for leaving her. Somehow, some way, she was going to convince her mother to move to Mount Weather. She sighed again and focused her attention to Leeroy.

After taking his saddle and bridle, she let him roll around on his back before leading him to the barn. Nikki put some cracked corn in a bucket and rubbed his nose.

"I'll come back later and brush you down, okay?"

Leeroy responded by nudging her hand out of the way in order to get to the corn.

Back at the butchering station, Nikki sharpened the fleshing knife and went to work on the hide. She thought about the hand grenade as she worked. Who did it? The first person she suspected was Drill Bit. When she'd arrived at the compound yesterday morning, Drill Bit was at the gate and gave her a hateful stare as she drove past. So, he knew she was there and probably learned that she intended to go hunting the next morning.

She was perplexed about his motive though. She knew that there was bad history between him and her parents, but she'd never been told of the specifics. Apparently though, Drill Bit was still sore about it, even years later. The harassment from him never ceased. One evening, almost a year ago now, she'd had words with him after she caught him harassing her mother. She squared off with him and challenged him to a fight. A small crowd had gathered, and he'd backed down, but not before making a few veiled threats. Did she bruise his ego so badly he felt that he needed to kill her?

Next on the list was BC. He hated her, she knew it. He was convinced, deep in his soul, that she had murdered his eldest son,

Colton. And he was an Army veteran, so it was conceivable he was well versed in hand grenades and booby traps. Collin, his other son, a year younger than Colton, was an idiot. He didn't like her and he hero worshipped his father. He'd willingly do whatever BC told him to do. She grimaced as she reflected back to that horrible day when Colton died.

The two of them had a big argument one night. It started during dinner. Colton had taken her only piece of cornbread off her plate and shoved it all in his mouth before she could grab it back. He frequently did immature things like that, and she'd had enough of it. She'd told him, loud enough for everyone to hear, she hoped he choked to death and stormed out.

He came to her the next morning, begging for forgiveness, like he always did because it always worked. He suggested they go horseback riding after breakfast and morning chores. Nikki had readily agreed. It was a hot day. They'd ridden for a mile to a nearby creek where they went skinny dipping and made love. Mad, passionate, makeup sex.

It was a fond memory and made Nikki smile for a moment. Fifteen minutes after, Colton was on the ground, unconscious, and bleeding from the head. A snake had spooked his horse and threw him.

He never regained consciousness and died the next day.

Colton's brother and father didn't believe her recounting of the events. They decided there was no way Colton could have been thrown from his horse. While it was true Colton was a hell of a rider, even the best can be thrown. None of that mattered to the grieving father and brother. They were certain that Colton died because Nikki had attacked him and hit him in the head with a rock or something.

It made more sense to them that way. Nikki was known for her temper and Colton was known for his skill with horses. They'd made more than one offhand comment that she'd pay for what she'd done. Collin was only a year younger than Colton. No military experience or anything like that, but BC could have taught him. The more likely scenario, if they did it, was that BC rigged the booby trap and Collin merely watched.

Nikki thought about Colton's dad; Barnabas Cart was his full name. He was a barrel-chested man with a full beard that didn't hide the constant scowl he wore. Colton had told her he wasn't like that before the plague. He was a family man, a farmer, a decorated war vet, and beloved in the community. Colton said he'd changed after Colton's mother and sister died.

"He could've done it," she muttered.

"Done what?"

Nikki jerked and pivoted around. It was Lou Ellen.

"Damn, Mom, don't sneak up on me like that," she exclaimed. "Why aren't you lying down?"

Lou Ellen gave a patient, disarming smile. "I'm sorry, baby. I can't lay down knowing you're out here working."

She walked closer and inspected the hide. "You're doing a good job."

"Thanks, Mom." She hesitated a moment. "Mom, I need to ask you something."

"What, baby?" Lou Ellen asked.

"Has Collin or his asshole father been making any threats lately?"

"Not lately, why?"

"Someone tried to kill me today. They rigged a booby trap," she said and explained. Lou Ellen listened, her expression turning from bemusement to concern.

"Are you sure someone wasn't simply using it to try and catch a deer?" Lou Ellen asked.

Nikki took her hat off and wiped her brow. "No, it was meant for me." She gestured at the deer with the knife. "This will keep Drill Bit or anyone else from saying you're not a contributor around here."

"I appreciate that, baby. I wish my back wasn't like this. I keep waiting for it to get better, but you know how that is."

Nikki nodded in understanding. When it'd all gone bad, Lou Ellen had taken a bad fall when fleeing from infected zeds. Her back had never been the same. It could've been something that was treatable, but that option did not exist back then. Ever since, the pain had been chronic and debilitating.

"Are you really leaving today?" Lou Ellen asked.

"Yeah."

Lou Ellen emitted a frustrated sigh. "I don't know why you can't live here. You've practically been here your whole life."

"Exactly, I've outgrown this place," Nikki said. There was no need to mention how BC and Collin had gone out of their way to make her life miserable. Lou Ellen was all too aware of it, even though she never mentioned it.

"Are you still living with that old cowboy?" Lou Ellen asked.

"Yeah, with Fred and his wife, and their baby. Little Sarah is cute as a button."

Lou Ellen scoffed. "You told me his wife is several years younger than him. It sounds like he likes his women young. He's probably got some ideas about you."

"It's not like that at all," Nikki retorted.

"Well, if you keep traipsing around with him people are going to start rumors and no man your age is going to be interested in you."

"I don't care anything about that," Nikki retorted, although it was a lie. The fact was, Nikki was lonely. She wanted a man in her life, but she wasn't going to fall for another Colton. This time, she was going to wait until she found a good man, someone she knew would be the one for her. And in the meantime, she was going to be self-sufficient.

They talked as Nikki worked, but it wasn't the conversation Nikki wanted. Lou Ellen continued to chide her about her living situation. She knew Lou Ellen loved her and was only trying to be a good mom, so she listened in silence while she finished up on the hide. It was a character flaw though. Her mom was a nagger. Always had been. Nikki could have brought in enough venison to last an entire year with Prince Charming riding beside her and her mother would still find something to nag about.

When Nikki was finished, the two women hung the hide on a drying rack. Nikki then hoisted the two buckets full of meat and carried it to the kitchen. When they walked in, a lot of people heaped praises on Nikki and her hunting skills. She smiled and graciously thanked them for their compliments, but then she spotted BC and his son. They were seated at the far end of the room. No compliments were passing through their lips. Instead, they sat silently, giving her a cold hard stare.

CHAPTER 5 – ZACH & THE ATTACK

The day after July 4th was pleasantly warm, a nice day for a picnic or going on a horseback ride, but not for the QRF. Today it was led by Gunnery Sergeant Merrit Burns. Merrit was somewhat of a loner, but tough, competent, and had good leadership qualities. He had the deuce-and-a-half loaded with the troops and exited the main gate within minutes. I jogged alongside of the truck until it reached the gate. Merrit looked over and gave me a salute as they drove away.

"What's going on?" Reese asked.

"South Mountain is a small community up in Maryland. They're under attack by zeds," I said.

"Oh, man. How long will it take for the QRF people to get there?"

"A little over an hour," I said.

"Oh, man," Reese repeated. "Will they be able to hold out that long?"

I didn't answer, but I was worried. There were only about forty of them living up there. The age demographics was across the spectrum, but most were over fifty and I wasn't so sure they could defend themselves against a horde. When we discovered them, they welcomed us and agreed to be a part of our network, but they mostly declined offers of assistance and they adamantly opposed being vaccinated. We kept in regular contact with them through the radio, but otherwise they kept to themselves. If there were indeed a horde of several hundred zeds attacking them, they were in grave danger. I turned to Reese.

"I don't quite know how the zeds communicate with each other, but we've seen past instances of coordinated attacks, so stay alert and keep everything buttoned up. I've got to inform the president."

"Roger that," he said and went to work closing the double gates.

Hustling back inside, I found Bob and Connie in the TOC. Kate had already notified them and was now in the process of putting out a broadcast warning to all of the other communities.

We sat in the room together, staring at the radio and getting the occasional update. About every fifteen minutes, Merrit's voice came over the air.

"Mount Weather, this is Quebec Actual. Passing checkpoint tango-two-two, over."

"Passing tango-two-two, out," Kate responded.

I glanced at the clock on the wall. "They're on schedule. They'll be there in fifteen minutes."

Bob and Conrad nodded in silence.

The minutes ticked by slowly. Precisely at the fifteen-minute mark, the radio came to life. There was gunfire in the background as Merrit spoke.

"Mount Weather, Quebec Actual. Contact made with several zeds. We're Oscar Mike. Stand by," Merrit said.

We all knew better than to respond and tell Merrit to tell us what was happening. He'd ignore us until they had the situation under control. And fifteen minutes later, he did.

"Mount Weather, Quebec Actual. SITREP, over."

The president grabbed the microphone. "For God's sake, tell us what's happening, Merrit!"

"Mount Weather, Quebec Actual. The threat has been neutralized. Please stand by while we search for survivors."

Bob was gripping the microphone so tightly his knuckles were white. He stared off into space for several seconds until I cleared my throat. That snapped him out of it. He looked over at me. I held out my hand and he handed the microphone to me.

"Quebec, this is Mount Weather, we are standing by, out."

Merrit, or his RTO, acknowledged with a click of the microphone. Zach sat with the other three, who would try to lessen their anxiety with small conversations.

"Merrit's a career Marine, a tough man," Bob remarked.

"Yes, he is," Conrad agreed.

I had to keep myself from scoffing. When I first came to Mount Weather, all of the politicians, Bob and Connie included, viewed the Marine contingent as people who were below their station, a necessary evil. I guess their attitudes changed over the years, especially in light of how the Marines had saved their asses multiple times. It took another thirty minutes before Merrit made contact.

"Enemy eradicated. Zero casualties on our end, but there are civilian casualties. We're going to be busy here for a while, but I should have a casualty count within an hour."

Bob gestured for the microphone again and cleared his throat before speaking. "Good job, Sergeant Burns. Please keep us updated and advise if a medical team needs to be dispatched."

Merrit advised there would be no need for a medical team, but a cleanup crew would be needed at some point. He also gave a preliminary body count of dead zeds and dead civilians. It was grim. Over three hundred dead zeds, a dozen South Mountain civilians dead or unaccounted for.

Leaving the TOC, I headed to the cafeteria. As I knew it would be, most people had partied late into the night and were only now coming to breakfast, or at this point, it would be considered brunch.

I wasn't in a good mood. This was the first attack by a sizeable horde in a long time. There were a handful of people in the cafeteria. The mood was mostly somber, with the exception of one particular table. There were four of them, including Jonesy. They were sitting there eating and laughing about something. I had no idea what, but I didn't care. I walked directly over to them.

Jonesy could be described as handsome, I guess. He was as tall as me, physically fit, dark brown hair which he kept trimmed short, brown eyes, and a square chin. He saw me walking over and his expression changed.

"Well, well. It's the Director of Operations himself, Zach Gunderson," he said.

"Good morning, everyone. I hope y'all enjoyed the party last night. Jonesy, you'll report to the TOC in fifteen minutes for assignment and I'll be directing the Officer of the Day to write you up for dereliction of duties. Any questions?"

Jonesy was about to speak but his buddy interrupted him.

"Dereliction of duties? What for?"

I stared at the person who asked the question. His nickname was Lock, short for Gunther Lockhart. He and Jonesy had been neighbors back when it all went bad, and if you believed their story, everyone in the neighborhood had been killed or infected, leaving only Jonesy and Lock to fend for themselves. Lock was the opposite of Jonesy. He was short and squat. He said he'd been a championship wrestler in school, which I suppose was possible. Like Jonesy, he was a bit of a blowhard and a malingerer.

"Because your boy missed guard duty this morning, that's why," I said.

"So, you're having him wrote up for being sick?" Lock asked.

"Sick? More likely hungover, but he seems fine now."

Jonesy's fake smile turned to a sneer. "You can't do that."

"I can and I will," I rejoined. "You've pulled this crap before and I'm not going to tolerate it. Kate will no doubt put you on a twelve-hour shift, so I recommend a hearty meal. No telling when you'll get to eat next." I started to turn away but stopped. "Oh, if you decide to refuse, go ahead and pack your bags because you'll be out of Mount Weather by sundown."

He was speechless. Lock and the other two were speechless as well. I showed him my back as I walked off and joined my family. Giving each kid a kiss before sitting beside Kelly and kissing her as well. I watched out of the corner of my eye as Jonesy and Lock walked out of the cafeteria, giving me a long hard stare before leaving.

"What's the latest on South Mountain?" she asked.

"The QRF neutralized the threat. They're reporting approximately three hundred dead zeds and a dozen or so dead civilians."

"Wow, didn't see that coming," Janet said.

Janet was a cynic, a pessimist, a hard person to deal with. Believe me, as my mother-in-law, I've had to deal with her for years. But she was also a realist and knew a small community of survivors were easily at risk of being overrun by a horde.

"When will we know something for certain?" Kelly asked.

"Gunnery Sergeant Burns is a methodical person. He'll be able to sort it all out."

"Where's the president?" Janet asked.

"Bob and Connie are sitting in the TOC with Kate. They're going to make a general announcement as soon as they know more," I said.

Kelly stared at me a moment and then frowned. "I know that look. You're going up there, aren't you."

My jaw tightened. "Yeah, they're going to need some help and the QRF can't stay there. They need to get back here as soon as possible in case something else happens."

"So, that would be a yes," she said.

I reluctantly nodded. When Merrit recommended a cleanup crew be sent to South Mountain, I immediately volunteered to lead it. Bob and Connie were reluctant for me to go.

"I would think that you are needed here," Connie said. "What if the zeds are using this as a ruse and intend to attack Weather?"

"First Sergeant Crumby is here and can handle it," I said.

"What do you intend to do?" Bob asked.

"Debrief the survivors, inspect the dead zeds. There hasn't been a mass attack in how long, over a year? I'd like to go up there and try to figure out why."

Bob glanced at Connie, who gave a slow nod of approval.

"Who are you taking with you?" Connie asked.

"I don't think I'll have any trouble rounding up a few people," I said.

"Are you taking the O'Malleys?" Bob asked.

"No, their services won't be needed, but I'll be taking one particular old cuss who'll know what to look for."

The two men smiled in understanding.

Kelly had reluctantly accepted my reasoning for travelling up there. "But that doesn't mean I have to like it," she'd said. She was about to add more to her disapproval when the P.A. system squawked to life and President Duckworth began speaking.

"May I have everyone's attention please. As I am sure you are aware, the community of South Mountain came under attack this morning by a horde of zeds. Our Quick Reactionary Force responded to the scene and encountered multiple zeds. Gunnery Sergeant Burns has also advised the community has suffered fatalities. Please join me in prayers for the survivors. I will keep all of you informed of any updates. Thank you for your time."

"He's not giving specific numbers, it must be bad," Janet remarked. It was, but I wished Janet had not pointed it out.

"It is bad, isn't it?" Kelly asked.

"I'm afraid so, which is why it's imperative that I try to figure out what's going on," I replied.

The P.A. system squawked to life once again. "TOC to Gunderson. You have visitors at the gate."

I frowned in puzzlement. Kelly did as well.

"Are you expecting someone?" she asked.

"No," I said, stood, walked over to the cafeteria's phone, and called the front gate.

"It's two people from Marcus Hook," Reese said. "Johnny G and Riley."

"Okay, let them in and tell them I'll be right there."

I went back over to the table where my family was and told them I'd be back later. Hustling to the front gate, I saw Johnny G and Riley patiently waiting. Both were wearing khaki cargo shorts and tee shirts with Nike logos on them. Johnny G's hair seemed to be a little grayer than the last time I saw him, but Riley looked as good as ever. They seemed to be a good match for each other, which I guess was a good thing.

"Hey guys. This is unexpected," I said.

"We were in the neighborhood and thought we'd stop by," Johnny G said with a grin. Riley simply stared with those fiery hazel green eyes.

"Glad you're here. Have you heard about South Mountain?" I asked.

Both of them stared. "No, we haven't," Johnny G said.

I updated them with what I knew. "We can head over to the TOC and see if there've been any updates."

Riley spoke up. "I miss the horses. Can we go visit them first?"

"Uh, yeah, sure," I said. It seemed like an odd request but I went along and led them to the horse barn. Once inside, Johnny G paused beside me while Riley checked all the stalls. They were empty, Sammy had the horses grazing out in the field. I realized she wasn't looking for horses, she was making sure there was nobody else in the barn. When she reached the last stall, she walked back toward us and gave Johnny G a nod.

"I know we're acting odd, but we need to speak to you alone," he said.

"This must be important," I remarked.

Johnny G nodded and reached into the satchel he was carrying. For a brief moment I wondered if he had a firearm concealed in it, but then his hand came out with a thumb drive and a piece of paper.

"First, here are the most up-to-date numbers for the trading post," he said. "The paper is a brief summation."

"Oh, thanks," I said and briefly scanned through the paper before looking up. "Something tells me there's more."

"Yeah, we need to talk to you," he said.

I frowned. "Let me guess, Philadelphia."

"Yeah."

Philadelphia had been a hotbed of zed activity, even after ten years. Back when it all went bad, the population of Philly was well over a million people crammed into about one hundred and forty square miles. We'd never encountered a survivor from Philly, which led us to believe those million people had either died or had become infected.

So, for years Philly was impervious to any scavenging. Until recently. The Marcus Hook group had created a secure corridor into the heart of Philly. The whole route had been reinforced, with various gates along the route, which allowed safe passage for the scavenging crews. They'd been highly successful, and they didn't want to share.

"That's our territory, Zach," Johnny G declared. "Everyone thinks they can simply come up to Marcus Hook and use our secured roadway to reap rewards. We are not going to allow that."

"Not at all?" I asked.

"There is going to be a mandatory tax put into place," he said.

This was concerning. The people he was referring to was us, the Mount Weather people.

"What kind of tax?" I asked.

"One hundred pounds of grain, per person, per expedition," he said.

"A five-man crew will be required to pay five hundred pounds of grain," Riley added.

"That's a lot of grain," I said.

"I'm sure some people will think that's unreasonable. What do you think, Zach?" Johnny G asked.

I thought a moment before responding. "A fee, or a tax, is not unreasonable. After all, you guys did all the work, but I would like to think that there's room for negotiation. Also, I think you already know, our goal is to advance from a bartering economy to reinstating a currency standard."

Johnny G responded with a shrug, which let me know that he wasn't going to commit himself at this time. I continued.

"I'll put it on the agenda for our next staff meeting. You're welcome to attend and present your plan."

"Do you think there will be resistance to it?" Riley asked.

"One point that will most certainly be made is that we did not charge Marcus Hook residents any kind of tax to travel the roads around here that we've repaved. And don't forget, we've almost completed the repaving project on I-81."

"It's almost finished?" Johnny G asked in surprise.

"I'd estimate ten more days. Oh, and we're moving some people into a place in Stephens City."

Johnny G nodded. "That'll make a good outpost."

I nodded in agreement. I didn't tell them of the upcoming meeting in Roanoke. Nobody from Marcus Hook had been invited because of the Fitzgerald family. Not everyone knew the Fitzgeralds were the prime suspects in the massacre, but the ones who would be attending the meeting certainly did, and their situation was one of the items on the agenda.

CHAPTER 6 – THE INVITATION

Melvin drove with steady deliberation and kept the odometer under thirty. The road he was currently travelling on had not been maintained since it all went bad, over ten years now, so he had to be careful of hazards, like potholes that were deep enough to tear the entire wheel off his truck. He also kept a keen eye out for zeds or hostiles.

Despite the recent attack on South Mountain, he was not overly worried about encountering a zed horde. If he was, he would've never left Mount Weather. It was his mission to find people and help them and nothing like a little horde of undead was going to deter him.

"Fear none but God," he muttered. It was the unofficial motto for his team, back before. The official motto for the Special Forces was De Oppresso Liber, but they'd come up with their own motto one night after hard partying and a barroom fight. He'd lived by that motto ever since.

His current mission entailed revisiting a group of survivors he'd discovered a couple of weeks ago. He and his two buddies, True and Dong, were on a scavenging outing. They'd come across a decent-sized subdivision that looked promising and began searching the houses. When he'd exited one of the houses while carrying some clothing, a girl was sitting on a palomino horse, eyeing him in wonderment. He dropped the clothing and threw his hands in the air.

"I surrender!" he said loud enough to forewarn True. He then turned on the charm. "I swear to goodness, I must be dreaming."

"What do you mean?" she asked.

"Because you're too beautiful to be a real person," Melvin replied.

He got the reaction he was hoping for, which was a big grin. He may have been laying on the charm, but he wasn't lying. She was a beautiful woman. She wasn't a glamour girl, she had natural beauty. Beauty that did not need to be enhanced with makeup. She was a petite girl, which made her look a lot younger than she was, which she'd later say was probably twenty-six or seven. She had a mass of curly brown hair, which had been blown around by the wind, a pert nose, freckles that were almost hidden by a deep tan, and bright hazel blue eyes that would make any man's heart skip a beat.

The girl continued grinning. "You surrender? Does that make you all mine?"

Melvin laughed. "What would you do with me?"

"I never had me a man before, I wouldn't know where to start."

"Let's start with names. I'm Melvin."

"I'm Hammy," she replied.

And that's how he met the Mackenzies. She took them back to her home that was near the town of Moorefield and introduced them to the rest of her people. There was Garth, Lynn, Poco, Mutt, Shirley, and a young boy named Ricky. There were no other children in the group, which seemed odd since all three women were still of childbearing age.

When the Mackenzies first met the trio, they were skittish, perhaps even a little afraid, but before long Melvin had won them over with his zany personality.

When Melvin drove up to the main house today, which was located on Old Route 55, Garth was sitting on a stump outside of his house, whittling on a chunk of cedar and doing nothing but getting slivers of wood all over himself. Melvin gave a friendly wave as he parked and killed the engine. This one was Garth. He was wearing the same stained jeans and sleeveless off-colored shirt he was wearing the last time Melvin visited. He didn't wave back, nor did he smile. Instead, he eyeballed Melvin like he was observing an unwelcome intruder. Melvin ignored the slight and got out and walked up to him.

"How're you doing?" Melvin asked.

"Fair enough," Garth replied.

Melvin waited for the man to say more, but he pointedly ignored Melvin and continued whittling. He tried a different tact and gestured at the piece of cedar.

"What're you carving?"

"A piano."

Melvin dutifully chuckled, even though he knew Garth was being a sarcastic smartass. "Where's everyone at?"

"Out and about. What brings you back here?" he asked.

"I've got some good news for you guys."

"What kind of news?"

"I got a new place for you and your people to live," Melvin said.

Garth narrowed his eyes. "New place to live? What do you mean, a new place to live?"

Melvin waved his hand around. "You people have had it rough this past year. I've got a place where you can move to and start over."

Garth spit. "You wasted your time coming here then, we ain't interested."

Melvin put on his thoughtful expression. "I suppose I understand. You mind if I stay for dinner? I brought something along."

Garth stopped whittling. "What'd you bring?"

Melvin motioned him toward the back of the truck and opened a large Igloo cooler. Inside were a dozen steaks.

"All of them are fresh cut. Over there in that other cooler I have some orange juice and a couple of gallons of milk. And see that box right there? Ten pounds of oats. You all can eat them yourselves, or you can feed your horses and fatten them up. Lord knows they need it."

Garth took it all in and then turned to Melvin. "I know what you're doing, you're trying to bribe us."

"Is it working?" Melvin asked.

Garth spit. "Welp, we sure won't turn any of it down, but we like it here. It'd behoove you to keep that in mind."

Melvin chuckled. "Behoove. You know, when I was in basic training, that seemed to be the favorite word of the senior drill sergeant. He loved using that word. I guess he thought it made him sound important."

Garth spit again and stared. "So, you was an Army man, was you?"

"That's right."

"I was too. I ain't gonna tell you some tall tale about how I was some kind of special forces hero."

"What was your MOS?" Melvin asked.

"Eleven bang-bang, leg infantry and proud of it. When everything was going haywire, me and a buddy loaded up with as much equipment that we could put on a deuce and snuck out one night. Technically, we deserted, but I ain't ashamed of it. It was the best decision I ever made."

"Looking back, I'd say that was an excellent judgement call," Melvin complimented.

"You're damn right it was," Garth said.

"Yep, and you guys have been surviving out here on your own for the last ten years."

"Yep," Garth agreed.

"But Mother Nature kicked everybody's ass back in February. I think the last time I've been that cold was during northern warfare training up at Fort Wainwright," Melvin said.

"I didn't ever do that training," Garth admitted.

"It was mostly small unit tactics training, only you were freezing your cods off the whole time."

Garth didn't respond, only nodded. Melvin continued.

"That month hurt us all, especially you guys. Y'all lost every one of your chickens, right?"

"Yeah, and we lost our two dairy cows when our barn collapsed, but you know that."

"Yeah, but I didn't see any need to mention it," Melvin said. He also didn't mention the fact that Garth and the others were skinnier than vegan pygmies.

"Yeah, we lost a lot. You don't have to remind me," Garth huffed. "And yeah, we've had a hard time getting back on our feet, so what?"

"So, we're willing to help you guys out, all you have to do is relocate."

The man wasn't sold, but Melvin knew he was at least listening now. He decided to add a few morsels. "Did I mention the place you'll be relocating to will have electricity?"

An hour later, everyone was sitting under the shade of a huge old oak tree listening to Melvin's sales pitch. Hammy was all smiles as he spoke, the rest of the group seemed uncertain, maybe even a little suspicious.

Poco raised his hand. Melvin nodded at him. "What's the catch, Melvin? Y'all ain't doing this out of the goodness of your hearts."

Melvin pursed his lips a moment before replying. "There is a catch, in a manner of speaking. If you agree to relocate and let us get you set up, you'll become part of the Mount Weather network."

"Network? What's that mean?" Garth asked.

"The location I have for you guys is not too far from here and about thirty miles from Mount Weather. You'll serve as an observation post and a way station for travelers. The place was a church, back before. We're going to fix up and repurpose it. If you don't like the church, there are plenty of old farms nearby. The catch is, if that's what you want to call it, is you'll be the eyes and ears in that neck of the woods."

Garth scoffed. "I knew it. I knew there had to be something."

"What's so bad about that?" Hammy asked.

"We'd be indebted to them, and it'd be a debt we'll never be able to pay off," he declared.

"What is it you think we'd make you folks do?" Melvin asked.

"Slave labor," Garth spat.

"Slave labor for what?" Melvin asked. "We don't need any slave labor. What we need is to expand our network. We can easily set up surveillance cameras, but we want people manning the place."

"What about marauders and them infected people?" Lynn asked.

"We have work crews that'll come in and fortify the place, and we'll arm you. Plus, we have what's called a QRF, which stands for Quick Reactionary Force. If you're ever under attack, you sound the alarm. The QRF is activated, and they hurry to you and take care of business."

Garth snorted. "Sound the alarm? What, you think one of us can yell loud enough to be heard from thirty miles away?"

Poco chuckled. Melvin laughed along with him.

"You'll have two forms of communication with Mount Weather. We'll start with a radio and eventually you'll be hooked up to the telephone system."

They stared at Melvin like he was talking about alien spaceships, but he assured them Mount Weather had an operating phone system. After a few more questions, there was an awkward silence. Melvin knew what that meant.

"Why don't I go wander around a little bit and let you folks talk it over," he suggested.

Lynn, who seemed to be the one who was the thinker of the group, gave him a nod.

Melvin walked off and soon found himself at a pond behind where the barn once was. He spotted Ricky, who had a cane pole and line in the water. The last time Melvin had been here, Ricky had not said a single word to him. Hammy had told him that his mother had committed suicide a month after giving birth and he seemed to be slow.

He walked up to him and stared into the pond. "How're they biting?" he asked.

Ricky shrugged. "Did you know this is the shit pond?"

"What?"

"That's why it stinks so bad. Back when our chickens and cows were still alive, we'd shovel up all the shit in the barn and dump it here. At least, it was. They're all dead now, but it still stinks."

Melvin stared down at the little boy, who never looked up from the cork bobber floating in the water. "What kind of fish do you think are in there?"

Ricky looked up now. "I reckon fish that eat shit."

Melvin chuckled, even though little Ricky was dead serious. He stared at Melvin a moment longer before refocusing his concentration on the bobber. Melvin realized Hammy was right, the young boy was developmentally disabled. He wondered if someone like Kelly could teach him the fundamentals. He made a mental note to bring it up as another selling point. Melvin sat with Ricky and the two of them watched the bobber for several minutes. Eventually, Hammy joined them.

"How's the discussion going?" Melvin asked.

"They have a lot of questions," she said.

"I'll be happy to answer them."

Ricky suddenly jumped to his feet. "No shit fish biting today. Guess I'll go."

"Good idea," Melvin said, getting to his feet as well.

Hammy insisted on intertwining her arm through his as they walked. It was a nice feeling, but it also made Melvin a little uncomfortable. When they reached the big tree where everyone was sitting, all eyes were on them. Everyone's expression seemed pleasant enough, except for Garth. Hammy sat beside Lynn. Melvin elected to remain standing and faced the group. He'd gone through this routine more than once and knew what the questions were going to be. Even so, he gave a smile and held his hands out.

"So, Hammy said you have a few questions for me. Fire away."

"What is this damned disease anyway?" Garth asked.

"We heard it was some commie plot to take over the world," Poco said.

Melvin gave a somber expression. "The intellectual folks back at Mount Weather have done a lot of investigating on that, and as best that they can determine, it's not a commie plot," he said and explained how the virus was believed to have originated in Egypt.

"We could only kill the sonsofbitches by shooting them in the head, but we don't have any bullets anymore. Do y'all have any?" Garth asked.

"Yes, we do, although not a lot. We have reloaders, but good quality gunpowder is getting hard to come by," Melvin said.

"Are we going to get any ammo in case we need to defend ourselves?" Lynn asked.

"Yes," Melvin answered immediately.

"Have y'all figured out any other way to kill them?" Mutt asked.

He'd been asked this before, and he always had the same response. "There was this jailer back in Tennessee. All his prisoners had become infected, and he decided to do some testing on them and wrote a journal about it. Let me tell you what all he did."

He then spent almost an hour describing all the experiments. As graphic as it was, this was a good question for Melvin. It allowed him to use his oratory skills and captivate his audience. This group was no different from the others. They listened intently.

"How many hordes have you seen?" Shirley asked. As best that he could tell, Shirley was hooked up with the man they called Mutt, which was a fitting moniker.

"Good question. I've seen quite a few over the years. As you can imagine, the big cities are where most of the hordes are. Have you people seen any lately?"

Poco grunted. "The last big horde was maybe four years ago. We used a lot of ammo on those stinking things and a couple of our people were killed. Since then, we've only seen a couple here and there. The last one was back last fall. I killed it with a pitchfork. Have you ever seen any of them come back to life?"

"Not after their brain has been severely damaged," Melvin answered. "Are there any other groups of people living around here that you know of?"

A couple of them shook their heads. Lynn spoke up. "So, if we're out at this new place and we come under attack, you'll send people out to defend us?"

"Yes ma'am. The QRF is a force of highly trained people and is led by battle hardened Marines."

All of them looked at each other. Lynn made the decision. "I think we'd like to explore this a little more, Melvin, but first I think we'd like to visit this place you want us to relocate to."

Melvin readily agreed. He planned with them to come back early in the morning and take them to Stephens City. He said his goodbyes and Hammy walked him back to his truck.

"I can't thank you enough for the food," she said.

"You're more than welcome." He pointed at his truck. "I can't fit all of you, maybe two or three. Y'all decide who wants to go and I'll be back early tomorrow morning."

"Thanks, Melvin," Hammy said and suddenly hugged him. Then she surprised Melvin by kissing him.

CHAPTER 7 – NIKKI THE BEAN GIRL

At about the time Melvin was being kissed by Hammy, Nikki had gotten Leeroy loaded into the trailer and exited the Shenandoah compound. Her mother tried to get her to stay, but Nikki wasn't having it. As she drove, she mentally replayed what happened at dinner. She was talking with a few people when Collin stood and sauntered over.

"How's it going, bean girl?" he asked with a smirk. "Have you been playing with any horse cocks lately?"

There was an immediate wave of laughter. Collin was referring to the time she was taught how to clean a horse's sheath by Norris, an old man in the group who was an expert with horses, but who had sadly passed a couple of years ago. After he died, the chore fell to Nikki. She didn't complain, but there were idiots like Collin who often ridiculed her about it. And here he was, at it again. It upset her, but she still had her wits.

"Oh, Collin, one day when you learn how to be a man maybe you'll lose your virginity."

There was an instant response of laughter. Collin's face turned red, and he balled up his fist. Nikki thought he might throw a punch. Her hand started moving toward her knife, which was sheathed on her belt, then BC suddenly appeared beside his son. He stared at her with pure hatred and gestured toward her knife.

"What's this? Are you going to try to murder my other son as well?" he asked and then made a small step toward her.

Nikki instinctively stepped back. BC frightened her. He was a big barrel-chested man with arms and a neck to match. In addition, he had an almost psychopathic temper. Back when she was a kid, a group of marauders had attempted to raid their compound. BC killed two of them singlehandedly with a knife. The others ran off. The big man took off after them and caught one. He hung the miscreant from the nearest tree and left him there for his friends to find. Since then, he had become the de facto leader of their group. He was an able man but was stubborn and pigheaded as well. Nikki was determined not to show fear. She stabbed a finger at Collin.

"You need to teach him some manners."

BC stared without warmth. "You are not the person to tell me what to do about anything. I'll warn you now to keep your distance, or else. Honestly, I don't even know why you're here. You're not needed, nor wanted."

He then walked by. Collin followed, smirking as he went by, following his father like a little puppy dog. Nikki stared as they passed and then noticed everyone was watching. Some were curious, but most seemed apathetic. BC was well liked, if not a little feared. He had leadership skills and was mostly a fair man. She was the exception though. For some reason, he had never liked her, and when she and Colton became an item, he disliked her even more.

The drive took a little over two hours and it was dark by the time she stopped at the front gate of Fred and Rachel's home. She had a key for the two padlocks, a testament of the trust they had in her. Once she drove through, she ensured the gate was secured and locked before driving on. She had no doubt Fred knew it was her, even so, she flashed her lights three times as she rode up the drive, using their protocol to identify themselves. She stopped at the barn and was unloading Leeroy from the horse trailer when Fred appeared. He helped unload the saddle as she put Leeroy in a stall.

"Run into any zeds?" he asked.

"A few of them tried to chase Leeroy, but they weren't any problem. No hordes though. It's almost like we're back to normal, sort of."

"How's your mother?" he asked.

"She's still down in her back. I think it's getting worse," Nikki replied.

Fred nodded in understanding. "I know we don't have any orthopedic surgeons here, but why don't you bring her to Weather and have the docs take a look? Maybe it's something they can correct."

Nikki frowned. "Lord knows I've tried, but she's stubborn." She changed the subject. "How's Rachel and Sarah?"

"They're both doing okay," Fred said. "I have a feeling that Sarah is going to take after her mama though, the little thing is noisy."

"Were you a quiet child?" Nikki asked.

"That's what my parents told me," he replied. "Sarah is due for a checkup, so we're taking her in the morning. You're welcome to join us."

"Yeah, I'd like that," she said and explained the booby trap. Fred listened, taking it all in.

"Find out who it is, and we'll take care of him," he said when she was finished.

"I'd like that. I thought I'd take the grenade over to Weather and show it to the Marines, see what they think about it."

"Good idea. Show it to Zach as well. See if he has the serial number on his records," Fred said.

Finishing up in the barn, the two of them walked into the house. Rachel met them at the door.

"Did you get it?" she asked. Nikki handed her a jar of homemade pickles, a gift from Lou Ellen. Rachel's eyes widened. "Oh, praise the Lord."

Jar gripped tightly in her hands, she hurried into the kitchen. Nikki and Fred followed. They watched in amusement as Rachel opened the top, plucked a pickle out, and rolled her eyes in ecstasy when she bit into it.

"Absolutely delicious," she proclaimed. "It's crazy, but I never loved pickles so much until I got pregnant."

Nikki smiled and sat at the table with Fred. He slid a book over to her. She eyed Fred curiously before picking it up. She read the title and gazed at him in question.

"It's the first in the Harry Potter series. Have you ever seen the movies? They play them frequently at Weather."

"Yeah, I've seen a couple of them, they're pretty good," Nikki replied.

"I had a crush on Luna Lovegood," Rachel said with her trademark mischievous grin.

"You did, huh?" Nikki said.

"She looked like she was a closet freak," Rachel said and giggled. "Who did you have a crush on, Fred?"

"I really liked Fang," Fred deadpanned.

Rachel furrowed her eyebrows. "Who was Fang?"

"Hagrid's boarhound," Fred said.

Rachel scoffed and dug another pickle out of the jar. "You probably had a crush on Bellatrix Lestrange. Now, that woman was a freak." She giggled again, which caused Nikki to laugh. Even Fred cracked a small smile but then got them back on topic.

"Anyway, the books are well written with a nice, easy flow. I've gotten all the audio CDs from Weather's library, so you can listen along while you read. I think this will be the best way to strengthen your reading comprehension."

"Were CDs all the rage back then?" Nikki asked.

"Yeah, for a few years, but they got replaced. Before CDs there were cassette tapes. Before that were eight-track tapes. Before that you had plain old vinyl records," Fred said. "Those were the best."

Rachel snorted. "Of course, you'd think that. Let me guess, I bet you had all the Hank Williams albums."

"I did, junior and senior," Fred said.

Rachel burst out in laughter. Nikki was confused. Fred explained.

"Hank Senior was a country music star in the forties and stayed popular years after his death. Hank Junior was born a few years before senior passed and followed in his father's footsteps later on. Both of them were great."

“Would I like listening to them?” Nikki asked.

Fred gave a slow nod. “I believe you would. I’m sure they have his music at Weather.”

Everyone was in bed by nine. Nikki lay awake in her bed, unable to sleep. The incident at Shenandoah still bothered her. Besides, she was kind of hoping Sammy would be at the house. She liked it when he was around.

“Who am I fooling,” she murmured.

The truth of it, she was a little lonely. No, it was more than a little. She ached for someone she could call her own. She resisted the urge to masturbate under the covers and eventually fell asleep.

CHAPTER 8 – MOVING DAY

The entire Mackenzie clan was waiting on the side of the road for Melvin when he showed up the next morning.

"Good morning," he greeted. "I believe it's going to be a hot one today, so I brought some water and a cooler full of ice."

All of them responded with wide eyes. "You have ice?"

"Damn right, I do," Melvin replied with a grin. "Now, we have a bit of driving to do and y'all know how the roads are, so let's go ahead and get going." He then gave them a sideways look. "I guess it's a good thing I brought along enough sausage and biscuits to feed a small army."

Poco laughed in joy now, as did Hammy. Garth scowled, as if Melvin was playing a cruel joke on them, but readily accepted a biscuit when Melvin offered. He stared at it only a second before wolfing it down.

It was decided that Poco, Garth and Hammy would accompany Melvin. They bid their goodbyes to the others and got in the truck. Melvin drove slowly and kept them entertained with various stories. Eventually, they made it to their destination. Melvin parked in the big parking lot and gestured.

"This is the place. It used to be the Shenandoah Valley Baptist Church but we're going to rename it the Stephens City Waystation and put a big sign out on the interstate. As you can see, there are already several outbuildings and even a barn. There's also plenty of open land around it for farming and raising livestock." He pointed east. "They've already created an exit road from the interstate leading straight to the parking lot."

"Why this particular building?" Poco asked.

Melvin explained. "It has to do with the interstate. It is a corridor between Mount Weather and Oak Ridge, which we have a partnership with. So, with that in mind, we thought it would be prudent to have waystations along the route. This will be our first one." Melvin pointed up the interstate.

"At first, we were going to use an elementary school a couple of miles north of here, but Zach discovered some significant structural damage." Melvin gestured at the church. "This one is smaller, but solid. There's no termite infestation and very little water damage."

"It's a big building," Garth remarked.

"Yeah, but you'll eventually need all the room and then some. Back when Zach lived in Tennessee, they converted both a church and a school to places where people could live. It will need to be fortified against zeds, but it's definitely doable. Look out yonder," Melvin said and pointed west. "Lots of open land for farming and livestock."

"What about water?" Poco asked.

"There's a creek nearby, but the work crew is going to drill a well and hook it up to the church."

"Has it been tested?" he asked.

Melvin shook his head. "Not yet, but the crew who does these renovations has testing equipment and people who know how to use it. They'll put a filtration system on it when they integrate it into the church's plumbing."

"You keep mentioning work crews, who are they?" Poco asked.

"Back before, there was a think tank of people who worked at Mount Weather. Their job was to think up doomsday scenarios and how to survive them. One of them created a model of work crews whose job was to go out and help survivors rebuild their community with self-sustaining survival in mind. They have fine-tuned the process over the years. As you can see, they've already started, but once you guys commit to living here, they're going to come in and get to work.

"Take this church, for example. They'll inspect the structure of the church and make necessary repairs. They'll get the electricity going, they'll dig the well, so you'll have a good supply of water, they'll fortify the place and put up fencing." Melvin paused so they could let the information sink in a moment before continuing.

"This will get you a decent place to live, and then you take over. I won't sugarcoat it, you have a lot of work ahead of you, and it won't be easy, but I can tell y'all are used to hard work."

"You mentioned electricity," Poco said. "Is it already wired up?"

"Not yet. We don't have unlimited manpower, but once you folks move in, they put it on the worklist. Right now, they're all tied up working on other projects, but they'll definitely get electricity to this place before the end of the summer." He paused again and smiled, knowing he had them hooked.

"Oh, and I don't know if I already told you, but they're going to set up some big storage tanks for diesel. We'll bring a tractor or two down here, which will allow you to till more land and grow extra crops."

Poco whispered something to Garth, who'd been quietly scowling the entire time. Poco whispered something else, and Garth shook his head.

"Hmm, I don't know about all this," he remarked.

Melvin kept himself from scoffing or rolling his eyes. If it wasn't for Garth, he was sure the rest of them would've already been packing their bags. He caught Hammy staring at him and offered a smile. She smiled back and didn't break eye contact.

The girl was really getting to him. In any other circumstance, he would've already been inviting her to go on a private, romantic picnic. He then reminded himself, once again, that there was a woman named Savannah who he loved and shared a bed with. He forced himself to look away, focusing on Garth and Poco, who were talking about the pros and cons of relocating, but Melvin was only half paying attention. After a minute or so, those intrusive thoughts were interrupted by an onslaught of questions.

"What's the vaccine you're talking about? It isn't like that COVID nonsense, is it? How many people are left in the world? What's up with that little Chinese dude? Is he a spy? Does he have that Wuhan COVID?"

Melvin answered them all while taking them on a tour of the church. After, he drove them around the area.

"Looks like all the buildings have been pilfered," Garth griped. "And what's with those marks on the wall? I've seen them on all the buildings."

"That's a FEMA symbol. We use it to identify the buildings we've searched," Melvin said.

"So, y'all have gone through here and taken everything," Garth said.

"Wouldn't you have done the same thing?" Melvin asked. Garth narrowed his eyes but didn't respond.

They drove around the Stephens City area until twilight and started their way back to Moorehead and it was well after dark when they arrived back at the Mackenzie homestead. Hammy had lingered behind after everyone else walked inside.

"I had a wonderful time," she said.

"That's great. I'll be back in a week with a moving crew, and we'll get you guys moved in one day. So, y'all need to have everything packed up."

"We will. Thanks, Melvin," she said.

There was a momentary awkward pause before Melvin reached out and hugged her. She returned the hug, pressing her body against him, and then they kissed again. It lasted longer than the first time they kissed. Melvin finally pulled away and said goodbye.

The kiss, both of them, occupied his thoughts as he drove. He was ashamed to admit it, but not only did he like it, he was tempted. Oh, Lord was he tempted. In fact, the kiss gave him an instant erection. He was aroused and a little embarrassed, but worst of all, he felt a tremendous amount of guilt. It was a good thing it was dark out, otherwise Hammy might have noticed.

He had driven almost twenty miles thinking about that kiss and how much it had unsettled him. Nobody knew it, but things had not been great between Savannah and himself lately. The time when she was held captive by the Blackjacks and repeatedly raped had caused a lot of unrepairable trauma. She'd be fine for days, and then something would trigger the memories. When that happened, she'd shut down. Her personality would change from warm and happy to cold and distant, sometimes within seconds. Melvin remembered watching videos of shellshocked soldiers and the similarities were troubling.

Needless to say, it had caused a troubling rift between them. They still slept in the same bed, but they'd not made love in months. He didn't complain and tried to be both understanding and supportive. But it was difficult, and he found thoughts creeping in that if not for Savannah's behavior, he wouldn't have given Hammy's flirtations a second's thought.

"Hammy. What kind of goofy name is that?" he muttered.

He slowed the truck to a crawl because he knew he was coming up on some particularly deep potholes. As he did so, two things suddenly and simultaneously occurred. The windshield shattered and a gunshot rang out.

CHAPTER 9 – THE FORT DETRICK RECON

Operation Fort Detrick was an ongoing reconnaissance mission that started back in April. In the words of Vice President Conrad Nelson, "We need to keep abreast of what the hell is going on up there."

Gunnery Sergeant James Lutz, commonly referred to as Joker, was picked to be in charge of the operation. He analyzed the mission objectives and decided a four-man team would be best. He then picked three new Marines, Cutter, Slim, and Flash, as his teammates.

He assembled his team two hours earlier than the normal departure time in the small conference room. None of them complained, they knew it was because of the South Mountain attack two days prior and none of them had slept well anyway. When they walked in, Joker greeted them and directed them to sit. Joker earned his nickname by always joking around, even after getting promoted, and yep, even after falling in love with Maria. The stern expression on his face was an indicator to him that this morning there would be no jokes.

"Alright, Marines. You know what happened at South Mountain yesterday. The zeds have decided to start attacking humans again. Zach and Fred are going up there to assess the situation and they'll update us as soon as they know more. Now you may be asking yourselves why we aren't delaying this recon mission, and the answer is, this mission is now more important than ever."

Flash raised his hand again. "Are we going offensive now?"

"No, Private. We'll only start shooting if we're attacked. Otherwise, this is still a recon mission. Understood?"

The three Marines nodded. Joker continued.

"Now, I know what you may be thinking. What if we're attacked by a few hundred or a few thousand zeds? What in the hell are we going to do then? The QRF will be on standby. We will be doing radio checks every thirty minutes. If we don't check in on time, they'll respond immediately. If something happens, say there's another attack somewhere else and the QRF has to respond elsewhere, we'll be immediately recalled."

Joker gave a few other directives before dismissing them for chow. "You have thirty minutes, then form up in front of the motor pool."

They left the main gate forty minutes later and were riding their bikes through the neighborhoods of Fort Detrick as the sun was coming up. At Joker's signal, they stopped at an intersection once known as Rosemont

Avenue and Baughmans Lane. They'd mounted a trail camera on the side of a utility pole the last time they were there and were going to have a look.

"What the hell," Cutter growled.

There, lying on the ground, was the broken remains of the camera. Flash hopped off his bike, picked it up, and brought it over to his teammates. The four of them examined it as Flash held it.

"Looks FUBARed," Cutter remarked.

"Yeah, but if the card is still good, I can download it to my laptop and see who busted it," Flash said.

Joker gave him a nod and directed his attention to Cutter. "Get the drone up," he ordered.

Cutter hopped off his bike and retrieved the drone out of his backpack while Slim scanned the area with the ACOG of his M4. Soon, there was the familiar buzzing noise as the drone was activated and began ascending. It was a smaller brand than military models. If the battery was fresh, it'd have a fifteen-minute flight time. But this battery was at least ten years old and only had enough juice for ten minutes, on a good day. Cutter knew this and didn't mess around. He deftly used the remote controls and had the drone complete a three-sixty around them in slightly over a minute. He then had it hover above them at five hundred feet until the battery ran low.

While he was doing that, Flash had his laptop booted up and inserted the camera's card. Soon he had a screen full of photos. He clicked on the last photo and opened it to a full face shot of a butt-ugly zed.

"I'm no detective, but I'd say a zed is definitely the culprit," Flash said.

The other two crowded close, looked at the screen, and agreed.

"Hey, zoom out, if you can," Joker directed. Flash did so, and now it showed four other zeds.

"Check that out. One of them is holding a couple of dead rabbits," Cutter observed.

"Yeah. It's another hunting party. They've gotten pretty good at it," Joker said.

"Alright, so they can hunt, but how in the hell did their brains recognize this trail camera?" Flash asked.

Joker gave a slight befuddled shake of his head. "Beats the hell out of me, but they're definitely able to think things out and identify things. I mean, why did they decide to attack a community where none of the people have had the vaccination?"

"Almost like they're thinking like humans again," Flash mused. "I wonder if, well, you know, they can smell blood, I wonder if they can smell the difference between a vaccinated person and an unvaccinated person."

"If they can, that's a scary situation," Flash remarked.

Joker gestured at the camera. "It's our fault for underestimating them. We'll mount the next one higher up. In the meantime, replay the drone video and let's have a closer look."

They played the recording at full speed and then half speed a couple of times, ultimately agreeing there were no zeds in the immediate area.

"If they know about trail cameras, they probably know enough to hide from the drone," Flash said.

"True enough, so don't let your guard down, stay alert," Joker replied. He stretched, looked down Rosemont and pointed. "According to the map, there's a nail spa down that way on Tollhouse Avenue. I want to see if there's anything there and surprise Maria."

"Waste of time," Cutter muttered.

Joker eyeballed him but didn't reply. He knew Cutter was still pining over Stretch. It'd been months since she dumped him, but he was still torn up about it. The others knew it as well and made no comment. Instead, Flash changed the subject.

"I wonder if there's anything left," he said.

"I hope they have some red nail polish that's still good, but I'll take anything," Joker said.

The rest of them shared a laugh now, but it was a quiet laugh, and their voices were barely above a whisper. Hard lessons had been learned in the past from being too loud. Ten years later those lessons were still valid, and stealth was a trait ingrained amongst the Marines. Joker thought back to his time in Marine boot camp. Back before when he was still a kid. During the bayonet training phase, yelling was encouraged, even demanded. One Drill Instructor's favorite saying was, "If you ain't loud, you ain't proud!"

None of that now. Noise discipline was vital. Orders were given either in a hushed voice or by hand signal. The only time shouting was acceptable was when someone's life was in danger or shots had already been fired.

They arrived at the nail salon ten minutes later and made a tactical entry. Once they were certain there were no hostiles of any kind inside, they relaxed a little and began searching the business. It took thirty minutes and all they found was a small cardboard box containing emery boards.

"Beats nothing," Slim lamented.

"Yeah," Joker agreed and glanced at the sun. "The way I see it, our reconnaissance has been executed. We still have plenty of daylight left and there's still plenty of structures that haven't been searched by any Mount Weather teams. What say we do some scavenging?"

The others agreed and started their search on Tollhouse, proceeded down North Street, back up Trail Street before turning back west on

Sharpes Lane and back to where they started. None of the structures had the FEMA markings, nevertheless all had been thoroughly looted. At the end of four hours the men were sweating profusely. Although they'd been keeping themselves hydrated, the heat and physical exertion had drained them. They dropped everything they'd found by the road and gathered in the outdoor seating of a restaurant that still had most of its awning intact.

"It's a hot one today," Flash remarked. "I'm almost out of water."

"Yeah, me too, but we still have the jugs in the van," Joker said.

"That water's probably a hundred degrees by now," Cutter griped. Joker eyed him but didn't respond. After all, he was right and if he'd thought about it, they could've found a creek and put the jugs in to keep their drinking water cool. He chastised himself mentally. A good leader thinks about things like that before the fact, not after.

"I'd rather have hot water than none at all," Slim said.

Cutter snorted. "Always the optimist."

"I think it's an admirable character trait," Flash said.

Joker changed the subject and pointed at their loot. "When we get back to the van, if the drone's battery is recharged, we'll send it up again."

"Are we going over to those labs?" Cutter asked.

Joker thought about it. "We'll get close enough for the drone to get eyes on the building, but that's it. If we spot the South Mountain people, great, but I'm not too worried about it. If Fred said they're with the zeds now, that's good enough for me."

The other Marines nodded in agreement. Flash gestured at the loot they had stacked in the road. It wasn't much. A few small kitchen appliances and other trinkets.

"Who would've thought that those are a good commodity?" Flash said.

"Not anyone that was here before us, that's for sure," Cutter said.

Joker nodded, mostly to himself. They were in high demand from the communities that once again had electricity. He directed them to load up and they began their trek back to where the van was parked. If they were to race, they would've made it back in perhaps twenty minutes, but racing was risky. They rode carefully, maneuvering around derelict automobiles, avoiding potholes, and fallen utility poles, all the while keeping a careful eye out for zeds, wolfpacks, and evil humans who were not a part of the Mount Weather community.

Only when they had everything loaded up and they were safely locked inside the fortified van did they speak at a normal voice level.

"Are you going to turn the a/c on?" Cutter asked.

Joker responded by starting the van and cranking up the a/c setting. He then pointed at the dash mounted camera. "Check and see if there were any visitors while we were gone."

Cutter punched the replay button and watched for a few minutes while putting his face close to one of the van's vents. After a moment he reset the camera.

"Not even a curious raccoon," he said. "But I've got to tell you, I'm still wondering about those zeds."

"Me too," Flash agreed.

"What do you mean?" Slim asked.

"They shouldn't be able to have any kind of upper-level thinking going on. I mean when a person becomes infected, they pretty much die, right? Their body starts decomposing and the virus takes over. They revert back to some kind of primordial state where all they want to do is chew on raw flesh, right?"

"But they've changed," Slim said. "They've evolved is what they're calling it."

"So, somehow their brains are working again," Flash surmised.

"In a manner of speaking, but not like they were before," Joker said. "They were able to figure out our trail camera, that's impressive. The thing is, they also know how to stack on top of each other to overcome obstacles. I wouldn't be surprised if we come back next week to another destroyed camera."

"If they figure out how to use guns again, we're going to be in some serious trouble," Slim remarked.

"Well, the good thing is we took all the ammo out of Detrick before vacating it," Joker said.

"We should set up an ambush and take 'em out," Flash declared.

"I hear you, brother, but these zeds aren't a problem for us, and we need to save our ammo for the ones that are."

"I guess so," Flash said. "But I don't like 'em."

"Nah, I don't like them either," Cutter agreed.

Joker consulted his map and found a good spot to park on Military Road. Cutter put the drone in the air, flew it around the Fort Detrick compound, and hovered it above the labs for several minutes before flying it back and landing it. The men sat in the cool air of the van and viewed the camera footage together.

"Nothing," Cutter said. The others agreed.

"If I didn't know any better, I'd say they're hiding from us," Slim surmised.

The others agreed with this supposition as well.

Joker thought for a minute. "You know what? I'm going to call it. We're not going to discover anything else by staying here an extra day."

Once more there was unanimous agreement amongst the other Marines. Joker directed Slim to drive, got comfortable in the passenger seat and spoke to his team.

"We need to invest some more time in training," he said.

Cutter peered at him with a frown. "Training? What kind of training? We've passed all the courses with flying colors. You know that."

"I know, but I think it's time for a little advanced training. One day, when we have the manpower and equipment, instead of deploying on missions in teams or squads, we're going to be executing platoon and company-sized missions. And you guys will be leading those missions. I think I'm going to get with the First Sergeant and set up some classes. I expect you three to pass them. If you do, I'll get you Marines promoted to corporal."

They discussed it for several minutes before veering off topic and started talking about other things.

"Do you guys remember Radar?" Flash asked.

"He's one of those dudes from Oak Ridge, right?" Joker said.

"Yeah. He said they came into contact with a group of people down somewhere in South Carolina that had started acting like zeds. They'd slather themselves up with rotting meat, and a few of them even skinned dead people and wore the skins."

"Damn, that's some Ed Gein shit right there," Flash said. "I can only imagine the smell."

"Oh, there's a word for that. Let me think, I read about it in a book about World War Two," Slim said and scratched his chin. After a moment, he shook his head. "Can't remember. Studs Terkel was the author of the book, but damned if I can remember the word."

"There's no way any of them are still alive," Joker surmised.

"Why do you think that?" Cutter asked.

"Rotting flesh has germs and bacteria and there's no way they wouldn't get sick," he said.

"I'm going to ask Doctor Salisbury about that," Flash said.

Joker grunted. "You do that. She'll barely speak to us white boys."

"Yeah, it's not like we've ever done anything to her," Cutter said. "Flash, you're friends with her. Why is she like that?"

"She encountered a lot of racism when she was growing up and it still messes with her," Flash replied. There was more to the story, but he didn't think the doctor would want him gossiping about her personal business.

"Didn't Radar say something about encountering pirates?" he asked.

"Yeah, he said they'd found some people in South Carolina who said there's pirates operating along the coast. If they caught you out deep-sea fishing, they'd make you pay them off and you were lucky if they didn't take your boat and dump you in the water."

"Ain't that some shit," Cutter remarked.

"Are any of you going back to the Trading Post anytime soon?" Slim asked.

Before anyone could answer, Slim slammed on the brakes a moment after rounding a curve.

"Would you look at this shit?" he exclaimed.

There were a dozen zeds standing in the road. All of them were motionless and staring directly at the van. As Flash readied his rifle and took the safety off, the zeds moved to the side of the roadway.

"What the hell?" Flash asked.

Joker drummed his fingers on his leg for a moment. "You know what they're doing? They're letting us know that they know we're here."

"You think so?" Flash asked.

"Oh yeah," he said and motioned for Slim to let the van creep forward. "They aren't attacking us, I guess that means something. There was a time when they'd attack a car or truck."

As they passed by them, the men peered out of the windows at the zeds. Patches of hair, rags for clothes, and their exposed flesh looked like scarred leather. Flash could never get used to their eyes. All zeds had the same eyes now. Most had a cloudy, yellow tint, probably from jaundice, but some of them had milky white clouds. Flash believed he could see something malevolent behind those clouds. It was hatred. He said as much.

"Yeah, maybe so," Joker agreed. "They used to see us as nothing more than something to attack and eat, but yeah, I think they're understanding better now. I bet they remember they used to be like us, and it makes them hate us that much more."

CHAPTER 10 – AMBUSHED!

Melvin instinctively ducked and mashed the accelerator. It didn't work out exactly the way he hoped it would. While he avoided being shot, the driver's side wheel hit the pothole far faster than it could safely withstand. Melvin tried to keep driving but it was no good. The wheel's violent impact had broken something, and the truck was having trouble moving. More gunshots rang out, shattering the windshield.

Melvin stayed low. His OODA loop was engaged, and he instantly determined the gunshots were coming from the front and to the right of the truck. Drawing his handgun from its holster, he opened the driver's door and slid out, leaving the truck running and the headlights on. There was another fusillade of gunfire, about ten shots, but he was crouched down by the front driver's side tire, putting the engine block between himself and his assailants.

He felt around the tire and the struts and knew it was FUBARed. He wouldn't be driving home in this truck.

"Damn," he muttered.

His mind was racing, analyzing the attack and his options. If his assailants were someone with tactical knowledge, one or more people would attempt to flank him. Or they were content with pinning him down here for the rest of the night. Or maybe they had their fun and left. As if sensing his thoughts, another shot rang out. This one hit the front of the truck and after a moment, he heard the trickling of fluid. Melvin assumed they'd struck the radiator. He believed that gunshot was meant to pin him down so that someone else could sneak up on him. He wasn't going to let that happen.

He low crawled backwards, away from the direction of the gunshots and out of the glow of the truck's headlights. He knew from memory that there was mostly weeds and a few trees on his left, the driver's side of the truck, and that there was a copse of trees up ahead on the right. He assumed that's where they were.

Melvin continued slithering backwards and to his left. Soon, he was burrowed deep in the weeds. The green light was given to the mosquitos, and they swarmed around him, landing and feasting. He ignored them and waited. He had his Glock in front of him, ready to shoot whoever came his way. A good tracker would see where he crawled backwards from the truck, and if they followed it, they'd get one between the eyes.

It took several minutes before he heard noises. Someone was near his truck. He heard some rummaging through it, and that's when Melvin knew he was dealing with amateurs. An assailant with skills would hunt down the threat and eliminate it before searching for the spoils.

Melvin waited patiently. Due to the weeds, he couldn't see everything, but he had a small opening that was illuminated by the truck's headlights. He held his gun in front of him, controlled his breathing, and waited. It took only a minute before a target presented itself.

Melvin was an excellent shot. Not a quickdraw artist like Fred, but hours upon hours on the gun range when he was in the Army, along with actual firefights, made him more proficient than most. When the man turned toward him, Melvin needed only a tenth of a second to squeeze the trigger of his Glock and put two bullets in the center of his chest.

The man crumpled to the ground without a sound. Melvin watched only a moment to ensure his target was down for the count and waited for the next threat. It only took a minute before he heard a voice.

"Daddy?"

It was a girl's voice and it sounded like she was over in the trees. So, the man he just killed was her father? Melvin wondered if there were any other family members lurking around. He kept quiet and waited. If the girl came to investigate, was he going to kill her too? He decided if she showed up with a weapon, he wasn't going to take any chances.

It didn't come to that. After a minute he heard her again. "Daddy, I'm going back to the house. If you're okay, come back home!"

It was a few seconds later when he heard the distinct sounds of a horse galloping away. Suspecting it may be a ruse, he waited several more minutes before circling around the truck, carefully searching for anyone that might be lying in wait. Satisfied there was nobody else around, Melvin approached the lifeless corpse and flipped him over with his booted foot. Blood oozed out of the two bullet holes and lifeless eyes stared out into the darkness.

He appeared to be in his forties, rough looking, unkempt, reeking of body odor, and hadn't shaved in years. He was either mixed race or spent a great deal of time in the sun. He then saw the Rambo style knife lying near him. Melvin picked it up and tested the edge. It was razor sharp.

"You were going to use that on me, weren't you, asshole?" Melvin muttered.

His thoughts then turned to the second assailant, the girl who yelled out for her father. He was certain now it was only the two of them and he wondered where she ran off to. Probably home. That's where all assholes run to when they lose.

Turning the engine and lights off, as if that mattered now, he retrieved one of his backpacks out of the truck. Fully loaded, it weighed over eighty pounds. Not a problem for Melvin, who was in superb shape, but he wanted to travel quickly. Dumping the contents, he found his penlight and used it to go through each individual item. He chose a canteen, extra ammo for his handgun, a poncho, a wool blanket, compass, a pack of homemade granola, and a TacLite. The total weight was no more than ten pounds. Securing the flaps and strapping the backpack to his shoulders, he retrieved one final item out of his truck, his Chinese war sword. The only lighting now were the stars and a quarter moon.

Tracking at night was not an easy task, but Melvin knew what he was doing. He used his TacLight sparingly. As he suspected, they'd set up their ambush in the little copse of trees. The spent cartridge casings lying on the ground left no doubt. Circling around the trees, he spotted the crumpled vegetation from the horse.

Only one horse? That's odd, he thought. There could've been any number of reasons for the two people to only have one horse. He ran through the possibilities in his mind and the only thing that made sense was one horse was all they had, which meant they weren't too well off.

So, what about the ambush? Were they tipped off by someone in the Mackenzie clan? He didn't think so. Melvin thought it was more than likely they heard the truck travelling along the road and he was merely a target of opportunity.

He inspected the area of the trees again and determined it wasn't a campsite. No, more than likely they lived nearby and when they heard the truck they knew of this spot and hustled out here. That meant that they lived up the road. The direction of the horse tracks confirmed it.

Melvin took an azimuth reading and started off at a brisk walk while continuing to analyze the situation. The road he was on had made a long, lazy series of curves. There were houses here and there on this strip of road, and it was conceivable someone could have been occupying one of those houses, heard his truck travelling slowly along, and they took a shortcut through the houses and yards to their little ambush spot.

That meant he didn't have far to go. No more than a half mile, maybe less. A walk in the park. He kept his TacLite off. The ambient lighting wasn't much, but it was enough for Melvin.

Melvin knew he didn't have to do this. He could've found a place to hole up and started back home in the morning. When he didn't make his morning radio contact, they'd send a search party out to find him. But he wasn't going to allow someone to ambush him without retaliation. And retaliation was exactly what he was going to do.

His senses were on high alert, and he was attuned to the night sounds while he walked with the stealth of an experienced hunter. Humans, zeds, wolves, any of them could be dangerous at night. Melvin was wary but not afraid. Fear was something he rarely felt anymore. After all, he was the apex predator out here in the wilderness.

He'd been walking approximately ten minutes when he began to see a dim light. Another minute and the outline of a house appeared. He stopped and took a knee. A dog started barking. After a few seconds, a door to the house opened, spilling a small amount of candlelight outside.

"What is it, Gumby?" a girl's voice asked.

Melvin recognized the voice. It was the same girl that called out to her father. Her daddy. The girl silhouetted herself in the doorway briefly, another amateur move. She was holding the dog by its collar and peering into the darkness. Melvin stayed as still as a statue. After a few seconds she shut the door back, and a moment later there was the distinct sound of a deadbolt being locked.

For some reason, Melvin chose not to shoot her, although he did not know why. Was it because she was a young girl? She couldn't have been more than fourteen or fifteen. Skinny, maybe malnourished. A lot like Savannah was when he found her.

When he thought of Savannah, he knew what he was going to do. Finding a suitable spot beside a tree, he took a long drink out of his canteen before pulling the blanket out and wrapping it around him.

It was going to be a long night. He hoped he wouldn't be visited by zeds or wolves.

CHAPTER 11 – ZACH GOES TO SOUTH MOUNTAIN

It was not yet zero-five hundred hours and Fred was waiting for me when I walked into the cafeteria, making me smile to myself. Eggs, toast, and bacon filled two plates and sat on the table, along with glasses of water. I pulled up a chair and sat.

"Yeah, I know. I'm predictable. Who fixed breakfast?" I asked.

"There's a crew in there cooking, but I didn't want to bother them, so I helped myself."

"I appreciate it," I said and dug in. Fred did the same and we were finished within minutes. After taking a few minutes to clean up our mess, we hurried to Fred's waiting truck. He had it all fueled up and a horse trailer hitched up. Aisha was in the trailer, nibbling on some hay. We were on the road a minute later.

"I didn't see any of the cleanup crew," Fred remarked.

"They'll be on the road in thirty minutes. I told them we were going to leave early."

Fred glanced at me. "Didn't see you talking to anybody."

"I told them last night. You see, you're predictable as well, and I knew you'd be here waiting on me at the butt crack of dawn."

Fred eyed me a moment, but his only response was a grunt.

The South Mountain survivor settlement started as neighbors who had nice houses and big yards. Some had a few hundred acres and they dabbled in farming or horses. They were all high-income people, back before. The end of the world terminated their high-paying government jobs and forced them to become survivors of another type.

The families continued living in their own homes, each of them had been fortified in some form or fashion, and they had essentially become isolationists. They were individualists, but eventually they chose a retired general as their leader. When we first made the offer to join us, they agreed, but only if we left them alone.

It took us almost two hours before we turned onto Pleasant Walk Road and stopped at the abatis barricade. It was constructed out of fallen trees. I pointed.

"The preliminary report said this is the point where the horde attacked."

"Looks like a good starting point," Fred said.

I nodded and parked the truck. Exiting, I walked around while Fred unloaded Aisha and saddled her.

"You want me to get a horse and ride with you?" I asked him.

I guess he sensed concern in my voice. He glanced at me as he adjusted the bridle. "This old man can still take care of himself."

I chuckled. "Alright, but if you aren't back in two hours, I'm coming to look for you."

"Better make it six, that'll give me time to find out what we need to know," Fred replied.

He adjusted the bridle before giving Aisha's nose an affectionate rub then deftly hopped on. Aisha was a splendid Arabian. Chiseled features, long arching neck, and a high tail carriage. All of which were trademark characteristics of the Arabian breed. She may have looked like a pretty show horse, but she was tough, and Fred had often bragged that she had more stamina than any other horse he'd ever had. He cared for her to the point of pampering her. As a result, she didn't like anyone else to ride her and she got downright jealous if the old man rode another horse.

Fred looked around, spotted something he thought was relevant, gave me a nod, and began walking south on Pleasant Walk Road. I watched him for a moment before going back to the truck and hailing someone on the radio.

"I'm parked at one of these roadblocks and will be walking from here. Let everyone know so I don't get shot by accident."

I was armed with a Glock handgun and a knife, but my primary weapon was a Kel-Tec Sub CQB rifle. It was an integrally suppressed 9-millimeter rifle, and when fired with subsonic ammo, was surprisingly quiet. Effective range with that type of ammo was only about a hundred yards, maybe one-fifty if I was braced. It was dependable and the suppressor kept the decibels down. Why? Because rule number two was still valid: They're attracted to noise.

I walked up on a cluster of zeds about twenty yards from the roadblock sprawled out in various forms of final repose. I ensured they were dead before crouching and inspecting the bodies. They smelled, they always do, but there were some things that were different about this group from zeds I encountered in the recent past. Noticeably different. Different enough to cause me concern.

I focused on one of them. He was a thirty-something man with long blond hair. He had it fixed in a ponytail with a length of five-fifty cord. That seemed a little odd. I mean, would someone who looked like a beach bum keep his hair tied back with cordage commonly found among military, campers, and preppers? I suppose he could've been ex-military when he became infected. It was something worth noting.

Another aspect was the decomposition. His didn't seem to be that advanced, much like the others. I inspected their footwear. There didn't appear to be a lot of wear and tear to any of them, which was both interesting and concerning.

Further inspection revealed that all of them were the recipients of single headshots, and most of the shots were between the forehead and the bridge of the nose.

"Damn good shooting," I muttered.

Yep, whoever killed these zeds was an excellent marksman. It was one thing to be able to hit a bullseye on a paper target, but to deliver these kinds of kill-shots to moving targets was at a higher level. Much higher.

The cleanup crew arrived and drove by as I was looking over the first kill zone. I saw Captain Justin Smithson driving one of the trucks and he gave me a wave. Walking toward the houses, I spotted the shooter's boot prints. They were several sizes smaller than my size twelves, and it instantly made me realize that this marksman was no man at all but a woman.

I was surprised, although I shouldn't have been. After all, I knew several women who were excellent shooters. Julie and Macie came to mind. My first wife and my first love. A flood of memories hit me, but I pushed them back to a far corner in my mind. I only thought about them at certain times, and it was no time to reminisce right now.

I looked at the boot print again. It could have been a kid, I guess, but I didn't think so. I peered over at the blonde man again. He'd been shot twice, which effectively canoed his face. The second shot was probably unnecessary, but the shooter must've felt it was. I'd have to ask about it when I met her.

I took a knee beside blondie, set my rifle down, and got out my knife. This part was going to be a little unpleasant. Some people might say it was unnecessary, like the double tap, but I knew it needed to be done.

Cutting open his shirt, I inspected his skin. It was the usual zed skin; decomposed and scarred over. I then cut him open and began inspecting his insides.

"Interesting," I mumbled.

I went to another corpse and performed the same actions. I did it to six more of them. It took me about thirty minutes before I made my way to the first house. There were dead zeds everywhere but somehow the zeds had made entry into the house. It didn't look like anyone had survived.

The next house, about a hundred yards down the road, was still intact. Many more zeds were dead. The closest one had not come within fifty yards of the house. A few people were sitting around a table on the porch. Captain Justin Smithson was one of them. He waved me over. I noticed the door had been damaged, as if the zeds had breached it during the attack. I decided to wait and ask about it later.

"I'm not complaining, but I'm surprised you're here," I said to Justin.

"Our esteemed president insisted I come," he replied. He gestured toward the house. "Twelve survivors inside. Two are women, a crotchety old fart who says he was a general once upon a time, and the rest are kids who were secured in a bunker under the house when the alarm sounded."

"Okay, good," I said.

He gestured toward the house behind me. "There was a family of six living there. They were overrun and four of them are missing. Three men and one woman."

My gut tightened. That was not good news.

"We need to start the burying process if we want to get it finished before dark," Justin suggested I nodded and was about to speak when we were interrupted.

"You won't be burying them anywhere around here!" an older man declared. He had walked outside as Justin was speaking.

"Where do you suggest we bury them then?" Justin asked, his tone of irritation clear.

"Anywhere but here," the man said and walked up to me. "I'm Major General Roland Fitzhugh, retired. Who the hell are you?"

"I'm Zach Gunderson. I'm the Director of Operations for Mount Weather."

The General sniffed. "You're a little young to hold that title. I'm calling bullshit. Where's Parvis?"

"He died of cancer a couple of years ago. I'm his successor," I said.

"His handpicked successor," Justin added.

The General glanced at Justin before refocusing on me. "I knew that."

"I'm sure you were simply testing me. Now then, let's get back to your statement."

"About those dead things? Yep, you're not burying them anywhere around here. They'll poison the land."

"Captain Smithson and I are open to suggestions," I said.

"I don't care what you do with them, but you will not bury them here," he growled.

The man irritated me, and I wasn't in the mood for stupid repartee.

"Alright, you've made it clear you don't want them buried here but you're not offering any plausible solutions."

"Not my problem," he said.

"Then I certainly won't make it mine," I said and turned my head to Justin. "You heard the man. We are not to bury any of the zeds. Leave them where they are."

The General's expression, which was I guess what you'd call resting asshole face, now deepened into an angry, confused scowl. "What? You can't leave them here. I forbid it."

"They're not ours and if you are not interested in suggesting solutions, we're not interested in what happens to them." I then leaned forward. "I am sorry for the loss of your people, I am, but if all you are going to do is hinder us with pedantic jackassery, we'll pack up and go home."

He scowled for a moment longer, and then his expression wavered. He sighed and it seemed to take all the juice out of him. Fatigue was etched in his features, and there were pronounced bags under the old man's eyes, suggesting he'd not had any sleep since the initial attack. I relented and gestured toward the work crew.

"We've brought a backhoe loader. I was thinking of a mass grave. Tell us a suitable location that's not too far from here and we'll take care of it."

He looked over and seemed to see the backhoe for the first time. "Why did you bring a backhoe here?"

"Two reasons. One, we've done this sort of thing before. Digging a mass grave is easier with a backhoe."

"What's the second reason?"

"Gunnery Sergeant Burns noted a weak area in your perimeter. He said he could fix it with some earthen embankments, which are easy to construct if you have a backhoe."

There was still a bit of defiance, but mostly he looked like a tired old man. He gestured back toward the front door.

"My granddaughter is inside. I'm sure she can show your people a spot." The door opened and he turned around. "Here she is." He waited for her to walk to us. "Gentlemen, this is Bailey Fitzhugh, my granddaughter."

I don't know why, but for some reason, when he first mentioned his granddaughter, I thought she'd be a teenage girl. But I was mistaken. Bailey was a gorgeous brunette somewhere close to my age. I guessed her at about five-seven, and she reminded me of the character Lara Croft, but with deep blue eyes. She was wearing a snug-fitting tank top and cargo shorts that showed long, muscular legs. Justin and I swapped a glance. She eyed me with a mixture of curiosity and perhaps suspicion, but what she said next somehow didn't surprise me.

"Who the hell are you?"

CHAPTER 12 - MELVIN MEETS MAL

As he suspected would happen, it wasn't until the sun had come up before there was any activity. Daylight confirmed the presence of a small subdivision of houses. There were no signs of fortifications or zed-proofing, no animal enclosures, and the only signs of gardening were a few flowerpots with tomatoes, which was unusual. July was usually too hot for tomatoes, but Melvin didn't give it much thought. What concerned him more was who was inside. Was it more than one person? How well armed were they? Would he have to kill that dog, what was its name, Gumby? He hoped not. Melvin had always liked dogs. Even ugly ones.

The door opened and the same young girl peeked out. The dog squeezed through the opening and ran out, stopping in the yard to urinate. If the mutt knew of Melvin's presence, he gave no indication of it. The girl watched Gumby through the door. Apparently satisfied there were no dangers, she walked outside, allowing Melvin to get a good look at her. Both her and the dog were dirty and emaciated. She stretched, then dropped her pants and squatted. Finishing, she walked around to the rear of the house and reemerged a moment later astride a horse, riding bareback.

Melvin waited a moment. He kept the tree between himself and the house, stood, and stretched. He knew she was going back to his truck to confirm what she suspected happened to her father. He also had no doubt she'd take everything she could carry and bring it back to the house. That was okay, he'd be waiting for her.

The lack of any noises or activity led him to believe none of the other houses were occupied, so he only focused on the one the girl was in. He found a pebble and threw it against the siding of the house. He waited a few seconds and repeated the process, a little harder this time. When nothing happened, he sprinted toward the house and stopped behind a wall that had no windows. He then listened. Hearing no sounds, he made his way to the door and walked inside.

The first thing he noted was the smell. It stunk in there, a combination of body odor, excrement, and dirty clothing. He methodically searched the house with effortless expertise. When he was finished, he learned a couple of things about his assailants. First, they were nasty. The nonworking toilets were filled with excrement. Second, there was no reinforcement or fortifications done to the house other than some plywood covering the larger windows, but there were gaps large enough to allow sunlight in, and to look outside.

The lack of strong, deliberate fortifications indicated the occupants only intended to stay here temporarily. When they'd done a thorough job of making it unfit to live in, they no doubt moved to a fresh house. Occupy, defile, move, repeat. Disgusting.

Based on what he saw, he was convinced there were only two of them and that his first guess about him being a target of opportunity was the correct supposition.

Melvin walked back over to the front door and paused. He had a couple of options. One, simply walk away. He had the radio in his truck. All he had to do was call them for a pickup. He'd be home in time for dinner with Savannah and little Prairie.

Second option, wait for her to come back and kill her. She'd already shown a propensity for cold-blooded murder. After thinking a moment, he decided he wanted to question her, and then decide what to do. Almost a second after reaching this decision he heard the clopping of horse hooves.

"Option three it'll be," he murmured.

He stood behind the door and waited. He knew the bright sunlight was going to diminish her vision when she walked inside, so he was going to use it to his advantage.

When she walked in the door, he did three things. He grabbed her by the back of the neck while simultaneously kicking the door shut, and then stuck his Glock up against her head. It would've been a nice touch if he could have cocked the hammer to add to the effect, but anybody who knows about handguns know Glocks don't have that feature.

"Do not move or I'll pull the trigger."

He said it slowly, in a low, ominous voice. Her breathing came in deep gasps. The only other sound was her dog outside, who was barking furiously and scratching at the door. He felt her tensing and she started to raise the AR-15 she was holding. He squeezed her skinny neck harder and shook her like a rag doll, causing her to whimper in pain.

"Drop it!" Melvin ordered. The rifle fell to the floor with a clatter, although Melvin was uncertain if she were complying with his command or if she was about to pass out from his grip.

He forced her to walk over to a spot where the sunlight was shining through a crack and looked her over. She had a knife in a sheath on her belt, which he promptly relieved her of. Only then did he loosen his grip. She slumped to the floor, causing Melvin to realize he was gripping her neck far tighter than he meant.

"Yeah, serves you right," he said.

He picked up the AR-15 and inspected it. It looked like it had not been treated well and it was dirty, much like the girl and her dead father.

He unloaded it, popped the rear take-down pin, and pocketed the carrier group. He gave her a glance before reassembling it and setting it on the floor out of her reach.

Melvin then activated his TacLite and pointed it at her face for a closer inspection. She was gaunt, and much dirtier than he realized. Her brown hair was unkempt and greasy, her face was dotted with blackheads, and the oversized shirt and pants she was wearing looked like they'd never been washed. He guessed she was a teenager, which meant she was a small child during the plague outbreak. He wondered how she'd been able to survive for ten years and decided he didn't care.

The dog continued barking. He ensured the door was secure so the mutt couldn't break in and attack him before dragging a chair over and sitting across from her. When she'd regained her senses, she spotted Melvin. Her face registered a mixture of pain, anger, and fear.

"Who are you?" she croaked.

"I'm the man you and your father tried to kill last night. Who are you?"

"You killed my daddy," she said.

Melvin noted she had a distinct backwoods Appalachian drawl. The kind of drawl that was usually attributed to inbred white-trash types.

"I certainly did," Melvin replied. "He was trying to kill me, and so were you. Should I kill you too?"

She narrowed her eyes. "You ain't killed me yet. That means you want something, and that means you're gonna rape me."

"Little girl, I'm not a rapist. What's your name, anyway?"

"Mal."

"Mal? Is that short for something like Mallory?" Melvin asked.

She responded with a shrug. "Just Mal. That's all my daddy ever called me."

"Where's your momma?"

Mal shrugged again. "I ain't got family, just Daddy."

"No other people at all?"

"There's been some people here and there. They weren't family and we didn't stay with them long. Daddy said don't never trust nobody," she said.

"Is that why you two tried to kill me yesterday?"

Mal shrugged again. "Daddy said anyone driving around these days have gotta be rich."

"Is that how you two survive? You go around killing people and take their property?"

Another shrug.

"How old are you?" he asked, to which he received yet another shrug.

"Daddy never kept up with the years. I know when it's summer and when it's winter. That's about it."

"Do you remember when the plague started, and everyone was getting infected? And don't give me a shrug, give me an honest answer."

Mal eyed him. "Sort of. Daddy came and got me from school one day. He said the world was full of monsters."

"Monsters. Yeah, that's one way to describe them. What grade were you in when that happened?" he asked. Mal held up two fingers.

"Second grade?" She nodded. Melvin had to think it through. "Let's see. That meant you were seven or eight, which puts you at seventeen or eighteen now."

"If you say so," she replied and stared with a blank expression. "Daddy said any man I saw I should kill them or else they'd rape me."

"I'm not going to rape you," Melvin said. "Although I'm not sure what I should do."

"What do you mean?" she asked.

"It means, I can't trust you as far as I can throw you."

"I don't know why you'd say something like that," she said.

Melvin eyed her, waiting for her to laugh at her joke. When she didn't, he gestured around. "How long have you two been living here, anyway?"

"A few days, I guess." She punctuated it with another shrug. It was beginning to annoy the hell out of Melvin.

"You don't seem to have a good concept of time," Melvin remarked, mostly to himself rather than her.

"Why'd you kill my daddy?" Before Melvin could respond, she started crying. "I ain't got nobody now," she lamented.

"That's your daddy's fault," Melvin said. "He should not have brought you up like this."

Mal stared at Melvin with a mixture of tears and antipathy. He didn't care and pointed a finger at her.

"I think the best thing to do is take you back to where I live."

"Why?" she asked.

"A couple of reasons. One, if I leave you out here by yourself, you'll die. Two, I'm going to show you how normal people live." Melvin waved a hand around. "Living like this isn't normal. When you see what normal is, you might understand how your father did not do right by you."

"What do you mean by that? I'm as normal as anyone," Mal said.

Melvin shook his head. "No, you're not. Murdering people for no reason other than taking what they have isn't normal." He gestured around the house. "Living in squalor isn't normal."

Mal frowned through her tears. "There ain't nothing not normal here, and you're the murderer. You killed Daddy."

Melvin was tempted to throttle her again but kept his temper in check and pointed at the door.

"We're going outside. If that dog attacks me, I'm going to kill it, so you better make sure it doesn't do it. Understand?"

Mal wiped her face and nodded. Melvin saw that her tears had cleaned off some of the grime on her cheeks. He was tempted to point it out to her, but instead, handed her the AR-15. She paused a moment before warily taking it. She didn't know he'd rendered it inoperative, and he was curious to see what she'd do. She continued staring at him and gripped the weapon tightly, but then surprised Melvin when she slung the rifle on her shoulder.

"Alright, let's go," he said.

He opened the door and motioned for Mal to walk out first. The dog immediately started growling at Melvin.

"Ssh, Gumby. It's okay."

Gumby stopped growling, and instead stared at Melvin and emitted a low whine.

"He does that when he's scared," Mal said.

"He's got mange," Melvin informed her. No surprise, his statement confused her.

"What's that?"

Melvin didn't bother explaining. "Let's go."

"What about my horse?"

"We'll come back and pick him up later," Melvin replied.

"Why?"

Melvin didn't answer. The truth was, he wasn't going to let her ride and have her gallop off, he wasn't going to ride and make her walk, and she smelled so bad he didn't want to share a saddle with her. He'd seen a creek nearby when he drove by it yesterday and was tempted to make her bathe in it but decided it'd be best to wait.

After walking along for about ten minutes, Melvin noticed smoke in the direction they were travelling. After a few minutes, he realized what the smoke meant. He stopped and grabbed Mal by the shoulder.

"You little shit, you set my truck on fire, didn't you?"

Mal shrugged.

CHAPTER 13 – TRUE & DONG TO THE RESCUE

Melvin stared at his smoldering truck, which by now had mostly burned to a charred shell of metal. After a few seconds, he turned to Mal. He was angrier than he'd been in a long time, but he managed to keep his emotions in check.

"Why did you do that?" he asked.

"You killed my daddy," she replied.

"I was defending my life, you fucking idiot!" he screamed. He then stopped himself and looked around. "Where's your father? What did you do with his body?"

Mal pointed at the smoldering truck. Melvin stared incredulously. "You put him in the fire?"

She nodded, which caused Melvin to wonder how this puny-looking girl could pick up a hundred and fifty pounds of dead weight and put the body inside the truck. He was impressed, sort of. He pointed at the truck.

"That was incredibly stupid and wasteful. I had a lot of good equipment in there, including food. We could've had us a nice meal, and you look like you haven't had one of those in a while."

"I had to do it," she said.

Melvin stared. "Why?"

"I had to keep my daddy from turning into a monster," she said, and the tears began again.

Melvin wasn't in a sympathetic mood and was about to give her more grief, but the distant sound of a vehicle's engine stopped him. There were only a few people around the area that had running vehicles, and they were all friendly. Melvin stood beside his truck and waited. When the vehicle came into view, he recognized it immediately.

"Awesome."

Mal eyed the approaching vehicle, a pickup truck, and then peered at Melvin. "Do you know them?"

"Yeah, I know them," he said and gave the hand signal wave, letting his friends know that it was safe for them to approach. True brought the truck to a stop ten feet away and turned it off. The two occupants, True and Dong, exited the truck. Dong walked over to Melvin.

"Hi, Melvin," he greeted with a big toothy grin.

"Hey, Dong," Melvin answered.

Mal frowned. "Dong? Is that his name? What kind of name is that? And what's wrong with his eyes?"

True gave her one of his cold stares for a moment before speaking to Melvin. "Who's your friend?"

"She says her name is Mal. She and her father tried to ambush me last night."

True's dark, armor-piercing stare went from cold to deadly. "Where's he at?"

Melvin pointed at his truck and brought them up to speed. Dong listened and offered an occasional nod while True kept his emotions buried deep within. When Melvin finished, he only had one thing to say.

"Why haven't you killed her?"

Melvin grunted. "Believe me, I considered it."

Mal glanced back and forth at the two of them, her expression nervous now. "You ain't really going to kill me, are you?"

Melvin ignored her and focused on True. "I'm glad you two showed up, but what brought you two out here?"

"Savannah was worried when you didn't come home last night. We were heading to Stephens City to find you when we saw the smoke," True said.

Dong agreed with a bob of his head. "Very worried."

"He's weird," Mal said.

"He doesn't stink, which is more than you can say," Melvin retorted.

Dong grinned and bobbed his head. "You stinky."

True had been scanning the area while they talked and suddenly pointed. "There's a horse."

They all turned to where he was pointing. Sure enough, there was a horse trotting toward them.

"That's Booboo," Mal exclaimed and gave out a whistle, causing True to grimace.

"Ain't nobody explained to her not to make loud noises, I'm guessing."

Booboo the horse trotted up to Mal and stopped. She squealed in joy and hugged him around the neck. True walked over and looked Booboo over.

"This horse has been treated badly. It's got scars from a whip and the hooves are in rough shape," he said.

"Yeah," Melvin agreed. "Mal's father was not a good man."

"He was too," Mal retorted.

Melvin scoffed. "By the way, where did you two get those bullets?"

Mal went back to her patented shrug.

"What does that mean? Are you refusing to tell me?" Melvin asked.

"A man gave them to Daddy. I don't know where they came from," she said.

"I see you didn't disarm her," True said.

Melvin pulled the bolt carrier group out of his pocket and showed it.

Mal saw it and frowned when she realized what Melvin had done. "You fucked up my gun?"

"What do you want to do with her?" True asked.

Melvin shrugged in exasperation. There was so much about her that he did not like, and yet, she reminded him of Savannah back when he first found her. He reached out and cupped her chin, forcing her to look up and make eye contact.

"You're free to go on your own, or you can come with us. It's your choice, but if you come with us, there are rules you'll have to abide by," he said.

Mal didn't move, nor did she try to get her face out of Melvin's grasp. Instead, a single tear hit her cheek. She was resigned to her fate at the hands of a man who had killed her father mere hours ago.

"Well, thanks to you I ain't got nobody anymore. I guess I can come with y'all."

Melvin let go of her then. "Alright, I guess we can do that. Now, as far as that horse and dog…"

Her face lit up in hope. "Can I bring them with me?"

Melvin glanced at True, who gave a slight shrug. He rubbed the horse's nose before lithely jumping up on it. "I'll ride him back to Weather. Ain't no way I'm going to ride in the truck with her. She stinks to high heaven."

CHAPTER 14 - ZACH & BAILEY

I wouldn't admit it out loud, but Bailey had me befuddled for a moment. Not only was she a good-looking woman, her whole demeanor exuded self-confidence. I cleared my throat. "I'm Zach Gunderson. I'm part of the team from Mount Weather."

Her stare was unwavering. I'm sure she made a lot of men uneasy with that stare. "I've heard your name. What's your function, Zach?" she asked.

"I'm the Director of Operations."

She continued staring. "Okay, you're the Director of Operations at Mount Weather. What are you doing here?"

"The scope of my duties are far more than simply ensuring things are running correctly at Mount Weather." I made a small head nod toward the work crew. "The work crews are an example. One of the things we can do to help you people out is to dispose of all these dead zeds. Your grandfather doesn't want them anywhere around here. I can understand that, but we need a suitable spot."

She stared a moment longer and then focused on her grandfather. "What about that rock quarry? We won't have to bother with digging a hole and burying them."

He thought about it a moment and then gave a nod of approval. "That's a good place. Out of sight, out of mind."

"How far is that from here?" I asked.

"About five miles," she replied.

I thought it over. Five miles was plenty of distance from their water supply. We'd have to make several trips with the deuce-and-a-half, but on the plus side, we wouldn't have to waste time digging a big ass hole in the ground and then burying them.

"It's doable, but it'll take some time," I said.

"Well, we better get started," she said. "You're going to pitch in and not stand around giving orders, aren't you?"

"Of course, but I need to interview a few of you, especially the person who first spotted them breaching the roadblock."

"That'd be me. You can ask me questions while we work," she said and without waiting for my response, turned to her grandfather. "Pops, go inside and lay down a while. We've got this."

The General put up a rather feeble argument, but Bailey shut him down with a stern lecture about his heart. From what I could see, I imagined everyone, her grandfather all the way down to the kids around here, toed the line when she was around.

We had the zeds stacked eight bodies high on the first load and strapped them down so they wouldn't fall off on the way to our destination. I questioned Bailey about the attack while we rode.

"I was walking the goats at the time, keeping guard over them."

I glanced at her. "Marauders?"

"Nope, there's a mountain lion living around here somewhere and she's been picking off our livestock. So, I guess I was about two hundred yards down the road from the blockade when I saw them. They were actually climbing over it, which I've never seen before. Have you?"

"Back a long time ago, but not recently. So, who was with you?" I asked.

"Just me and the goats. I picked off as many as I could before running out of ammo. I got most of the goats rounded up and ran them back to the house. They'd heard the gunshots, so everyone was ready, but there were so many of them." Her voice drifted off a moment and then she refocused. "Has there been a final count?"

"A little over three hundred dead, but it appears some of them broke contact and left. One of our men is tracking them as we speak," I said.

She furrowed her brow as we bounced up and down in the cab of the truck. "Only one man is tracking them? Does he have a death wish or something?"

Justin and I chuckled. "No, I wouldn't say that at all. Quite the opposite."

She grunted. "I hope he's a good shot and has a lot of ammo."

"He is and he has plenty. So, you're the one who shot those zeds at the blockade?" I asked. She nodded. "At two hundred yards? That is some impressive shooting. Beyond impressive, all I saw were head shots."

"Thanks. Back when I was a kid, I was a competition shooter. I won my first match when I was eleven. Dad and Pops were hopeful that I could compete in the Olympics one day," she said.

"You're certainly good. Better than me I'm guessing, and I'm no slouch."

Justin chuckled. Bailey received the compliment with a small smile. "So, who's this man who's going to take on all those zeds by himself?"

"His name's Fred McCoy. He used to be a competition shooter back before as well. It was cowboy shooting though. No Olympic stuff."

She nodded. "Aha, I've heard of him. I thought he was dead."

"Oh, he's still around. It'd take a hell of a lot to kill that man."

"Very true," Justin added.

"I'd like to meet him," she said.

"He'll be back in a few hours. I'll introduce you. Getting back to the zeds, are there any other peculiarities you guys noticed about them?"

"Yep. Some of them were kind of running."

"Running?" I asked.

"Well, not really running. They were, hmm, loping? Loping. I guess that's what I'd call it. It's like they were trying to run, but their legs and muscles weren't fully cooperating, so they had this kind of hunched over loping gait. They weren't fast, but faster than walking."

I puzzled over that. It was even more peculiar than I thought. Bailey noticed my confusion.

"Is that odd or something?" she asked.

"Yes, it is. Have you ever seen them loping like that before?"

"Zach, the last time we saw any zeds has been almost two years ago. It was three of them and it looked like they were starving. We put them out of their misery, and we haven't seen any since. The only threats we've had are from coyotes and that damned mountain lion. Do y'all have any down at Mount Weather?"

"We haven't seen any mountain lions, but definitely coyotes and a few wolves were seen back in the spring."

Bailey gave directions as I drove, and soon we were turning onto Benevola Church Road and then into the drive of the rock quarry. Bailey got out and directed me to back up to the near edge. We then climbed up on the back and lobbed the bodies over the edge of the quarry into the water below.

"Here's some company for you, Anson," she said, barely above a whisper.

"Anson?" I asked.

"My ex. He was a couple of years older than me. He was the proverbial rich kid. Handsome, athletic, the life of the party type of guy. He had a scholarship lined up at Washington and Lee. But he couldn't keep his dick in his pants. Back before, I caught him cheating on me."

"Did he survive?" I asked.

"Yep. He and his family lived down the road from me. I forgave him because I'm a dumbass, and he was my one and only throughout the chaos. I'd been told he was cheating on me again, but I didn't believe it until I caught him in the act with my ugly ass cousin."

"I'm sorry to hear that," I said.

"That was two years ago. No and no."

I eyed her in bemusement. "No and no what?"

"No, I haven't been with anyone since, and no, I'm not looking, so don't ask."

I smiled. "Okay, I won't."

She scoffed. "Yeah, right."

"Seriously, I won't. I'm happily married with three kids and another on the way."

She stared at me a moment before speaking. "Well, good for you. Anyway, the two of them went out in his Range Rover one day and haven't been seen since. We haven't even located the car." She pointed at the quarry. "I had a dream one night that they were in the Rover at the bottom." She shrugged. "I've decided to go with it."

I had a sudden thought about that zed that she'd shot twice in the face. "Was Anson blonde headed?"

She arched an eyebrow. "Yeah, how'd you know?"

"Just a guess," I said.

"His hair was like yours," she said and eyed me with an unreadable expression.

CHAPTER 15 – SQUEAKY CLEAN

"Sweetie, please don't be upset," Melvin begged.

He was standing outside of the women's locker room, attempting to assuage Savannah's anger. Judging by the angry expression on her face, it wasn't working.

"Why would I be upset, huh? You went traipsing off by yourself, like you usually do, and you come back home with a skinny little girl who smells like a pig. And then I find out from Dong that she and her father tried to kill you and she set your truck on fire. Why would I be upset over any of that?"

Before Melvin could respond, Kelly stuck her head out of the locker room door.

"This is going to take a little longer than anticipated. Apparently, she's never had a shower before with hot water and a flexible shower head."

Savannah gasped when a loud moan could be heard from the locker room. "Is she masturbating?"

Kelly started giggling. Melvin and Savannah laughed as well until she hit Melvin on the shoulder.

"You shouldn't be laughing. This is your fault."

"What was I supposed to do?" he asked.

Savannah didn't answer verbally, instead she gave him a disapproving stare.

"Okay, well, I have things to do, like go find a new ride," Melvin said.

Savannah eyed him. "Don't you dare go out that gate by yourself."

"No, ma'am, I won't. I'll take True and Dong with me."

"How long will you be gone this time?" she asked.

"No more than a couple of hours. I've already got a vehicle in mind. It's not too far from here. I'm borrowing a tow truck from Jorge and will bring it right back."

Melvin hurried off before he caught any additional grief from Savannah. He knew she was more upset than she let on about him being ambushed, which he supposed meant she still loved him. So, even though she was mad at him, he was smiling to himself as he headed outside and over to the motor pool.

After they succeeded in getting Mal out of the shower, they dressed her in some hand-me-downs consisting of jeans, a plain tee shirt, socks, and a bra that Mal curled her nose at.

"What the hell am I going to do with that?" she asked.

Kelly tried to explain the purpose of it, but it didn't make sense to Mal. So, she shoved it in her pocket and the two women led her to the infirmary for a medical exam. Doctor Salisbury greeted the women, inquired about Kelly and her pregnancy, and then led Mal through the doors leading to the examination rooms.

"At least she's squeaky clean for the exam," Kelly said to Savannah with a chuckle.

Savannah nodded, but her mind went back to this same scenario with herself. What she remembered the most was being told she'd had an STD that went untreated for too long and now she couldn't have kids. She glanced over at Kelly's growing bulge and was envious. It seemed like everything that happened lately reminded her of her past, back when she'd been abducted by the Blackjacks. It was the most horrific time of her life.

"That girl reminds me of an annoying child who constantly asks questions," Kelly said.

"Do you think she's ever had a physical before?" Savannah asked.

"She had to have one or two when she was a child. It seems like she would've had inoculations too," Kelly answered.

As if to punctuate their questions about inoculations, they heard a yelp of pain coming from the back.

"Sounds like she got her vaccination," Kelly quipped.

CHAPTER 16 – ZACH & FRED

We managed to get the rest of the zed corpses loaded up on the second trip. It was hard work; dirty and physically demanding. At the end of the day, we were all spent. Fred had come back when we were on our second load. I showed him some of the corpses and what I'd discovered.

"He cut some of them open, in case you were wondering," Bailey said. "Is he always this way?"

Fred gave me a glance.

"I took pictures too, although I was thinking maybe we should've kept a couple of them to take back to Weather so they could properly autopsy them," I said.

Fred grunted. "I don't want them anywhere near Aisha."

I chuckled, then realized Fred wasn't joking. "Okay, understood."

"I have a question. You've cut them open without wearing any type of safety equipment. Why aren't you worried about becoming infected? Or are you simply stupid?" Bailey asked.

Justin scoffed. "Didn't you know? Zach is completely immune."

Bailey eyed me. "Are you now. What about those six kids of yours? Are they immune too?"

"Three, plus one on the way, and yes, they are. I don't let them get exposed though."

She eyed me a moment longer, a glint in her eye now. "Something tells me you're a pretty good dad." She then changed the subject and pointed at the camera. "So, what have you figured out about them?"

"The muscle tissue shows some evidence of regeneration, although there's a lot of scar tissue as well. Also, I don't know if you're aware, they're able to digest food again. We've seen this before but haven't been able to understand it. There is a rather complex theory about it."

"What kind of theory?" she asked.

"That the virus has mutated into a virophage."

"A virus that infects other viruses," Bailey surmised.

I looked at her in surprise. "Exactly. Viruses hijack the host's cellular mechanisms to replicate themselves, often taking pieces of the host's DNA in the process to create the next generation of progeny. There is a study that was conducted back before that showed some of those viruses had the capability of tissue regeneration.

"The theory is a superbug has been created from phages which caused some kind of low-level regeneration of the digestive system. From what I've seen, it could be theorized that the same thing is happening to the infected person's muscles."

"What about bacteria?" she asked.

Now I frowned in puzzlement. "Bacteria?"

"Bacteria is a living organism and it's already been proven that bacteria can regenerate tissue," she noticed my expression. "My mom was a high school biology teacher. She continued teaching me even after it all went bad."

I nodded. I was impressed.

"What about you?" she asked.

"What do you mean?"

"You talk like an educated person. My guess is you were about fifteen or sixteen when it went bad?"

"Yep," I said.

"So that means somebody made sure you continued your education."

I shrugged. "I've always been a voracious reader and I have an excellent memory." I then pointed at Fred. "My greatest education came from this old man and a couple of others like him."

Fred was staring off into the distance saying nothing. Bailey gave Fred the once over.

"I've seen you before, Mister McCoy, back when I was a kid. I think I was six or seven. My family went to a county fair at the Carroll County Ag Center. You were a trick shot artist in one of the shows. I remember you did all kinds of shots, but the one that stuck out the most is you shot two quarters out of the air. It was the most amazing thing I'd ever seen."

Fred stared and gave her a small nod. We stared back, waiting for him to tell us all about it, but Fred wasn't the type to talk much about himself. He only offered us a morsel.

"Yeah, that was a few years ago. Doubt I could do it these days," he said and looked off into the distance, perhaps thinking of the past. His reverie lasted only a couple of seconds, then he turned to me.

"We best get going," he said.

It was not something that was up for debate. Fred was ready to go home and that was that. I turned to Bailey.

"Please convey my condolences to the people who lost their loved ones. Despite the circumstances, it was a pleasure working and talking with you."

"I appreciate it. I'm sure we'll see each other again. It's been a while since any of us have visited Mount Weather. Maybe I'll bring my pops down one day. He's been wanting to speak with the president and give him some advice."

I chuckled. “I’d like to be a witness to that.”

The sky was clear, which meant dusk lingered a little longer, allowing for me to spot any road hazards a little quicker. I rolled down the window and welcomed the influx of wind. It’d been a hot day and I’d been bathed in sweat most of the day. I glanced over at Fred. He’d taken his hat off and was also enjoying the breeze.

“I’ll have to slow down once it gets dark,” I said.

Fred gave one of his micro nods, but otherwise remained quiet. It seemed like there was something on his mind. I kept talking.

“It’s a nice evening. Reminds me of back when I was a kid. When it was like this, my grandmother liked to sit on the back porch after dinner. I’d sit with her, and she’d tell me stories of her childhood.”

“Yep. I was the same. Me and my little brother would run around in the back yard chasing lightning bugs while our parents sat on the porch having a beer and laughing at us. Good times.”

“Yeah,” I agreed. “What else are you thinking about?”

“Those zeds.”

“So, where did you follow them to?” I asked.

“East.”

“I know that, but did you follow them all the way back to their destination?”

“Nope, but I didn’t need to. I knew where they were going,” he said.

I glanced over at him in the growing darkness. “Where?”

“Have you had any dreams of that girl lately?” he asked.

“Not a one since I got the lab reopened for her. Why?”

“About fifty or so went back the way they came. My guess is they got spooked when the QRF arrived and started killing all of them.”

“And where did they come from?” I asked. He was beginning to annoy me.

“You know where.”

It took me a moment, but then realization sunk in. “Fort Detrick?”

“Yep.”

My jaw tightened. “Shit. Shit, shit, shit.”

Fred waited for me to get it out of my system before speaking again. “Isn’t there an ongoing recon patrol of that area?”

“Yeah. Joker is in charge of it. He and his team go up there once a week.” I thought a moment. “Their last patrol was a day before the attack. There was nothing in his report that indicated anything out of the ordinary, other than the fact the zeds busted a trail camera they’d set up.”

Fred glanced at me. “If they busted it up, they know what that camera was doing. I think I’d call that a little out of the ordinary.”

"Yeah, I guess you're right. I always thought it was only a small percentage that have any cognitive thoughts. Like any group of people. Most of them are dummies but one or two might be smart."

"Sounds like the people at Mount Weather," Fred remarked. After a moment, he spoke again. "There's something else. They walked across an area that was still damp from some recent rain."

I glanced at him again and waited. Sometimes he was like this, and I had to pry it out of him. "Alright, what is it?"

"My guess is you have a few of those South Mountain folks who are unaccounted for."

I frowned as I looked at him. "Yeah. Are you saying some of them were bitten and turned?"

Fred gave a small nod.

"Shit," I growled, and then had a thought. "You know, they turned down our offer to vaccinate them."

"You think that's why they were attacked?" Fred asked.

"I don't know. Honestly, they were a soft target. They're too spread out and their defense works are minimal. But still…" I left the sentence unfinished.

"So, what are you going to do?" Fred asked.

"I'll be meeting with Bob and Connie in the morning and brief them. Then, Bob and Connie will be meeting with the senators, and they'll talk about it for hours before coming to some kind of bullshit resolution. Then, as a result of their bullshit resolution, they'll issue some bullshit directive which I'll be tasked with implementing."

While I talked, Fred made a face like he had gas pains. Even in the growing darkness I could see it. I knew all too well what he thought of the politicians, it's one of the reasons he and Rachel moved out of Mount Weather.

"I'm sure they'll come up with a brilliant solution," he quipped.

I scoffed. "Yeah, I'm sure they will. What would be your brilliant solution?"

Fred continued staring straight ahead, but his words were succinct. "The only good zed is a dead zed." He then glanced over at me. "Out of all your rules, that's the most important one."

CHAPTER 17 – MAL MEETS CIVILIZATION

"You've never been to a doctor?" Doctor Salisbury asked.

Mal shrugged. "I might've when I was little, but I don't remember it."

The doctor stared at her patient a long moment. She knew that childhood memories generally faded with time, but this girl was still a teenager.

"Do you remember a time when you became extremely sick?" she asked.

Mal's eyes widened. "Yeah, I remember that. Daddy said I got a fever and hoosinated."

Doctor Salisbury narrowed her eyes. "Would he have perhaps said you had hallucinations?"

Mal shrugged. "Could've been. He said I was going crazy and seeing things that weren't really there."

"How old were you when that happened?" the doctor asked. Mal's response was another shrug.

The doctor made a mental note to include that in her report and then inspected Mal's upper arms, looking for the telltale scar of the smallpox vaccination. Finding none, she added it to her list.

"Have you ever had any worms?" the doc asked.

"I ain't sure. How do you know if you've had worms?"

She didn't reply. If a person had ever had worms, they'd know. Doctor Salisbury changed the subject.

"You appear to be in good health, but you will need to undergo a round of inoculations. I hope you don't have an aversion to needles."

"What does aversion mean?" Mal asked.

The doctor didn't answer that question either, but Mal soon learned what she was talking about. Kelly was waiting for her when she was done. When she walked into the small waiting room, Kelly noticed she was a little pale.

"How are you feeling?" she asked.

"Aversioned," Mal answered.

Kelly frowned and peered at Doctor Salisbury for clarification.

"The inoculations may leave her feeling a little woozy, otherwise, she's healthy. Malnourished, but healthy. She may need to lie down for a little while, but I strongly suggest a strong nutritional program for her. The girl needs calories."

"I ain't eaten in a day or two," Mal said.

"A day or two? Oh, lordy. Why didn't you say something earlier?" Kelly asked. Mal's reply was a shrug.

"Okay then. How about you lie down a little while first?" Kelly suggested.

"I'm really hungry. I'd like to eat first, if that's okay," Mal said.

"Understood," Kelly replied and looked to Doctor Salisbury for guidance, who responded with a shrug and then realized what she'd done.

"Certainly but keep it light. Anything heavy or spicy may give her an upset stomach."

"I understand," Kelly said.

The cafeteria was not yet officially open for the dinner crowd, but since everyone liked Kelly, she had no trouble sweet talking one of the staff into whipping up a couple of chicken salad sandwiches for Mal.

Sitting, Mal took a tentative bite. "This is wonderful, what is it?"

"Chicken salad. In addition to the chicken, it's a mixture of mayonnaise, celery, and I think the chef adds lemon juice into the mix. Eat up," Kelly encouraged.

Mal gobbled down the first sandwich and used fingers to wipe the excess off her face and into her mouth. She started to reach for the second sandwich when Kelly reached out and put a hand on hers.

"Honey, we need to teach you some table manners. First, wipe your mouth with the napkin, and slow down a little bit. We have plenty to eat here."

Mal stared at Kelly in confusion. "What am I doing wrong?"

Kelly gave a patient smile and spent the next hour teaching table manners and etiquette. Mal complained that such things seemed unnecessary but tried to follow Kelly's advice. After eating, Kelly showed her to the dorms and got her set up with a bed and locker.

"It's co-ed, but don't worry, nobody will try to rape you or anything like that."

"I ain't worried," Mal replied.

Kelly withheld any snarky response. "I'll see you in the morning then."

Mal stood beside the bed and watched Kelly walk out. There were a couple of others in the dorm, a man and woman who weren't much older than her.

"Are you new here?" the young man asked. Mal nodded. "Well, welcome."

It seemed like he was about to say more but the woman whispered something to him and then they ignored her. Mal was undecided if this was a good thing or a bad thing. She felt like this wasn't her world and she wasn't sure if she wanted to make friends with anyone.

Her full belly made her sleepy. She barely remembered taking her shoes off and crawling into bed. She slept deeply and awoke an indeterminate number of hours later to some strange sounds coming from four bunks over. It took her a moment to realize that two people were making love, although she'd never heard that expression. Her father and King Rat simply called it fucking.

As quietly as she could, she crawled out of bed, found her shoes, and crept out of the dorm. After wandering the hallways for a few minutes, she stopped someone and asked where the exit was. Once outside, she found the barn where Booboo and Gumby were.

"Hey, you two," she said as she entered the stall.

Gumby was lying in some hay but stood and greeted her with a wagging tail. She saw an empty plate lying on the ground. Somebody had fed him, causing her to feel guilty for eating and not even thinking about the little mutt. She gave Booboo a nose rub before sitting in the stall and hugging Gumby.

"I'm sorry I haven't been around," she said. "I promise I'll do better."

She was awakened the next morning by someone shaking her shoulder. Looking up, she saw a young man standing over her.

"Hey, what're you doing here?" the man asked.

She sat up and stretched. "I was sleeping with my horse and dog."

The young man frowned. "Well, I guess that's okay. My name's Slim. I don't think I've ever seen you around here before. Are you new?"

"I came here yesterday. Melvin brought me. I'm supposed to be questioned or something. Then they'll decide if I get to stay."

Slim nodded in understanding. "Ah, you're going to be interviewed. I went through the same thing when I first got here. What's your name?"

"Mal. I don't think they're gonna let me stay."

"Why's that?" Slim asked.

"Cuz me and my daddy tried to kill Melvin."

Slim frowned again. "Ooh, not a wise move. What happened?"

"He killed my daddy," Mal lamented.

Slim gave a slow nod. "I'm not surprised. There're a few men around here who you shouldn't ever tangle with. Melvin's one of them."

Mal stared but said nothing.

"When's your interview?" Slim asked.

She looked out of the open barn door and estimated the time. "Sometime this morning."

"Welp, good luck with it. Oh, if you don't mind me putting in my two cents worth, you might want to get cleaned up first. It looks like you got some horse manure on you."

Mal looked down at her clothing and realized she must have rolled over in it while asleep. She almost started to cry.

"They put me in a dorm, but I don't know how to get back inside."

"Oh, that's no problem. I'll show you. You can get yourself cleaned up and be looking all spiffy for your interview. Okay?"

Mal nodded and wiped her tears away. "You're nice."

Slim grinned. "I try to be. The good Lord blessed us with life, and we should cherish it. There's no reason to be full of hate, right?"

Mal stared. "I ain't ever thought of it like that."

CHAPTER 18 – ZACH & THE GRENADE

The briefing with Bob and Connie about the South Mountain attack took place after I'd returned home last night. It went like I thought it would. The two men listened to my report, asked several questions, and then said they'd have a meeting with the senators in the morning after breakfast. I'm glad they didn't insist I sit in on it. It would have been an enormous waste of my time, but I didn't tell them that. Bob would no doubt give me a summation later.

As I stood in the breakfast line engaging in small talk with First Sergeant Crumby, I never expected what would happen next. Nikki Mullins walked up to us. She was dressed in her usual attire, jeans, cowboy boots, and a dark green tee shirt that was tucked in so as not to impede her holster. Her signature hat was missing, making me wonder if she'd finally thrown it away.

"Good morning, Nikki. How's it going?" I asked.

"Fine," she answered and stared a moment at me before focusing on Jeremiah. "You're a Marine, right?"

Jeremiah chuckled. "Been one since you were still wearing diapers."

"Good. I want to show you something." She pulled the small backpack off of her shoulders and dug into it. A moment later, she came out with an olive drab cylindrical-shaped object. A grenade.

"Whoa," he exclaimed in surprise before reaching out and taking it from her outstretched hand.

I hastened a subtle look around the cafeteria and lowered my voice. "Let's quietly take it over to the TOC."

Jeremiah agreed with a nod, put the grenade back in Nikki's pack, and the three of us left the cafeteria as casually as we could. Once inside the TOC, I motioned them toward a plain, army issue table that was surprisingly the same color as the grenade. "First Sergeant, why don't you do the honors."

Nikki put her backpack on the table. Jeremiah opened it and pulled it out with a chuckle. "I've got to admit, when she first showed it to me, I was worried, but she's got the safety pin secured and bent over so it won't accidentally fall out."

"I see that," I replied as I picked it up. Inspecting it, I looked up at the first sergeant.

"It's one of ours, isn't it," Jeremiah said.

"It's a distinct possibility," I replied.

"What do you mean? How would you know that?" Nikki asked.

"We've gone on multiple scavenging missions over the years, including the military bases around here. Although most of the bases have already been looted, we've had some success in finding things." I gestured at Jeremiah. "The First Sergeant found a couple of cases of hand grenades on one of those missions."

I rotated it until the serial number was facing up. "You see this?"

"A serial number," Nikki said and gave me a look to indicate she thought I was about to mansplain something.

"What you may or may not know about me is that I am a stickler about details."

Jeremiah agreed by snorting. I gave a small smile.

"Yep, I am. One of the things that I insist on is dutifully keeping an accurate record of all items that are scavenged, and oh boy do I like serial numbers."

"Yep, you certainly do," Jeremiah added.

I paused in my lecturing and reached for the TOC's laptop. Logging in, I soon had the appropriate spreadsheet open and entered the serial number into the search function. The only hit was from a lathe. I modified my search to the first three numbers and this time I got a partial hit.

"It's a close match to that case of grenades we recovered from the University of Virginia's ROTC armory. That was one of your missions, right?"

"Yeah, that was one of mine," Jeremiah said. "I still wonder why a college ROTC unit would have the need to have hand grenades. Think about it, those were college boys and girls, not a combat unit. I guess that'll forever be a mystery."

"Yeah, no doubt," I said and faced Nikki. "Have any of you guys been on scavenging missions in Charlottsville?"

Nikki frowned. "I don't know specifically, but they used to go out on looting runs back when they had working vehicles. BC finally called it off when a crew got attacked by zeds and three of them were killed. Besides, they don't have any real mechanics, and nobody seems interested in building up a fleet of diesel vehicles." She shook her head. "There's this mindset there that they'd like to go back to the 1800s, where the men rode around on their horses and the women stayed home cooking, weaving on the loom and servicing their men."

"Yeah, that's one of the negatives of this damned apocalypse. It seemed to make sexist and racist beliefs even stronger," Jeremiah said. "That's why I hooked up with a white woman."

He kept a straight face. Nikki stared a moment and then gave me a questioning look. Jeremiah then howled with laughter.

"I'm just messing with you, girl. Well, I mean my girlfriend is white, but it has nothing to do with any of that other stuff."

Nikki gave an uncertain smile. "So, getting back to this hand grenade, would it have killed me?"

"Absolutely, if you were close enough. The manual says it has a kill radius of five meters and a casualty radius of fifteen meters," Jeremiah said.

"Tell us how it was rigged up," I suggested.

Nikki gestured at it. "It was tied to a tree. A fishing line was tied to the pin, and it was stretched across the road and tied off to a fallen tree on the other side of the road. Whoever did it left a scuff mark on the bark of the tree, that's how I spotted it."

"Where was the grenade mounted? Near the ground or higher up?" I asked.

"I had to reach up to it, so maybe six feet off the ground."

Jeremiah gave me a look. "They knew you were on horseback. That's why they put it up so high. If you'd have activated it, you would've been killed. Your horse too, most likely."

"Do you know who did it?" I asked.

Nikki gave a slight shrug. "I don't want to name anyone until I'm certain."

"I'll get on the radio and ask BC about it," I said and started to stand. Nikki instantly shook her head.

"No, don't do that," she said.

I stopped and peered at her. She made a pained expression.

"It's possible he's the one who did it," she said and then she told us of the death of Colton and how he blamed her for it.

"Okay, I understand. Alright, I'll get Liam and Logan to start an investigation," I said, and Nikki once again shook her head.

"I want to figure it out myself," she said.

I swapped glances with Jeremiah. He shrugged his shoulders.

"Your call," he said.

"Alright, but let me caution you, we are attempting to have a society of law and order. Frontier justice is frowned upon."

"Thanks guys," she said and stood. "Okay, well, I have some things to do and then I'm heading back to Fred and Rachel's."

I waited until she left before speaking to Jeremiah. "What do you think?"

He scratched his head before responding. "It ain't random. I think there's somebody out there at that Shenandoah community who wants to kill her, but they don't want anyone to know they did it."

"Hence the reason for the booby trap and not simply lying in wait and shooting her," I said and thought for a moment. "Sniping her would have required a lot of time to set up and wait on her. Whoever did this did not have that amount of time."

"Staying gone from their people, or their work detail, would have raised questions. If she turned up dead from being shot, the first thing that'd be asked was who was absent during the time frame she was killed," he said.

I nodded. "Yep, exactly. And they had to have access to a hand grenade."

"Sounds like a job for the O'Malleys, but she doesn't want that," Jeremiah said.

"Yeah, she wants to figure it out for herself."

Jeremiah let out a low chuckle.

"What?"

"That part about frontier justice. Now that was funny, especially coming from you."

I allowed him a small smile. Yeah, one could say I'd committed more than one act of frontier justice in my time, but Nikki didn't need to know that. I wondered if she knew how many acts of frontier justice Fred had committed. I stretched and then stood.

"We're interviewing a new arrival in about an hour. After that's done, I'll advise Bob and Connie about Nikki and her grenade. They'll want to talk it over at length, but I'll convince them there's not much else we can do for the moment."

Jeremiah stood too. "Sounds good to me. I've got things to do too, but I'll be around. Give me a shout if you need me."

I headed to my office, which would normally take less than five minutes, but I was stopped several times by people who had questions or needed something. Being the Director of Operations, I felt it was my responsibility to listen and act, even if a lot of it was frivolous nonsense, like one person complaining about having potatoes served five times a week. I'd make a point of earnestly listening and discussing whatever issue they had. Most of the time, I could get it resolved, but not always.

I finally made it to my office where Kate was diligently typing away. She looked up when I walked in.

"I'm glad you're here. I have questions," she said.

I took a seat at my desk. "What kind of questions?"

"This computer program for the food consumption model wants specific demographics, like the ages and gender of everyone living in and around Mount Weather. Where do I get all that?"

"Oh, that should be easy enough. There is an Excel file that's titled, 'Census.' It has all the demographics you need. There should be a way to merge it into the program. Let me see what I can do."

It took me twenty minutes to figure it out and then the computer programing took over. It was updated less than a minute later. Kate smiled when the data cells began automatically populating.

"Wow, that's awesome. I'll actually be done with this by the end of the week."

We began discussing the data sheets for a couple of minutes until my phone rang.

"Hi sweetie," Kelly greeted. "I've got Mal with me and we're in the conference room."

I looked up at the clock and realized the meeting was starting in five minutes.

"I'll be right there," I said.

"You better," Kelly said and hung up. Kate overheard the conversation.

"Who's Mal?" she asked.

"A new girl that Melvin found," I said and briefly explained the circumstances.

Kate arched an eyebrow. "And Melvin didn't kill her? Interesting."

"Yeah, go figure. I guess he decided the father was the bad guy and not this little girl. Anyway, I'll be sitting in on the interview. Do you need anything else from me?"

"Nothing that can't wait. You better get going. Oh, if I may add, there's too many young single boys around here that're so horny even the chickens are nervous. A new female added to the Mount Weather population couldn't hurt."

I grinned. "Point taken."

CHAPTER 19 – ZACH & MAL

We didn't know Mal's last name, and she claimed not to remember it. I briefly saw her at breakfast, sitting with Slim and wolfing down food like there was no tomorrow, and now she was sitting at the conference table, looking around like she'd never seen anything like it. Then, she confirmed it.

"I ain't never been in a room like this before," she said. "And y'all got lights? And hot water? Does everyone get to take showers here?"

"All of the above," Bob said with a patient smile.

Kelly and Savannah had already briefed us on her demeanor. They couldn't decide if it was her semi-feral upbringing or if she was simply stupid. I looked her over. She was skinny, not unlike a lot of people who we've rescued in the past. She wasn't ugly, but she wasn't exactly pretty either. She had plain, sorrel-colored hair that reached down past her shoulders and hazel-colored eyes. Her teeth were not pleasant to look at. I guessed they had probably not had the pleasure of a toothbrush in years.

"Melvin has a weakness for strays, just look at me," Savannah quipped. She remembered the night Melvin found her. It was raining. She was handcuffed and fleeing for her life. Melvin found her when she was about to be killed by zeds. And he was naked as a jaybird when he killed the zeds and rescued her. She wondered if he was wearing anything when he found Mal.

After taking her for a physical, Kelly fixed her up with fresh clothing, got her fed, and then found her a bed in the dorm for the evening. I don't know how she met Slim, but he was nice enough to get her to breakfast. Kelly and Savannah then brought her here for her formal interview. Sitting her down, Kelly motioned for me to follow her into the hallway.

"Doctor Salisbury said she's malnourished, but otherwise, she's fine. No signs of infection."

"Alright, that's good," I said.

"Are we keeping her?" she asked.

"We're going to interview her and see if she's a good candidate, but I'd say it's merely a formality."

Kelly nodded in understanding. She was also aware of the lopsided male-to-female ratio around here.

"We should send her to Marcus Hook or somewhere else," Savannah remarked.

I peered at her. "You don't like her?"

Savannah stared and gave a slight shrug. "She tried to kill Melvin and she's dumber than a box of rocks. There's not much to like."

Kelly and I laughed. Savannah was going to say more, but the approach of the president and vice president stopped her.

"Hello, ladies," Connie said with a smile that could rival any used car salesman. That was Connie, always complimenting the women, hoping for an opening. Kelly gave me a knowing look.

"So, is this young lady all cleaned up and ready for her interview?" he asked.

"Yep. Lucky for you she likes showers. She smelled like the ass end of a pig when she first got here," Savannah said and glanced at me. "Something tells me she's going to be here for a while, and I have better things to do. See you guys later," she said and gave Connie a cool glance before walking off.

"I'll be in my classroom," Kelly said and gave me a kiss before leaving.

I faced Mal and motioned toward the door. "Alright, let's go."

When we sat, Connie was his usual self and gave Mal a warm smile. Almost to the point where he was leering. I wouldn't have been surprised if he was already fantasizing.

"Hi, Mal. I'm Conrad Nelson, but everyone calls me Connie."

She scrunched her face at him. "Are you the president?"

His smile faltered, but he recovered and gestured toward Bob. "He is. This is President Robert Duckworth."

"Hello, Mal," Bob greeted. "Connie is our country's vice president, and this is Zach Gunderson. He's the Director of Operations."

"Well, I feel special getting to meet y'all. Kelly said y'all want to ask me a bunch of questions."

"Yes, we do," Bob answered.

"What about? I ain't got much to tell that you probably don't already know."

"How about you start with telling us about yourself?" Bob replied.

"Like what? Y'all already know my name and y'all know that Melvin killed my daddy."

"Yes, tell us about that," Connie said.

"Well, back the other night, we saw a truck driving down the road. We hadn't seen anyone driving anything in a long time, so Daddy said we should set up on them."

"So, your father made the decision to ambush Melvin," Connie said.

Mal frowned at Connie's question. "Melvin used that word too. What's an ambush?"

"It's when you hide and then surprise a person and kill them," I said. "Isn't that what you and your father did with Melvin?"

Mal seemed to think it over and then slowly nodded. "Yeah. Daddy shot at him and made him wreck his truck. Then, when he went up to the truck, Melvin shot him."

"Why did he go up to the truck?" Connie asked.

"To finish him off, I reckon," she said matter-of-factly. "But Melvin killed him instead. Can't y'all punish him or something?"

"We're not going to punish Melvin for defending himself," I said. "Maybe it's you that needs punishing."

"For what?" Mal asked in surprise.

Bob held up a hand. "Perhaps we can revisit that issue later. First, I want to hear about your childhood. Where did you grow up?"

Mal scrunched up her nose. "I ain't really sure. Somewhere around here, but Daddy never told me exactly where," she said and scratched her face. "I remember it called a trailer park. That's where we lived. I don't remember where it was at though."

"Do you remember the beginning of everything going bad?" he asked.

"Sort of. I was in the second grade. Daddy came and got me out of school one day during Miss Tipton's English class. He said the world was going crazy. Miss Tipton didn't like that too much and told Daddy she was going to call the police, but Daddy took me anyway. I was real scared but I never saw no police."

"What was the name of the school?" I asked.

Mal shrugged. "It was some man's name."

I wanted to press her on it, but Bob changed the subject.

"Who was with your father?" he asked.

"It was only him. He had the car packed up with stuff," she answered.

"Where did the two of you go?" he asked.

"Some church that was out in the country. I remember asking Daddy why we didn't go home and get Momma, but he said Momma had already turned into a monster. So, we went to a church. There were some other people there. I remember everyone was scared," Mal said and paused a moment to pick her nose before continuing. "Everyone was always scared. That's what I remember the most, and there were always men running around with guns. We weren't even allowed outside for a long time, but then one day the kids were allowed to go outside and play. Even then, they told us not to make any noise. Then, one day there was a big argument among the men and Daddy said we had to leave."

"Did he say why?" Bob asked.

Mal shook her head. "If you're going to ask us what we did next, I don't really know. We traveled around some, and we found some people who let us stay with them. I think we stayed with them through the cold weather. When it got warm, we left but our car didn't work no more so Daddy took a couple of horses."

"Where did you go next?"

Mal shrugged. "I don't know. We wandered around a lot."

"Did you kill people you encountered?" I asked.

Mal looked down at her fingernails. "Kelly had perfect fingernails. She said she could fix mine up just like hers."

"That's nice, Mal. Now, how about you answer my question," I said.

She looked up at me, although I could tell she was reluctant to do so. "It wasn't like that all the time. Mostly we just snuck around and took from people when we could. There ain't many people around here no more though."

"Where did you get the rifle and ammunition?" I asked.

"Huh?"

"The rifle and ammunition you and your father used to shoot at Melvin. Where did you get it?"

"Oh, from Rat King," she said.

"Who is Rat King?" I asked.

"He's a man that comes to visit sometimes. He brings us stuff to eat, like fish. If it weren't for him, we would've starved to death I reckon. I like crappie the best. Do y'all have crappie?"

"So, he gave you and your father the ammunition," I pressed.

"Yeah, and the rifle. The one y'all took from me. He said we needed to start killing people to earn our keep."

"Describe this man," Conrad said.

She gazed at the vice president. "He looks a little like you, but he has long gray hair. He keeps it tied back and he has a bushy beard." She rubbed her neck. "It always scratches me up."

"Does he talk about himself, like does he say where he lives?" I asked.

Mal shook her head. "He didn't say, and I didn't ask. Daddy said he's mean. He said that on the outside he acts all nice and friendly, but on the inside he's black hearted. So, I never asked him no questions that might've made him mad."

Conrad had leaned forward in his chair. "What did you mean when you said his beard scratches up your neck?"

"When he's on top of me and kissing on me. Daddy loans me to him to get food and stuff."

I frowned. Looking over, I saw the vice president frowning as well.

"When you say your father loans you to him, what exactly do you mean?" he asked.

"So's he can have his way with me. Sometimes he's nice, sometimes he ain't so nice. Daddy said he liked me though. He said that's the price I have to pay for him to bring us food. And then, when he brought us the gun and bullets, that's when he told us to go out and steal and kill for him."

"By ambushing people," I said.

Mal nodded. "I didn't like it, but Daddy said it'd be okay. But now he's dead." Her eyes began tearing up now. Her father sounded like a piece of trash, but even so, he was her father and I'm sure she loved him. She then stared at the president.

"I kind of like it here. Well, some of the people seem a little off, if you know what I mean, but I met a boy this morning and he was nice to me. And y'all have hot showers. Those are nice too. Are y'all gonna let me stay?"

Bob stared back. "That depends."

"On what?" she asked.

"On you. You've got to be truthful with us about everything and you have to learn how to be a productive and honest person. Can you do that?"

She paused for several seconds and wiped her nose with the back of her hand before responding. "I ain't really sure what you mean by productive. I guess there's a lot for me to learn, but yesterday Kelly taught me a little bit about manners, and she said I learned real quick. Does that count?"

CHAPTER 20 – A VISIT TO THE TRADING POST

Team Joker, minus Joker, exited the main gate ten minutes before Zach, and arrived at Marcus Hook an hour later. After stopping at the barricade and saying hello to the guards, they drove to the former soccer stadium and parked.

The three men, Flash, Slim, and Cutter, stared in silence, taking it all in. It was mostly open, but there were also individual business kiosks, several large tents, and the upper areas where fans used to sit and watch the game was undergoing a remodeling process where the seats were slowly being replaced by structures of various sizes.

"Welp, we made it," Slim said. "Too bad Joker didn't want to come."

"He's a husband and dad now," Cutter said. "No more fun stuff for him. A good reminder to never get married."

Flash murmured something that could've been an agreement or maybe he was only acknowledging Cutter's opinion about marriage. He changed the subject and gestured around the area.

"I didn't think there'd still be this many people here considering that zed attack last week."

"I wonder if the whores are still here," Cutter mused.

"I think they prefer to be called adult entertainment specialists," Flash quipped.

"Whatever, if they're still here I might have to hire some entertainment," Cutter replied.

"Reese said they're ugly," Slim said.

"Sometimes, you got to play the hand you're dealt," Cutter rejoined. "Good thing I have condoms."

"They probably expired five years ago," Flash said.

Cutter shrugged. "No matter. I need the company of a woman. I might last all of two minutes, but it'll be worth it."

"What're you gonna trade for?" Flash asked, which caused Cutter to frown.

"I hadn't thought of that. I have my weed stash, maybe that'll work."

"We don't need to be messing with them," Slim said. "If we catch some kind of sex disease, everyone at Mount Weather will know about it fifteen minutes after going to the infirmary."

Flash chuckled at Slim's warning and gazed around the place. Trader Joe was calling it an agora these days. There were a couple of fenced in areas which contained a couple dozen sheep. There was a livery stable with at least two blacksmiths plying their trade, a cobbler, a basket weaver, a creamery, several horse-drawn wagons filled with various types of items. Pots and pans, tools of all kinds, secondhand clothing, homemade clothing, you name it. And, wouldn't you know it, the sound of a banjo being played could be heard.

"It's impressive," Flash remarked.

"It is," Cutter agreed. "I hope I can find some decent boots in my size."

"I think I might find one or two things to purchase," Slim said. Cutter eyed him.

"What the hell are you going to trade for?"

Slim chuckled. Cutter cut his eyes at him. "Well, they ain't going to give away their shit for free and you don't have any weed."

"Did you happen to notice that tote bin I put in the back of the van this morning?" Slim asked.

"Yeah, what'd you bring?" he asked.

Slim held a finger up and opened the back doors of the van. The tote bin was a thick black plastic bin with a yellow top. Slim opened it, showing the bin was divided into multiple sections with carefully cut out cardboard. Each section held individual items.

"Fishing gear?" Cutter asked.

"Don't knock it," Slim replied and waved a finger at the contents. "Those are hand crafted lures."

"They look brand new. Where'd you get them?" Cutter asked.

"He made all of them," Flash said.

"Some of them," Slim corrected. "Some of them are refurbished, but they're better than new, if I say so myself."

Cutter picked up one of them and scrutinized it, slowly turning it in his fingers. Slim cleared his throat.

"That one's called a nymph. It's designed to travel a few inches under water and is used for fly fishing. You can catch trout all day long with that little beauty."

Cutter admired it a moment longer before looking up. "That's some nice workmanship."

Slim beamed. "Thanks."

"What do you think you can trade them for?"

Slim's grin faltered. "Welp, I don't know, but I suppose I can ask around and find out. There's got to be some fishermen here. Or fisherwomen, whatever you call them." He scrunched up his face in thought a moment before snapping his fingers. "I have a thought. Let's ask Trader Joe. He knows everyone here."

There was a chorus of agreement among them. They found Trader Joe sitting under an open canopy tent near the entrance, drinking some kind of dark beverage with Irina and a couple of men whom they did not recognize.

"She's showing them off, as usual," Cutter whispered to his buddies. He was referring to Irina's ample breasts. Today, she was wearing a bright orange tank top that was probably a size too small, and no bra.

Technically, Irina Fleming was still married to Clay Fleming. But when Clay was banished for killing a young man who he mistakenly thought raped his stepdaughter, she ghosted him and stayed at Marcus Hook. Eventually, she made her way into Trader Joe's bed. Cutter thought she was a manipulative snake in the grass, but if he had to be honest with himself, he'd sleep with her in a minute.

Joe looked the same as he always did; long salt and pepper hair pulled back in a ponytail, graying beard, and an easygoing smile. The beard was neatly trimmed for a change, which looked good on him.

"Howdy, boys," he greeted.

"Hey, Joe," they chorused.

Cutter waved a hand around. "This place is doing great."

Joe gave a pleasant smile. "Well, thank you for that. We've worked hard to make this a success. Personally, I think it does more for the rebuilding of America than anything else that's been done so far."

"Can't argue with that," Cutter said.

"So, what are you men up to today?" Trader Joe asked.

Flash and Cutter traded a nervous glance. Cutter plowed ahead and motioned for Trader Joe to follow him with a head nod. He waited until they were far enough away from everyone else so nobody could hear.

"I'll be honest. We came here to see if there were any women around. You know, single women."

Joe's smile returned. "There're a few fillies here. The Mennonites seemed to have brought all their eligible girls. The oldest is twenty-two and the youngest is fourteen."

He saw Cutter frown and explained. "They're looking for husbands to come live and work on their farms."

"Oh, shit, we're not looking for wives," Flash said.

"We'd just like to get laid," Cutter added. Flash gave a nervous chuckle and Slim blushed.

"Well, boys, you're in luck. There's a couple of working girls that came down from Jersey and made themselves at home here." He leaned forward and lowered his voice. "My advice though, use condoms."

"What do you think they'll charge?" Cutter asked.

"Oh, that one's easy. They're hardcore stoners. They love the herb, which I kind of understand because it's a highly sought after commodity."

Cutter grinned like the cat that ate the canary. "Well, we're in luck then. I bet we can work something out with them."

Trader Joe gave an approving nod. "That's good, that's good, but be careful with your generosity, they'll smoke it all up before you can even get a happy ending." He pointed. "You can find them over by that section where there's a couple of men working on trucks. Don't show them how much you have though, they'll take all of it."

"Thanks, Joe," Cutter said and the two of them headed off, leaving Slim standing alone.

"What about you, Slim?" Trader Joe asked.

"I don't smoke, and I don't think I'd like those kinds of girls anyway," he said.

Trader Joe gave a fatherly smile. "Good for you, son. I take you for a man who'd like a nice lady to settle down with. Now, if I was a young single man like you, I'd probably mosey on over there to the Mennonites. Those girls are pure as the driven snow, if you know what I mean."

Slim cleared his throat. "I have a question."

"Ask away, Slim," Trader Joe said.

"Do you know if those Mennonites like to fish?"

CHAPTER 21 – ZACH VOTES FOR MAL

I'd sent Mal off with Kelly so the three of us could talk about her and decide if she could stay.

"She's rather crass," Bob said after Mal had left the conference room.

"And uneducated," Connie added.

"She is at that," I agreed.

"Doctor Salisbury said she's capable of having children, right?" Bob asked. I nodded. "Well, that's something then."

Connie cleared his throat. "Zach, let me ask you. Is she a complete moron or do you think she's capable of learning?"

"I think she can be educated, to a point. She'll never be a doctor, or president, but I think there's a good possibility of successfully integrating her."

Honestly, I amazed myself on how well I could speak like a politician. The truth of it, she was dumb, but she was a young woman of childbearing age, and I'm sure there were plenty of men around the area who wouldn't care what her IQ is.

"If you're asking me, I think we should let her stay here on a trial basis. If she's not crazy or a troublemaker, she'll have her a man before Christmas. Hell, she'll probably be pregnant before that."

"You think it'll take that long?" Connie asked with a sarcastic chuckle.

"So, it's decided then?" Bob asked.

Connie and I exchanged a glance and then agreed with a nod.

"Good. I'll let you give her the news," Bob said.

I stepped outside to the hallway and motioned for Mal to follow me.

"Where are we going?" she asked.

I didn't answer and led her to the classroom where Kelly taught. It was empty at the moment and Kelly was sitting at her desk, studying something on her laptop. She looked up when we walked in and gave me a smile.

"Let me guess, she's been accepted."

"Yes, but on a probationary basis," I said.

"What's that mean?" Mal asked.

"It means you have to behave yourself and not cause trouble," I warned.

"Oh."

I focused on Kelly. "The dorm she slept in last night, were there any problems?"

"Not that I know of," Kelly said. "What do you think, Mal? Was the dorm to your satisfaction?"

"I guess so. The bed was comfortable," Mal answered. She didn't mention being awakened by the couple that were having sex.

"Good," I said. "I'll let Lydia know of our newest member here and get her put on the work roster. Okay, I'm running late. I'll see you this evening."

"Bye sweetie," Kelly replied and gave me a kiss.

I saw Mal staring in puzzlement as I left.

"Is he your sweetie?" I heard Mal ask as I jogged down the hallway.

As I hustled to the motor pool, I mulled over the interview. Mal seemed to have a lot of memory gaps. The question I had was, were they genuine or was she intentionally being vague about some aspects of her life? If she was, that probably meant she was smarter than she was letting on. It was something I felt I needed to figure out, and more importantly, I wanted to find out who this King Rat character was and if he was part of a larger problem. Was he a lone wolf, like Mal alleged, or was he part of a gang? I needed to find out.

Approaching the motor pool, I saw Melvin, True, and Dong already waiting for me.

"Sorry I'm late," I said.

"No problem. We have everything ready to go. How'd Mal's interview go?" Melvin asked.

"Our leaders have decided to let her stay," I said.

True scoffed. "They weren't going to turn any fertile woman away, no matter how crazy she might be."

"I agree, she's a little out there, but I think it's because of how her father raised her. Time will tell, I guess."

"A classic example of Bronfenbrenner's Ecological Systems theory," Melvin remarked.

I peered at him. "One might argue that Lerner's Social-Contextual Perspective theory would also explain her lack of social development."

Melvin nodded. "A good point, Zach, a good point indeed."

"What the hell are you two talking about?" True asked. "On second thought, I don't want to know. You two babble too much."

Melvin and I shared a smile. True was scowling, he didn't like it when Melvin and I engaged in intellectual debates, so I changed the subject.

"Hey, let me ask you guys something. Have you ever heard of anyone called King Rat?"

"I've never heard that name," Melvin remarked.

True shook his head. "Me neither."

"Me neither," Dong parroted.

"Yeah, same here," I said.

"Is he connected to Mal somehow?" Melvin asked.

"Yeah," I said and explained.

"Don't tell me any more, I'm starting to feel sorry for her," True said, eliciting a chuckle from Melvin.

I made a mental note to send out a discrete inquiry to the surrounding communities. Over the years, we'd had people who lived around the Virginia and West Virginia areas turn up dead or go missing. It was one of those hard truths of life in post-apocalyptic America, and undoubtedly all over the world. Lawlessness was the norm. I wanted to change that. At least in our area of purview.

Melvin waved a hand at the two box trucks we acquired for our mission.

"What do you say we saddle up and get on the road?" he asked.

He was impatient for some reason, but we were running behind, thanks to me, so I didn't say anything. We loaded up and were on the road to Moorefield in minutes. It took us two hours to get there, but there were no major issues and even though neither truck had cold air to offset the summer heat, the drive wasn't that bad.

The Mackenzie clan seemed happy to see us, mostly. The one named Garth was in a sour mood, as if he thought this big move was wrong. Melvin seemed to sense what I was thinking.

"He's always in a bad mood. I think he has hemorrhoids and possibly an overly enlarged prostate."

"Could be," I said with a chuckle.

"Of course, he might've had a deficient childhood too," Melvin quipped.

"Don't start that shit," True huffed.

Moving furniture and stuff is a little different than it was back before. Back then, you could hire a moving company or go down to the U-Haul and purchase boxes. Cardboard boxes were a rarity these days, so we used handmade wooden crates, or we simply stacked everything in the back of the trucks and hoped not to cause too much damage.

With all hands doggedly motivated, it only took us a couple of hours to fill up the trucks. Because we had full loads, we had to drive slowly, which limited the breeze through the open windows. When we arrived at the church, Hammy clapped her hands in joy.

"We're home!" she exclaimed and then pointed. "Who are all those people?"

"Our work crews," I said and pointed at a team filling makeshift gabion baskets with rocks and similar materials. "Those are defense works, which you keep improving in the ensuing days. There's also a team who are working on the plumbing and there's a barn raising operation going on out back. I bet there are a few people working on the inside as well. C'mon, let's go see."

One of Mount Weather's oldest members, Norman Marnix, exited the building and walked out to us.

"We've made some progress," he said and looked over the group. "Hello, new people, I'm Norman. My team's mission is to get this place up to speed for you to live in. I'd say we have one or two more days of work before we're finished. After that, it's all up to you."

"We can do it," Poco said with a determined expression. Hammy nodded in agreement.

Norman stared at them over his bifocals. "I hope so, we need hardworking honest people around here, not lazy assholes."

The response from everyone was positive, with the exception of Garth.

"When are we going to get some cattle out here?" he grumbled.

Norman eyed him like he was looking at a pile of manure before walking off.

"When you're settled in, we'll bring some livestock out here," I said, trying to placate him. I can't say I liked him, but it was going to go easier if he were onboard.

"Chickens too, but we need a secure coop and make sure the fencing is good before we bring them out. I don't know about Moorefield, but around here we're having a problem with coyotes. We send out hunting parties when cattle or chickens are killed, but those rascals are like cockroaches, you never can kill off all of them."

"You got that right," Garth replied.

When he agreed with me, I took it as a good sign. By the end of the day, Garth seemed to be in a more positive mood. As I looked over everything, I surmised this operation was going to be a successful endeavor. I sure hoped I was right.

CHAPTER 22 - SLIM & THE MENNONITES

Slim heard Trader Joe's words, but he was watching his friends make a beeline over to the Winnebago Joe had pointed out. As he watched, two rough looking girls exited the RV and gave his buddies come-hither smiles.

Slim scoffed to himself. "No, sir, that's nothing but trouble," he murmured.

As he walked around and took it all in, he had to admit that it was a hell of a place. There was electricity, running water, and the restrooms worked. He didn't even try to guess where the refuse went, seeing as how the city sewer system was inoperative, but he didn't detect any foul odor, so he guessed it was all good.

It wasn't long before he meandered over to one of the open stalls where a girl was making a rhythmic thumping with a wooden butter churn. She smiled as Slim approached. Slim deduced from her homemade dress and head scarf that she was a Mennonite. She was cute too, maybe too cute for him, he thought, but he couldn't stop staring.

"Do you fancy yourself some homemade butter?" she asked. "Ours is the best around."

"I'm sure it is," Slim replied, "but, well, they make butter back at Mount Weather. I don't guess I need any."

"Why don't you try a taste," she suggested, and before Slim could turn her down, she turned to a table beside her and used a kitchen knife to cut a thin pad of butter off a larger block. She grasped the butter between her thumb and index finger and held it out for Slim.

She gazed at him with a sweet smile and bright hazel blue eyes that made Slim's heart skip a beat. He tried to keep his hand from shaking as he reached out and put it in his mouth.

"Wow, this is delicious," Slim said. "Tastes a little bit like you got some honey in it."

"Indeed, we do," she said, still smiling. "And what did you bring along to trade with?"

"Um, I have a tote bin full of fishing lures I've made. Now all I have to do is find people who enjoy fishing."

"Fishing lures, you say?"

Slim turned toward the voice. It was a man standing with a group of other men, all dressed similarly and wearing broad-brimmed straw hats with a black band. The man who spoke was tall and lean, with a long gray beard and eyes similar in color as the cute girl who had given him a taste of butter. Slim guessed him to be in his late forties and was more than likely this girl's father. He walked over and held out a hand.

"The name's Nicholas," he said.

Slim shook his hand, noting the strong grip and calloused palm.

"Everybody calls me Slim. It's nice to meet you, sir."

Nicholas frowned. "Slim? Is that your Christian name, son?"

"No, sir, it's my nickname because I can eat all day and never gain weight."

"I see. What is your Christian name?" he asked.

"Joseph," Slim replied, though it was a lie.

He was named after his father. Back before it all went bad, his dad had been sentenced to seventeen life sentences because he was a serial killer, and his name was well known by anyone who watched the news or surfed the internet. Slim wasn't sure if Mennonites had ever watched TV, but he didn't want anyone to ever know who he was related to.

Nicholas nodded. "Joseph, a good Christian name. Tell me, Joseph, have you accepted Jesus as your Lord and savior?"

Slim shifted on his feet. "Um, well, honestly, I don't know. My parents never took us to church, and I haven't had much time to study on it, but I can tell you that in these past ten years I've done an awful lot of praying."

"Haven't we all," Nicholas said with a somber smile. "We can talk more of that later if you'd like. So, what's this I hear about fishing? Are you a fisherman, son?"

"Yessir, I am. I've developed a hobby I guess you'd say of making fishing lures. I have all types and thought I'd bring them along, hoping to trade them for stuff I might need."

Nicholas nodded thoughtfully while continuing to stare at Slim through a pair of horn-rimmed glasses.

"We Mennonites have been known to do a little fishing. Why don't you show us what you have?"

Slim practically ran back to the van and returned a short time later with his tote bin. The men had gathered around him, and more importantly, the girl was still there. Whether she was genuinely interested in the lures or him, he wasn't sure. Whatever the reason, he was happy for her presence. Slim opened the box and explained each lure and what fish they were best used for. Nicholas listened with interest and inspected almost every lure Slim had.

"That is some fine craftsmanship, young man," he said. "We have a lot of lures, but nothing on this level. I believe we might be interested in doing some trading if you're willing."

"Yes sir, absolutely," Slim said and glanced over again at the girl. Nicholas also noticed and gestured at her.

"This is my daughter, Esther," he said.

"I'm very pleased to meet you," Slim said, proud of the fact that he said it without getting tongue tied and even more giddy when Esther gave him another flirtatious smile.

"Joseph, we were about to take a break and prepare lunch. Would you like to join us? Perhaps we can observe this appetite you are famous for."

Slim grinned. "Yes sir, I'd like that."

Esther's smile broadened. Nicholas and his people had folding tables assembled and food laid out with swift efficiency. Esther insisted he sit beside her. Once seated, she had a plate full of food in front of him and a napkin tucked into his shirt before he could even say please and thank you.

Slim was peppered with questions while he ate. He was asked almost everything about himself. How he had survived, whether or not he'd ever been married or had kids, what he thought about the Mennonite lifestyle, everything. They were friendly and polite, but he knew they were interrogating him. It took him a few minutes before he understood why.

After lunch, Slim leaned back in his chair and stretched. "Thanks for the meal, it was delicious."

"Did you get enough to eat?" Esther asked.

"Lord yes," Slim replied. "I believe I'd like to walk around." He turned to Esther. "Would you like to join me?"

"I would like that," she said.

Slim didn't know it yet, but before he left the Marcus Hook Trading Post, he was going to be hopelessly in love with a cute Mennonite girl by the name of Esther.

CHAPTER 23 – HORSE TRADING

After finishing her daily chores, Nikki fed Leeroy some grain and then sat in the stall with him. She found it a comfortable place to listen to one of the Harry Potter novels while reading along in the book. She'd listened for almost an hour and today, she only jotted down one word that she wasn't familiar with. She was looking it up on a well-used pocket dictionary when she heard the barn door open.

"Nikki?" Fred said.

"Over here," she replied.

Nikki didn't look up when she heard the footsteps approaching. It only took her a moment before she recognized the second set of footsteps. "Is that Sammy with you?"

"Yep. Your skills are getting better and better," he said and looked down where she was sitting. "What word are you looking up?"

"Quandary," she replied.

"Good one. I am in a bit of a quandary myself right now," Fred said.

"You are?"

"Your Shenandoah people have agreed to trade a mare and her colt to me. The problem is Rachel is not feeling well, and I need to stay here. Sammy has volunteered to go get them, but the folks at Mount Weather have said since Melvin's close call and the recent zed activity, there won't be any more one-man excursions. Two people minimum at all times. Would it be possible for you to go with him?"

She stood and glanced at Sammy, who stared back stoically. She liked Sammy. He was a little on the quiet side, but nice. And handsome. He was freshly bathed with clean clothes. She'd seen him out one day with his shirt off and was impressed. He didn't seem to have an ounce of fat on him and although he was lean, his muscles were well defined. She secretly envied Serena but made sure to never let anyone catch on that she felt that way.

"Yeah, sure, I can do that," she said.

"I figure if there aren't any problems, we'll be back well before midnight," Sammy said.

Nikki nodded at his response, but internally she was wondering about Sammy's significant other, Serena. Was she okay with Sammy going on a day trip with another woman? She was tempted to ask but decided not to. After all, it might cause him to have second thoughts about going and then he'd ruin her day by changing his mind.

"I'd kind of like to get going right away, if that's okay with you," he said.

Nikki glanced at Fred who gave a small nod. Nikki brushed the dirt off her pants and squared her shoulders. "Okay, let me get my kit together and I'll be ready."

Nikki went inside and went directly to the restroom. She washed her hands and face, brushed her hair, and inspected herself in the mirror. She guessed she was presentable enough and exited the restroom. She then filled her canteen, grabbed her favorite rifle, her go pack, and hustled outside.

Sammy and Fred had hooked up a horse trailer to her truck. He too had a backpack similar to hers and he had already put it in the back of her truck. She looked at his long gun, which he'd put in the passenger seat. She eyed Sammy with curiosity.

"A twelve-gauge pump instead of a rifle?"

"Yeah, I love it," he said. He saw her eyeing it. "It's a Winchester SXP Defender. I've gotten pretty good with it. I've got a slug barrel on it and can put one in a zed's head at a hundred yards, and I have plenty of double-ought buckshot for closer encounters," he said.

"Impressive. Where'd you pick that up from?"

"Zach found it somewhere and gave it to me for a birthday present a few years back. Don't tell anyone, but it's the best birthday present I've ever gotten."

Nikki nodded, wondering what kind of presents Serena had gotten him over the years. "Alright, I have to ask."

Sammy glanced at her. "Ask what?"

"Your girl, Serena, did she not want to go with you?"

"Nope. There's a group of people who get together once a week and play cards. She didn't want to miss it."

"Oh, that's…"

Sammy glanced over again when she didn't finish the sentence. "What were you going to say?"

"I don't know, maybe it's me, but it seems like she'd rather want to go with you."

"Yeah, you'd think so. It's okay though," he said.

Secretly, he was glad Fred suggested Nikki come with him. He thought she was attractive, and he liked talking to her. Besides, he needed some space from Serena. It'd gotten to the point where they argued often. It seemed like anything he said, no matter how innocuous, she'd disagree with him. He didn't know how to fix it, and worse, he wasn't sure he cared enough anymore. Sammy decided he didn't want to think about it and changed the subject.

"Tell me about the grenade," he said. "Fred said it was rigged up with a trip wire."

"Yes, it was."

"And it was meant for you?" he asked.

"I believe so," Nikki said and explained the circumstances.

"Damn," Sammy said when she'd finished. "Who do you think did it?"

"There are a couple of people who come to mind. One is Barnabas Cart."

"BC? The man who runs the place?" Sammy asked.

"Yep, he blames me for Colton's death," she said. "He's a military vet, so I would guess he knows about hand grenades and he's a tough man who'd kill someone who he thinks has wronged him. And then there's his son, Collin. He's Colton's younger brother. He also blames me for Colton's death."

"Why do they blame you?" Sammy asked.

Nikki let out a sigh. "It's a long story."

Sammy gave a small smile. "We have time, unless it's too personal."

"Alright, you asked for it. Colton and I were a couple. In fact, he was my first ever boyfriend. We went on a ride one morning. Just the two of us. His horse got spooked and threw him. When he landed, he hit his head, and it ended up killing him. BC is convinced I made up the story and in truth, I murdered him."

"Why in the world would he think that?" Sammy asked.

"Because Colton was an excellent rider and because we would sometimes get into huge fights." She glanced at Sammy. "I can be a little hotheaded and Colton was the same way. So, BC has it in his head that we got into another one of our fights and I hit him in the head with a rock or something."

Sammy thought about what she said a moment before speaking. "I don't think you killed him. I mean, I'm pretty good with horses and I got thrown the other day. I remember once, back a few years ago, Fred got thrown, and he's awesome with horses."

Nikki widened her eyes in surprise. "Fred got thrown off a horse? I would've liked to have seen that."

Sammy chuckled. "It was pretty cool, actually. He got bucked way up in the air, about five or six feet, but he landed on his feet, stood there a moment, and then got back on the horse like he meant to do the whole thing."

Nikki laughed. "You know, I'm not surprised."

"Alright, who's the other person you're thinking of?" he asked.

"A certain asshole by the name of Drill Bit," she said.

"Drill Bit?"

"It's a nickname. Don't ask."

Sammy smirked. "Alright, I won't. Why do you suspect him?"

Nikki frowned in thought a moment. “It’s kind of hard to explain, but there’s history between him and my stepparents. I don’t know all the details. He and Herman used to be good friends, but they had a falling out. Ever since then, he treats Mom like shit. About a month ago, I was visiting and walked in on him giving my mom hell about her back. I gave him a piece of my mind and warned him to leave Mom alone. He didn’t like it and told me I better watch myself.”

“Not a lot to go on,” Sam remarked.

“No, it’s not, but I’m positive it’s one of those three. My mom and I get along with everyone else unless there’s something I don’t know about. Anyway, those are my suspects and I’m not sure about how to find out which one of them did it.”

“If you do find out, what’re you going to do?” Sammy asked.

“To be honest, I’m not sure.”

There was a silence of several seconds before Sammy spoke up. “If you ever figure out who did it, and you want to do something about it, I’ve got your back.”

Nikki glanced at Sammy, who was staring straight ahead. “That’s, um, I don’t know what to say. Thanks for the offer.”

“I mean it,” Sammy said.

Nikki stared at him a moment longer before she hit a bump in the road and refocused on driving. She decided to change the subject.

“So, you’re nineteen.”

“Yep. Born August thirtieth. What about you?”

“I’m nineteen too. Born in October. On the fifteenth, I think,” she said.

“So, I’m the older one,” Sammy said.

“Yeah, but I’m cuter,” Nikki retorted.

“Yes, you are,” Sammy rejoined, causing Nikki to laugh. “So, I’ve noticed you also refer to your parents as stepparents sometimes.”

“Yeah, Lou Ellen and Herman were our neighbors back when I was a little kid. They took me in when my parents became infected. I’m not certain, but I think Herman killed them. If he did, he was doing it as an act of mercy. Anyway, we ended up at the church with a bunch of other scared people.”

“No siblings?” Sammy asked.

“I was an only child, but my parents adopted my dad’s nephew when he was a kid. He was a few years older than me and went into the Army right out of high school. He visited once when he graduated basic training and then I never saw him again. What about you?”

“I don’t remember a whole lot,” Sammy said. “I remember the birthday party my mom had for me. It was in the employee breakroom at the casino where she worked.”

“That sounds like an odd place to have a birthday party.”

"Yeah, well, she was a single mom, and she couldn't afford to take off work or do anything fancy for me."

"Was it a good birthday?" Nikki asked.

"I guess so. None of my friends were there, only people my mom worked with. Not too long after that, the plague swept through. It seems like it happened sometime around Thanksgiving. We took refuge in the casino. And then Mom was killed."

Nikki glanced over. "Killed? Did the zeds get her?"

"Nope. An ex-boyfriend murdered her."

"Oh shit. That must have been rough on you," she said.

Sammy shrugged again. "Yeah, I guess. I don't remember much about it. So, Kate and Kyra kind of adopted me. Things had gotten bad at the casino, so they decided to leave. One of them had a boyfriend who went with us, but he ended up getting killed and we were stranded. That's when Sarah found us."

"Sarah, as in the Sarah that Fred and Rachel were involved with?"

"Yep, the same Sarah they named their daughter after. You would have liked her, she was cool, and tough. Tough as nails."

"I've heard about her. She was a pilot in the Air Force, wasn't she?" Nikki asked.

"Yep."

"How did she die?"

"A sniper killed her. She never stood a chance. Fred got revenge though."

"Oh wait, I think I heard the story. Didn't he hunt them down and scalp them?"

"Yep," Sammy answered.

"Holy hell that's incredible."

"Don't try asking him about it though. It's not something he'll talk about," Sammy said. "He's a good man, a great man, but by God don't get on his bad side."

Nikki nodded in agreement. That's what she admired about Fred, and she found herself seeing a lot of the same character traits in Sammy. She also caught herself glancing at him frequently. If he noticed, he didn't let on.

They arrived as the sun was starting to disappear behind the western tree line. The gate was open and there were several people milling around. Nikki pointed at a woman who appeared to be in her late forties. She was medium-sized and had brown hair with streaks of gray. She was also standing funny, which made Sammy think she had back or hip problems.

"That's my mom. C'mon, I'll introduce you."

When they approached Lou Ellen, the two of them hugged. When Nikki pulled away, the look on her mother's face caused her to frown in concern. "Is something wrong?"

"Janey is missing," Lou Ellen gushed.

CHAPTER 24 – ZACH IN STEPHENS CITY

We worked until it was dark and then built a fire outside. Everyone was hot and sweaty. Melvin tossed fresh pine needles into the fire which created a lot of smoke. It helped keep the mosquitos at bay. Mostly.

Dinner consisted of a big pot of beef stew that Norman's wife, Lois, had premade and we used the fire to reheat it. Nothing special for beverages though, only water. Nobody complained.

The Mackenzie clan mostly seemed excited and enthusiastic about their new home. The little kid, Ricky, seemed especially excited about it and asked if there was a choir that was going to be singing. Poco and Lynn had Norman's ear and pestered him with questions. Their upbeat attitudes gave me a good feeling about them. Well, expect for Garth. He worked, but he was a stick in the mud.

One thing I noticed that seemed a little odd was Hammy. She seemed to go out of her way to be wherever Melvin was and even sat next to him at dinner. My curiosity was stoked, but I also knew that whatever was going on with them, if anything, was none of my business. We talked as we ate.

"I'm curious to know what our function will be here, Mister Zach," Poco asked.

I knew Melvin had already gone over this, I guess he was trying to see if there were any contradictions. I gave Melvin a subtle glance before answering.

"You'll be expected to be self-sufficient by this time next year. Everything we're giving you now is sort of a loan. You'll be expected to pay back in the form of barter and work. Oh, any selling or bartering on the side is perfectly acceptable.

"You'll also be expected to run this place as a layover stop and provide temporary lodging to travelers. Mostly, we want you to observe and report. Any human movement, zed movement, animal movement, severe weather, anything that might be of interest. Observe it and report it. You'll be part of the Mount Weather network."

"That's doable, what else?" Poco asked.

"At the present moment, that will be all that's required of you. After you get established, there will be more responsibilities, but that won't happen for at least a year."

"Like I said, there's strings attached," Garth said.

"There's no catch," I countered. "You'll simply earn your keep. If that's untenable to you folks, I understand. Tomorrow, we'll come back with moving trucks, pack you up, and move you back to that farm where all of you were barely eating enough to live."

Garth scowled. Poco and Lynn weren't too happy either. My last sentence may have chafed them a little, but it was the harsh truth, and they knew it. I continued.

"Think of it like this. You'll eventually be paying taxes for the electricity, the fuel, the work crews, all we're currently doing for you and will continue to do for you. But, and this is a big but, we're not going to tax you into starvation. The goal is to improve your lives, not oppress you."

Garth cleared his throat and spat. "What about fightin'? Are y'all going to want us to do your fightin'?"

"We already have a military force in place. If you live at Mount Weather, you're required to participate in military training in the event we encounter hostilities. For you, it'll be entirely voluntary, at this time. Garth, it's my understanding that you're an old infantry soldier."

"Yep," he said.

"That's good. At some point, when the population in this area increases, we may want to draw upon your knowledge and expertise to form a local militia unit."

I watched him mull that one over and slowly nod. The truth was, we'd probably never utilize him for something like that. Melvin had already confided in me that he didn't trust him, and I had to agree.

We talked until late and did not arrive home until almost midnight. I was tired, but I wasn't going to bed until I'd cleaned myself up. I took a quick shower and tried to crawl into bed as quietly as I could, but I still woke Kelly up.

"How'd it go?" she asked.

"We got about ninety percent of their property moved. We'll loan them a box truck and they can take care of the rest."

"Are they going to work out?"

"I think so. They may need a little coddling for a month or two though. Any incidents with Mal?"

Kelly gave a sleepy chuckle. "She's getting on Savannah's last nerve, but other than that she's only been wandering around like a curious cat."

I grunted as I worked my arms around her. "I'll talk to Lydia in the morning and put her butt to work." I thought for a moment as my eyelids began to grow heavy. "You know what? I think I have a pretty good idea."

I turned my head in the dark to explain, but Kelly was already asleep.

CHAPTER 25 - ZACH & REESE

I waited at the elevator doors for Reese to arrive. When they opened, he stepped out and looked around in wonder. "I've never been down here."

"Technically, it's a restricted access area. Why don't I show you around?" I suggested.

His eyes lit up. "Yeah, if it won't get you in trouble."

I chuckled. "I'm the Director of Operations, basically the number three around here, it'll be okay."

I started with the mechanics of the building, the alternative living quarters, the crematorium, almost all of it. I omitted a visit to the room where the supercomputer was located because, well, not everyone needed to know about that.

After the tour, I led him back to my office. He took a moment to admire all the maps and the multiple lists written on the whiteboards before sitting.

"Okay, you've buttered me up with the tour, but I've got a feeling you've got something in mind," he said.

"Yes, I do. Have you met Mal yet?" I asked.

He pursed his lips a moment. "Is that the skinny new girl?"

"Yep, that's her," I said.

"Yeah, I think I've seen her around."

He was playing coy, but I already knew he was aware of her. I'd seen him glancing at her more than once during breakfast. Mal wasn't my type, but others remarked that she was a cute girl, once she had cleaned up. She was still skinny as a rail and her teeth needed cleaning, but Reese was definitely interested.

"The Mount Weather life is all new to her and I suppose she's a little bit overwhelmed," I said.

"I can imagine."

"Kelly's been mentoring her, but between her day job and our kids, she has enough to do. That's where I'm hoping you can help out."

Reese cocked his head. "How so?"

"I'd like for you to befriend her and kind of mentor her about Mount Weather."

"Oh, that's easy. Sure, I can do that."

"There's more," I said.

Reese grinned. "I thought there might be."

"When we interviewed her, I felt like she was withholding information from us."

"Oh, I got you now. You want me to get her talking and find out her secrets," he surmised.

"Exactly. So, here's the situation. Have you heard how Melvin met her?" I asked.

"Yeah, I heard the story. That's some crazy shit. I'm kind of surprised he didn't kill her," Reese said.

I nodded. "Yeah, but instead of killing her, he took pity on her and brought her home."

"That was nice of him. Everyone says he's a great guy."

"He is. So, he discovered an interesting thing with her. She and her father had a rifle and ammunition that matches ammo we have in our inventory. We asked her about it, and she said a character who calls himself King Rat gave it to them."

Reese stared for a moment and then understanding spread across his face. "You want to find out more about King Rat and any other secrets Mal may be hiding."

"Exactly," I said. "It seems inconceivable to me that a man and a little girl could survive out there on their own for ten years by themselves. There has to be more to it, and like I mentioned, she had a lot of memory gaps during her interview. I want to know more, and I want you to be the man to get it."

Reese nodded slowly. "I can do that."

I nodded in satisfaction. "Good. Bear in mind, this will probably be a long-term mission."

"How so?" Reese asked.

"I don't think you'll get all her little secrets out of her within a day or two. It'll take time."

"What do I concentrate on first, King Rat?"

"Yeah. I think this man lives around here, somewhere close, and I want to identify him. So, gain her trust, become her best friend. I want to know everything about her. I want to know who he is, and anything else she knows that might be of interest. She said she didn't know where he lived, and I have a feeling that was true. So, my plan is to put the two of you on the logistics team."

From his expression, I don't think he understood what I meant, so I explained. "A lot of communities around here don't have the manpower or diesel to travel much, so we have a delivery system where we travel around picking up and delivering various items to each of the communities. I'm going to put you and Mal on one of those trucks and have you visit these communities in hopes of finding this guy. And, as you visit each location, try to jog her memory, see if she's been to any of the places before."

Reese gave a nod. “I’m your man. I do have a question though. How do you know that ammo and rifle came from here?”

“The rifle looks like one of ours, but the serial number had been scratched off. The ammo is a little more concrete. The headstamps match ours and the ammo was shiny, like fresh out of the box shiny.”

Reese frowned. “Zach, I’m embarrassed to admit it, but I have no idea what a headstamp is.”

I gave a patient smile. “Back in the day, an ammunition manufacturer put markings on the rim of the casing. Here, let me show you.” I opened a desk drawer, rummaged around a second, and came out with a couple of bullets. I turned them on end and showed Reese.

“You see, these letters are an abbreviation for the manufacturer and these numbers are the caliber. What you have here is a nine-millimeter bullet manufactured by Federal. Now, if you inspect closer, you’ll be able to see that this particular bullet is a reload. See the little telltale markings? Not an uncommon trait nowadays. Those casings found at Melvin’s ambush site were not reloads. That makes me almost positive they came from Mount Weather.”

“Okay, that makes sense, I guess. I obviously have a lot to learn.” He ran a hand through his hair and scratched his face. “Okay, the identity of King Rat is the primary goal. That seems like an odd name to call yourself.”

“Have you ever heard the story of King Rat?” I asked.

Reese stared. “There’s a story?”

“There are actually two that I know of. One is a novel written by a great author named James Clavell. It’s a semifictional story of a World War Two prisoner of war camp in Singapore. The main character is Corporal King. While all the other prisoners are suffering, he thrives through wheeling and dealing, manipulating, lying, whatever it takes. So, he takes on the name King Rat. There’s a copy of the book in our library if you’re interested.”

“I suppose I could give it a read sometime. What’s the other story?” Reese asked.

“The other King Rat is an old story about rats that have somehow had their tails intertwined and there is one rat that sits on top of them and rules them all. There’s an allegory in there somewhere.”

Reese studied the maps on the wall behind me, but I could tell he was thinking about what I said. After a moment, he held up a finger. “I think this dude is relating to the character in the book. He’s a user, a manipulator.”

“Yeah, and no doubt he’s a psychopath, but who is he exactly? We need to find out.”

“Alright, I’ll do it,” he said.

"Good man," I said. "So, like all new people, she's currently assigned to latrine duty. I'll give Lydia a call and tell her to pair you two up."

Reese made an exaggerated sigh. "Oh boy, latrine duty."

"Oh, by the way, we have an advanced firearms training class that's offered in September. Melvin teaches it. You ought to consider taking it."

After talking with Reese, I found Melvin hanging out in the motor pool talking with Josue and Jorge. When he saw me, he pointed out a truck I'd not seen before.

"Check it out. I spotted it back a few months ago under a carport over in Manassas."

It was a late model white Ford F250, and it looked practically new. Melvin pointed out the lift kit, skid plates, brush guard, and two LED light bars. One was mounted in the brush guard, the other on the roof.

"The previous owner put it all on. Check out the engine." He lifted the hood and showed the big block diesel motor in it.

"Four-wheel-drive, all the bells and whistles. This is a good truck," he said. "I think I'm going to put a camper top on it, I'm not sure yet."

I peered at Josue, who gave a small expression of approval.

"It's got computers on it. If a computer goes bad, it won't run," he said. Jorge chimed in.

"But we've got the software to diagnose everything. If there's some kind of feature that's a pain in the ass, we'll disable it. Like the door chimes."

"And that little girl isn't coming anywhere near it," Josue added.

"Amen to that," Melvin agreed.

CHAPTER 26 – REESE & MAL

Reese found Mal at the main supply room where she was staring at the shelves of cleaning products. It looked like someone had trimmed her hair and had done a nice job of it. When he walked up and stopped, she stared.

"Hey, I'm Reese. It looks like I've got latrine duty with you," he said.

"Can I ask you something?"

"Sure, what's up?" Reese said.

"What's the difference between a latrine and a shitter?"

Reese chuckled and then realized she was serious. "Well, latrine is a French word. I believe the correct definition is that a latrine is a toilet or group of toilets for use by the public instead of a single toilet which is meant only for private use."

"Is a toilet the same as a shitter?" she asked.

"Yeah, I believe it is. Let's get started," Reese answered and realized this was going to be more challenging than he originally thought.

"I have another question," Mal said.

"Okay."

She waved a hand toward the items in the closet. "I ain't sure what is what. I ain't never used any of this stuff before."

"Oh, well, let me help," Reese said and picked out the items he thought they'd need and put them on the cleaning cart.

The two of them spent the next four hours cleaning the various restrooms and locker rooms at Mount Weather and talked the entire time. Reese found it easy to talk to her, even if she was a little on the naïve and ignorant side of the spectrum.

"Is this what I'll be doing the rest of the time I live here?" she asked at one point.

"New arrivals have to do it for the first couple of months. It's kind of like an initiation for living at Mount Weather. If you do well, you'll be switched around on assignments. Guard duty, gardening, trash duty, kitchen duty, there's always something. When I first got here, I was assigned duty with Hog Head Harold."

"That's a weird name, who's he?" Mal asked.

Reese chuckled. "He and his wife run a hog farm nearby. They're nice people but it's dirty work. There are regular work assignments but sometimes you're put on a work crew and do some kind of special duty.

Right now, there's one crew that's doing road work and a couple of other crews are doing farm work. It changes around."

"I have to be honest, I ain't never done no work duties before, except for hoeing the weeds out of a garden," Mal said, causing Reese to smile.

"Don't worry, I'll show you what to do. I don't know if Lydia told you, but the sooner we finish, we'll have the rest of the day to ourselves. Lydia will come by and inspect behind us, but mostly she's looking for people who only do marginal work, and that's not us."

Mal tucked some hair behind an ear. "So, we won't have to be doing this all day?"

"Not if we work hard and fast," Reese said.

"Well, I'm glad you're helping me then."

It took Reese only a few minutes to realize despite her roughness, she was easy to talk to and took directions well, which made it easy for him to converse with her. He asked innocuous questions while they worked.

"Did you and your father have indoor plumbing where you lived?" Reese asked.

"We did when I was little, but that seemed like a long time ago. What about you?"

"Yeah, back before, when I was a kid. You take things like that for granted until you don't have it anymore."

"How does it work? I mean, how does water get in here and where does it all go?" she asked.

Reese gave a patient smile and spent the next thirty minutes trying to give a simple explanation.

"Daddy explained it all to me once, but you've told it a lot better. Does everyone around here have indoor plumbing?"

"Not everyone. We didn't have it where I used to live. We had outhouses instead. What about where King Rat lived, did he have indoor plumbing?" Reese asked.

"I don't know. I ain't never seen where he lived. How did you know about him?"

"The Mount Weather grapevine," Reese said.

"What's a grapevine?"

"It's a word used to describe how people pass along information on an informal basis. Apparently, somebody found out that you mentioned a man named King Rat when the president was interviewing you. I think it's created something of an interest because nobody knows who he is."

"Oh."

"How often did he come visit?"

"Oh, about once a month. Daddy said it wasn't important to keep up with the days anymore, but I kind of kept up with it in my head."

"Was he always alone?" Reese asked.

Mal nodded. "He'd bring us stuff in exchange for whatever we found, and I'd service him."

Reese frowned. He thought he knew what she meant, but he needed to make sure. "What do you mean, service him?"

"I'd lay with him, and he'd stick his ding-a-ling in me," she answered.

"Your daddy was okay with that?" Reese asked. Mal nodded. He shook his head in disgust. "That's awful."

"Why?"

"Your own father was pimping you out."

"What's that mean?"

"He was letting another man have sex with you in exchange for property or favors," Reese said.

Mal shrugged as she flushed the toilet she'd been scrubbing and watched the soapy water swirl. "If you say so, but it wasn't so bad. He brought us stuff."

Reese eyed her, hoping he wasn't overdoing the questioning. "What kind of stuff?"

"He was good about bringing us food. Sometimes, he'd bring other stuff. One day he brought me a dress. He made me put it on. He and Daddy really liked it."

"Did you like it?" he asked.

Mal shrugged again. "It was okay when it was hot out, and it made it easier when I had to squat."

Reese forced out a laugh, but he realized he was having feelings of empathy for her. She'd been treated like shit, and she didn't even realize it. Even so, he stayed focused on his mission.

"So, King Rat, what kind of guy was he?"

"He could be nice, but he could be mean too. There was once this boy who was kind of living with us. King Rat killed him."

"Why?" he asked. Mal shrugged again.

"I dunno. He didn't like him, I guess."

"Have you seen him kill anyone else?"

"Yeah, a couple of people," she said.

"And you don't know where he lives?"

She shook her head. "The president already asked me them questions."

Reese filed away the information and decided not to push it any further, otherwise she might shut down or start making things up.

"Why did you leave where you used to live and come here?" she asked him.

"We had it rough the last couple of years and last winter was especially tough. A couple of the older people didn't make it. We were running out of food, and we knew about Mount Weather, so a few of us headed out and came here. We didn't know if we would've been welcome or not, but they took us in."

"Are your friends still here?" she asked.

Reese nodded. "Yeah, they're here, but back in April they found a house nearby they liked and decided to move."

"Why?"

"Because if you live here at Mount Weather, you're expected to work. There's a lot of stuff to do and sometimes there are long days and nights. Also, there's a little bit of a pecking order. When you've been here long enough, you'll see that the original inhabitants don't do stuff like latrine duty, and there is a certain amount of control. For example, if you wake up tomorrow and you don't feel like doing anything, you'll have to explain yourself. My friends are good people, but they wanted to be on their own."

"I bet they aren't allowed to come visit or anything," Mal surmised.

"On the contrary. Homesteading is encouraged and they're allowed to visit anytime they want. In fact, Zach has been checking on them and keeping them supplied."

"Oh. Well, I guess that's nice. You didn't go with them though. Why not?"

"I like it here and I don't mind hard work," Reese said.

"Have you got a girl that you're poking?"

Reese arched his eyebrows in surprise. "No, I'm not poking anyone."

"Why not? It ain't like you're ugly or nothing."

"Thanks for the compliment, I guess, but most girls around here that're my age are already taken."

They completed their rounds and ended at the women's locker room by the dorms. After Mal ensured nobody was inside, Reese walked in and they got right to it. When they were finished, Reese stretched.

"All done, and if I do say so myself, Lydia will give her approval without complaint."

"Does that mean we don't have to work anymore today?" Mal asked.

Reese grinned. "Yep. We've got the rest of the day to ourselves. Is there anything you'd like to do?"

Mal eyed him a second and then began undressing.

"What are you doing?" he asked in surprise.

"I want to shower again. I'm sweaty and it feels good. You want to get in with me?"

Reese, who'd not been with a woman in a while, a long while, stared like a hungry man ogling a juicy ribeye steak. Soon, Mal was completely nude. She peered at Reese, who was still staring, and grinned, showing her yellow teeth. He quickly looked away, but Reese was, after all, a healthy young man with raging hormones. He debated on what to do, but he realized the decision was made as soon as Mal took her pants off.

"Lord help me," he whispered to himself and began stripping. When he entered the shower, she turned to him and grinned.

"Girl, you need to gain some weight," he said as he grabbed the soap. He'd wait until later before saying anything about her teeth.

CHAPTER 27 – THE SEARCH FOR JANEY

Nikki frowned. "How long has she been missing?"

"She hasn't been seen since right after breakfast," Lou Ellen replied.

Marvin walked up while the two women were talking. "Hey Nikki. I didn't know you were coming to visit."

"We're here to pick up a couple of horses for Fred McCoy," Nikki said.

"Oh. I thought he was coming himself. Anyway, your mother told you Janey's missing, right? Did you see her on the drive down here?"

"No, we didn't," Nikki said and looked to Sammy for confirmation.

"Is she out riding around?" Sammy asked.

"Nope, all the horses are accounted for," Marvin said. "The mare and her colt are in the barn over yonder. They're ready to load up."

"Thanks," Nikki said and turned to her mother. "What kind of search effort is being made?"

"We got people out on horseback looking for her. The rest of us have searched all over the compound and walked around outside the perimeter. That girl has just plain disappeared."

"Is everyone else accounted for?" Sammy asked.

Marvin stared in thought. "That's a good question, young man, but we've taken roll. Nobody else is missing that I know of."

"Who's out on horseback?" Nikki asked.

"There're three teams. Janey's father and mother are one team, Drill Bit and Rori are the other team, and then there's BC and Collin. They're going to stay out until dark, so that means they should be coming back any minute now."

Nikki thought that wasn't enough, everyone should be out looking except for a couple of people guarding the compound. It's a shame they didn't bother with handheld radios, which Mount Weather would have supplied to them, but eschewed things like that. She kept quiet though. Her opinion no longer mattered around here, if it ever did.

Everyone was milling around the front gate, making small talk while waiting for the search teams to return. Marvin suggested that maybe they ought to search the buildings again, but before they could do so, a couple of riders on horseback came into sight. It was Drill Bit and Rori. They were approximately a hundred yards out, and once they saw a small crowd standing at the gate waiting for them, they prodded the horses into a canter. They arrived a few seconds later and started talking before the horses had even stopped.

"We didn't see anything. No tracks of zeds, nothing," Rori said. "What about y'all?"

"Nothing yet," Marvin said. "You two are the first ones back. Maybe one of the others found her."

Drill Bit remained quiet and simply stared off into space. Soon, Janey's parents returned with the same news. Nikki saw that Janey's mother was visibly distraught, but otherwise she was holding it together. A few minutes later, BC and Collin returned.

"We spooked a couple of coyotes eating on a rabbit, but that's it," Collin said.

"Where is she then?" Janey's mother said. "If there aren't any of those dead things wandering around, what happened to my Janey?"

She began weeping now. Her husband got her off the horse and led her inside. BC noticed Nikki and gave her a cool stare.

"What are you doing here?" he asked.

"We're here to pick up the horses for Fred," she said.

BC stared a moment longer before nudging his horse and walking by them. Collin lingered behind, giving a cold stare to both Nikki and Sammy. Lou Ellen got his attention.

"Was there any sign of other people? Horse tracks or car tracks?" she asked him.

"Nope, nothing," he said and continued staring at Nikki. "I don't suppose you two saw anything."

"Nothing," Nikki said.

He scoffed, like he didn't believe her. "This is some coincidence that you and some punk show up the day a girl goes missing."

"Watch your mouth, little boy," Sammy said.

Collin scowled but was at a loss for words. He wasn't accustomed to someone standing up to him. He didn't know Sammy and didn't know that Sammy was raised by Zach and Fred. Two men who taught him not to take any crap. He stared at Sammy for a few seconds, sizing him up. Sammy was slightly older and a few pounds heavier. Sammy was obviously not intimidated and stared the young man down. Collin broke eye contact and focused on Nikki.

"You should take care of whatever it is you came to do and get the hell out of here. Neither of you are welcome here." He nudged his horse and walked away before either of them could respond.

"Nice guy," Sammy muttered.

"He's a punk," Nikki said.

"Are you two going to stay the night?" Lou Ellen asked.

"I don't think so, Mom. We're going to load up the horses and head back," Nikki replied.

Lou Ellen's disappointment was obvious, but she didn't complain. "Well, at least stay for dinner."

Nikki made a pained expression. "I don't know, Mom. We really need to get back."

"Why don't I go get the horses and load them up while you two talk," Sammy suggested.

At Lou Ellen's insistence, Nikki agreed to go to her cabin for tea. Sammy said he'd catch up when he got the horses loaded and headed to the barn. He listened to the talk from the other people while he walked. There were numerous opinions being bantered back and forth but it was obvious nobody had a clue what'd happened to Janey.

Sammy lit a kerosene lamp before opening the double doors to the barn and walked in. The mare stared at him and stood between Sammy and her foal.

"Hi, girl," Sammy said in a low, soothing voice.

He hung the lamp on a nail and ensured that it was secure before softly walking over to the mare, speaking softly to her as he did so. When he extended his arm, she stuck her head toward him and nuzzled his hand.

"That's a good girl," Sammy cooed as he began caressing her neck. She sniffed him a bit and he knew she wasn't going to be any trouble. As he rubbed her, he looked down at the small colt. He was only a few months old, but Sammy could already tell he was going to be a handful. Currently, he was playfully pawing at a pile of hay. Sammy smiled at him as he attached a lead to the mare's halter. When he walked over to the young colt to put a tether on him, his breath caught. It took him a moment to realize what he was seeing.

Peeking out of the hay, a lifeless face stared back at him.

CHAPTER 28 – FINDING JANEY

"Tell me again what exactly you were doing when you found her?" BC asked, although his tone made it a demand rather than a question. Collin stood off to the side of his father, a smirk on his face.

"I was getting the horses to load them up," Sammy said. "The little colt was playing around and had dislodged some hay, which exposed her face."

BC stared a moment at Sammy before crouching down in front of the corpse.

"Is it Janey?" Sammy asked.

"I'm afraid it is," BC replied.

He separated the hay from Janey's body and set it off to the side. The removal of the fodder revealed that Janey was nude from the waist down and when he held a light close, one could see distinct fingermarks on her throat.

"Has she been murdered, Dad?" Collin asked.

"That's what is looks like," BC said. After a moment, he stood and brushed the hay off.

"What are we going to do now?" Collin asked.

"We have to figure out who murdered her," he said.

Sammy held up a hand. "Mister Cart, if I may suggest, there are two men back at Mount Weather who are the official police force. Both of them were veteran cops in Pittsburgh, back before. We should get on the radio and have them come investigate."

Collin scoffed. "What a stupid idea."

BC looked at his son a moment before staring at Sammy. "Who are you, exactly?"

Sammy stood a little straighter. "My name is Sam Hunter. I came up to Mount Weather with Zach and his group."

"So, you're with Gunderson," he said.

"I consider him a good friend, yes."

BC stared in silence. After a moment, he motioned for them to follow him and exited the barn. Almost all of the members of their settlement were gathered around.

"People, I have unsettling news. Janey is in the barn, and she's been murdered."

"Are you sure? How do you know?" someone from the crowd asked.

"Because there are finger marks on her neck. It looks like she's been strangled."

There was a collective gasp from the crowd followed by everyone talking at once. BC held up a hand.

"Alright now, everyone quiet down." He gave the crowd a studious gaze as he waited for everyone to shut up. When they had done so, he spoke again. "This is a most serious matter and must be investigated."

He paused for a moment and glanced over at Sammy, who was standing with Nikki away from the gathered crowd. The crowd's murmuring had grown louder now and soon became a loud cacophony. BC emitted a loud whistle, causing the crowd to hush.

"I believe it will be in the best interest of this community to call Mount Weather and request the assistance of their police officers."

Drill Bit scoffed. "Why in the hell would we do that?"

"Because you are all considered suspects," Nikki said. "I know that sounds harsh, but it's true. I've met the O'Malley brothers. They're good men and I've no doubt they'll figure out who murdered Janey."

BC paused a moment, as if considering something. He then nodded to himself. "Alright, let's take a vote. Give me a show of hands for all those who agree to request the police to investigate Janey's murder."

Almost everyone raised their hands.

"All opposed?" BC asked. Nobody raised their hand on this. "That settles it. Rori?"

"Yes, BC?" Rori said. Rori had always been a nervous type of person, but Nikki seemed to think she was even more anxious than normal. BC didn't notice or didn't care.

"Get on the radio and inform Mount Weather of our situation. Ask for those two policemen to come here as soon as possible."

Rori nodded and hastened out of the barn. BC once again gazed at the crowd.

"Like they used to say in the movies, this is now a crime scene. Everyone out. You," he said, pointing a finger at Sammy. "Stay here a moment."

BC waited until everyone left before turning to Sammy. "Why did you really go to the barn?" he asked.

"Nikki wanted to get out of here. I was trying to expedite things," Sammy said.

BC stared at Sammy without emotion. "You have feelings for her."

"I like her and respect her," Sammy replied. "And, if I may add, your perception of her is tainted by the death of your son."

His eyes furrowed. Maybe it was a scowl, Sammy wasn't sure.

"I'll give you some advice, young man, be careful of that girl. She has a temper and she's dangerous."

Sammy gave a small nod. “I appreciate your advice, sir. Now, if I may, I’d like to give you some advice. This world needs people like Nikki. She’s tough and she’s smart. She may have a temper, but for what it’s worth, I’ve been around her long enough that I don’t think she would kill a man she loved.”

BC gazed at Sammy with an unreadable expression before motioning for him to follow him out of the barn.

“I’d like for you to guard the barn and keep anybody from going in,” BC said.

“I’ll gladly do so, but you might want to warn people that I’ll shoot anyone who tries to get past me,” Sammy warned.

BC stared a moment before giving Sammy a nod and walked off. One would think that Collin would have followed his father, but he decided he had something to say first.

“You know, it’s funny. This is only the second person who’s been murdered since my father created this place and Nikki is the only one who was present during both of them.”

Nikki glared at him in the growing darkness. “You’re an idiot, Collin. An idiot with a mouth that’s going to overload his ass one day.”

“I’d like to see you try something with me,” Collin said.

“Why, what will you do?” Sammy asked. “Are you saying you’d have no problem committing violence on a woman? Interesting, I’ll be sure to let the O’Malleys know that.”

Collin’s mouth dropped open. “That’s not what I said!”

“Go away, Collin,” Nikki said.

Collin knew he’d lost this verbal joust and didn’t like it. He gave them his best scowl before walking off.

“I really do not like him,” Sammy said.

“That makes two of us,” Nikki agreed. “Alright, enough of him. It looks like we’re going to be here a while.”

“Yeah, looks that way,” Sammy agreed.

“I’ll go get us some dinner. Be back in ten.”

Sammy found two folding chairs and placed them in front of the barn doors. Although a few people glanced his way as they walked by, nobody came near him. Nikki was back in nine minutes with two plates of pork chops, mashed potatoes, and green beans.

“All we have to drink is water,” she said.

“That’s fine,” Sammy said and put a big forkful of potatoes in his mouth. “I didn’t realize how hungry I was. Thanks. If you want to spend time with your mom, I’ll be fine.”

“I think I’d like to sit here with you instead,” Nikki said.

CHAPTER 29 – ZACH GOES TO ROANOKE

I liked Bob, I really did, but now that he was the president, he felt it incumbent of him to be the people's president. That is, he went out of his way to greet someone, shake their hand, ask how they were doing, and all that happy horse shit. I suppose he was trying to atone for the sins of the previous presidents. He was indeed well liked, but his behavior could be bothersome at times.

This morning was a good example. We were supposed to leave immediately after breakfast, but Bob got involved in a conversation with Jorge and Josue about car parts. I have no idea why he thought that was important enough to delay our departure, but I kept my opinion to myself and waited patiently.

Finally, with no small amount of coaxing, we got everyone loaded up and on the road. It was a caravan of two passenger vans capable of carrying up to ten people, and two armored vehicles. We didn't expect any trouble, but when you had the president, vice president, and most of our senators onboard, a heavily armed escort was the correct thing to do. One only had to remember the murder of President Rochelle VanAllen and her entourage to see the wisdom of having an armed escort.

I was driving the Mercedes Sprinter van that Bob, Connie, and their respective wives were in. There were also a couple of the senators who, in my opinion, were as worthless as teats on a boar hog. I slowed and spoke as I drove.

"We're coming up on Stephens City. There are two items of note about this location. First, this is the starting point for Project Asphalt. If you look over to your left, you'll see an old strip mall and the parking lot appears to be destroyed. That's where we harvested asphalt to repair the interstate. There are places like this all along the interstate corridor."

"I don't understand, Zach."

The person who said this was the First Lady, Angela Duckworth. She was a prim and proper lady, born and raised in Utah. She was now sixty or more, but still an attractive woman. She eschewed salon treatments, and her hair was a silvery gray. She had the perfect look and demeanor for the First Lady role, and I had no doubt she was aware of it. I liked her and gave her a patient smile.

"The work crew uses machinery to bust up the asphalt. We use other machinery that can grind up that old asphalt and heat it up with a small mixture of new asphalt cement. The machines are capable of producing approximately two thousand pounds of fresh asphalt every fifteen minutes, and we have twelve of them."

"Oh my," she said.

"We aren't at maximum production level, but so far we've been able to repave almost two hundred miles of roadway and we've only lost one piece of equipment due to wear and tear," I said.

"That's impressive," she said.

"Yes, ma'am, it is," I replied.

"Is this where the way station will be created?" she asked.

"Yes ma'am. It's going to be a church that's in the process of being repurposed and a group of people are being moved in there."

"We should go pay a visit," the senator from New York said.

"Unfortunately, we're running behind schedule, but I'm sure we can arrange a visit at a later time."

In fact, it was on the itinerary, but our late departure cancelled it. I wanted them to visit the church. It would have been good for the Moorefield people to see how important it was, but nobody asked me. The senator waved a hand at me.

"Why did we choose this location for a waystation?"

"Our goal is to have some type of waystation or community every thirty miles, which will mean we'll need fifteen of these between Mount Weather and Oak Ridge. So, why every thirty miles? That's about the furthest a human can walk in one day, if they're in good physical shape, and I don't know about your experience in riding horses, but thirty miles in a saddle is about the maximum one can endure, unless you're someone like Fred McCoy."

That drew a few chuckles and began a long conversation about waystations, observation posts and how they helped in the effort to rebuild America. It was an oft repeated conversation, but that was okay, it occupied Bob and Connie all the way to Roanoke.

It was an overdue meeting. It'd already been delayed due to the zed attack on South Mountain. Exiting the interstate, we headed to our destination, a huge estate located on Timberview Road. When I slowed to turn into the gated driveway, I could see the barrels of machine guns in both guard posts. The New York senator whistled as two people hustled out and opened the gate.

"Those are fifty caliber machine guns. Our armament is no match for that," he said.

"I guess it's a good thing we're friends then," I deadpanned.

Doc Kreis had originally introduced us to this group of survivors a few years back. The estate was owned by the Russets, a wealthy and powerful Virginia family, back before. They'd made disaster preparations long before the plague was nothing more than a virologist's wet dream. Their preps included things like the machine guns at their gate, and they'd seen extensive use against zeds and bad guys.

I saw a welcoming committee waiting for us as I drove the Mercedes Sprinter up the hill, the other Sprinters followed. They were armed, but I knew them all and did not suspect any ill will. Doc walked up to the driver's door as I got out.

"Good to see you, big guy," he greeted and offered a fist bump.

Doc was the leader of Oak Ridge and probably the smartest man I've ever known, including Parvis. In addition, he was related to the Russets, who owned this estate. He gestured toward the house.

"Miss Ellie has already said for everyone to come inside as soon as you people arrive," he said.

"You don't need to tell us twice," one of the Marines said. "It's hotter than Hades today."

He was right. It was in the high nineties, and I happened to know that the air conditioning system at the Russet estate was in excellent working order.

There were approximately a dozen more people waiting for us inside. Standing in the middle was Eleanor Russet, commonly known as Miss Ellie. She was a stately woman in her seventies and the resident matriarch. She'd always been a pleasant woman, a little stand-offish but pleasant. My conversations with her in the past indicated a keen intellect, which was not surprising considering who she was related to.

"Welcome, Mister President, Mister Vice President, Senators," she greeted. "And the rest of you. Welcome to our home. Please, follow me."

She led us to a dining room big enough to host a sizeable black-tie affair, if there was a call for such a thing anymore. An equally large dining table was in the middle. Once we were seated, a staff of people brought in big bowls of food and set them in the middle.

"Help yourself, folks," a man urged.

The food was served and soon everyone was eating and making small talk. Bob, Connie, and their wives felt like they needed to carry the conversation while we ate.

"I couldn't help but notice the solar panels," Bob commented as he sipped his tea.

"They've been a Godsend. Thankfully, we had them upgraded a short time before the pandemic hit. And, we have an excellent engineer." She made a head gesture toward a fifty-something man who was helping himself to a helping of mashed potatoes. "Dimitri, remind me again where you went to school?"

"Virginia Tech," he said and promptly focused on the potatoes.

"Yes, Virginia Tech. He has a degree in mechanical engineering," Miss Ellie said.

"And electrical, but mechanical is my first love," he added.

The food was delicious and eventually everyone was sated. Without being told, four people stood and with quick efficiency had the table cleared. Miss Ellie watched and waited until they were through before speaking.

"Does anyone need to powder their nose, or shall we get started?"

Bob glanced at Angela, who gave him a small nod and a smile.

"By all means," Bob replied.

Miss Ellie made a head motion, and I heard a whirring sound at the far wall and saw a projection screen drop down.

"That's my cue," Doc said and activated a laser pointer he was holding.

"This is from our scout team that recently returned from their long-range mission, which was dubbed Operation I-75. As you all know, they went due south on the interstate all the way to Florida. And, as you can see from the video, they recorded a lot of destruction of buildings and roadways. Some structures were decimated by fire, but most appeared to have been destroyed by wind and water."

"Hurricanes?" Bob asked.

"Yes, Mister President, that's the conclusion they reached. To continue, the further south they went into Florida, the heavier the flora. Everything is overgrown. That's an indicator of little human activity. Also," he clicked his mouse and another picture appeared of a dozen or more gators sunning themselves on the side of the road. "There is a plethora of alligators and pythons. The only thing that kept the population of those two species in check back before was human intervention, so obviously they're thriving down there."

"No humans around at all?" I asked.

Doc clicked on another picture. "They found evidence of human habitation in Ocala, but they had no contact. However, on their way back home, they encountered a group in Valdosta, Georgia. They consisted of twelve men, all between the ages of twenty-five and thirty. It was a civil encounter, but our squad leader was of the opinion that they only acted friendly because they were outgunned. In fact, the only type of weaponry they had were compound bows, spears, and knives."

I nodded to myself. Ammunition and reloading supplies were becoming a rare commodity these days. I doubted there were many survivor communities that had ammo at all. I listened as Doc continued.

"They were agreeable to be interviewed. I've already sent a report, so I'll summarize. They claim to be part of a larger group of survivors who live in central Georgia. They wouldn't be more specific, nor would they provide numbers or demographics. They advised there is still zed activity, but it's rare. Also, a family of four somehow became infected last fall. They killed them and burned the bodies."

Doc paused and hastened a subtle glance at me. He was waiting to see if anyone noticed that nothing was mentioned about vaccinations or blood samples being obtained. The team had claimed to have forgotten to execute these actions. Doc and I had already discussed it and I suggested simply leaving it out of the report. He did and the silence seemed to indicate that nobody had noticed. He continued.

"Alright, moving forward with Project Tire. Dimitri, would you like to start it off?" he asked.

Dimitri nodded and wiped his mouth with a cloth napkin before speaking. "I'll keep it short. All of you are aware of the Yokohama plant a few miles from here. I've inspected it and if we have the electricity and manpower, I can get the plant running again."

"How many people do you think you'll need?" I asked.

"A hundred would be nice," he said. Apparently, he saw a lot of frowns, me included. "Let me say this. I know you all are smart people, but I'll keep it simple. The composition of a tire consists of multiple ingredients, including rubber. Those components are mixed together using machinery that is similar to a big furnace which creates heat and pressure. Those furnaces require several hours start up time and they have to be monitored the entire time. It's not a nine-to-five job. And that's only the first couple of steps in the creation of a tire. There are other complex assembly processes. During the production run we'll need to have the factory staffed twenty-four hours a day. Also, we'll only be able to make one size tire. I have chosen one that was the most popular size, back before. If anyone disagrees, feel free to fire me and do it yourself."

This led to more talk. More discussion. Needless discussion. Oxygen depleting discussion. At the end of it all, nothing changed. What Dimitri said could not be disputed, altered, or modified. Sometimes people talk too much instead of listening. Because, if they had listened to Dimitri and acknowledged he knew what he was talking about, they would've saved themselves a lot of time. Even in this post-apocalyptic world, we still had too many of those types of people.

CHAPTER 30 – DETECTIVES O'MALLEY & O'MALLEY

Most members of the Shenandoah community were always up at sunrise. Some were in the dining hall, some were milling about, some were taking care of business in one of the four outhouses. When the alarm sounded at the front gate, all of them responded. They had not been attacked by zeds or marauders in a long time, but with the death of Janey, tensions were running high. What they saw on the other side of the gate may have comforted some while others may have become a little more anxious.

Two burly-looking men were standing there. They were dressed similarly in olive drab cargo pants, military-style boots, and black short sleeved shirts that did little to hide their broad chests and hairy muscular arms. Both had dark beards which brought out their hazel eyes, and equally dark hair tied back in ponytails. The men were armed with semiautomatic weapons which were currently contained in tactical thigh holsters.

The guard was a teenage boy who had no idea what to do, so he sounded the alarm. BC was the first person to reach the gate. He believed he knew who they were but wanted to make certain.

"Who are you?" he demanded.

"We're the O'Malleys, from Mount Weather. You put in a request for our services," Liam said. "Oh, and we had good weather on our ride here. No issues."

BC gave the men a nod and directed the boy to open the gate. Liam was carrying a gray Pelican case. They paused at the entrance and looked around. Liam spotted Sammy.

"Well, there's someone I recognize. How are you, Mister Hunter?"

"I'm glad you two are here," Sammy replied.

"This seems like a nice place, maybe we can get a tour later," Logan said. "Let's get down to business first. Take us to this poor young lady."

BC led them to the barn and opened one of the double doors. They started to step in when Liam stopped and turned to the crowd. "I hope everyone's cooperative. My brother and I would prefer not to kill anyone today."

Sammy smiled to himself. He knew the O'Malleys well. They were nice guys, always joking around, not cold-blooded killers, but he also knew they were tough and capable.

Liam turned to Sammy. "Alright, Mister Hunter, show us what you have."

Sammy led them through the doorway. Nikki was standing immediately inside and greeted them. "I'm glad y'all are here," she repeated and pointed to where Janey's body was lying.

"What time was she discovered and by whom?" Logan asked.

"I found her," Sammy said. "I'd say it was about twenty-one hundred hours. I immediately went to get Nikki and we contacted BC."

"Was the scene protected?"

"Yeah, for the most part. When she was first discovered, a few people came in and looked her over, but then BC told everyone to stay out. Nikki and I guarded the barn the rest of the night," Sammy said.

"I'm guessing you two haven't slept yet?" Liam asked.

"We swapped off and got an hour or two," Sammy said.

Liam gave a grim smile. "I understand. Good job, you two. If you want to go catch a little shuteye, we will certainly understand. Or you can hang out and maybe help us out, if needed."

Nikki and Sammy swapped glances. "We'll stay," both of them said in unison.

Liam nodded. "Alright, brother, let's see what we have."

The two men then started inspecting the barn in a slow, methodical sweep with their taclights, taking photographs as they did so. They whispered some things between themselves, but neither Nikki nor Sammy could hear what was said. After about ten minutes, they turned their attention to Janey.

"Tell us the circumstances of how you found her," Liam said.

Sammy cleared his throat. "Fred had purchased a mare and her colt. Nikki and I came here to get them and take them back. Somebody put them up in the barn here and I came inside to get them. The little colt was messing with the pile of hay that she'd been buried under. He'd knocked some of the hay off her face and that's when I saw her."

"Why did you two think to fetch BC?" Logan asked.

"He more or less runs the place, so it seemed like he was the one to go to," Nikki said.

While she was talking, Liam took some pictures and pulled Janey further out of the hay. He inspected her closely, including turning her over and looking under her shirt. When he was finished, he rolled her onto her back and stood.

"Was she raped?" Nikki asked.

Liam studied Janey a moment longer before answering. "Raped and strangled, it looks like. I can see a dried substance on her genitalia and thighs. It's probably semen. Close that barn door so it's a little darker in here and perhaps we can find out."

The barn door was still partially ajar. Nikki walked over and closed it completely. It was a typical wood barn. There were narrow gaps between each individual slat. With the door closed, it was darker, but not completely without light.

Liam opened the case they'd brought in and retrieved an object that looked like a typical flashlight. When he turned it on, instead of emitting a normal light, it was an ultraviolet light. Shining the light over Janey's corpse, the dried substance gave off a faint glow.

"I think I can safely say that's semen," Liam said.

He knew it wasn't a conclusive scientific test, but these days you made do with what you had. He shone the light all over the barn but had no other positive readings. Putting the light away and closing the case, he stood.

"Do it here, brother?" Logan asked.

"It's the best place, I'm thinking. The shock of looking at Janey's body might encourage some truthfulness."

"What are y'all going to do?" Nikki asked.

"We're going to interview everybody, one by one, right here in the barn," Logan said. He spotted the folding chairs Sammy and Nikki had been using when they were on guard duty.

"We need one more of those," Logan said.

Nikki retrieved one that was leaning up against the barn wall. Logan thanked her, knocked the dust off it and then set up the chairs. He put one on either side of Janey and the third chair a couple of feet away, facing the other two and the body. He then stared at Nikki.

"So, do we understand correctly that the two of you were not even here during the time Janey was killed?"

"Yeah, we didn't get here until later," Sammy said.

"And the first person you notified was Mister Barnabas Cart, correct?"

Both of them nodded.

"I believe he'll be the first person to interview then. Would one of you go fetch him, please?"

CHAPTER 31 - REESE & MAL IN MARCUS HOOK

"That sure is a funny sounding name for a place to live. What's it all about?" Mal asked.

Reese smiled. After spending most of the day and evening going around and putting eyes on every man at Mount Weather, Zach decided what was next. He had them assigned to the logistics team and once Reese was taught how to drive a tanker truck, he and Mal were sent to Marcus Hook. Reese explained as he drove.

"The way it was explained to me, when it all went bad, there was a group of people who'd formed together and created a stronghold," Reese said, gesturing his hand around. "They said it wasn't much to begin with, but they have an old man leading the place by the name of Roscoe Sidebottom. He ran all of the petroleum plants around here, back before. He's one of those people who is smart as hell. They eventually were able to renew the production of petroleum. And as for why it's called Marcus Hook, I have no idea."

"Why go to all that trouble?" Mal asked.

"Roscoe was convinced that after everything went bad, diesel fuel would be rare and valuable. They're the only ones I know of that make it."

"That makes them powerful, right?" Mal asked.

Reese shrugged. "I don't know. Mount Weather is one of their biggest customers, so maybe, yeah. The trading post sure has made them popular."

Mal frowned. "Trading post? What's that?"

"I'm going to show you, but first, we need to check in." He smiled. "You'll get to meet Jimbo. He's a good guy."

Reese drove up the road linking Mount Weather to Marcus Hook. It was once a series of roads, various lefts and rights, but when you had access to heavy equipment and an unlimited supply of diesel, it was fairly easy to convert those roads into a direct freeway. Stopping at the barricade, Reese smiled when Jimbo came out to greet him. The first time they met, Reese had taken a liking to him. The man was stocky, the kind of guy who loved to hang out at a bar that served hot wings, cold beer, and had scantily clad waitresses. Jimbo gave a broad grin as he walked up.

"Hey, hey, Mister Reese. How's it hanging?"

"Doing great. Jimbo, this is Mal, she's our newest member of Mount Weather," Reese answered.

Jimbo peered through the open door of the box truck. "Hey there, Mal. Welcome to Marcus Hook."

Mal squinted at him. "So, you're Jimbo."

"Yep."

"Reese said you're a good guy."

Jimbo's grin broadened. "I'd like to think I am."

"Well then, I'm happy to meet you," Mal said.

"Is there any chance you can give Mal the grand tour?" Reese asked.

Jimbo glanced at Reese, and then back at Mal, who was smiling at him. "Yeah, I believe I can do that. Let's get the truck unloaded first, and we've got some things for you to take back to Weather."

"Oh, yeah? Good stuff, I hope," Reese said.

Jimbo nodded. "We've pulled in some respectable hauls and we're sharing the wealth I guess you'd say." He then looked around and lowered his voice. "Don't tell anyone, but we've got an order in for a hundred tires, and we want them before anyone else."

Jimbo punctuated it with a grin and a slap on the shoulder. "Alright, let me show you two what Marcus Hook is all about." He gave them the grand tour, including the petroleum manufacturing facility. Reese was impressed, Mal was in awe.

"I didn't think things like this were a thing anymore," she said.

The tour ended when Jimbo got called in for work. After leaving Jimbo, they went to the trading post. Mal looked around in wonder.

"This is something else. What're we going to do here?"

"There's a married couple that were running a barber shop the last time I was here. I traded some snap beans for a trim and a hot shave."

"A hot shave? Why'd you get that?"

"Because I'd never had one before. I heard they felt wonderful."

"Was it?" she asked.

"Oh yeah."

"You should have gotten a haircut too," she said.

Reese acted offended. "I got a trim, why? You don't like my long hair?"

"It looks girlish."

Reese chuckled. "Maybe I'll get it cut shorter this time. Oh, and they built a sauna. You can have a steam bath if you want."

"A steam bath?"

"Yeah," Reese answered. When he realized she had no idea what a steam bath was, he explained.

Her eyes went wide. "Can we do that?"

Reese grinned. "Sure, but first we need to walk all around and see if you spot King Rat."

Reese expected Mal to return his smile. Instead, she frowned. "Is something wrong?"

"It just seems like all of y'all got your nads in a knot about finding out who he is," she said.

"It's important to the president and Zach."

"Why?" she asked.

Reese bit his lip. He wasn't sure if he was supposed to tell her but decided maybe it was the only way to fully gain her trust. After a few seconds of thought, he came to a decision.

"Okay, let me explain." He spent the next five minutes telling her about the ammunition.

"I already told them I don't know how he got them bullets," she said.

"They believe you. That's why they want to know who King Rat is. Once he's identified, then they can find out how he got it."

"How're they going to do that?" she asked.

"I imagine they'll interrogate him. I think they believe he somehow stole it from Mount Weather, and they want to figure out how." Reese hesitated a moment. "And, um, I think they want to know what other crimes he's committed."

Mal stared. "You weren't supposed to tell me all that, were you?"

Reese shook his head. "Nope. The way it was explained to me, the less you know, the harder it'd be to lie to me and get away with it."

"I ain't gonna lie to you. You're my only friend. Besides, we're shower buddies."

Reese laughed now. "Yeah, we are. You know what? We don't have to look for King Rat right away. How about we go do one of those saunas first? You're going to love it."

CHAPTER 32 – THE INVESTIGATION

Barnabas Cart was seldom intimidated by anyone or anything, but sitting across from the O'Malley brothers, he couldn't help but feel a little uneasy. He wasn't going to let them see it though and fixed his face into a scowl.

"So, you two were cops once," he remarked.

"We once worked for the Pittsburgh Police Department," Liam said. "Most of our family were cops."

"Hmph, from what I see, you two were probably part of a goon squad. I've heard of big city police departments having those. You two look like you'd be on one."

Liam eyed him. "What exactly do you see?"

BC gestured at him with his finger. "Both of you are big men. You have scarred knuckles, and other scars. It looks like both of you have had your noses broken at one time, and you have some cauliflower on one of your ears. Yeah, you two were brawlers, enforcers, goons. Bad cops."

Liam gave a patient smile. "I got the cauliflower ear back when I was on the high school wrestling team. Most of the scars my brother and I have occurred after the world went to hell. Pittsburgh was our home, and we didn't want to leave, but it was a rough city. The plague brought out the worst in people. My brother and I fought both zeds and bad guys in order to survive. When we were cops, we weren't dirty, we weren't enforcers, nothing like that. We were good cops who were damned proud to wear the badge. But enough about us. Let's talk about Janey."

BC stared as he digested Liam's words, trying to determine if he was telling the truth. The two men seemed sincere enough and after a moment he decided to cooperate. "Okay, ask your questions."

"Nikki said she and Sammy came to you when they made the discovery."

"They did," BC replied. "When they told me they'd found her, I immediately went with them to the barn and had a look. I confirmed it was Janey and that she was dead."

"What did you observe?" Logan asked.

BC worked his hands together. "I saw the marks on her neck, like she'd been strangled. I didn't see any other injuries." He thought for a moment. "She was stiff. What do they call that, rigor?"

"Rigor mortis," Logan said. "How stiff do you think she was?"

"Well, I was able to move her arm when I tried to take a pulse, but on a scale of one to ten, I'd give it a five as far as stiffness goes."

"Alright, based on the amount of rigor mortis and the lividity, it could be surmised she was killed sometime yesterday morning. When was the last time you saw her alive?"

BC slowly nodded. "Yesterday, at about six. She was at breakfast. She was sitting with her mother and father, as usual. I left before them, so I don't know what time she finished," BC said.

"We'll follow up with her parents about that. Where did you go?" Logan asked.

He paused a moment, as if searching for the correct answer. "Four of us spent the day cutting firewood and lumber at a grove of trees about a mile from here. My son and I left a little after six because we wanted to do some riding before working all day cutting wood. We met the other two men at the grove around eight. We were summoned back to look for Janey at around three," he said and named the people who were with him.

"Tell us about this young lady," Logan asked.

"Typical teenage girl, I guess. Sometimes I'd see her wandering around like she was daydreaming. I don't know if she was sweet on anyone. My son didn't care for her because he said she was stupid. I don't know if she was or not, but she certainly seemed to have her head in the clouds all the time."

There was a pause in which the two brothers glanced at each other. Logan gave Liam a slight nod.

"Who do you think did it?" Liam asked.

BC thought about it as he absently rubbed his beard. "I'm not sure. Am I considered a suspect?"

"My gut says no," Liam said.

"Same here," Logan said.

"Well, I'm not. I've killed before, yes, that's true, but I'm not a man who would rape and murder a little girl." He pointed at the two men. "You two have a difficult task. Being able to prove someone committed this murder is going to be impossible without a confession. Believe me, I know."

"Why do you say that?" Logan asked.

"You see, I once had two sons. There's Collin, whom you've met, and there was Colton, my oldest. He died not too long ago. He was murdered and I know who did it. The problem is, I can't convince anyone around here that it was a murder, so if I meted out punishment it would most likely work against me."

"I believe I've heard this story," Logan said. "Colton and Nikki used to be an item. They went out on a ride one day and he was thrown from his horse."

"That's her story, but I don't believe it. She's a hothead and more than capable of murder."

"You're certain she killed him, and it didn't happen the way she said?" Logan asked.

"I am," BC said with a defiant stare, as if daring them to disagree with him.

Liam did not want to get bogged down in something that had nothing to do with this case and changed the subject.

"Let me ask you, has there been anything else unusual happening around here lately?"

BC shifted in his seat. "We've seen tracks here and there."

"Zeds?"

"I believe so, but I can't be certain. We haven't actually seen any zeds since last fall, around October. One day a couple of them wandered up. We killed them and burned the corpses."

"What about strangers?" Logan asked.

"Other than Mount Weather people, nobody." He paused for a moment. "We've also had a rifle and ammunition turn up missing back about May."

"Tell us about it," Logan asked.

"An AR-15 and about a hundred rounds of ammo. I brokered a deal with Zach on the ammo. We traded some lumber for it. That was done sometime around the end of April, and it turned up missing a couple of weeks after."

"Did you figure out who took it?" Liam asked.

BC shook his head. "Someone around here took it for themselves. I figured the rifle would turn up eventually, but so far, no luck. I didn't record the serial number of it, but I bet Zach has it on file."

"Yeah, I'm sure he does. Anything else odd been happening?" Liam asked.

"No, I can't say that it has. We're only trying to live a peaceful life out here. We're not as advanced as you folks at Weather or at Marcus Hook. Speaking of which, I do have something I'd like you to relay back to Zach. I want to know if and when they're ever going to get us electricity."

"I'll pass it along," Liam said. "Although I can tell you it may be a while. They've got a big project going on at Roanoke to get a tire plant up and running again. That's going to require a lot of electricity and we've only got that one hydroelectric dam in operation."

Logan cleared his throat. "They need people to run that plant and all the other stuff that goes along with it. Y'all should consider relocating to Roanoke. I mean, I like this little settlement you people have, but it's a little off the beaten path and my guess is that getting electricity to you is going to be low on the list of priorities."

BC frowned. "I don't see how working for someone would benefit us."

"You'll have electricity, diesel fuel, and running vehicles," Logan said. "There are going to be a lot of services needed besides running the tire plant. With the influx of people there will be a need for food and lodging. It'd be a great business opportunity to grow and barter food. Maybe even get one of the hotels in town up and running."

BC picked at his beard. "It sounds intriguing, but honestly we like the solitude here."

"I suppose I understand," Logan said, although mentally he believed BC was probably only speaking for himself. "Zach wanted me to suggest it and to tell you if you want to know more to get in touch with him."

"I suppose I can do that. Are there any other questions?"

"Not at the moment. If you don't mind, on your way out, send the next person in please, sir," Liam said.

BC slowly stood and glanced down at Janey. He shook his head.

"Senseless, absolutely senseless," he murmured before leaving the barn.

The interrogations lasted until well after lunch. They saved Janey's parents for last and took a moment to cover her body before having them come in. As expected, they were overwhelmed with grief. The only useful information they got was Janey's chores for the morning were to feed the chickens and clean the coop. Neither task had been accomplished but they pointed out the wooden barrels where the chicken feed was stored, which was in the very barn in which she was murdered.

When they were finished, it was the two of them, alone in the barn with Janey.

"Are we going to do an autopsy, brother?" Logan asked.

"I don't think there's any need. It's obvious she was strangled to death. If you look closely, you can see that her trachea is crushed."

Logan scoffed. "Of course. I was waiting to see if you saw it. So, Rori."

"Yeah," Liam replied. "What are we going to do about it?"

Logan's response to his brother's question was a shrug.

"You know, brother, our record as the first post-apocalyptic police force isn't so good. We know exactly who killed Rochelle VanAllen and her entourage, and yet, we've not made an arrest. Is this going to be a repeat?"

Liam sighed. "I don't know, brother."

CHAPTER 33 – THE FAUX PAS

After the two policemen had their private discussion, Liam exited the barn and summoned BC, Nikki, and Sammy to rejoin them. Collin followed his father in, even though he was uninvited.

"Have you figured it out?" BC asked as soon as he walked in.

Logan glanced at his brother a moment before speaking. "Why don't you tell your son to go outside and count horse apples or something. This is grown-up talk."

Logan had not met Collin before today, but the young man's obvious self-entitled attitude annoyed him. Collin stared in disbelief a moment before responding.

"Who the hell do you think you are? I'm just as much a man in here as anyone, and that includes him," he said as he pointed at Sammy.

"I beg to differ," Logan said. "Mister Hunter here is one hell of a man. You're a child who has a lot of growing up to do."

Nikki snickered, which angered Collin even further. BC didn't like it, but he turned to his son.

"Go back to the dining hall. I'll be there in a few."

Collin was angry and had a few choice insults for Logan on the tip of his tongue, but he knew from experience that to not obey his father would have dire consequences. The last time he did, he was thirteen, he got a slap that sent him stumbling across the room. He gave Nikki a hateful scowl as he walked out. The brothers waited several seconds after Collin closed the barn door before speaking.

"The first thing we can say is that nobody from outside snuck in this place and hurt that girl. It wouldn't be hard to do it, security is rather slack around here, but it didn't happen."

BC narrowed his eyes. "How would you know that?"

"We had a little look around before we announced ourselves," Logan said. "Nobody spotted us, and we weren't even trying to be sneaky."

"So, somebody here is the killer," Liam said.

BC continued frowning. "Alright, who?"

Logan held up a hand. "Allow us to lay the groundwork before we name the person who we believe is the culprit."

BC seemed annoyed but went along. "Alright."

"According to Janey's mother, her chores for the day were tending to the chickens. She said Janey's quick about getting it done so she can spend the rest of the day free."

"Yeah, she's like that," Nikki said. "She'll wander around talking to people. Sometimes she'll help them with their chores, but mostly she wanders around like she's in her own world."

BC nodded. "Yeah, that sounds about right. Back in the day, they called it being on the spectrum, or something like that."

Logan continued. "So, she was last seen wandering around and eventually went into the barn."

"What about her murderer?" Nikki asked.

"I'm glad you asked, Nikki. There are two possibilities. Her assailant was in the barn already or he followed her in. She knew him and wasn't frightened by his presence. We're speculating a little here, but the sudden appearance of a stranger would have frightened her. She would have screamed or runaway."

"Assuming she wasn't ambushed, but there's no evidence indicating that happened," Liam said.

"Correct," Logan said. "Her assailant was known to her, and his presence did not frighten her. He more than likely attempted to engage her in conversation in the hopes that it might lead to a more intimate encounter."

"And when it didn't go as planned, he turned violent," Nikki surmised.

The two brothers nodded. "That's what we believe. If you were to feel her head, there are bumps under her hair, like he gave her a good punch or two," Logan said.

"He hit her there so there wouldn't be any marks on her face. Oh, and it was to the left side of her head, which means her assailant was probably right-handed," Liam added.

"And he raped her?" BC asked.

"Yes, he did. We can't really determine at what point he strangled her to death. Perhaps she tried to resist and started screaming, perhaps he killed her and then raped her," Logan said.

"With limited forensics, we'll never know for certain the sequence of events without a confession," Liam said. He then pointed toward Janey. "Tell them about the marks on her neck, brother."

"Like my brother said, we have limited forensics. Even so, it's obvious her assailant had average-sized hands," he said and gestured toward BC's hands. "Definitely not big mitts like you have."

BC glanced down at his hands. "Is this the point where you're going to name the suspect?"

"Yep."

"Who?" he asked.

The brothers once again swapped glances before Liam gave BC a somber stare.

"Why don't we get Rori back in here?"

BC frowned in confusion and then his eyes widened in apparent understanding. "Are you certain?" he asked. The brothers did not answer and kept staring.

Standing, he went to the barn door and yelled for Collin. He instructed his son to find Rori, escort her back, and then guard the barn door. Collin looked around at the others and started to ask questions, but his father put a firm hand on his shoulder and pushed him out. Collin hurried off. BC faced the O'Malleys.

"I want to be present during this," he said.

Logan nodded. "We insist on it. In fact, we have a plan in mind."

BC started to ask another question, but Rori appeared in the doorway. All of them could see the anxiety and worry etched in her features.

"You wanted to see me, BC?" she asked.

"Please, come in," Liam invited and motioned toward the chair.

Rori tentatively walked in, and after some gentle coaxing, sat in the same chair she'd sat in a couple of hours ago during the O'Malleys's initial interview. Once seated, the others also sat.

"What's this all about? I've already told you everything I know," she said.

"Unfortunately, that's not true, Rori," Logan said.

"What I'm about to say is a compliment, but you are a terrible liar," Liam said. "You're a good person, it's obvious, and a good person cannot lie well. So, with that in mind, it's time for you to come clean."

Rori frowned, as if confused. Liam continued.

"You see, back when we were police officers in the fine city of Pittsburgh, we received extensive training in the art of interviewing people. We learned to detect the subtle nuances of deception." He stared somberly. "Rori, you show all the signs. You know more than you're telling us."

"It's time for you to tell the truth," Logan added. "Poor Janey deserves it."

She began stuttering. "I…I…"

"It's okay, Rori," Liam said. "You're not in trouble. All we need is the truth. We know Drill Bit is responsible for this. All you need to do is tell us what you know."

Rori's face was a mixture of fright and unease now. She felt trapped. Liam sensed it and tried to work that angle.

"You're wrong for covering for him, but you can make it right. All you have to do is tell the truth. Tell us, Rori. Nobody will blame you."

She was so nervous now her hands were visibly shaking, and tears welled up in her eyes.

"I can't," she said. "I, I…"

Her stammering trailed off and she stared at the O'Malleys like a deer caught in the headlights of an oncoming eighteen-wheeler. She then did something nobody expected. She lurched to her feet, causing Logan to jump to his feet as well. Rori backpedaled from him, tripping over the chair.

The gun, a small two-shot derringer, appeared from nowhere. They'd later discuss the incident and agree it was small enough to be easily concealed in her pants pocket, hence their faux pax in never noticing it. She shoved it into her mouth and gave them one last desperate look before pulling the trigger.

CHAPTER 34 - RORI

The sound from the small weapon wasn't particularly loud. Even so, Rori's head snapped back like she'd been hit with an uppercut by Mike Tyson. The momentum caused her to fall backwards and collapse on the dirt floor. Logan and Liam rushed over to her. Squatting beside her, Liam removed the derringer out of her clinched hand while Logan stabilized her head.

The brothers exchanged a glance. She was still breathing, but they knew she was a goner. After all, a traumatic gunshot wound to the brain was often fatal even when there was a level one trauma center available.

BC shouted for his son, who immediately entered the barn. Upon seeing Rori, he skidded to a stop and stared wide eyed.

"Wha-wha…"

"Go get Anita!" BC yelled.

Collin stared at Rori in shock, and continued staring until BC yelled again, springing him into action. Soon, he reappeared with an older woman with a weathered face and flaxen gray hair. Others followed but stopped in the doorway. Liam and Logan would later learn that Anita was the de facto doctor for the community but originally, she was a midwife by trade. They watched as she directed a few people to pick up Rori and carry her off. Almost everyone followed, but a few lingered behind, including Drill Bit. He stared at the blood on the ground a moment before looking up and fixing on BC.

"What the hell happened?" he asked.

"She shot herself," BC said.

The O'Malleys paid close attention to Drill Bit. He stared with a mixture of incredulity and concern. "Why?"

Logan made an ambiguous gesture with his hand toward the spot where only minutes before Rori was lying. "She knew something that was weighing heavily on her."

Drill Bit stared in fright for only a moment before his eyes narrowed into a wary stare. "And what would that be?"

"The murder of Janey," Liam said.

Drill Bit stared only a moment longer and turned to BC. "I'm going to be with Rori."

He then hurried out of the barn. The three men watched the open barn door for several seconds, wondering if Drill Bit was going to suddenly reappear, perhaps with a gun. After what seemed to be a long time but in fact was only about a minute, BC cleared his throat.

"Do you two really think he killed Janey?"

"Without a doubt," Liam replied.

"But how?" he asked.

The two policemen spent the next twenty minutes explaining their thought process and how they reached their conclusions. BC listened thoughtfully, if not a little nervously.

"How would you describe Drill Bit?" Liam asked him when they had finished.

BC cleared his throat. "Before all of this I would have said he's a solid man. He's a hard worker, tough, independent. It's not uncommon for him to saddle up on a horse and go out by himself for a few days."

"Where does he go?" Logan asked.

"Fishing and hunting. He says it relaxes him. Nobody complains when he does it. He'll frequently come back with something. A burlap bag full of fish, a fresh deer kill, or he'll have stuff he's scavenged." BC reached up and ran his hand over his beard. "He has a temper though, but he's always kept it in check. Mostly." He thought for a moment and glanced at Nikki. "He had a falling out with Nikki's stepfather back a few years ago. I never heard the whole story, but it doesn't matter. Herman's passed on. That's the only problem I've ever known about."

Nikki stared but remained silent. She knew BC was well aware of Drill Bit's animosity toward both Lou Ellen and her.

"So, he's never done anything sketchy toward any of the ladies around here?" Logan asked. When BC shook his head, he peered at Nikki.

"He'll make little offhanded remarks on occasion," she said.

"What kind of remarks?" Logan asked.

"Remarks about a woman's looks, things like that."

"Would they be considered complimentary, or do they go beyond complimentary to sleazy?" he asked.

Nikki hesitated. She didn't like Drill Bit, but she wasn't going to lie. "They're right on the edge of complimentary and sleazy, I guess."

Logan gave a slight nod of his head. "Interesting. That's something we'll definitely follow up on."

"What's next? Are you going to arrest him?" BC asked.

"Although we strongly suspect him, we're not yet at the level of proof known as probable cause," Logan said.

"We need more," Liam agreed.

"What are you going to do then?" Nikki asked.

"We're going to continue our investigation," Logan said. He looked outside. "Where would everyone be right about now?"

"It's close to dinner time. I expect most of our people will be in our dining hall right now. We can go there, if you'd like," BC said.

Logan and Liam stood. "Lead the way, sir."

The cafeteria was located in the basement of the church. It also served as their shelter against storms and zeds. With the exception of Drill Bit, Anita, Rori, and the lone guard manning the gate, everyone else was present and going through the motions of eating. When Anita walked in, all eyes were on her as she walked directly to BC and whispered something in his ear. BC gave a slight nod and dabbed at his face with a napkin before standing.

"It is with great sadness to tell all of you that Rori has died. The death of a loved one is never easy, and our community has suffered with not one, but two tragedies. Janey and Rori's deaths has brought back all the pain I felt when Colton was murdered not so long ago. Tomorrow, we will have a funeral for these two beautiful ladies and mourn together."

He then sat heavily and stared at his plate of uneaten food.

"Who killed Janey?" someone asked. The question was repeated, this time to the O'Malleys.

"That is the question, isn't it?" Liam said.

Liam got a confused stare from the woman who posed the question, but then she turned to a man sitting beside her and spoke in a low voice, but not low enough that others could not hear.

"I heard they think Drill Bit did it."

There was more hushed talking, everyone seemed to have something to say, but they were worried about too many people hearing what they had to say. Liam and Logan sat quietly, watching, listening. They learned many interesting things about Drill Bit during this impromptu meeting, and none of it was good.

Then, it was as if a lightning bolt struck. Everyone realized Drill Bit was not among those gathered in the dining room. A couple of people went looking for him. After several minutes of searching the compound, they realized Drill Bit, along with his horse, were gone.

CHAPTER 35 – ZACH GETS A BOX

It was late evening, and I was hanging out at the main gate with the current guards, Kyra, and Shanika. Neither one of them were my favorite people but I was being polite and engaging in small talk while I awaited the return of Reese and Mal. It was well after dark when they finally arrived. Reese put the truck in park and jumped out.

"They loaded us up with four hundred gallons," he said. "Also, Jimbo sent you a present." He handed over a cardboard box.

"What've we got here?" I asked as I looked in it.

"DVDs. He had to explain what they were to Mal," Reese said with a chuckle.

"I've never even seen them before," Mal said.

There was a couple dozen in the box. I pulled one out and read off the title.

"The Man Who Laughs."

"Yeah, I've never heard of half of them. Jimbo said you liked the old classics."

"I do indeed. This one is a movie adaptation of a Victor Hugo novel. I've read the book but haven't ever seen the movie."

"Jimbo said you'd like them," Reese said. "They found a house or business in Philly that had a few thousand of them and he immediately thought of you."

I laughed. "Did he tell you why he's giving them to me?"

"He wants first dibs on the new tires."

"Yep. Well, he certainly knows my weakness," I said and glanced at Mal. "Mal, why don't you go get yourself something to eat. I need to speak to Reese in private."

"I've told her everything," Reese said.

I blinked. "As in…"

"He told me you wanted him to keep it secret why we were paired up," Mal said. "It's okay, I understand. I guess I ain't the trustworthy type, seeing as how my daddy and I tried to kill Melvin."

"Yeah, that sums it up," I said. "Do you disagree with that sentiment?"

Mal frowned and glanced at Reese, who made it easy for her.

"Zach is asking if you think you can be trusted."

Mal stared at Reese for several seconds, and it seemed to me that she desperately wanted his approval. She eventually focused on me.

"First, I want to say thank you for letting me stay here and for telling Reese to be my friend. I'm telling you that you can trust me, but I'll understand if you don't and make me leave."

I thought for a moment she was going to cry. Reese saw it too. He reached out and grabbed her hand.

"That won't happen. Right, Zach?" he asked.

I kept my face passive and didn't tell them what I was thinking. Nope, I didn't trust her, but…

I reached out and gave her a slight, reassuring pat on the shoulder. "If I make you leave who'd be left to keep an eye on Reese, right?"

My quip made them both smile in relief, which is what I hoped for. Mal was still on probationary status, but I didn't feel the need to reiterate that point. I pointed at the tanker truck.

"Let's get this baby to the motor pool and parked. Then we can sit and talk."

Parking the truck, we sat in some chairs that were outside the entrance to the motor pool. It was a pleasant evening with a slight breeze that made the thick humidity tolerable.

"It feels like we may have rain on the way," I said. "But enough about the weather, let's hear it."

"Short answer, no sighting of King Rat," Reese said and went into their activities of the day, starting with their meeting with Jimbo and ending with the trading post. "I think I can safely say we put eyes on every man in the place."

"What about Trader Joe?" I asked. It's not that I suspected him, but he sure matched Mal's description of King Rat.

"Him too," Reese replied.

"I liked that trading post, we had a lot of fun there," Mal said with a grin.

"Good," I replied and glanced at Reese, who was also sheepishly grinning. I suddenly realized that they had gone a level beyond friendship. I wasn't sure if it was a good thing or a bad thing, but I hoped it was the former.

"Alright, I'm glad you two are getting along, because you're going to be spending a lot of time together. Starting tomorrow, you two will be going on delivery runs. Priss is in charge, so don't show up late, unless you enjoy getting your ass chewed out." I thought for a second. "One of the stops is to a small group of people who recently relocated to Stephens City. There's one man there whose name is Garth. He matches the description a little bit."

"We'll make sure to meet him," Reese said.

"What if that ain't him?" Mal asked.

"We're going to keep at it until he's found. Now then, I suspect you two are hungry. Dinner's still being served for the next thirty minutes, so you better get going."

"Ain't you eating?" Mal asked.

"I've already eaten. I'd sit with you guys, but I have some work to do," I said.

We said our goodbyes and parted company. They headed toward the cafeteria while I headed to the library to meet Justin. He was sitting in the reading area, looking over a handwritten list.

"What do you have there?" I asked as I sat.

"Jorge gave me another wish list."

I nodded. Every patrol was sent out with a list of the makes and models of cars that Jorge and Josue needed parts from. If a particular vehicle was spotted, they were tasked with taking a picture and recording the location of it. If they had time, they scavenged the parts needed off it, otherwise Jorge and Josue would go get it with their tow truck. I absently drummed my fingers, lost in thought. Justin noticed.

"Got something on your mind?" he asked.

"I have a question for you. We've known each other a long time."

"Ten years and some change," Justin said. "Is that the question?"

"The question is, do you think I may be overreacting with this King Rat character?"

Justin scratched his face. He had the proverbial five o'clock shadow. Being a career Marine, whisker stubble annoyed him. "No, I don't think so. Let's see, how many evil bastards have you encountered over the years? That guy who called himself the captain was the first one, wasn't he?"

"Yeah," I agreed. Technically he wasn't the first evil bastard, but he was an evil psycho. And mean. In fact, he was within a second of killing me before my friend Andie killed him. Justin continued with his list.

"Those dudes you knew from high school." I nodded in agreement. "Let's see, those cannibals you told me about. Then there was that serial killer, what was his name?"

"Geoffrey Thompson. Fred took care of him." I didn't know the specific details, but when Fred advised Geoffrey Thompson would never hurt anybody again, one did not have to ask any further questions.

"Yeah. Okay, after him was who?"

"Colonel Coltrane, but you know all about him," I said.

"I was kind of hoping you'd forgotten about that," he replied.

Justin once served under Colonel Coltrane, and in fact assisted in kidnapping me, but that was long ago, and many things had happened since. I changed the subject.

"After that was an unfortunate encounter with an old friend of mine. Then there was a gang led by a turd who called himself King Ro. Then there was the Blackjacks."

"Ah, yeah. Fred took care of them too," Justin said.

"Yes, he did. Then there was General Fosswell, some nut who called himself The Professor, although I never met him, and then there were the Freitag brothers." I grunted. "We know what happened with them."

Justin gave a dry chuckle. "Yeah, Fred. So, there you have it. This is a no-brainer. There's ample past history to justify your concern with this guy. He may be nothing or he may be a credible threat. He may be one man, or he may be the tip of the iceberg. I agree with your concerns."

There were others I'd not mentioned, but Justin was aware of most of them. I nodded in gratitude. "I appreciate that."

"You're welcome," Justin said. "Now, if you're asking me what should be done next, I believe we should conduct some patrols in the area where Mal was found. It might flush this guy out."

Grace walked in while we were working up mission plans for the patrols.

"We've received a radio transmission from Logan. He said to tell you he found out where the assault weapon and ammo came from."

My eyes widened. "Where? Shenandoah?"

She nodded and then updated me on the status of their investigation. I thanked her and waited for her to leave before speaking to Justin. "Well, this is an interesting development."

"I'm surprised you didn't have a match with the serial number," he said.

I shook my head. "The rifle taken off of Mal had the serial number scratched off. I have her making supply runs tomorrow, but I think I'm going to take her to the Shenandoah community instead. You want to ride along?"

"Sounds like fun. What are you going to do if this King Rat is there?" he asked.

I drummed my fingers on the arm of the chair. "That's a good question. I'll go over the legalities with the O'Malleys, but he's definitely going to be brought back to Mount Weather."

"Agreed," Justin said and stood.

Walking out of the library, the intercom came to life with the sound of Lydia's voice.

"Mister Gunderson, come to the cafeteria at once! All available Marines, respond to the cafeteria at once!"

The sense of urgency in her voice was plain to hear. Justin and I took off at a sprint and entered the cafeteria a minute later. When we pushed through the cafeteria doors, I was surprised at what I saw.

Several people were gathered around First Sergeant Crumby. He had a cut on his cheekbone and was standing over a man lying on the floor. Another man, Jonesy, was standing a few feet away from the First Sergeant, blood running down his nose, shouting profanities at him.

I then saw Reese. He was sitting in a chair. He too had a bloody nose, and one eye was already starting to swell shut. Mal was standing beside him, looking lost and befuddled.

"What's going on?" I asked.

Jeremiah pointed at Jonesy. "I walked into the cafeteria and spotted Jonesy beating the snot out of this young man. When I intervened, he thought he could put his hands on me. And that asshole sucker punched me."

He pointed at the man on the floor when he said it. It was Jonesy's buddy, Lock. I took my foot and rolled him over. He looked so addled he probably didn't even know what day of the week it was. I faced First Sergeant Crumby with a look of surprise. He was grimacing and holding his right hand.

"I think I broke my damned hand on his head," he said.

"Head to the infirmary. We got this," I said.

"Yeah, okay," Crumby replied. He gave the two men a baleful stare before leaving.

I turned to the two men. "Alright, we'll do this the easy way and you two can walk to the brig on your own, or Captain Smithson and I will beat the ever-loving shit out of you two and then drag your sorry asses to the brig."

Jonesy scowled at me and then stabbed a finger at Reese. "He threw the first punch. That makes me the victim of assault. It's him that should be arrested. And Crumby, he needs to be arrested too!"

"Not so fast." We all turned to the voice. It was Lydia. "I witnessed the whole thing and he's no innocent victim."

I gave a small smile. "An eyewitness. I like that. Alright, Ms. Creamer, what did you observe?"

She pointed at Jonesy. "He walked by this little girl, made a horrible remark about her breasts, and then had the audacity to grope them. Reese tried to defend her and got beaten for his trouble. And as First Sergeant Crumby advised, when he tried to break it up, Mister Jones punched him, and then Mister Lockhart in a cowardly move, sucker punched the First Sergeant." She then stabbed a finger at Jonesy. "Mister Jones committed a sexual assault against this young lady."

Jonesy stared in disbelief at the accusation and then his face turned to a scowl. "She's lying!"

"No, she's telling the truth," Reese said.

"Yeah, she's telling the truth, I saw it too," someone else said.

Other people then began parroting what Lydia stated. I gave Jonesy a pointed stare. He stared back and smirked.

"You can't do anything. Only the cops can."

Justin spoke up. "They're not here, so the law enforcement duties fall to me in the event of their absence. So, Zach gave you two a choice. What's it going to be?"

By now, a couple of Marines had come in and walked over beside Justin.

"We got word someone attacked our first sergeant, sir. What can we do to help?"

Justin gave them a small smile and then stared pointedly at Jonesy and Lock. "What's it going to be, gentlemen?"

Jonesy and Lock didn't like it, but they were smart enough to know the crowd was not on their side, and if they resisted, they'd get their asses handed to them. After all, First Sergeant Crumby had already knocked the hell out of both of them. They threw out a few threats before walking out with Justin and his Marines. I focused my attention on Reese. One of his eyes was already swollen shut and it looked like his nose was broken.

"I've seen worse. Hell, I've had worse, but we're going to get you to the infirmary," I said.

He wiped some blood off his face. "The doc won't keep me overnight or anything like that, will she? We've got a supply run to a new place tomorrow."

"Don't worry about that. I think we have a strong lead on King Rat, and we'll follow up on it when the time's right. Let's get you fixed up first."

"What's going to happen to those two assholes?" he asked.

I gave a pointed stare. "Don't worry, I'll take care of everything. Trust me."

CHAPTER 36 – JANEY & RORI

The double funeral was conducted after lunch. It would've been earlier, but BC needed time to hastily build two coffins. It was a sullen affair, more than anyone could have imagined. To add to the sorrow, the day was sunless, bleak, laden with dark clouds, exaggerating the sense of heaviness and gloom. It did not go unnoticed that Drill Bit had not returned from wherever he went.

"Where is he?" somebody would whisper.

"Is he the one who killed Janey?"

"I always thought there was something about him."

"He always gave me the creeps."

The whispering and murmuring, along with a lot of crying, continued throughout the service. After, people began openly speculating about Drill Bit's disappearance. Some said it was due to grief, but most of the voiced opinions named Drill Bit as Janey's murderer.

Liam and Logan listened in silence, but they definitely listened. Intently. As Logan would say later, it was amazing what you could learn about people if you kept your mouth shut and your ears open.

The church cemetery was located next to one of the community gardens. Somebody had the forethought to rope off the gardens so the cabbage wouldn't be carelessly trampled.

Everyone watched as Marvin and BC lowered the coffins in the newly dug holes and the dirt was shoveled back in. The finishing act was the installment of simple wooden crosses at the head of the graves. As BC pounded them into the ground with a sledgehammer, Collin walked up behind Nikki.

"Remember when we buried Colton?" he asked while pointing at Colton's nearby grave. "You acted all sad and cried those fake tears, but Dad and me know the truth, and the truth is going to catch up with you one day. When it does, you'll be lucky if all that happens is you die."

Nikki turned around and stared with contempt. "The truth? You wouldn't know the truth if it slapped you in the face. You don't even know what day it is, you moron."

She could not hide her anger but knew this was neither the time nor place for a confrontation. Sammy sensed her mood and put a gentle hand on her shoulder.

"Come on, let's get out of here," he suggested.

"Yeah. Let's," Nikki replied. She turned away from Collin, grabbed Sammy's hand, and walked back to her mother's cabin at a fast pace, forcing Sammy to do the same. She packed her things quickly, throwing everything into her go-bag. Sammy did the same. Lou Ellen watched with trepidation.

"You don't have to leave so soon. Why don't you stay another day?" she pleaded.

Nikki stopped for a moment and faced her mother. "Mom, I swear to God, if I stay here any longer, I'll punch his lights out."

Lou Ellen gave a worried look. "Hush now, honey. Don't let anyone hear you talk like that."

Lou Ellen didn't like it, but after listening to Nikki, she agreed it might be for the best if she left. They hugged tightly before Nikki hopped in the truck. Getting seated, she offered Sammy a smile.

"I bet you're ready to get back to your sweetie and your kid."

Sammy's face darkened. Nikki noticed. "Is something wrong?"

"No, it's nothing. Let's get going," he said.

Marvin waved as they exited the compound and closed the gate behind them. Nikki watched out of her sideview mirror.

"I swear, if it wasn't for my mother, I'd never come back here again." She sighed heavily and peered at the sky. "The sky's gotten darker. The clouds look…" she paused, searching for a new word she'd learned. "Ominous, they look ominous."

"Nimbostratus clouds," Sammy remarked.

Nikki glanced at him. "Nimbostratus?"

"Yeah, at least, that's what Zach calls them."

"I always heard them called thunderheads," Nikki said.

Sammy shrugged. "I like thunderheads better."

Nikki smiled and realized Sammy had made her anger go away. She glanced over at him. He looked back and returned her smile.

"No doubt we're going to get some rain," he said.

They'd not travelled more than a couple of miles when it started. At first, it was a spattering of large drops and within a minute it turned into a torrential downpour. Nikki turned on the wiper blades, only to have the wiper on the driver's side break off.

"Damn it," she said, a little louder than she meant to. She turned the wipers off and stopped the truck. "I think it'd be better if we didn't try to drive in this rain. Knowing my luck, we'll end up in a ditch."

"We can wait it out," Sammy said and pointed at a side road. "That looks like a decent spot."

"Yeah," Nikki said and did as Sammy suggested. As she parked, a bolt of lightning shot out of the sky, followed by a clap of thunder a few seconds later. Killing the engine, she faced Sammy.

"We might be here a while."

"I don't mind," Sammy said. "It's funny, I've always liked thunderstorms. I like your company too."

"Thanks, I enjoy yours too," Nikki said, hesitated a moment, and changed the subject. "I feel like I said something that offended you earlier."

"Oh, no, it's not you. To be honest, Serena and I haven't been getting along for quite a while now. I doubt she even cared that I've been gone."

"I didn't know, I'm sorry," she said.

"No worries. Only a few people know about it."

"Yeah, he's definitely not a gossip. Was it always that way with you and Serena?" Nikki asked.

Sammy shook his head in the dark. "We've known each other since we were little kids, and there was a time when we were very close. Then, I can't tell you the exact moment when, something changed in Serena's behavior. We started arguing about everything. Nothing I said or did was right, and to top it off, I'm pretty sure she had an affair with Connie Nelson."

Nikki stared wide eyed. "The vice president?"

"The one and the same," Sammy said.

"Isn't he married?"

"Yep, and he's old enough to be her father."

"Wow. Have you confronted them?" she asked.

"Not him but I asked her one night after we'd had an argument. She was mad at how I was doing something with the baby, and I point blank asked her if it was my child. She wouldn't answer. Anyway, I know she's not in love with me anymore and I can't say I'm in love with her either. I'm only still with her because of the baby. A baby that probably isn't mine."

Nikki arched an eyebrow. "Not yours?"

"The affair I suspect them of having started around the time of conception."

"Ouch, that sucks," Nikki said. She'd thought of a few more colorful expletives to label Serena but didn't. It wasn't her place.

"Yeah," Sammy agreed, his voice low. "One day I'll probably leave Mount Weather."

She stared in surprise. "Really? Where will you go?"

"I don't know. Maybe Oak Ridge, or maybe I'll strike out on my own."

"That's why I convinced Fred to mentor me," Nikki said. "I want to learn how to survive on my own. The people at Shenandoah think women exist to serve men. Even the women think that way."

"You don't like living with Fred and Rachel?" Sammy asked.

"I do, but I want to get out and explore. I had planned on being gone by now, but I don't think I'm ready. Besides, Rachel hasn't admitted it to anyone but me and Fred, but giving birth took a lot out of her. She's still not at a hundred percent, so I'm not going to leave until she's better. But one day, I'm going wandering."

"Where would you go?" Sammy asked.

"Oh, all over. I want to see the ocean again, and one day I'd like to go see Minnesota and Montana."

Sammy found himself nodding in the dark cab of the truck. "I think that sounds wonderful."

Time seemed to have stopped when they were caught by a lightning strike staring at each other. Neither could say who initiated the kiss. It was sudden and intense. They kissed again and again, and at some point, their hands began clawing at the other's clothes. The rain beat down and the thunder reverberated. They didn't care, and it may have even encouraged them, almost like Zeus himself was orchestrating the event.

When it was over, they held each other tightly. Sammy was the first one to speak.

"I should probably be feeling remorseful right about now, but I don't."

"You don't regret this?" Nikki asked.

"Not one iota. What about you?"

"You don't even know how many times I've avoided looking at you because you were hitched up with Serena. At least, I thought you were."

"You liked me?" Sammy asked in surprise, which caused Nikki to laugh.

"Yeah, I liked you. You're cute, and Fred and Rachel think the world of you."

"They think the world of you too," Sammy said. "And you're cute as hell."

Nikki grinned. "Thanks."

"So, what now?" Sammy asked.

Nikki stared intensely, ignoring the beads of sweat that were trickling down her bare chest. "It's still raining, so we're not going anywhere for a while. Why don't we recline the seat this time?"

CHAPTER 37 – SUPPLY RUN

Sammy kept his head under the spray for several minutes thinking of recent events. He was reluctant to wash Nikki off, but it wouldn't go well if Serena were to happen to catch a whiff of another woman on him. Even he knew that.

Nikki was only the second woman he'd ever slept with. Hell, she was only the second woman he'd ever passionately kissed. Once upon a time, he believed Serena was his one and only. The love of his life. He was pretty sure she had felt the same, once. Not anymore.

She didn't even look at him the same anymore. She stared at him like he was an annoyance and someone to be loathed.

He finished showering, dressed, and headed to the cafeteria. He had a lot to do today and even though it would've been nice to have breakfast with Nikki, he knew it wasn't going to happen. Besides, she was currently with Fred and Rachel.

He didn't see Serena in the cafeteria, which didn't surprise him. She was a late sleeper and always one of the last people to eat. He was grateful and chose to eat breakfast with True and Dong.

"I understand I missed a big kerfuffle last night," Sammy remarked.

"Yeah, that's what I heard," True replied.

After a moment of silence, Sammy glanced at Dong, who gave Sammy a grin before diving into his eggs. Realizing True wasn't going to talk about it, he changed the subject.

"What're you guys doing today?"

"Reese is still in the infirmary, so I volunteered to do his supply run for him. We're supposed to take Mal with us, but she said she's not leaving Reese."

"She said she protect him," Dong said in his thick accent.

"Have you met her yet?" True asked. Sammy shook his head. "She's a piece of work. So, what about you? What've you got going on today?"

"I've already fed the horses and checked them out, so my duties are done for the day. I suppose I could check in with Lydia and see if there's anything I could help out with."

"Why don't you join us?" True asked. "We could use the help if you're willing. We're heading out in thirty minutes."

Sammy thought about it. He knew Nikki would be with Fred and Rachel all day and he wanted to avoid Serena, or worse, Serena's mother. "Yeah, count me in."

Mal walked in the cafeteria and looked around. Spotting True, she walked over to the table. "A mean woman told me I have to go with y'all," she said.

True stared at her for a moment with those dark, armor-piercing eyes. "You probably shouldn't."

"Why not?" she asked.

"Because I don't like you."

"She said if I shirk my duties I'll be kicked out," Mal lamented.

Sammy peered at Mal. It was obvious True's words hurt her, and he thought he saw the beginnings of tears form. He didn't know her, and he wasn't sure he was going to like her either based on what he'd heard about her. Even so, he'd never been a bully.

"I don't know, True. With the zeds being active these days, an extra set of eyes couldn't hurt," he said.

True finished his breakfast and wiped his mouth before looking again at Mal. He pointed a finger at her.

"You tried to kill Melvin and you said some shitty things about Dong. Both of them are my friends. Why should I overlook that?"

Mal dropped her head. "I reckon you shouldn't."

True stared at her for five long seconds before speaking. "Alright, you can go with us, but you do exactly as I say. If you do anything stupid, it won't go well for you." He gestured at her loose-fitting clothes. "Don't you have any clothes that fit you?"

"This is all they gave me," Mal replied.

True scoffed. "You better sit down and eat then, get some meat on your bones."

Sticking to True's schedule, thirty minutes later they were loaded up in a Ford F-450 Super Duty crew cab and ready to go. The back was full of various items. True drove and Dong manned the front passenger seat. Sammy sat in the rear with Mal.

"First stop is Leesburg," True said as they approached the gate.

"I've already been there," Mal said. "King Rat ain't there."

True glanced at her. "What're you talking about?"

"That's why I'm going with y'all. Didn't nobody tell you?"

"Tell us what?" Sammy asked. "Who's King Rat?"

Mal hesitated, wondering if she'd said something she wasn't supposed to.

"Speak up," True said.

"That's the whole reason I've been put on the supply runs. I'm supposed to be looking for a man who calls himself King Rat. It's supposed to be a secret mission."

"Who put you on this secret mission?" True asked.

"Zach," she said and dropped her eyes. "I don't think I was supposed to tell y'all."

True grunted. "Too late for that."

Sammy knew True well enough to know he wouldn't elaborate, so he jumped in.

"We've been with Zach a long time. Well, Dong is a recent arrival, but True and I have known Zach since we all lived in Tennessee."

"So, y'all are friends?" Mal asked.

"Yes, we are," Sammy said. "I have a great deal of respect for Zach and True. If Zach said it's supposed to be a secret, we'll abide by it."

"Okay, I hope I didn't get myself in trouble," she said.

"You'll be fine," Sammy said.

As True drove, Sammy passed the time by telling Mal about their lives in Tennessee. Mal was full of questions about how they lived and was amazed at Sammy's stories.

"It sounds like y'all had a lot of fun," she said.

Sammy scoffed. "I don't know about that. We had some hard times. Right, True?"

True didn't respond. Instead, he slammed on the brakes.

"Guns out! Lock and load!" he ordered as he threw the truck in reverse and began hurriedly backing up, eyeing his mirrors as he did so.

While Mal stared at True in confusion, Sammy and Dong instantly reacted to True's order. As rehearsed many times in Mount Weather, Sammy focused on his predesignated field of fire, which was immediately outside of his window, as he racked his shotgun and put the safety selector on fire. Seeing no immediate threat, he hastened a glance in front of them and saw what alerted True.

They'd been travelling along Leesburg Pike, which was their normal route. They had rounded a curve in the road and there were no less than six derelict cars that were blocking the road.

"Damn," Sammy muttered.

"Them cars weren't there the last time we came up here. What's going on?" Mal asked.

"Possible ambush," Sammy replied. "Now be quiet and keep your eyes open for hostiles."

True continued backing the truck until they were back around the curve. Dong had been staring intently toward the front.

"Contact!" he shouted, along with rapidly speaking in Chinese and leaned out of his window with his rifle.

As he did so, a staccato of gunshots rang out. Dong returned fire as True put the truck in park, opened his door, and took up a shooting position. "Watch our flanks, Sammy!"

Sammy scanned for any threat, but it was difficult. This particular section of Leesburg Pike was nothing but overgrown trees and bushes.

"Do you see anyone over there, Mal?" he asked.

Mal was crouched down in the seat, sticking her head only high enough to see outside. "I ain't seeing nobody," she said.

"I shoot one," Dong exclaimed.

True grunted. "Yeah, but I think he had a buddy with him."

"He shot at us," Mal exclaimed. "They was trying to ambush us."

Sammy glanced over at her. The expression on her face was like she'd had a sudden epiphany of what it was like to be on the receiving end of an ambush.

"Cover me, Sammy," True directed.

He exited the truck and dropped down to a crouch. After scanning the area, he duckwalked to the front of the truck. After a moment, he came back to the open driver's door.

"He put a couple of rounds through the front of our truck," he said and cursed under his breath as he grabbed the microphone and called Mount Weather.

"SITREP follows, over."

"Send it, over."

"Contact with at least two hostiles. They tried to ambush us. One hostile is down, another one is at large, over."

"Copy that, advise status, over," the TOC asked.

"No friendly injuries. Our vehicle has been disabled, over," True said.

"Roger that. QRF response time, thirty minutes. Make updates every two mikes, over."

"Roger, out," True replied and placed the microphone back on the holder.

"Thirty minutes. Long time," Dong said and made a running motion with his fingers. "Cocksucker run away."

"Yep," True said and eyed Dong. "What do you think?"

Dong said nothing but made a head gesture toward the front of the truck.

"Yep," True said and faced Sammy.

"You and Mal wait here with the truck. Tell whoever is in charge of the QRF that we'll be back before dark."

With that, Dong exited the vehicle and joined True. They took a moment to check their rifles before taking off at a jog. Sammy watched in wonder and badly wanted to go with them, but he knew True expected him to stay with the truck, protect its contents, along with protecting Mal. He got into the front seat and motioned for Mal to do the same.

"Keep watching for hostiles," he said.

"Where're they going?" Mal asked.

"They're going to hunt down the people who tried to ambush us," Sammy said.

"Then what?" she asked.

Sammy glanced over at her. "True is not as forgiving as Melvin. Whoever's out there will be dead by the end of the day." And he'll probably cut their heads off to send a warning to others, Sammy thought.

"Why do they call him True?" she asked.

"That's his name. Or, I should say, that's his last name. Only a few of us know his full name and I don't think he wants anyone else to know it. But it's a good name for him. As long as I've known him, he's never spoken a lie." Of course, there's been many times where he didn't answer a question either, Sammy thought, but that was his prerogative.

"Daddy said you can't trust colored boys. They'll kill you in your sleep and then rape the women," Mal said.

Sammy took a moment to give her a stare of contempt. "Your father was an idiot."

"Take it back," she demanded.

"No, I'm not going to take it back. I never met your father, but from what you told me, he wasn't a good man." Sammy gestured toward the front window. "True is a good man. I'm proud to call him a friend. Making disparaging remarks about a person based solely on the pigmentation of their skin is indicative of a true idiot. An imbecile, a moron, a fucktard, all of the above."

Mal stared at him for a few seconds before responding. "You use a lot of words that I don't understand."

"That's because your father didn't teach you," Sammy said. "He was not a good father. If he was, you'd be smarter and a better person."

"Did your father teach you all that stuff?"

Sammy sighed. "No, my father left my mother not too long after I was born. He wasn't ever a part of my life."

"Who taught you then?"

"A lot of people. Some you know, like Zach and Melvin."

"They taught you things?"

"Yep, they did. I've been lucky to have people like them in my life," Sammy said and gestured toward the front of the truck. "True has too, although learning from him comes from watching him rather than listening to him. He's not much of a talker."

"I ain't never had anybody else," she lamented. "Unless you count King Rat."

Sammy glanced over at her again. This time he felt sorry for her. "There's a lot of nice people at Mount Weather. I'd encourage you to make friends. There're classes you can take too."

"Are you taking any?"

"I just finished taking a calculus class and Jorge has been teaching me auto mechanics. Is there anything that you want to learn?"

Mal responded with a shrug. Sammy took a moment to radio in an update, although he didn't tell them what True and Dong were doing. He then continued with Mal.

"How're your basic education skills? Reading, writing, arithmetic?" he asked. Mal shrugged again. "Well, if I may suggest, you should enroll in school. Not many people are aware, but if you're in school, you don't have as many work assignments."

"I don't know," Mal said.

Sammy was about to say more, but then he heard two gunshots in the distance. It came from the direction that True and Dong had jogged toward. There was a pause and then one final gunshot. Sammy knew what that meant.

"They'll be back soon, but we still need to keep a look out for any other possible hostiles," he said.

"You know what I think? I think they killed them all," Mal said after a minute.

"Yep," Sammy agreed.

Mal surprised him by chuckling. "Good."

CHAPTER 38 – ZACH & THE BANISHMENT

Before I could enjoy breakfast, I had to brief Bob and Connie about the status of the murder investigation, the possible lead on King Rat, and then discuss the situation regarding Jonesy and Lock. Surprisingly, they agreed with my recommendations without any unnecessary discussion. I then had a pleasant breakfast with my family and was heading toward our holding cells when the intercom blasted to life with the warning alert used specifically for activating the Quick Reactionary Force. I hustled over to the TOC to see what was going on. Priss was manning the radio when I ran in and didn't waste words.

"Attempted ambush on the supply truck approximately ten miles outside of Leesburg. The QRF should be on the way within the next minute or so," she said. "Leesburg is also sending a response team."

"Who's on the truck?" I asked.

"True, Dong, Sammy, and Mal. They advised contact with one or two individuals, not zeds."

I didn't like it. "We should've sent an escort team with them."

Priss nodded. "I agree, but with all the projects the president has on the plate, we're a little shorthanded, but you know that."

I sighed. "Yeah."

"Besides, with True, there's nothing to worry about, right?" Priss asked with a grin.

"That's very true, no pun intended."

Priss groaned. "I knew you were going to say that."

It took an hour before we received the all-clear. Nobody was surprised that True had hunted down and took out the hostiles. Mal was not supposed to be on the supply run, but I'd forgotten to inform Lydia about it. It turned out okay, but I needed to take her down to the Shenandoah community as soon as possible to see if Drill Bit was indeed King Rat. I'd planned on doing it today but got caught up in other duties.

"Alright, I have something that needs taking care of," I said to Priss. "You've got this."

She gave me a knowing look and nodded.

"It's about damn time," Jonesy griped when I walked in. "We should've been released hours ago. This is a bunch of bullshit, Gunderson, and you know it."

"Apologies, gentlemen. The president thought it best to let you two spend the night here and reflect upon your sins. Good news though, as of this morning, the situation has been resolved."

Jonesy eyed me with suspicion. "How so?"

"I want you to know, it was my idea, but the president and vice president both signed off on it. There will be no trial."

"There won't, huh?" Jonesy said. "Fine, let us out."

"This is the part where I say, oh wait, there's more. Since the two of you have already been put on notice due to prior disciplinary matters, this last incident has sealed your fate. Both of you have been officially banished from Mount Weather."

Jonesy's brow furrowed in a mixture of confusion and suspicion. "What the hell do you mean, banished?"

"Yeah, what the hell are you talking about?" Lock asked. He'd been lying in his cot in the next cell, acting like he was asleep, but all of a sudden, he was wide awake and staring intensely.

I stared back, and then sighed. "You know, when you two were found and brought to Mount Weather, I had high hopes. I thought y'all would be a great fit. But there've always been issues, haven't there? Small things at first, showing up late to work details, inappropriate comments to some of the women here, and as time went on, it kept getting worse, didn't it?"

Neither one of them answered. Instead, they stared with angry scowls. I continued.

"Alright, so here's how it's going to go. You have two options. You two can relocate to Roanoke where you'll be employed at the tire plant. At some point in time, if you two display exemplary behavior, you'll be allowed to visit Mount Weather, but you won't be able to live here anymore."

"What's our other option?" Lock asked.

I stared pointedly. "You'll be taken out of here and dropped off wherever we decide."

"That's bullshit, we haven't done anything wrong," Lock said.

"Your declaration of innocence is both idiotic and pathetic," I said. "If you choose the second option, you'll never be allowed back on Mount Weather grounds. Not even as a visitor. Oh, and I already checked with Marcus Hook in case you had a notion of moving there. They said they don't want either one of you. Same with Oak Ridge."

Both men had sat up now. Jonesy stood, walked over to the door, and stared out at Lock.

"Fuck working in a tire plant," Lock proclaimed.

"There you have it, shithead, we aren't working in a tire plant," Jonesy said. "We'll take option B. Give us a vehicle and provisions and we're out of here."

"No," I said. "You two get to take your personal belongings and that's it."

Jonesy stared with pure hatred in his eyes. "I'll get you for this, Gunderson."

I stood and was about to walk out but paused a moment and stared back. "If you want to think of me as your enemy, go ahead. I don't give a shit."

Little did I know how those words would come back to bite me where it hurt the most.

CHAPTER 39 – ZACH & TRUE

True's team arrived later in the afternoon. I met them at the gate and took them directly to the small conference room where Bob and Connie were waiting.

"Alright, we'll have a formal briefing later, but in the meantime tell me what happened," I asked.

"We kill those cocksuckers," Dong said with a grin.

True grunted. "We've been watching the Deadwood series. That's his favorite word now."

Dong grinned and bobbed his head up and down. True took a breath.

"Anyway, there were two of them. They were originally from some little shithole north of Harrisburg…"

"Pennsylvania cocksuckers," Dong said.

True gave Dong one of his patented stares before continuing. "Dong shot one and we caught up with the other one. When we caught him we had a little talk with him."

"You talked with him?" Mal asked. "I thought you killed him."

True ignored her and stared at me. I understood. True didn't take kindly to being shot at and he didn't take prisoners.

"He said they were living around Harrisburg. About a dozen of them. They had trouble and had to leave. He and his buddy were the only two left. They'd seen the occasional car traveling on Leesburg and thought they'd ambush one. You know the rest."

"Two dead cocksuckers," Dong said.

I saw Bob looking at me but didn't reply. I'd talk to him about it later and remind him that True was not a forgiving man.

"Tell me about the men," I asked.

"The one Dong shot was in his late teens or early twenties. He was skinny and filthy, kind of like somebody else I recently met," he said while looking at Mal.

"What about the other one?" I asked.

"Forties or fifties, filthy, only a few teeth left, and he had a goiter."

That fact was interesting. Goiters were believed to be caused by iodine deficiency. Thankfully, Mount Weather had a stockpile of iodized salt.

"What's a goiter?" Mal asked.

Everyone ignored her. I focused on Sammy. "What's your take of it?"

"If not for True's quick thinking, it could've been worse. I don't think there were more than two of them. If there were, they would've tried to get to the truck."

I nodded. I already knew Sammy would say something like that. I asked so Bob and Connie would hear it. I turned to the two men.

"Do you have any questions?" I asked.

"Did you have to kill him?" Bob asked.

"Yes," True said.

Bob waited for True to defend himself and explain his actions. True simply stared, silently conveying there would be no explanation forthcoming. When Bob realized True wasn't going to elaborate, he chose to change the subject.

"Okay, it's been an eventful day for the four of you. I imagine you'd like to get cleaned up and maybe decompress before dinner. I look forward to reading your report, Mister True."

True nodded, stood, and walked out. Dong gave everyone a grin before following his friend. Sammy and Mal followed.

"Is True a person we should be concerned about?" Connie asked after they'd left.

"I'd trust my life with True anytime, anywhere," I said. "He's a good man."

"What's our next course of action?" Connie asked.

"I think it'd be prudent to conduct some patrols in that area. I'll see if True's interested in handling it," I said.

"Excellent," Bob said and looked at the clock on the wall. "Alright, get with True and line up a meeting in the morning." He looked at Connie and grinned. "Are you ready?"

"Yep,' Connie said and stood. He saw me gazing at them.

"We're on work detail in ten minutes," he said.

I widened my eyes in surprise. "What work detail?"

"We're on kitchen duty," he said proudly.

CHAPTER 40 – SHENANDOAH

Logan glanced over at Reese. The left side of his face was a deep purple now, and even though his nose had been set, he could see a bit of crookedness to it. Reese noticed him staring.

"Yeah, I know. I look like shit."

"I wish I'd have been there, my man. I owe that asshole a fist sandwich," Logan said.

"What for?" Mal asked.

"At the July Fourth party he made a few lewd comments to Grace when I wasn't around. She didn't tell me until a couple of days ago." Logan's jaw muscles clenched. "Yeah, I owe him for that."

"Grace is your girl?" Mal asked.

"Yep."

"Did he know?"

"Yep."

"Well, that ain't right. He should've been respectful."

"Yep."

Logan still fumed at the thought of it. To top it off, Grace was pregnant, but that didn't stop him from trying to put the moves on her. He said nothing more about it, glanced at his watch, and reached for the radio's microphone. His clicks were met with clicks. Satisfied, he spoke into the mike.

"Nothing here," he said.

"Same," Liam replied.

Logan glanced at Mal, who was standing outside of their vehicle beside the driver's window. She'd been scanning the area with a pair of binoculars.

"All I've seen are some squirrels and a fat groundhog," she said. She lowered the binoculars and looked at Logan. "You ever eat a groundhog? They're awful."

Logan stared back. "I can only imagine. I haven't seen any horse tracks, what about you?"

Mal shook her head. Logan picked up the map and looked it over before speaking into the microphone. "We're going to head toward the Shenandoah community."

"We'll do the same," Liam said.

Logan motioned for Mal to get in the vehicle. When she did, she set the binoculars in her lap and peered at Logan. "I ain't the smartest, but this doesn't seem to be working. If King Rat is anywhere around here, he's already seen us and he's hiding."

Logan glanced over at her. "Sometimes you have to work with what you have. All we have is you telling us that this area is his bailiwick. Now, if you have a better idea, I'm all ears."

Mal stared at him. "Well, I guess I need to think on it. By the way, what's a bellywick?"

It took them a little over forty minutes. When they arrived at the community, the two people manning the gates opened them without comment. BC and his ever-present son greeted them as they exited the truck.

"BC, this is Mal," Logan said. "We're thinking that maybe she lived here with her father once, back a few years ago."

BC squinted down at her, but it was Lou Ellen who recognized her.

"Her name's not Mal, it's Melody. You were a sweet little girl. Where's your father at?"

"He's dead," Mal said.

Lou Ellen gave a sad, slow shake of her head before turning back to BC. "She's Luther's girl. You remember him."

BC frowned. "Yeah, I remember both of them. We had to run Luther off. Drill Bit said the two of them got attacked and eaten."

"Ain't no monsters eat either one of us," Mal said. "We had a few close calls, but they didn't get us. Are you sure you got the right person, lady? I don't never remember being called Melody."

"Oh, yes, I remember you. A few days after arriving here, you got deathly sick. Fever. We thought for a minute you'd been infected, but after a day or so, the fever broke." Lou Ellen peered at the O'Malleys. "Where on earth did you find her?"

"It's a long story." He faced BC. "Perhaps we should go somewhere private and talk."

BC motioned with his hand and led them to his cabin. It was simple and utilitarian with only the bare necessities, but clean. There were only two chairs, so they stood and explained everything.

"Drill Bit is King Rat," BC surmised after the O'Malleys had finished their story.

"That's what we suspect," Liam said.

"It's him. I've heard him refer to himself as King Rat before. That was a few years ago. He was talking to himself one day and when I asked him who King Rat was, he claimed I must have misunderstood him, he was merely talking about a rat he'd seen. I didn't misunderstand him though and it stuck with me all this time."

"Has he come back since the funeral?" Logan asked.

"He might have. This morning, we discovered a piece of fence that'd been cut, and some things are missing."

"Like what?"

"Food and ammo. Not a lot, about enough that one man can carry out of here without being seen," BC said and rubbed his meaty paws together. "If I catch him, you won't have to worry about him anymore."

Liam and Logan swapped glances. They'd already had a meeting with all the politicians, and they impressed upon the brothers the need to apprehend him without killing him and show everyone the Mount Weather criminal justice system worked effectively.

"We understand, but we need him alive, if possible," Logan said.

"There are other crimes he may have committed, and we need to try to find out."

"I understand, but I'm not making any promises," BC replied.

Before leaving, they had Mal eyeball every man in the community to ensure King Rat was not in fact someone other than Drill Bit before making the drive back to Mount Weather. Reese asked to drive one of the vehicles with Mal. The brothers agreed on the condition they stay right on their bumper.

Mal was being abnormally quiet on the ride back. Reese noticed and tried to engage her in conversation.

"So, your real name is Melody," he said.

"I reckon it is," she replied.

"And your father's name was Luther," he said. She didn't respond. "So, I guess I'll be calling you Melody now."

"No, don't do that. I'm Mal."

Reese chuckled. "Okay, Mal it is. Do you have any memories of that place?"

Mal frowned. "I sort of remember the church and I sort of remember that woman, but that's it. I remember my daddy telling me I got a bad fever once and I got ambrosia."

Reese frowned and glanced at her. "Do you mean amnesia?"

Mal shrugged. Reese chucked again. "Amnesia, that's what it's called and that would explain why you don't remember much from your childhood."

It would also explain her seeming low intelligence, he thought. He still couldn't decide on that. It seemed like she was possibly challenged, but she picked up on things without having to be told twice. He glanced over at her and smiled. He doubted she'd ever use the word ambrosia again.

It was dark when they arrived back at Mount Weather. Once they parked the vehicles at the motor pool, Reese approached the two brothers.

"We're going to eat dinner, what about you two?" he asked.

"Yeah, we radioed ahead, and our two girls are waiting on us. You two are welcome to join us."

"Sounds good. What about it, Mal?" Reese asked and turned to her. Mal was staring up at the sky. He repeated himself. "What about it, you want to eat with them?"

"I think it's almost time for a full moon," she said.

The three men peered up at the sky. It was clear, not yet fully dark. The moon was not yet in the sky.

"Yeah, could be," Reese said and glanced at the brothers. It was moments like this when he thought maybe she was a moron after all. Logan seemed to understand and cleared his throat.

"You know, Grace is well versed in astronomy. We can ask her, is it important?" he asked.

Mal took her eyes away from the sky and focused on him. "I reckon it is. It'd be a way for us to find King Rat."

Reese stared in surprise and mentally retracted his earlier thought about her. He glanced at the brothers again who seemed as surprised as he was.

"Tell us what you're thinking," he said.

CHAPTER 41 – ZACH & THE MISCREANTS

Justin and Jeremiah insisted on being the ones to do it. They, along with their Marines, escorted Jonesy and Lock to a deuce-and-a-half, put them in the back, and drove off. There was a small crowd of people who were waiting at the main gate when they were led out and they all clapped as the duo were hauled off. When they radioed that they were returning, I waited for them at the main gate.

"We dumped them on the outskirts of Baltimore," Justin said, which caused the rest of the Marines to erupt in laughter.

"You should've seen Lock. The man was begging us to take them back to Mount Weather. He actually had tears in his eyes." He paused to wait for my reaction. It brought a smile to my face. "We gave them the supplies, like you ordered. Honestly, Zach, I never thought I'd see the day when you'd be so nice to a couple of assholes."

"Did you make the offer?" I asked. In addition to the supplies, I told Justin to extend the offer to make them observers for the Baltimore area.

"Yeah, Jonesy told me to go eff myself," he said with a chuckle. "Just as well, I'd never believe any reports they sent."

"Yeah, I suppose you're right," I said. I guess I should have known better. When the two of them were brought to Mount Weather, they seemed like good guys. Tough, seasoned survivors of the apocalypse. But they'd proven to be, well, assholes. Selfish, self-serving assholes.

"Bad apples, huh Zach?" Jeremiah asked.

"Yeah. Unfortunately," I replied. There'd been others who were like them over the years, and I knew we'd get more.

"Alright, I'm going to spend some time with my family before bed. The next few days are going to be tough."

"Yeah, I'm sure you've got some tough reports to write out," Joker quipped with a friendly grin.

I grinned back. "Something like that."

I found my work crew in the main lounge, hanging out with a few other teenagers. I knew them all. They were mostly good kids, but lately a few of them had discovered a rebellious streak within them and had gotten themselves into trouble. Nothing major, but enough to cause a stir. I stepped in and volunteered to mete out an appropriate punishment for their latest act of defiance.

Stopping at the table, I took a moment to eye the five miscreants: Theo, Dwight, Robert, Shelly, and LaToya. I eyed them for a long three seconds before speaking.

"Ah, the Mount Weather troublemakers. Are you ready for tomorrow?"

"Do we really have to go through with this?" Shelly asked.

"You will find that in life there are always consequences to your actions." I cocked my head. "Let's see if I can think of a good example. Oh, yes. Using Sharpies to write disparaging remarks about people on the walls would be an excellent example. Now, you must atone for your sins."

My verbiage was met with a collective sigh. I smirked. "Theo is the only one of you that has hauled hay. He'll tell you that it's dirty, physically demanding work. I would suggest going to bed early and getting a good night's sleep. Theo and Shelly, first thing in the morning, get two water coolers from the kitchen, fill them with ice water, and carry them to the motor pool. We leave at zero-six hundred hours."

LaToya looked at me like I'd told her she was uglier than a bucket full of assholes. "Six o'clock? That's too early!"

"Yeah, we don't even eat breakfast until eight," Dwight added.

"You'll come in early and fix your own breakfast. And, for that matter, you'll be responsible for your own lunch. We're going to be working all day. Ask Theo if you doubt it."

They grumbled and complained, but that was to be expected. Theo was the first one to arrive in the cafeteria the next morning. He saw me and walked over.

"Are any of your friends planning on not showing up?" I asked.

He stifled a yawn. "They talked about it, but they'll be here."

"Good. Grab something to eat. It's going to be a long day."

We started with some fields off of Morgan's Mill Road, using pitchforks to load the hay on the back of a trailer being pulled by a tractor. I let them rotate between driving, which gave them a little bit of a break from the physical part. It didn't help much. It wasn't even noon yet and it was already sweltering hot. The kids made a point of letting me know it.

"Why can't we use the hay bailers?" Shelly asked.

"We ran out of netting and baling rope back about five years ago," I answered and waved a hand around. "Now we do it the old-fashioned way. You know, the Amish have done it this way since before all of us were born. No tractors, just wagons pulled by mules."

"I ain't Amish," LaToya griped. Her shirt was soaked with sweat, causing it to cling to her upper torso. The boys unabashedly stared. Dwight also happened to be Shelly's boyfriend and she made it clear with her eyes that she was not pleased.

"This is bullshit," she said under her breath, but loud enough for me to hear.

"Alright, I suppose we can take an early lunch. Park it under those trees," I said, pointing to a couple of Locust trees near the roadside.

I made sure they drank plenty of water. The boys doused themselves, as did LaToya. Shelly probably felt a little insecure because LaToya was more developed up top than her and abstained from doing so, calling it stupid. Spreading out and sitting under the trees, we talked as we ate.

"Be honest, Zach, did you ever do this shit when you were our age?" Robert asked.

"Yep, sure did," I replied.

"Bullshit," LaToya said. "I bet you were a rich, pasty white boy who went to all the best schools."

I smiled. "You're way off the mark. I attended public school, lived with my grandmother in a tiny little house, and supplemented her small social security check by working on a farm."

"Really?" Shelly asked.

"Yep. My grandmother died shortly before the outbreak hit Tennessee and I went to live on the farm with an old Vietnam vet. He's the only reason I survived."

"What happened to him?" she asked.

"He died of a heart attack that Christmas."

It sounded good, it's possible Rick really did die of a heart attack, but the truth was, all I know is he died in his sleep after he'd polished off a bottle of whiskey.

"Oh, man, that must have been tough," Theo said.

"It was. I was all alone for a while, but eventually found other survivors, including Fred."

"What was Mister McCoy like back then?" Theo asked.

"I'll tell you all about him, but you have to keep it between us," I said. The five of them stared in rapt attention. After all, Fred was a living legend around here. Nobody outside of the Tennessee group knew anything about him. I kept a straight face and drew the moment out by drinking some water.

"Fred McCoy has always been a tough man. He was a rodeo man, a trick shot artist, and had a college degree in engineering. Nobody, and I mean nobody, has ever crossed Fred McCoy and won. The most important thing you need to know about Mister Fred McCoy is this, once you have his respect and friendship, you can count on him for anything. That's a character trait I try to emulate, and you should as well."

There were some nods of agreement and it looked like Theo wanted to ask more questions, but LaToya suddenly stood and pointed across the hayfield.

"Zeds!"

CHAPTER 42 – ZACH, THE MISCREANTS, & THE ZEDS

I counted seven of them. They were on the far side of the field and making their way toward us. The way they were walking seemed to confirm LaToya's announcement, but I wanted to be sure. I hustled over to the tractor, and then realized I didn't have my scoped rifle with me, only my Kel-Tec and five handguns. I motioned them over.

"Strap up," I ordered, and then directed them to take up positions around the tractor.

"LaToya, you stand on top of the trailer and keep an eye out. They may have some friends that'll try to sneak up on us from behind."

She gave me a nod. A slight breeze had kicked up, but I don't know if it was that or the thrill of the moment, but her nipples were sticking out like pencil erasers. Robert and Dwight had forgotten about the zeds and were fixated.

"Hey! Pay attention!" I admonished.

When the zeds were a hundred yards away, I brought my rifle up to my shoulder, but then it occurred to me that this would be an excellent training moment. I held the rifle out to Theo.

"Shoot the one who's out front," I said.

Theo took the rifle with uncertainty and aimed. His first shot kicked up some dirt about ten feet in front of the zed.

"Aim a little higher and try again. Don't rush your shot, make it count," I said.

His second shot hit the zed in the chest, knocking him down.

"Good, but he's not dead yet. We'll come back to him later. Pick another target and fire."

Theo did so, successfully hitting the second one in the forehead. The zeds started running toward us now, and LaToya shouted.

"There's a bunch of them coming!"

I turned and saw almost a dozen coming from the opposite side of the road, which was another hay field that had been cut, but not yet raked up. I grabbed my rifle from Theo's grasp and went to work.

I focused on the four who were running at us and picked them off in a matter of a few seconds. LaToya had already started shooting at the second group and had ordered the others to focus their fire on them. I reloaded with a fresh magazine and started to take aim. But there was only one left. The kids focused on the last remaining zed and put almost a dozen rounds into him before I shouted for them to cease fire.

They stared in wide-eyed wonderment at the dead zeds. After a moment, they were euphoric and began whooping and giving each other high-fives. I had to smile. Killing zeds didn't cause this kind of reaction in me anymore, but their reaction brought back memories.

"Alright, good job, everyone. Reload and check your weapons. LaToya," I said. She swiveled her head and stared.

"Damn good job," I said.

LaToya beamed at the compliment, but I heard Shelly scoff. A younger Zach would have jumped her ass at her attitude, but I kept my anger in check.

"Shelly, get on the radio and call in a SITREP."

"How do you do that?" she asked.

I stared at her in puzzlement. I was certain all of them had received training on radio procedure, including her.

"I'll do it," LaToya said and went into the cab of the tractor.

"Let's go check them out," Robert said and started to walk over to the group of zeds on the opposite field.

"Not so fast," I said. "We're going to wait for the QRF to respond, then we'll have a look."

"What about that one?" Shelly said, pointing at the first zed that Theo had shot in the chest. He'd gotten back on his feet and was now shuffling toward us, snarling as he shuffled. I walked over to the trailer and grabbed one of the pitchforks.

"Which one of you wants to finish him off with this?" I asked.

I was going to hand the pitchfork to one of the boys, but LaToya suddenly grabbed it from me and sprinted toward the zed yelling like a banshee.

It wasn't exactly what I wanted, but I admired her grit. Even so, I brought my rifle up and got a good aim in case it didn't go so well for her. I needn't have bothered. LaToya ran up to the zed, who was almost a foot taller than her, dropped into a semicrouch as she neared it, and brought the pitchfork up under the zed's chin. She continued the upward thrust, which pushed two of the pitchfork's tines into the zed's brain.

The zed fell backwards like a sack of day-old shit. LaToya turned around and raised her hands in victory, giving us all a big grin. Her friends cheered like she'd scored a touchdown.

CHAPTER 43 – MELVIN & MUTT

Melvin exited the main gate of Mount Weather as Zach was rounding up the teens and exited I-81 onto the newly created gravel road a little before zero-seven hundred hours. It led directly to the church, which had now officially been renamed Stephens City Waystation. They even had a hand-painted sign. When Melvin neared the church, he was surprised to see Shirley and Mutt standing outside. He waved, parked his truck, and walked over to them.

"Good morning," they greeted.

"Good morning," Melvin replied and stared at the direction where they had been looking.

Mutt pointed down the road. "Could've swore we saw some movement. It might've been deer, but it sure looked like people to me."

"They were too far away to tell for certain," Shirley added.

Melvin stared toward where he gestured. "There's been some zed activity the past few days. I'll go drive down there and check it out."

"By yourself?" Shirley asked.

Melvin pointed toward the east. "There's a Mennonite community not too far from here. They sometimes get out and explore. It's probably them and they know me. If it's zeds, it's probably only a few of them. If a horde was nearby, we'd already know about it."

"Mennonites? I didn't know they survived," Mutt said.

"Oh, yeah, they've done well," Melvin said. "Friendly folks, but they like to keep to themselves. They believe the whole apocalypse was God's doing because people had become too advanced and had strayed too far from the path. I'll see if I can arrange a meetup one day. In the meantime, I brought everything you need to build a decent-sized chicken coop. Let's get the truck unloaded."

Mutt nodded and gave a short whistle. The others emerged from the church and began helping out. Garth looked over the lumber with a scowl.

"It's all rough cut," he grumbled.

"No need for fine cut wood when all we're using it for is the chicken coop," Melvin said and glanced at Mutt, who shook his head at Garth's complaining.

The men unloaded the truck and after a few minutes of discussion over where the coop should be built, which should have already been decided, Melvin suggested a location near an already existing storage building.

"It's out of the way but close enough to the back door where you don't have to walk a long distance to fetch eggs every morning," Melvin said and then waved a hand at the materials. "They tell me we can build this in about three hours. I got step-by-step instructions printed out. Let's see if we can do it quicker."

Melvin didn't tell them he'd already built three other coops using the same blueprints and instructions. He could do it by memory now. Thankfully, Garth kept his complaints to a minimum and everyone listened to Melvin's directions. They had the coop built in a little over two hours, which seemed to boost morale. Melvin congratulated them.

"I knew y'all could do it," he said while they admired their accomplishment.

"I've come to love raising chickens," Mutt said. "I'm the first to admit, I shed a few tears when ours died."

Melvin gestured at the new coop. "This one can hold a dozen easily and the wiring keeps the coyotes and hawks out. Once you get settled in and start to develop your new home, you can expand it. We've got some hens and a big old rooster that'll be brought down in a day or two."

"My mouth is watering at the thought already," Mutt said with a grin.

"I don't know what you all had in mind for dinner, but I've got a butchered pig in that big Igloo cooler in the back of the truck. It's already been cooked, but it needs to be reheated."

"Hammy and I can take care of that," Lynn said.

"Make it a low temperature and the meat won't dry out," Melvin advised.

Lynn scoffed. "Melvin Clark, I may not be much, but I know how to cook."

"Yes, ma'am," Melvin replied with a grin. He got the cooler and carried it inside the church to the newly renovated kitchen. Hammy followed closely and helped him unload the meat.

"This looks wonderful, you better stick around and eat with us," she said.

"Absolutely, but first, I think I'll take a drive down into Stephens City and make sure there aren't any zeds hanging around."

"I'd like to come along, if you don't mind," Mutt said.

"I'd be happy for the company," Melvin replied.

The two men were soon travelling down Valley Pike toward the heart of Stephens City.

"Was Garth right? Has everything around here already been picked through?" Mutt asked.

"My guess is about ninety percent. There should be the FEMA X on any structure that's been searched."

"So, there's nothing left, like Garth said," Mutt grumbled.

"What you have to do is go back to these businesses and houses and look for hidden booty. For example, my buddy and I were in a convenience store a while back and although it was obvious it'd been picked clean, we found a big pack of toilet paper hidden in the ceiling of the bathroom."

Mutt frowned. "In the ceiling?"

"Yeah. You know those suspended ceilings with tiles? Someone hid the TP up there. It was a goldmine."

Mutt chuckled. "I can't remember the last time I used real toilet paper."

"Can I let you in on a little secret? True and I kept it all."

"You didn't turn any of it over?" Mutt asked.

"Not a single roll, and I'm not ashamed to admit it," Melvin said, which elicited another chuckle from Mutt.

"If you find something like that, keep it," Melvin said and laughed some more.

The two men continued discussing the wonderful aspects of manufactured toilet paper as they approached a blue building that was once a used car lot. A FEMA X was spray painted on the front wall immediately below an a/c unit. Mutt pointed at it.

"I don't even know what all those markings stand for."

"It's fairly easy to understand. I can explain, if you want."

Mutt shrugged. "Sure, I guess."

"The left side of the X is where you identify who did the search. In this case, you see my name written there."

"Okay."

Melvin continued. "Yeah, I've searched a lot of these. On the top is a date indicating when it was searched."

Mutt stared at the symbol. "You were here a year ago."

"I was. Now, on the right side of the X is where you notate any hazards."

"You wrote down rats."

Melvin nodded. "Some people don't like rats, so if they were looking for a place to sleep for the night, this wouldn't be a place they'd like."

"Nice of you," Mutt said.

"I try to be. That leads to the bottom part of the X. If I were to find dead bodies or zeds, I'd put that info right there. It's an easy formula, but it gets hard when people use abbreviations that nobody else understands. In this case, I put the universal symbol of a big zero with a hash mark through it. No dead bodies, no zeds."

"Are we allowed to search through all these places?"

"Absolutely. You may find things that were missed by other people. Hell, in that building, there may be gold bullion hidden in the walls. The only requirement is that you use the FEMA sign. If there's a FEMA sign already there, all you do is update it."

"Why?" Mutt asked.

Melvin shrugged. "Zach requires it. He's our Director of Operations, you've met him. He's a meticulous, organized man. He plans out everything and has a lot of reasons that justifies this requirement."

"Well, I can't promise anything," Mutt said.

Melvin nodded, but inwardly he was beginning to wonder if these people were going to get along with the Mount Weather administration. They continued riding around the area, looking for signs of human or zed activity. After thirty minutes, Melvin stopped the truck.

"If there were any people or zeds out here, they appear to be long gone now. I suppose we should get on back."

"That sounds good. We appreciate everything you've done for us, Melvin."

"I'm more than happy to help good people, but I feel like I'd be remiss if I didn't remind you all that there will be things that are required of you. If you don't meet those requirements, you won't be able to stay here."

Mutt turned in his seat. "Why do you say that? Has something happened?"

Before Melvin could explain his statement, he spotted movement down the road at a building that was once a post office.

"We have something," he said and moved the truck along at a creep and into the parking lot.

Parking, Melvin armed himself with his Chinese war sword. Mutt stared in disbelief.

"You've got a gun on you, what're you going to do with that thing?" he asked.

Melvin gave him a wink and started walking toward the post office. As he did so, two zeds came around the corner. Melvin noticed two items of interest at the same time. First, they did not appear to be in advanced stages of decomposition. Second, they were sprinting toward him at a speed he'd never seen from a zed before.

Melvin had been in life threatening situations so many times in the past, he wasn't frightened or deterred. He sidestepped, pivoted on the ball of his right foot, and swung the war sword in a lightning fast three-sixty. The razor-sharp blade caught the zed in the neck and cut completely through, decapitating him.

The second zed turned toward Melvin and reached out, coming within inches of grabbing him. Melvin continued swinging the sword and connected it with one of the zed's outstretched arms, nearly severing it. Melvin frowned.

"That was sloppy," he remarked as he stepped out of the zed's reach.

Recovering, he swung again, this time severing the zed's other arm. Melvin then aimed low and took off the zed's left leg an inch above the knee. The zed fell to the ground. He still tried to get at Melvin, but with only one functioning leg, all he did was move his torso in a slow circle. The black ooze that used to be blood secreted out onto the asphalt. Mutt walked up while Melvin was examining them.

"I would've helped, but I didn't want to get in the way of you and that damned sword," he said.

Melvin glanced at Mutt and then gestured toward the live zed. "He doesn't look like he's been a zed for too long, does he?"

Mutt stared down at the thing that used to be a young man. The zed had ceased his attempts to stand and was now staring at the men while emitting an occasional snarl.

"No, I don't guess he does. I wonder where he came from?"

"Look at the clothes. That's Mennonite clothing. That group I was telling you about declined to be vaccinated. I wonder how many of them are infected now. It'll be something I'll need to report. In the meantime, let's put this poor bastard out of his misery."

Melvin lifted the war sword and buried it in the zed's head. The two men watched as the zed succumbed to lifelessness. Mutt pointed at the sword.

"Why'd you use that? Why didn't you just shoot them?"

"Ammunition is at a premium these days, my friend," Melvin said. "That ammunition we supplied you with, use it sparingly. If they decide you're wasting it, you won't get any more."

"We won't? Who gets to decide something like that?" Mutt asked.

"The president, mostly. Zach is the one who keeps up with the numbers, so the president's decision will come from what Zach tells him. My advice, if you have occasion to shoot something, keep a record of it and how much you use. And keep target practice at a minimum."

"That don't seem too fair, if you ask me," Mutt lamented.

"Times are tough. There's material shortages of all kinds. If you guys ever find any ammo, unused cartridge casings, gunpowder, anything like that, there'd be a nice reward for you."

Mutt gave a slow nod. "I'll keep that in mind. So, what do we do with these two mopes?"

"The best course of action is to burn them. I need to take some pictures of them first. Y'all are going to need to build a burn pit somewhere around here for situations like this."

"We sure do have a lot of work to do, it seems," Mutt remarked.

"Yes, you do, but I want you to think of it like this. There's a plate full of food waiting for us both, right? If not for Mount Weather, would things be different?"

Mutt grunted. “I suppose you make a good point. It’s just that we’ve been on our own for so long we’re used to doing things our way.”

“There’s nothing wrong with that. Your independent nature is what kept y’all alive all this time. It’s part of the reason why I suggested to the president that y’all would be a good fit for this outpost.”

Mutt stared. “You vouched for us? I didn’t know that.”

“Yep. I want you to think of it this way. While there will be certain things required of you and your people, you’ll have a lot of autonomy here. You get to make the rules for visitors. If they don’t follow them, you will be well within your right to kick them out.”

“I suppose that makes sense.”

Melvin grinned. “We can deal with these bodies later. What do you say we head back and get something to eat?”

CHAPTER 44 – ZACH & JEREMIAH

The First Sergeant looked around in admiration. "Looks like you and your crew took care of business. Didn't even need us to respond."

"The kids were top notch," I said, then lowered my voice and gestured at LaToya. "You got yourself a Marine right there. Trust me."

Jeremiah arched an eyebrow and then focused on her. She and the other kids were over by the trailer, talking and laughing over their zed encounter. "What's her name?"

"LaToya Greenwood."

"Greenwood, get over here!" the First Sergeant shouted.

LaToya's grin vanished and she hustled over. Stopping in front of us, she stared at us, wondering what she'd done wrong. The First Sergeant made a slight gesture toward me.

"Mister Gunderson was singing your praises to me just now about how you acted with the zeds, and that says a lot. Do you know why?"

"Why is that, sir?"

"Because he's killed a gazillion of those things, starting when he was about your age, did you know that?"

LaToya glanced at me. "I've heard things."

"So, if a man like Mister Gunderson says good things about you, that's got to mean something, right? What's your plan, Greenwood?"

"What do you mean, sir?" she asked.

"What do you want to be when you're all grown up? Are you one of those girls who wants to be a beautician or some shit like that?"

"Oh, hell no," she exclaimed.

"Well then, you might want to consider becoming a Marine."

Her jaw dropped. "A Marine?"

"That's right, a Marine. It's a tough life and it's not for everyone. You think about it. Maybe talk it over with your parents. When you've decided, come see me."

"Yes sir, I will," she said. I could see a little bit of bewilderment in her expression. I think the First Sergeant saw it too.

"Alright then, in the meantime, you and your friends get back to work. That hay isn't going to get put in the barn by itself, right?"

Jeremiah chuckled under his breath as she jogged back to her friends. "You weren't exaggerating, were you?"

"Nope, she's got some grit to her. Let's get a closer look at these zeds."

Jeremiah agreed and the two of us walked over to the first group. We crouched down and looked them over. "Some are old."

I nodded. "Yeah but look at that one. He doesn't look old at all. I'd say he's a fresh infection. That's concerning."

"Do you recognize any of them?" Jeremiah asked.

"No. How about you?" I asked.

Jeremiah responded with a shake of his head. He then had his QRF personnel look them over to see if they might have recognized anyone. None did, which I suppose was a positive sign, but it also made me wonder, where did they come from? DC perhaps?

"That couldn't be right," I muttered.

"What's that?" Jeremiah asked.

"I'm wondering where these came from. These are fresh infections, so DC would be out of the question, right?"

"From somewhere else then," he surmised.

"Yeah, but from where?"

CHAPTER 45 – MELVIN & HAMMY

"Those were some mighty good pork chops," Melvin remarked. He only ate one. He could've eaten two or three, but the food was meant for them. He could eat plenty back home.

"I have no doubt," Hammy said with a grin. "Do you want some more potatoes?"

"I believe I'm full. Thanks though," Melvin replied, stood, and stretched. "I believe I'm going to head back while there's still a bit of daylight."

"Will you be back tomorrow?" Hammy asked.

"Tomorrow or the day after. I don't know what they have planned for me. Either way, I'll make sure you get your chickens tomorrow," Melvin said. "Alright, I think today has been a good day. Very productive. Hopefully, I'll see everyone tomorrow."

"I'll walk you out," Hammy said.

Everyone said their goodbyes to Melvin, even Garth, although he was giving Melvin the stink eye when Hammy joined him. After they'd walked outside and closed the door, Hammy intertwined her arm in his and pressed close. Close enough where Melvin felt her breasts against his arm.

"What was Mutt talking about with the houses and businesses around here?" she asked. "You mentioned getting credits. What does that mean?"

"At some point, you're going to have time to go scavenging. I'll be the first to tell you, most everything around here of face value has already been taken, but that doesn't mean there's nothing left. Besides, there are other things of value, like the copper wiring out of a house.

"Anything you find is yours. However, you may discover items that you have no use for. If that happens, you have the option of giving these surplus items to Mount Weather where they will be assigned a value, and that value will be put on your account. Credits. Kind of like money, but the money is only numbers on a ledger sheet."

"Is that important?" she asked.

"It will be when you find the need for something, like maybe an extra thousand pounds of grain. That's how you'll be able to pay for it."

Hammy scoffed. "So, there's only so many freebies we'll get from Mount Weather."

"Correct. You make it sound bad, but we don't have an unlimited supply of resources." Melvin opted not to explain further. Maybe one day.

"Oh," Hammy said and then walked closer to Melvin. "I'd like to request something right now."

She leaned in and kissed Melvin. Instead of returning the kiss, Melvin pulled back.

Hammy frowned in confusion. "Don't you like me?"

"Yes, yes I do, but there's something I haven't told you," Melvin said. "I have a girl back home. Back at Mount Weather."

Hammy eyed him. "Don't you think that's something you should have told me before you ever kissed me?"

Melvin stared at the ground a moment and then looked her in the eye. "You're right and I apologize."

"You should apologize, leading me on like that. It doesn't matter though. There's something you should know," Hammy said and waited for Melvin to make eye contact before continuing. "I already knew you had a girl."

"You did?"

"Yep, the way you acted; I knew it was something like that," she said. "And you want to know something? I don't care that you have a girl back home. You have a girl right here, if you want her."

Melvin was tempted. Sorely tempted. But his only girl was Savannah, and that was that. Did it matter if things weren't going well between them? For better or worse, that's a vow they would've made if a preacher were around to marry them and by God he was going to abide by that vow even if they hadn't actually spoken the words.

"Hammy, you're a beautiful woman, and if I were a single man, I'd be coming to visit every day. But I'm not single and I can't. I'm sorry for leading you on the way I have."

Hammy stared. "Yes, you led me on. When I first laid eyes on you, I thought you were the most handsome man I'd ever seen, and I thought you felt the same way about me. You sure talked like you did."

"I know and I apologize for that. I was sweet-talking you to get on your good side, but honestly, I really do think you're a beautiful woman."

"What about your girl?" Hammy asked.

"She's a beautiful woman too."

"How did you two get together?" she asked.

"I happened upon her one night out in the middle of nowhere. She was skinny as a rail but still beautiful. We've been together ever since."

"But y'all ain't getting along," Hammy accused. "Otherwise, you wouldn't have given me a second glance."

Melvin struggled to find an appropriate response, but he had none. Hammy leaned forward and kissed him again. "Maybe you're confused, maybe you're liking me a little bit more than you're willing to admit."

She waited for a response, but Melvin remained silent. She sighed, placed a hand on his chest, and rubbed it gently. "You figure yourself out. I want and need me a man. I ain't settling for Garth, but before too long we're going to start having regular visitors, right?" Melvin nodded. "One day, a man is going to come along, and he'll be almost as handsome as you. You think about that."

He made it back to Mount Weather by nineteen hundred hours, found Savannah at the Tennessee table, and sat down beside her. She looked up when he sat. He smiled and gave her a peck on the forehead.

"How're the people at Stephens City?" she asked.

"They're coming along. We got the coop built and ready for chickens. They're going to need a couple of donkeys to protect their livestock though. I'll speak to Zach about it. Has anyone seen him?"

"He's meeting with the doctors and scientists," Kelly said. "They want to talk about the zeds some more."

"Well then, they'll want to hear what I have to tell them," he said.

Janet piped in. "Why, what's going on?"

"I came across a couple of zeds over in Stephens City earlier. Two teenaged boys and they were dressed in Mennonite clothing."

"Were they old or new zeds?" Janet asked.

"If I had to guess, I'd say they've been infected no more than a couple of months," Melvin replied. "I should really talk to them about this. Are they in one of the conference rooms?"

"I believe they are. The small one," Janet said.

"Thanks," Melvin said and started to stand.

"You haven't even eaten," Savannah said.

"I ate a bite with the Stephens City folks. I might get something later. See you in a little while."

Savannah watched as Melvin hurried off. Melvin was always hungry. It seemed to her that the real reason he left was he didn't want to be around her. Deep down, she knew why, but that didn't mean she had to like it or accept it. So, with nothing else to do, she hung out with Janet, an unlikely friendship, until they both started yawning. She bumped into Melvin in the hallway on the way back to their suite.

"Are you coming back with me?" she asked.

"Yep, I'm dog tired. How about you?"

"I'm a little tired too, I guess," she said.

The two of them walked to their suite in silence. Once they got inside, Melvin began undressing and then turned to her. "I've been out in the heat all day. Maybe I should shower before bed."

"Yeah."

Savannah watched him finish undressing and disappear into the bathroom. When she heard the shower turn on, she found herself wondering why she was standing there doing nothing. She hurriedly stripped and joined him. Melvin had his eyes closed and head under the spray. He jumped when she touched his back and turned to her.

"This is a surprise."

"It is?" she asked.

"Well, I mean, we haven't showered together in a while." Or anything else, he thought.

"I guess that's my fault."

"It's nobody's fault, love," Melvin said. The last thing he wanted was to quarrel.

Savannah said nothing. She knew it was indeed her fault. She'd been cold and argumentative lately. At times, she was downright hateful. She knew it was uncalled for but couldn't explain why she was behaving that way.

She grabbed the bar of homemade soap and began lathering him up. She worked her way down from his chest and then paid extra attention to a certain area. Melvin held his head back and moaned.

It wasn't a big shower stall, so making love in it required a little bit of give and take, but make love they did. After drying off, they went straight to bed and spooned like they used to always do.

"This is nice," Melvin said.

"I'm sorry I've been so mean lately," Savannah said.

"It's okay."

"Have you found someone else?" she suddenly asked. She felt Melvin stiffen at the question. "It's okay if you have, I understand."

"There's nobody else," Melvin said. "You're my girl, period, end of story."

He wrapped his arms tightly around her and Savannah melted against him. She wanted to cry. She felt like that a lot lately and she wondered, not for the first time, if Melvin would be better off without her. She snuggled closer to him. He was snoring already, but her movements had caused him to become aroused again. She believed it was an indicator he wasn't sleeping with anyone else.

Melvin would never know that his nocturnal arousal caused by Savannah's closeness was the only thing that kept her from going into the closet and hanging herself with one of his belts.

CHAPTER 46 – ZACH & FORT DETRICK

I can't say that I was calm, cool, and collected as I sat in the driver's seat of the lead vehicle in the convoy. In fact, I was a little nervous. Call it a psychic phenomenon, call it bullshit, call it whatever you wanted, but up until recently, I possessed some kind of connection with the zed we called Eve.

But not anymore. I'd not had a single dream about her since I'd opened up the labs for her. There had been no hostile actions by her group of zeds for the longest time, so the attack on South Mountain came somewhat as a surprise.

We had over a hundred people on this op. Security squads deployed around Fort Detrick, drones in the air, and two mortar teams. The main force, led by Justin, made entry onto the grounds at precisely zero-six hundred hours. It took us almost five hours of painstaking searching to learn that nobody was home. They'd all left.

"It's a bust," one of the troops remarked.

She was right. Well, almost right. We'd saved the best for last, the labs. We entered them slowly, carefully. When we entered the last lab, all of us let out a collective gasp.

"Oh, my God," Ruth whispered.

There were corpses on four tables. Or, should I say, there were the remains of four zeds. Female zeds. They were splayed out and had been eviscerated.

"What in the bloody hell were they doing to them?" Justin said. "What do you think, Zach? Were they torturing them?"

I walked over to the nearest one and used my TacLight to inspect closer. After a minute, I inspected the other three. All four were females, and all four had their internal organs cut out.

"They may have felt the pain, but I don't think torture was the goal," I said.

"What then?" Ruth asked.

"It's only a guess, but I think they're trying to figure out how to get the females to reproduce," I said.

"This is crazy," Ruth said. "It's more than crazy, it's downright evil. How are they able to conceive of this shit and actually eviscerate the women?"

Justin glanced at her. "Remember what those two drunk scientists said?"

"What are you talking about?" I asked.

"The July 4th party. Ruth and I were in the party barn playing darts with the two scientists, Lowery and Fitzhugh. They were pretty drunk, and we got to talking about the zeds. They had some interesting things to say about them."

"Like what?" I asked.

"Fitzhugh was going on about how the zeds were an evolved species of humanoids. I asked him what he meant, and he began going on about the history of man and viruses. He said when man first began domesticating animals, people would become infected with different types of poxes."

I stared at the dissected corpses. "That's true."

Justin frowned. "Really? I thought he was full of shit."

"Take a look at history. Humans first began domesticating animals around ten thousand years ago, or more. But they weren't knowledgeable about good hygiene back then and would become infected after handling the animals. They found evidence of smallpox in mummies which were over three thousand years old. Smallpox has been responsible for the deaths of millions of people. There are numerous types of poxes that've been identified. Chickenpox, herpes, the list goes on. Over the years, we began developing immunities without the assistance of vaccines."

"Yeah, that's what he was saying and that zeds were the future of humanity."

I scoffed. "I wouldn't agree with that at all. We're the future of humanity. The uninfected humans are the future. Even now, our children are developing antibodies."

I scoffed again. I knew Fitzhugh. Highly educated he was, but half the time he was drunk and blathering on with wild theories. He was sort of right. In the ten years since the plague infected most of the human population and either killed them outright or turned them into undead, flesh-eating monsters, they'd definitely changed. Evolved or mutated, I'm not sure what the correct term would apply. They had developed a collective sense of survival, as evidenced by their organized hunting parties, and I've personally seen glimpses of emotion from them, but I sincerely doubted they'd ever regain their humanity and I said so.

"Why do you think that?" Merrit asked.

"First, they have sustained permanent brain damage. They have no sense of empathy, which is an indicator that the anterior insular cortex is no longer functioning, and that part is located deep in the center of the brain. Also, I don't know if you guys have noticed, but they have no sense of personal hygiene. Even a rodent will clean itself."

I could've continued, but we had arrived at the outer boundaries of Fort Detrick. The vehicles were spaced an adequate distance apart in order to have good sectors of fire. We slowly rode up and down each street, hoping to draw the zeds out into the open. When all the teams confirmed there had not been a single sighting, we parked and began a building-to-building search. It was slow, painstaking, exhausting. It took most of the day, and when we were finished, we had not come into contact with a single zed.

"You were right about the hygiene stuff," Merrit remarked. "The buildings where they were living stunk to high heaven, and there were piles of excrement everywhere."

It gave me a thought. I went around and asked each team if they had encountered any fresh piles of turds.

"Well, we didn't spend much time studying on them, but there didn't seem to be any fresh juicy ones, no," Slim had said, eliciting laughter from his teammates. He continued. "There's plenty of animal carcasses, but they all looked old too."

Justin had listened with interest. "They've definitely left Detrick," he said.

I nodded slowly. "I want to send Joker's team on a recon."

He stared a moment before giving Joker a shout. Joker, who was sitting under a tree with his team, stood and trotted over.

"I want you to take your team east on 70 for a few miles. Have Slim utilize his tracking skills and see if he notices anything."

Joker gave a clipped nod and trotted back to his team. A moment later, they'd loaded up in their vehicle and driven off.

"What're you thinking?" Justin asked.

"I think they fled to DC," I said.

Justin eyed me. "Why do you think that?"

"DC was decimated during the initial outbreak. There probably wasn't a single survivor. No humans anywhere around there. A good place for a zed to live without fear of being hunted," I said.

We sat around and talked while we waited. After an hour, the radio came to life with the information I was waiting for.

"So, they are heading to DC," Justin remarked.

"Yep. They're probably there already," I said.

"That whole place is a hive of zeds, the last time anybody checked," Justin said.

"Yep, exactly," I said.

He pressed the button on the microphone and ordered the team to return. "I hate to say it, but I smell a recon mission to DC in the near future," he mused.

"We should send Melvin," Merrit said.

Justin gave his Marine compadre a quizzical look. "Why's that?"

"Simple. I have a theory about Wildman Melvin."

"Oh, yeah? Do tell," Justin said.

"Back when everything was sort of normal and I was living in the barracks at Camp Lejune, guys in my squad passed around some paperbacks. They were a series of stories about a Roman soldier named Casca."

"Ah, Casca, the eternal mercenary," I said.

"You've heard of it?" Merrit asked.

"Heard of it? I've read all of them. Casca Rufio Longinus, the soldier who drove the holy lance into Jesus, who in turn cursed Casca to live until his second coming. I loved that series."

"Yeah, me too. My theory is, Melvin is Casca, and that means he's immortal," Merrit said.

"What kind of weed you been smoking?" someone asked.

Merrit was undeterred. "Think about it. He's been on more missions than anyone else and always comes back home with a bunch of dead zeds in his wake and not a scratch on him."

There was a chorus of chuckles and agreements.

"You might be onto something," I said with a grin. "After all, the series was written by a man named Barry Sadler who was a Special Forces soldier in Vietnam."

"Maybe Melvin is Barry's illegitimate child," Justin quipped, causing more laughter. "I have to say though, you're right, I've never seen or heard of him getting injured, and he's done some crazy shit."

"I bet we don't know about most of his adventures," Merrit added.

"So, it's settled then. We send Melvin to DC with his war sword and tell him he can't come home until he's killed all the zeds," I said.

"He'll be home by dinnertime," Justin replied.

I laughed along with them, but that didn't mean I was without worry. In fact, I was both puzzled and concerned about the activities of our local zeds. Why did they attack South Mountain? Why did they then leave Fort Detrick? And, most importantly, would an offensive operation into DC be the best course of action?

Tough questions that I didn't have answers to. Justin was right, our esteemed politicians would declare we needed to conduct recon missions in the DC area and find out more.

"Zach, you seem like your mind is a million miles away. What are you thinking?" Justin asked.

"I need to talk to you two," I said and motioned for them to follow me and didn't say anything until we were out of earshot from the others. "The decision has already been made."

Justin's expression was hard. "Let me guess. The meeting in Roanoke."

"Yep. Well, let me explain. This mission is what was talked about in Roanoke. The gist of it was, go in and kill them all. The thing is, Miss

Ellie had an idea that the zeds would've already fled, and a contingency plan was drawn up."

"So, DC then," Justin said.

"Yep. We can do it right now, but I don't think we have enough people to pull it off. What do you think?"

"Why do you say that?" Merrit asked.

I gestured around. "According to the recon reports, there were under a thousand zeds here. There's something you guys don't know. Melvin has already been to DC."

"I knew it!" Merrit exclaimed.

"Yeah, he ventured over to Dulles a while back and decided to have a look around DC. He said there's thousands of them."

"Even ten years later?" Justin asked.

"I know, I thought they would've all died out by now as well, but they haven't. The bottom line is, we're going to need to double the size of this assault force. I'd like to go back home, sit down, and plan it out. We'll need to get volunteers from other communities. I know a way to get some from Marcus Hook, but we'll need more."

The two men nodded in agreement. Merrit then spoke.

"Can we still become infected? I can't stop thinking about those people from South Mountain."

"They were unvaccinated, and unvaccinated people are definitely at risk."

"Knuckleheads," Merrit quipped.

I instantly thought of Bailey. She was a lot of things, but she was definitely not a knucklehead. Stubborn, perhaps, but intelligent. Even so, she was one voice. The rest of them were a different story. Especially her grandfather.

"Their rationalization is the vax had not been properly tested, which is true, but I think the results speak for themselves. We've had absolutely no adverse side effects other than a few people reporting migraine headaches and nausea. So, the answer to your question is no, I do not believe anyone who has been vaccinated is at risk of becoming infected."

"What's going to be done with the people still living at South Mountain?" he asked.

"When the time is right, I'm going to meet with them and convince them to get vaccinated. I'm going to start with Bailey. I think she'll listen to reason. If we get her on board, she'll convince the others."

"Good luck with that. I can tell you from firsthand experience, she doesn't care much for what other people think," Justin said.

"Yeah, that's the impression I got, but I'll still try to talk to her about it."

"Alright, getting back on the subject at hand, is this our mission now? Kill all the zeds?"

I looked around to see if anyone else was listening in on our conversation. Nobody was, but I still lowered my voice before speaking.

"I once thought the only good zed was a dead zed. I started thinking differently when I had that thing with Eve, but that was a mistake, they're more of a threat now than they ever were," I said.

"How so?" Merrit asked.

"The attack on South Mountain was organized and planned, like some of their previous attacks. We can't simply go on with our lives believing that we can live in symbiosis with each other. We have to act."

"Doctrine dictates we take it to the enemy. We don't wait for them to come to us," Justin said and eyed me. "Sun Tzu, right, Zach?"

I smiled. "I believe that is one of his rules."

"Alright, tell us the truth, do you still have some sort of bond with Eve?" he asked.

"At one time I'm certain I did, but not anymore."

"I wonder what they're up to," Merrit mused.

"I bet I can answer that," Justin said. "They're looking to replenish their ranks."

Merrit smirked. "They're conscripting new soldiers. Right, Zach?"

"I can't say that I disagree with your theory. It makes sense. Some of them have actually rotted away and died, and we've killed a lot of them."

"Plus, they can't reproduce," Justin said. I nodded. "I wonder how they're going to react when they realize our intent is to wipe them out." Justin thought for a moment. "Do we have enough ammo to do that?"

I stared somberly. "I'm not sure."

CHAPTER 47 – TEAM JOKER

"This is going to test our mettle, Marines," Joker proclaimed as they exited Mount Weather's main gate.

"How?" Cutter asked. "It's just another recon mission."

"It's more than that," Joker said. "We're going into the belly of the beast. The zeds at Fort Detrick numbered in the hundreds, DC has thousands. We had a drone that was bigger than the one we have now. It had more range and flying time. We flew it into the heart of DC. Thousands of them. And somehow the drone crashed."

"The zeds got it?" Flash asked.

Joker shrugged. "We don't really know, but that was our best drone. So, let's go over this one more time. We have a thousand rounds of ammo, 5.56 only. Captain Smithson emphasized the importance of firing only if absolutely necessary." He pointed a thumb toward the back of their armored van. "We have enough rations for a week, eighty gallons of water, and a cooler full of ice."

"Seems like overkill, although I'm grateful for the ice," Cutter said.

"I hope it is overkill," Joker said. "We discussed it and decided it's necessary in case we somehow get stranded. We could use more water, but we don't have the room. What I'm trying to emphasize is, this mission has the potential to go sideways."

"We won't let that happen, Gunny," Flash said.

Joker eyed them. "I hope so. No messing around on this mission though, keep it tight."

The team voiced their agreement, and they chitchatted about Mount Weather as they rode. The journey was rather uneventful until they neared I-495. Flash, who was in the passenger seat, pointed.

"Zeds at our one o'clock."

Joker, who was driving, brought the van to a stop. "I believe that area is called Tyson's Corner."

Flash gestured. "I'm counting a dozen over in that parking lot."

"I bet there's a lot more lurking around in the buildings," Slim said.

As if the zeds heard him, more started appearing. Joker frowned.

"I wanted to set up near the Potomac," he said.

"What's stopping us?" Cutter asked.

Joker watched as more and more zeds started spilling out of buildings and making their way toward them. "They know we're here. We've got to move. Get on the radio and give them a SITREP," Joker said as he accelerated. He swerved around a large pothole as he heard Cutter on the radio. "Advise them we're proceeding toward OP One, but it appears any other OP will be unreachable."

Cutter did as Joker instructed him. Outwardly he kept a calm demeanor, but inside he was nervous. This was the most zeds he'd seen in a long time. He glanced in the sideview mirror. Some of them had already made it up to the Dulles Access Road and more were coming. There were a lot of derelict vehicles on the road, which limited their maneuverability. As Joker zigzagged through the cars, a group of zeds, maybe a dozen, jumped in front of their vehicle.

"Damn it!" Joker shouted.

He knew this odd zed maneuver. They'd continue massing together to form a zed blockade, preventing the vehicle from moving. Joker's answer to this dilemma was to push on the accelerator and run the zeds over. Their van jostled its occupants around as it ran over the zeds, and then something unexpected happened. The van got hung up on some of the zeds Joker had run over.

"Oh, shit," Joker growled as he tried reversing the van.

"Are we stuck?" Cutter asked as he wildly peered at the zeds who were now surrounding them.

Joker alternated between drive and reverse several times, but during his attempts to free the van, more and more zeds approached. Soon, they were completely surrounded. The van was fortified, and the window openings had metal straps across them, preventing the zeds from breaking the glass and making entry. Cutter had rolled his window down and now stuck his rifle barrel between the metal straps. Joker noticed.

"Hold your fire, it won't do any good right now," he said.

After several attempts to free themselves, Joker put the gear shift into park and turned the van off. He took a slow deep breath before speaking.

"Cutter, call it in. We're stuck and it appears we've been surrounded by several hundred zeds." He pointed out of the front window, which was now completely covered by disfigured, snarling zeds. "Give them some reference points to our location. We're a hundred yards west of the 495 Interchange."

As the men listened to Cutter call in their SITREP on the radio, they watched as the zeds began stacking up around the van. Within a minute, they heard zeds on the roof of the van.

"Oh shit," Flash said.

"Oh shit what?" Cutter asked.

"I know what they're doing," Flash said. "They're going to try to suffocate us."

Cutter jerked his head around and stared back at Flash. "What do you mean?"

“They bottlenecked us with the derelict cars, limiting our movement. Once they got us stopped, they started dogpiling us. If we leave the van running, it’ll overheat and quit on us, and after a while we’re going to run out of fresh air.”

“And then we’ll die?” Cutter asked and then realized Flash was right. “Holy shit! How did they figure out how to do this?”

Joker turned the van off, which caused Cutter to jerk his head toward him. “What the hell are you doing?”

“Flash is right. If I keep the van running, not only will it kill us with carbon monoxide, but it’ll burn up the engine.”

Slim had been watching the zeds. “It’s already getting hot in here. How much time do we have, do you think?”

“Don’t know but I’m not ready to die today,” Joker said and then paused a moment. A zed had stuck its face against the window mesh and snarled at him. “Marines, it’s my fault we’re in this predicament. I should’ve anticipated this. I apologize for letting you down.”

“Not your fault,” Flash said. “We’re all in this together.”

“Damn right,” Slim added.

Cutter nodded in agreement. “We’ll have a good laugh about this later. In the meantime, let’s concentrate on staying alive. Slim, get us some cups of ice out. We need to stay cool.”

The men drank iced water and tried to relax, even though the fetid odor and unstopping snarling from the zeds was making it difficult. Joker noted the tension and spoke to them while they listened to the main force call out whenever they passed a phase line.

“The new girl is doing okay. Any of y’all know her well?” he asked.

“What’s her name?” Slim asked.

“LaToya. Her and her family used to live over near Bluemont,” Flash said. “She’s alright, a little immature but I think the First Sergeant will work that out of her.”

“She’s a good-looking heifer,” Cutter remarked.

Flash didn’t answer. He in fact liked LaToya and had been trying to figure out a way to speak to her but all she liked to do was hang out with her small circle of friends. It didn’t seem like any of them were her boyfriend, but any time he’d tried talking to her it went nowhere.

“There’s something I’ve got to tell you guys,” Slim said.

“What’s that?” Flash asked.

“I wasn’t going to say anything until later, but I think I’d like to get it out while we’re all still alive,” Slim said.

“Oh shit, this has to be something about a girl,” Joker said. “Unless you’re coming out.” When he said it, the other men turned toward Slim.

“Yeah, it’s about a girl,” Slim said. “You see, back at the trading post, when you two were getting friendly with those working girls, I found my own girl.”

"You did? Who?" Flash asked.

"Her name's Esther. Her father and brother came to Mount Weather to visit the other day," Slim said.

"Why?" Flash asked.

"They were getting to know me better, and they even spoke with the president about me. Before they left, they handed me a letter. Esther had written it."

The other men continued staring, which compelled Slim to explain. "Well, the bottom line is, they invited me to come live with them and Esther wrote that she'd consider marrying me if I was willing. And I'm going to."

"Holy shit," Cutter drawled.

"Well, congratulations, big guy," Flash said. "I guess that means we better not get ourselves eaten alive then."

Slim noticed Joker had not commented. "What do you think, Gunny?"

"I think you have a wonderful life ahead of you, just don't name your firstborn after Cutter."

The other three men erupted in laughter.

CHAPTER 48 – ZACH & THE TOC

After returning from Fort Detrick, we put together a plan. Operation Eradicate DC was the name it was given. We recruited volunteers from other communities. Marcus Hook provided twenty people on the guarantee of the tires. With a total of two hundred people, we assembled at Mount Weather and commenced the operation two days after Detrick.

I'd already expressed my concerns on such an operation back during the big summit meeting at the Russet estate. We had enough ammunition, but we stood a good chance of depleting it all, which would leave us vulnerable against future attacks.

Doc came up with the idea of a massive artillery strike, which I thought was a fantastic idea. We'd kill most of them and then come in with troops and mop up.

Ultimately, the politicians voted this down. It was unconscionable to them to destroy Washington, D.C. and all that it stood for. I could have told them no human had been able to live there in over ten years, but it wouldn't have mattered. They had decided and there was no dissuading them.

Back to the present. The president was adamant that I would not be part of the group that was going into DC. He said I was too valuable of an asset, but I strongly suspected Kelly had cornered him and ordered him to keep me at Mount Weather.

I could have argued, or simply ignored him, but I didn't. Instead, I declared myself Officer of the Day and took command of the TOC.

The First Sergeant was in the lead vehicle of the multivehicle convoy and led them out of the Mount Weather compound promptly at zero-four hundred hours. LaToya, the newly assigned radio operator, promptly announced it.

"Mount Weather TOC, this is Alpha-One-Romeo. We are exiting the main gate, over."

He had assigned LaToya as the radio operator. She made regular radio transmissions of status and location, and although she'd made some procedural errors, the politicians were eating it up. And then came a radio transmission we didn't want to hear.

"TOC, this is Joker One Romeo. SITREP, over."

All of us recognized Cutter's voice.

"He's stressed," Priss remarked before she answered his call. "Send it, over."

Cutter advised they had visual contact with multiple zeds on the Dulles Access Road. We acknowledged and the First Sergeant acknowledged it, advising Joker and his team they were forty minutes away. Five minutes later, Cutter radioed in and advised their vehicle was disabled and the zeds were dogpiling onto their vehicle.

"What exactly are they trying to do?" Connie asked.

Before I could respond, Cutter got on the radio and answered, even though he did not hear the question.

"Guys, be advised they're attempting to suffocate us and there is a good possibility that they'll succeed. We'd appreciate some assistance ASAP."

The First Sergeant's radio operator answered Cutter and advised him they were thirty minutes away. I saw Connie out of the corner of my eye. He was frowning.

"Zach, did I hear Cutter correctly?" he asked.

"If you're referring to him saying the zeds are trying to suffocate them, yes. Somehow their vehicle became disabled. I'm speculating here, but I believe the zeds are stacking themselves around and on top of their van in an attempt to deprive them of oxygen."

Connie scoffed. "They can't be doing that on purpose. They're not smart enough."

"At one time I would have agreed with you, but remember the attack at Fort Detrick and how they dogpiled on the phalanxes? I think that's what they're doing to Joker's team."

Connie continued frowning. "If you're correct, that would mean a higher level of learning, would it not?"

"Yessir," I replied. "That contaminated vaccine has had some interesting side effects."

I looked around and only then did I notice the others staring at me in rapt attention. I decided to take advantage of their concern. I pointed at Kate and Kyra.

"I need you two to personally visit each guard post. Make sure they're alert and even though I've already gone over it, reemphasize the possibility of an attack."

The sisters jumped up immediately, acknowledged me, and hustled out. Connie watched the women's backsides as they left. He then turned to me.

"What do you think happened with Eve's baby? Did it survive?"

"I don't know. Lots of unanswered questions with that situation. Did it survive? Has it been growing like a normal child? Is it infected? Is it a normal human that's immune or is it some kind of advanced zed? The list goes on."

The radio came to life. LaToya was the speaker, and she sounded a little nervous. "Mount Weather, this is Alpha One Romeo. The First

Sergeant advises the zeds are attacking us in waves. No friendly casualties reported… yet."

I grabbed the microphone, hailed Joker, and asked for an update.

"They've packed themselves pretty tight around the van," Joker said. "I don't know what'll get us first, the lack of oxygen or the heat."

The next voice on the radio was Justin. "Hold fast, Marines, we're coming."

CHAPTER 49 – ZEDS & PLOWS

"This isn't how I hoped it'd be," the First Sergeant muttered.

LaToya, who was standing beside him in the open turret of their armored vehicle, glanced over. "It isn't?"

"The plan was to go kill some zeds and then I'd take you new people to Eighth and I."

"What's that?" LaToya asked.

"It's the oldest active post in the Marine Corps. Or it was, before the world went to hell. It served a special purpose in the Corps, and I was stationed there. Maybe one day it will be active again. Not in my lifetime, but maybe yours." Jeremiah was silent for several seconds before giving his head a sharp shake. "Give me that microphone."

She did so and watched as the First Sergeant stared out at the roadway a moment, took a deep breath, and began speaking.

"Alright, listen up. Our mission has changed slightly. We're still going to kill zeds, but our priority is rescuing Team Joker. When the zeds get thick, use the plows. When we get to Joker, the lead elements will employ the grappling hooks. We haven't tried it before, but it should work. If you're not using the grappling hooks, that means you're either dead or you're shooting. Concentrate and keep in mind our Marines are trapped in a van at our twelve o'clock. It's been modified, but it's not completely bulletproof. Therefore, make your shots count. Don't spray and pray. We're coming up on Team Joker's position. Get ready."

He handed the microphone back to LaToya and checked his weapon.

"Um, First Sergeant?"

Jeremiah glanced at LaToya. "What is it, Private?"

"Would now be a good time to tell you that you didn't follow proper radio protocol?"

He glanced at her again and grunted. "You can have me do pushups when we get back. Now, your primary job is to monitor radio traffic and make sure I don't miss hearing any important comms. But if it gets thick, I expect you to kill zeds."

"Aye, sir," LaToya said.

They saw the zeds first. LaToya audibly gasped. "There're thousands of them!"

She was right. Thousands of them crammed onto Dulles Access Road. The two lead vehicles rode side-by-side, mere inches separating them. When the First Sergeant mentioned plows, he was referring to the modification that had recently been made by Josue and Jorge. They were wedges of steel that were angled at forty-five degrees and attached to the vehicle's framework. The vehicle on the left had their plow angled left, and the vehicle on the right was the opposite.

When the two vehicles made contact with the zeds, they went flying off to either side. The First Sergeant, whose vehicle was immediately behind the two lead vehicles, gave a loud Marine Hoo-Rah. LaToya did the same, which caused Jeremiah to grin.

"Alright, tell everyone I don't hear enough zeds dying."

When she said it, the amount of gunfire intensified.

CHAPTER 50 – TEAM JOKER

"You men hear that?" Slim asked.

The four of them had passed out, or fallen asleep, depending on who was asked about it later. The combination of the lack of oxygen and the sheer heat was doing a good job of killing them. Slim was the first to hear it. It sounded like a distant thump-thump-thump. He believed he was dreaming at first. Slowly, his brain began working and he forced himself to open his eyes when he understood. Flash was beside him. Slim nudged him and then violently shook him.

"Wake up, Marines!" he shouted at the top of his voice.

He had earplugs in to alleviate the maddening sound of the snarling and started to take them out, but he had a better idea. The windows were closed. He opened his now. A couple of zeds had their faces stuck against the meshing. He stuck the muzzle of his assault weapon against the forehead of one of them and fired. That zed slumped, but only slightly. The force of the other zeds behind him kept him pressed against the van.

Slim shot another one, all the while yelling at the others to wake up. He had a splitting headache from the heat and lack of oxygen, and part of him was telling him to go back to sleep, that it would all be over soon. He kept firing, and kept firing, hoping his bullets were causing lethal damage to the zeds packed around the van.

When he paused to reload, he felt a tap on his shoulder. It was Flash.

"What're you doing, bro?" he asked in a gravelly rasp.

"The cavalry is here! Can't you hear them?" Slim shouted.

It took Flash a moment to understand what Slim was saying, but when he did, he mimicked Slim and began firing out of his own window. The continuous and loud gunfire brought Joker and Cutter around. Slim yelled at them, which caused Cutter to shout in glee. Joker then yelled.

"Damnit, Marines, I was dreaming about my first piece of tail, and you had to wake me up!"

Despite them being in bad shape, each laughed.

"Alright, cease fire, cease fire!" Joker shouted. When they stopped firing, he explained. "We're kind of shooting blind and we don't know how close our rescuers are. We might inflict friendly fire casualties, and we don't want that."

Cutter stared out of his window. One zed was still stuck with its face against the mesh, but the other one had fallen, a fresh snarling face had taken its place.

"So, what do we do?" he asked.

"What we should've done already. Get your bayonets out," Joker said.

CHAPTER 51 – THE RESCUE

Captain Justin Smithson was in the rearmost vehicle, and it was the last place he wanted to be. The wedge was working in spectacular fashion and the lead element was making more kills than they could count. But, they still had action. Zeds were coming in behind them. Some were barely walking; some were running in that peculiar loping movement.

Two seasoned men were riding with him. They weren't Marines, but they were no rookies. Each had done their share of killing zeds in the past, and they were making a good show of it now. They were older, and their maturity showed. They didn't rush their shots, and Justin noticed every time one of them fired, a hole appeared in between a zed's eyes before they dropped to the ground.

Zed bodies were lying on either side of the roadway as they drove, and every teen feet or so, three zed corpses were lying in the middle of the road. Justin smiled to himself. If not for the fact that Team Joker's lives were in peril, he'd be having a buttload of fun. He realized he missed this action.

"Message from the First Sergeant," Ruth yelled. She was both the driver and the radio person. "They've reached the van!"

Justin wanted to yell back to her to tell them to surround the van and get his Marines to safety as quickly as possible, but he knew that order was not necessary. Jeremiah knew what to do. He gave another order instead.

"Get as close as you can," he directed Ruth.

He wanted to be part of the rescue, but if his Marines were dead, he needed to be there also. The thought of that possibility angered him. He took aim and shot three zeds in the blink of an eye. The man to his left noticed.

"Damn good shooting, Captain!" he shouted, and then shot three as well.

When Justin's vehicle had reached the rest of the vehicles, all he could see was a few patches of the top of the van. He watched as they continuously threw out the grappling hooks and pulled dead zeds away from it. It seemed to take forever, and there were also other live zeds to contend with.

When the last zed dropped, Justin ordered three teams out of their vehicles to get to the van. While they were doing it, Ruth was on the radio trying to raise Joker. There were so many zeds, they had to create a trench through the corpses.

The first person they brought out was Cutter. Two of them half carried, half dragged him along the trench. Once they were out, two more ran in. It was repeated four times until all of them were out. Justin walked up to the four Marines, who were lying on their backs, taking deep gulps of air. Two medics were busily putting IVs in their arms. Justin squatted by Joker.

"Are you going to live, Gunny?" he asked.

"Oh, yeah. They haven't killed me yet."

"Good thing. For a minute I thought I was going to have to take Maria as my second wife."

Joker chuckled. "After she's had this magnificence, she'll never be with another man. You got anything to drink stronger than water?"

Justin reached into his flak jacket and came out with a flask. Joker reached for it and took a swig.

"What is it?" he asked.

"George Dickel. I got it from Jimbo at Marcus Hook."

Joker chuckled. "That man is always finding good stuff." He sat up now and tried to hand the flask back. Justin waved him off.

"Share it with your Marines, they deserve it."

"I believe I will," Joker replied. Cutter was the closest to him. He rolled a little to the left and handed it off to him. After taking a generous swig, he handed it to Flash, who did the same and handed it to Slim.

"So, my man is going to marry a Mennonite girl," Flash said.

"Yep," Slim said and took a small swig, which caused him to cough.

Cutter shook his head as he took the flask back. "You know, back when everything was sort of normal, there was dating involved before marriage."

Slim looked around at the plethora of dead corpses. "Hoss, there ain't nothing normal anymore."

Joker was standing now. He bent over and took the flask. "Don't give your man a hard time. Be happy for him. Hell, we're lucky to be alive. Here's to Slim," he said and drank from the flask.

CHAPTER 52 - ZACH HAS AN ENCOUNTER

My morning ride was pleasant. The birds were singing, and I even encountered a group of beautiful butterflies that flew along with me for a couple of minutes. No zeds, no strangers, no odd tracks that'd indicate we were being visited or otherwise surveilled. It was a wonderful ride.

I took Sparkie out this morning. Technically, he belonged to Brisco, the resident electrician of Mount Weather. Since he was the only electrician with a master's rating, he was the unofficial manager of our power grid. Which meant he travelled a lot. Currently, he was in Roanoke getting the electricity sorted out in order to power the factory. He didn't mind. He was well compensated for his work, and I happened to know that in addition to being friends with benefits with Kyra Redbank, he had similar arrangements with other ladies in both Marcus Hook and Roanoke.

I needed this ride. I needed the solitude and the openness to help me think. Operation Eradicate DC had been deemed a success among the politicians. The final body count was over four thousand. After rescuing Joker and his crew, the rest of the team went into the heart of DC. Most of the zeds were already dead, so it became a mop up operation.

The old politicians were ecstatic that they could go back to their offices and reminisce, or whatever. In fact, they were there now, along with the First Sergeant and a contingent of Marines guarding them. Bob and Connie wanted me to go with them, but I begged off. I was interested, but there were other things here at home that needed my attention. Namely, my family. We'd planned on a picnic together with the McCoys and I was looking forward to it.

I spoke a couple of minutes to the gate guard before walking Sparkie to the barn. That's where they were waiting for me. It was a good spot to jump a person. Out of the way, no prying eyes. Good for them, bad for me.

When I walked in, Jonesy was standing there, a taunting look on his face. He started walking toward me and I knew we were about to fight. His ruse worked. I was concentrating on him when I should have been watching my back. I was about to grab my gun out of my holster, but Lock had come up behind me and grabbed it with both hands. That's when Jonesy began his assault and punched me several times while I was wrestling for my gun.

I couldn't keep taking punches, so I relinquished control over it and began fighting back. It's hard to say if I had made the right decision. When I felt my gun being pulled out of my holster, I at least managed to knock Jonesy off his feet. My smugness lasted maybe one second. As I turned to face Lock, he hit me in the side of the head with my own gun. I fought back and got in some good punches, but it was two against one and they were no pushovers. I knew I had to do something. Jonesy attempted to get me in a heel hook. I managed to escape, roll, and was about to get to my feet when Lock caught me with a hell of a kick to the head.

I saw stars and fell back onto the barn floor. As I lay in the dirt, I at least managed to land a good punch to Jonesy's jaw. I looked up to see Lock about to stomp me in the face. I jerked my head to the side and he missed the first one. Jonesy grabbed me and tied up an arm. Lock's boot was raised, waiting for the right moment. Jonesy started punching me in the side again and Lock stomped me. He smirked as he raised a boot to stomp me again when suddenly, I heard something akin to a watermelon being smashed and Lock's head snapped forward.

He slumped to the ground, and that's when I saw Josue standing there, a crowbar in his hands. He brought it up again and hit Jonesy on his right knee. Jonesy screamed out in pain. Josue said something in Spanish and hit him again.

The sudden appearance of Josue gave me a second wind. I rolled over on top of Jonesy and began pummeling him until my fists were throbbing in pain. Josue watched without comment until I rolled off of Jonesy and lay on my back, gasping for air. After a minute, Josue helped me to my feet. He then gestured at Lock with his crowbar.

"I saw that asshole sneak in the barn after you. I knew it was no bueno, so I brought along my little friend." He held up the crowbar for emphasis.

"Thanks, amigo," I said.

I wiped some blood out of my eyes and stared at the two men. I could see gray matter peeking out from the split in the back of Lock's skull. Jonesy's face was a bloody pulp but surprisingly, he was still breathing. Josue noticed as well.

"He might live. We'll worry about him later. Let's get you to the infirmary."

CHAPTER 53 – ZACH & GRANT

I was hurting all over, one side of my face looked like a bloated football and an eye was already swollen shut, but I still had my wits. Grant Parsons, a man who was once an enemy but now was my friend, looked my face over with a penlight.

"I'm sure I look better than I feel," I quipped.

Grant grunted. "Well then, you must feel like death warmed over." He poked me once or twice and then put his penlight back in his breast pocket.

"Broken ribs, multiple contusions, and a possible concussion. I think you should spend the night here," he said.

"Nah, I'll be alright," I replied.

Grant shook his head. "I know you pretty well, Zach Gunderson, and you know I do. If you walk out of here, you'll feel the need to show everyone you're fine and you'll work all day. And then your kids are going to bug you all night. Nope. You need to stay out of the public's eye, and away from your kids for at least the next couple of days. I'm going to have some x-rays done and see how badly those ribs are broken." He gave my swollen cheek a gentle poke, which made me wince with my good eye.

"Mmhmm, that orbital socket may be fractured as well. That's it, then. You're staying here until at least tomorrow evening."

"I agree with Doctor Parsons."

I looked over at the voice. President Duckworth had entered the room along with Captain Smithson. The two men walked directly over and stood close.

"Captain Smithson has informed me what happened," he said with a somber expression. Justin took his cue.

"Lock is dead, in case you're wondering." He hooked a thumb toward the hall. "Jonesy's in the next room, under guard. He's all beat to hell, but it looks like he's going to live." He eyed me. "He looks worse than you, but not by much."

"What happens now?" I asked.

"Oh, he'll have a fair trial," Bob said and then lowered his voice to a whisper. "And then we'll banish his ass forever. Again. Justin said this time he's going to take him several hundred miles away and dump him with nothing more than the clothes on his back. Between you and me,

I'm thinking Justin is going to make sure he'll never be seen again. I like that idea."

Even though my face was aching, I cracked a smile. Bob smiled back.

"I'll have him dropped off in some toxic shithole city with a canteen of water and a loaf of bread," Justin said.

"That sounds only fair," I said. "But in the meantime, I think I'm ready to get out of here."

Kelly, who had been standing off to the side, spoke up. "You're not going anywhere. You're going to stay here the rest of the day and tonight, like Grant directed you to."

The men grinned. "Sounds like the boss has spoken," Bob said.

After everyone left, Kelly sat on the bed and softly stroked my swollen cheek. "Seems like we've been through this before."

"Yeah," I replied.

"Janet is watching the kids. I told Grant I'd stay with you and keep an eye on you," she said.

"All this seems totally unnecessary. You can keep an eye on me back at our place."

Kelly wrinkled her nose. "You know that won't work. The kids will be full of questions, and they won't leave you alone."

She was right. I worked so much, whenever I was home, I made sure to pay as much attention to the kids as I could. They ate it up and I was thankful, but the broken ribs were causing me a lot of discomfort and the kids always wanted to horseplay when Daddy was around.

"Alright, I guess I can stay here," I said.

Grant reappeared, this time pushing a wheelchair. "Alright, time for x-rays." He held up a hospital gown. "You're going to need to change into this too."

That elicited a laugh from Kelly. "Oh, you'll look so cute."

"Gee, thanks."

"Are you hungry?"

I realized I'd not even eaten breakfast and my stomach was grumbling. "I could eat."

"Good. I'm going to go to the cafeteria and get you a plate. I'll be back before the x-rays are done."

The x-rays confirmed I had two broken ribs and a hairline fracture of the orbital socket. Grant whispered to me conspiratorially.

"Jonesy has a broken socket as well, some missing teeth, a broken nose, and his kneecap is fractured. Did I ever mention I always thought he was an asshole, and I may have accidentally poked and prodded a little harder than what was necessary?" He grinned when I looked at him. "Alright, Zach. You're banged up pretty bad, but nothing permanent. My advice is to simply take it easy for a few weeks and you'll be fine."

Kelly kept her promise and brought me a plate of food. I had a multitude of visitors throughout the day. Everyone had offered their condolences and wanted a piece of Jonesy. True came in and declared he was going to assist Justin with Jonesy's relocation. I knew then that Jonesy was a dead man.

Kelly finally directed everyone out and that I was to have no more visitors. I slept for a while. When I awoke, Kelly was sitting in a chair beside the bed.

"What time is it?" I asked.

"Almost six. Everyone is probably eating right now."

"Why don't you go eat? I'm fine," I said.

"I might later. Right now, I'd like to stay with you, and you're not fine. You were groaning in your sleep." She then peered back toward the door. "I know a way to make you feel better. Don't move."

She then lifted the bed sheet and ducked her head underneath. I involuntarily moaned in pleasure. She was right, I was feeling better within seconds. Despite my discomfort, Kelly's loving ministrations caused me to climax within a minute. Pulling her head out from under the sheets, she motioned toward the door, and gave me a wink before walking out. I assumed she was going to the restroom and clean up. I watched as she walked out, thinking about how much I loved her.

I was nodding off when I heard the door open. I assumed it was Kelly coming back in the room and didn't bother opening my eyes. Not until I felt the cold hard edge of a blade pressing against my throat.

Jonesy's face was battered and swollen. His eyes were swollen, one of them was completely shut, but I could still see the malevolence, the hatred, as he stared at me.

"How's the knee?" I asked.

"Hurts like hell," he growled. "I'll take care of that greasy Mexican later, but right now I'm going to deal with you."

I was a dead man. No doubt about it. I was going to try something heroic, something macho. I grabbed at his wrist and struggled with him, but to be honest, he had me. I felt the pressure of the blade increasing. Suddenly, a rabid wolverine jumped on Jonesy's back.

"You sonofabitch!" Kelly screamed as her fingers dug into his eyes.

Jonesy howled in pain. He'd forgotten all about me and attempted to get Kelly off him. I grabbed at the knife, but only managed to get my hand sliced open. The sudden infusion of adrenalin blocked all pain receptors, and I shot out of the bed. Spotting the chair sitting near my bed, I grabbed it and swung it with every ounce of strength I had. I made solid contact with Jonesy's head, and he stumbled forward against Kelly. I swung again and this time he went down.

I raised the stool to hit him again, but instead, I doubled over in pain as a feeling similar to a hot poker shot through my side. I assumed it was my broken ribs. I raised my head up and spotted Kelly, who was leaning against the wall. When my brain registered what I was seeing, my mouth went dry.

CHAPTER 54 - KELLY

"Zach?" she said in a raspy whisper. She had stumbled back and was leaning against the wall. Jonesy's knife, a hand-forged Bowie knife that was around seven or eight inches long, had been plunged into her chest, about an inch below her sternum.

I hobbled over to her as quickly as I could and gently guided her down to the floor.

"I can't breathe," she said and coughed, spraying my face with blood.

I struggled to say something, but I too was having trouble breathing. A little voice was telling me one of my busted ribs had penetrated a lung.

The door opened and I looked up in fright, wondering if somebody was coming in to finish the job. It was one of the guys who'd come to Mount Weather with Reese. His name was Paul. His last name escaped me at the moment. He was a little older than Reese, a quiet man who seemed depressed most of the time. He stared in apparent confusion.

"What happened?" he asked.

"Get the doctor! Now!" I shouted, which caused another bolt of pain to shoot through me. I fought down a wave of nausea and looked back down at Kelly. Her face was pale and her breathing came in fitful gasps.

"Hang in there, love," I said and looked around. The only thing I saw that might help was my bedding.

The pain in my side was so intense, it took everything I had to walk over to the bed. I tried to pull a blanket, but only had the strength to grab a sheet and feebly pull it off the bed.

It was almost impossible to crouch down beside Kelly. Waves of nausea hit me, but somehow I squatted and began working a sheet around the knife in the hopes that it would control the bleeding. I knew she was bleeding internally, but I had to do something. I talked to her as I worked.

"I can't pull it out. We've got to leave it in, but that's okay. When they operate on you, they'll be able to remove it without you bleeding to death."

I hastened a look at her and was going to offer a smile, but I stopped. Kelly was staring into space with lifeless eyes. I honestly don't know if I stared stoically or screamed out in agony because somewhere during that, I passed out.

I dreamt. I dreamt of people yelling, screaming. I was in a dark whirlpool. I couldn't see anything. I only felt an overwhelming sadness.

The infirmary had no windows. When I awoke, I didn't know if it was still night or if I'd been out longer than a few hours. I tried clearing my throat and suddenly Justin was standing there.

"Hey, big guy, good to see you awake," he said.

I looked around and saw Cutter, True, and Dong. All of them were armed. I tried to sit up but a stabbing of pain from the ribcage stopped me.

"Easy. The doc says you need to stay still and let your ribs heal a little bit."

I stared at him. "Tell me what's going on, Justin."

When I spoke, it came out like a croak. I tried swallowing, but my throat was dry. Cutter noticed.

"You want some water? I'll get you some."

He didn't wait for my response, hurried out, and returned a moment later with a glass and a straw. "Here, man, take some sips. It'll help."

I did as he said and sipped. The cool water refreshed my mouth and throat, but not my soul.

"Okay, tell me what's going on. How long have I been out?"

"How long have you been out? About sixteen hours," he said. "Your left lung had collapsed, and you had some internal bleeding. Grant can give you a more detailed explanation."

"Lock is dead, but you know that. Jonesy too." He took a slow, deep breath. "Kelly didn't make it."

I knew that, but there was one thing I didn't know, and he was avoiding it. "How's the baby?"

Justin gave a slow shake of his head. So, there it was. I was kind of hoping he was going to tell me they saved the baby and then Janet would come in the room holding the little tyke and we'd all share a happy moment, but that kind of thing only happens on TV.

"Zach, I can't begin to tell you how sorry I am that I let you down. I should've had one or two of my Marines guarding that asshole from the start." He leaned his head forward and lowered his voice to a whisper. "Cutter and I were the first ones here, and we made sure Jonesy did not survive. I know you may never forgive me for what happened to Kelly, but I hope this is a start."

"Okay," I said.

He stared a moment longer before straightening. If he expected me to say anything else, I don't know, but I couldn't talk at the moment. Kelly and my child were dead. I knew it was a fact, but it seemed surreal. If not for the pain wracking my body, I might have thought I was having a bad dream.

"So, as for everything else going on, Fred and Rachel have your kids. Janet is helping with them, although I have no idea how Fred allowed her into his house. The president has ordered the flags flown at half-mast for the week. Everyone is torn up over this. Hell, everyone loved Kelly."

I nodded silently.

"Nothing else has happened," Justin said. "I believe there is a general consensus that we were far too lenient for too long with Jonesy and Lock. The president said there will be a review of the behavior of everyone in and around Mount Weather. As you might imagine, some of the slackers are so nervous they're going to Lydia and asking for extra work."

I nodded again, which was a bit painful. "Anything else?"

"The funeral is in two days, unless you don't think you can attend, the president said we can delay it as long as needed."

"Two days it is," I replied. "Anything else?"

Cutter cleared his throat. "Liam, Logan, and Melvin came by earlier. They wanted to talk to you, but you were asleep, and we didn't want to wake you. They said Mal came up with a way to find King Rat. They came up with a plan and wanted your approval before they did anything."

I listened as Cutter explained it. "The president likes it, but I guess he's deferring to you on the final approval. Mal said they have to do it no later than tomorrow. Do you have any questions you want me to ask them? I can run them down and bring them back."

I thought it over for a moment and glanced at Justin. "I like it," he said.

I gave Cutter a nod. "Tell them to do it. Now, the only thing I want is to see my kids."

Cutter jumped up. "I'll take care of everything." He started to rush out but stopped in the doorway.

"I don't have many friends. Kelly was one of them and now she's gone. Joker, Slim, Flash, and now you, all of you almost died. I consider you a friend, Zach. I hope you feel the same about me."

He darted through the door before I could reply.

CHAPTER 55 – MAL & KING RAT

Mal was awakened by a gentle hand shaking her shoulder. She opened her eyes to see Melvin staring down. She reclosed her eyes, but Melvin shook her shoulder again. Not as gentle this time. It took one or two more rough shakes before Mal reluctantly sat up and rubbed her eyes. The only light was from a low wattage exit sign down at the end of the hall. She looked around and saw everyone else was still asleep.

"What time is it?" she asked, her voice groggy.

"Zero-four hundred," he answered in a hushed voice. "C'mon, we've got to get going."

She forced herself out of bed and stretched. All she was wearing was a black tee shirt. It used to belong to Reese. Melvin watched as she threw the blanket off her, revealing bony legs. He noticed they were shaved, a big difference from those two furry toothpicks he saw during their first encounter. She stretched before standing and stared at him.

"Can I take a shower first?"

"Make it a quick one. Ten minutes, no more," Melvin said.

She nodded and headed toward the locker rooms, scratching her ass as she walked. Melvin shook his head and picked out some clothes for her; socks, a pair of jeans, a plain gray tee shirt. He didn't see any bra or panties in her locker and didn't worry too much about it.

An hour later the two of them were in Melvin's new replacement truck, horse trailer in tow. Reese had guard duty and gave a hopeful wave as they drove out. Melvin drove cautiously but still reached their prearranged spot. He parked, killed the engine, and stared out at the burnt remains of his old truck. It still angered him, but he forced himself to keep his emotions in check.

"Ain't much left of it, is there?" Mal remarked.

"You sure did a number on it. I still haven't replaced all my gear that was in it."

"Sorry," she muttered.

"Are you having any second thoughts?" he asked her.

Mal shook her head. "I reckon I need to do the right thing. Right?"

"Yep."

"Are you sure those cops are out there?"

"They are. Are you positive this is the day?" he asked.

She nodded. "The full moon started last night. He'd always show up the next day. He probably doesn't even know he did that."

Melvin eyed her for a moment. “Alright, go get your horse ready. I’ll be out in a minute.”

He waited until she exited the truck before reaching for the microphone of the CB radio. Ensuring he was on the proper channel, he gave the push-to-talk button a quick five clicks, waited a couple of seconds, and clicked it five more times. There was an immediate response of four clicks. He made two clicks and received a response of two clicks.

Melvin nodded to himself. The O’Malleys were in place, and everything was ready. The radio discipline probably wasn’t necessary, but they were taking no chances this time.

Melvin exited the truck and helped Mal finish saddling Booboo. He then gestured at the kit he’d tied on the back of the saddle.

“You know how to work the recorder?” he asked. She nodded. “And you know the sign to give when you’ve talked him into admitting he killed Janey, right?” She nodded again. He eyed her for a long three seconds before speaking. “Alright then, you better get going.”

Mal looked east. “Sun’s coming up. It looks like it’s going to be a nice day.”

“Yep. I imagine it’s going to be another hot one.”

“There’s something I want to say,” she said. Melvin stared and waited. “Me and Reese have had some long talks, and I reckon you were right to go and kill my daddy.”

Melvin paused a moment, making sure she was sincere before responding. “I appreciate that. When we get back, I think we need to sit down with Savannah and square things away with her too.”

Mal didn’t answer and hopped up on Booboo. Once seated, she nudged him into a canter, her ugly dog following along behind her. Melvin watched her ride, noting how natural it came to her. Her dog still had bald patches from the mange, but it was clearing up.

“I guess it’s good I didn’t kill you,” he muttered.

Ten minutes later, Mal arrived at the abandoned house that had once been her home. It hadn’t changed any. Thankfully, one of the plastic pails had some rainwater in it. She led Booboo over to it and hopped down.

Untying her kit, she unwrapped the contents from the blanket, set the items aside for the moment, and laid the blanket out on the driveway. Sitting on it, she got a couple of biscuits out of her lunch box. Nibbling on one, she pulled the digital tape recorder out of the same box and eyed it. She’d never seen one before and Liam had to show her how to use it.

Finishing the biscuits, she washed them down with water from her canteen. She wanted to go inside and take a nap, but she knew one of those cops was in there, hiding. So, she stretched out on the blanket and closed her eyes.

She dozed off, although she didn't know for how long. It didn't matter though. Her dog's soft growling immediately awakened her. She sat up and saw a man down the road riding a horse. She knew instantly it was King Rat. She gave a wave before quickly grabbing the digital recorder, pushed the little red button, and hid it under the blanket with only the little part where the microphone was located sticking out. A minute later, King Rat ambled up and stopped beside her. He looked around and then stared pointedly.

"What're you doing, girl?" he asked.

"Just relaxing. What're you doing?" Mal answered.

"I came to see you two. Y'all weren't here the last time I came by. Where've you been?"

"I've been staying with some people who live up north of here a little ways."

King Rat eyed her and looked around again. "Where's your daddy? He inside?"

"Naw, he got himself kilt."

His eyes narrowed. "Killed? Who killed him?"

"A man by the name of Melvin. We was trying to ambush him, but he got the better of Daddy."

King Rat stared a moment, probably wondering if she were kidding, then smirked. "Well, sucks to be him, don't it. What'd you do with his body?"

"I set it on fire."

King Rat frowned, but then gave a thoughtful nod. "Good idea, I suppose." He dismounted and dropped the reins to his horse, who promptly walked over to Booboo and began eating grass. He continued looking around before stretching and focusing on Mal.

"You've put on a little weight since the last time I visited. You must be eating good."

"Yeah, they have good food. They have hot showers too. You ever taken a hot shower?"

King Rat narrowed his eyes in suspicion. "Where did you say you were staying at?"

"It's a place called Mount Weather."

He kept staring and after a moment gestured at the house. "Why'd you come back then? Are you alone?"

"Me, Booboo, and Gumby. Why?"

"So, you're all alone out here," he said. "Why'd you come back?"

"I was getting antsy and thought I'd go on a morning ride. I ended up here."

"That's a fair distance to ride on a horse. You aren't scared of the monsters getting you?" he asked.

"I reckon I can outrun 'em on Booboo. Why're you here?"

"Well, like I said, I thought I'd come visit. Plus, I need to get paid for that gun and ammo I gave you two. Where is it?"

"The people at Mount Weather took it. They said it belonged to them and it was stolen," Mal said.

King Rat's expression turned hard. "That's unfortunate."

He continued giving Mal a hard stare for a moment and once again looked around. "So, you're out here all alone, huh?"

He didn't wait for an answer. He walked closer to Mal and squatted beside her. Staring, he reached out and ran his fingers through her hair before leaning closer and sniffing her.

"You got your hair cut and smell a lot better than you usually do. King Rat approves. Why don't you pull those britches off, and we can have a little go around?"

"You're wanting to diddle me?" Mal asked, causing King Rat to chuckle.

"You always say some of the stupidest things. Of course I want to diddle you. What else is there to do around here? So, take those damn clothes off."

Mal stared a moment before pulling off her shirt, exposing her small breasts. She watched King Rat staring hungrily at her.

"Ain't you gonna get undressed?" she asked. He responded by standing and taking off his hat, dropping it on the corner of the blanket where the recorder was hidden. Mal kept her face impassive, but inside she wondered if the recorder could still work with his hat on top of it. Even though she was concerned, she stuck with the plan.

"I have a question though. The people I've been staying with said you raped a girl and killed her over in some settlement not too far from here."

King Rat scoffed. "Rape hell, that bitch was begging for it." He leered as he continued undressing. "You know, I'm going to let you in on a little secret. Back when you were still a little wormy-looking girl, you and your daddy used to live there."

Mal acted like this was news to her and gave a confused frown. "Where?"

"The same place I'm living now," he said.

"We did?"

"Yep, but your daddy was a piece of shit who kept stealing from everyone, me included, so he was kicked out. You were supposed to stay with us, but he took you with him. I found you two one day, out here, starving to death. I've been helping you out ever since."

"Why?" Mal asked.

"Because your daddy's my cousin. Now I know you're too stupid to understand, but technically, that makes you my first cousin once removed. And to think, I've been putting it to you ever since you've been growing hair down there," he said and chortled.

Mal stared at him with growing antipathy. She'd told Reese about this man and Reese made her realize King Rat was no friend. She did not know what incest was all about, but she intuitively knew there was something evil about the man. She kept talking.

"So, you admit you diddled her."

King Rat chuckled. "Why, you jealous? You don't think you're the only piece of tail King Rat has at his beck and call, do you?"

"But you killed her," Mal rejoined.

King Rat scoffed. "Yeah, I put my hands around her neck and squeezed the life out of her. The bitch started going crazy on me. No respect whatsoever. You start going crazy I'll do the same to you. Now, get those pants off."

"Okay," Mal said, and then raised both her arms, as if she was stretching.

Logan exited the house as Mal was removing her pants. He briefly noticed she wasn't wearing panties before focusing on King Rat, who was now wearing nothing more than socks, an erection, and a surprised expression.

"Hello, King Rat, or should I say, hello, Drill Bit," Logan said.

Drill Bit continued staring in surprise. He glanced down at Mal and then back up at Logan. It only took him a few seconds to understand the dynamic. Mal had elicited a confession out of him, and he knew that Logan had heard it.

"Well, not only have you caught me with my pants down, but you've also convinced the love of my life to betray me," he said and then gazed sadly at Mal. He intentionally kept his eyes off his handgun, which was sitting under his pants. "You're going to regret doing that."

"The only thing I regret is ever knowing you," Mal said.

Drill Bit gave a slow nod of his head and then faced Logan.

"So, what now?" he asked.

"You are hereby under arrest for the rape and murder of Jane Wilson," Logan said. "You'll be taken back to Mount Weather whereupon you will stand trial."

Drill Bit stared for a moment and then burst out laughing. He laughed long and hard. "Do you think anyone will actually believe this bullshit?" He pointed at Mal. "It's my word against hers and I don't think you heard things correctly."

"You said you raped and strangled her," Mal said.

Drill Bit laughed and shook his head. "She's so stupid nobody will ever believe her." He laughed some more. "It's her word against mine. Don't think for a moment that I'm some ignorant hillbilly. If I'm going to be tried in a legitimate court of law, this case will be thrown out immediately."

"There is other proof," Logan said.

"Like what?" Drill Bit asked.

"The fact that you disappeared without even going to the funerals."

"I couldn't go, I was overcome with grief," Drill Bit said and winked.

"There's one other thing," Mal said.

Drill Bit turned to her and saw a small rectangular box in her hand. It was a satin silver color and appeared to be plastic. His mind refused to identify it, but his demeanor darkened.

"What've you got there, Mal?" he asked.

"It's a digital recorder," Logan answered. "Back when I was a cop, we used them on occasion. Is it still recording, Mal?"

Mal glanced at it. "Yep, it sure is."

Drill Bit understood now. It was no longer her word against his. She got him to admit to it and recorded it. He'd been duped. Mal was stupid but she'd set him up good. Sweat broke out on his brow. He furtively glanced at Logan's sidearm. It was still secured in its holster.

He lunged at Mal in an attempt to get the recorder away from her. Mal was quicker than he thought, she deftly rolled away from him. When he tried to get to her again, Logan knocked him to the ground with a hard right cross.

Drill Bit was addled, but only for a moment. He sat up and rubbed on his chin.

"Nice one," he said.

"Thank you," Logan replied.

"So, you're going to arrest me, huh?"

"Yes, I am," Logan said.

Drill Bit seemed to mull it over before speaking. "Okay, you got me. At least let me put my clothes back on."

"Certainly," Logan said.

Drill Bit acted casually as he reached for his pants. Logan caught Mal's attention and motioned for her to move toward him. As soon as she had done so, Drill Bit straightened. He started to bring his gun up but never got a chance. A 5.56 caliber bullet caught him under his shoulder and knocked him to the ground.

He was gravely wounded, he'd be dead within a minute from trauma and blood loss, but for the moment he was still conscious. He tried to raise his handgun again, but Logan rushed toward him and deftly took the firearm out of Drill Bit's hand.

"Any last words?" Logan asked him.

Drill Bit struggled to say something, but all that came out of his mouth was blood and spittle. After several seconds, he emitted a gurgle and then stopped breathing. Mal walked up and stared at him.

"He thought he was going to kill you, didn't he?" she asked.

"Yep."

"Who shot him, Lynn?"

"Liam, his name is Liam," Logan said. "Yeah, he shot him."

Logan pointed toward the location Liam was hiding, which was about fifty yards away in the open garage of another house down the street. After a moment, Liam emerged and walked toward them.

"He's a pretty good shot," Mal said.

"Yep, he always has been," he said with a bit of brotherly pride. He then looked at her. "Would you do me a favor and put your clothes back on?"

CHAPTER 56 – ZACH & THE FUNERAL

It was a beautiful morning. Fictional books were always full of silly tropes when it came to funerals. Bad weather, mysterious people showing up, somebody causing a scene. Nothing like that with Kelly's funeral. Great weather. High seventies. Sunny. A gentle breeze coming in from the east. Everybody was on their best behavior. Kelly would've loved it.

The funeral was delayed a couple of days so I could heal up a little bit. I still looked like hell though. We didn't have a mortician, nor any embalming materials. So, the casket was sealed shut. We had pictures though. Not photographs. Jpegs were projected onto the wall behind the casket. Ironically, these days, it was easier to use a computer and a projector than it was to develop photographs.

With the exception of the assigned guards, everyone was present for the service. People from all around came. Oak Ridge, Marcus Hook, everybody. Not surprising. Kelly was loved. She had no enemies. One could even say Jonesy liked her. He wasn't intentionally trying to kill her. She wasn't his enemy. I was.

It was like I was in a daze as I watched the pictures segue from one to another. There were dozens. The last one was a closeup portrait of her, her long dark hair flowing around her face, and her left hand caressing her cheek. Her ring finger had the big diamond ring I'd given her so long ago. Nobody knew it, but I'd got it off a zed I'd killed. An infected bride. She was still in her wedding dress. I cut her finger off to get it. How long ago was that? Seven years? It seemed like an eternity.

Kelly found me after I had escaped my imprisonment. After the massacre. She was the only survivor. Well, Fred had survived too, but we didn't know it at the time. We'd gotten drunk one night and made love in front of a crackling fire. I'd recited a poem to her later from memory. Upon the hearth the fire is red, beneath the roof there is a bed. That's how it started. It was a Tolkien poem. It wasn't about making love, and we were on the floor, but close enough.

I was sitting in the front row of the auditorium. Stoic, somber, squared shoulders, hiding the pain I felt deep inside. Those who had not reached out to me before to offer their condolences were doing so now. I played the game. I stared solemnly at each person and thanked them for their presence. In reality, I wanted to be far, far away from here.

Bob and Connie each spoke, giving homage to my beautiful wife. I had originally planned to as well, but I couldn't. I knew the words wouldn't come out. As the eulogies were given, my mind wandered into the past. I thought of Julie. I thought of Macie. I thought of how Kelly and I were thrown together and how much we'd been through. We clicked immediately and it worked for us. I couldn't remember a single heated argument between us. Can't say the same with Macie or Julie. Macie was my first love and she'd dumped me for another man. Julie and I had our moments. I loved both women, but not as much as I loved Kelly.

I went through the motions of a grieving husband who was gracious and thankful for all the kind words. It was over after an hour or three, I'm not sure. All I know is that Janet had guided me back to our suite, the kids clinging to me as if their lives depended on it.

"Do you need some alone time?" Janet asked. "I can take the kids out for a stroll."

"No, I think I want to be with them," I replied. Little Macie loudly agreed, declaring she wasn't going to go anywhere without me.

Janet said she understood, excused herself, and left. The four of us, and Zoe of course, were alone now. Macie cried some more, which caused Hardy to cry as well. We all ended up sprawled on the bed, each kid attached to a leg or arm and Zoe stretched out at the end of the bed. It wasn't long before they were sound asleep. Not me, even though I was fatigued, both from the recent attack and the deep grief I was experiencing, I couldn't sleep.

The memories of us started. The struggles, the good times, the birth of Hardy. I looked down at him, he was snuggled up in the crook of my arm on my uninjured side. He looked like me, but he also had Kelly's features. He had her calm temperament too, which was nice. My other two kids took after Julie and me, and sometimes they could be hellions.

At some point I fell asleep. I dreamt of her. Kelly, that is. I didn't dream of Eve anymore, and I had not dreamt of anyone else in a long time. It was a deep but restless sleep. When I awoke, my biological clock told me it was well after midnight but before sunrise. Looking over at the clock confirmed it was almost four in the morning.

I eased out of bed and took a shower. Janet was asleep in Macie's bed. I woke her and told her I was going out and I'd be back later.

Walking down the hallway, I heard some people talking and hid until they exited the building. Nobody was yet in the cafeteria, not even the morning crew. Still too early for them. I went into the kitchen, found a tea kettle, and started boiling some water. I heard the swinging door open as I was steeping some oolong and looked up. It was Bailey from South Mountain.

"I didn't know you were here," I said.

"We came for the funeral," she replied. "I didn't know what to say to you, and besides, you looked like you were in a fog."

"Yeah, I guess I was. Probably still am." I gestured toward a chair. "Come join me. Would you like some tea? This is oolong, but we have other varieties."

"Oolong is fine," she said and sat. "So, you couldn't sleep either?"

I shook my head. "I've slept enough for a while."

"Yeah, me too. I know it's the last thing on your mind but the attack on our people has really affected me."

"Yeah, I'm sure."

She stared at her cup of tea for a moment and then looked up. "Enough about me, how're you holding up? You've still got bruises."

"I'm sure they won't go away for a few more days. My ribs hurt like hell though. I'm okay with looking like hell, but these ribs need to heal up before I go nuts."

Bailey gave me a small sympathetic smile. "How are you mentally?"

I shrugged. "I'm not sure yet. When my first wife died, I was deeply depressed. Kelly helped me through it, and we eventually ended up together. We never officially married, but I considered her my wife. Honestly, I'm not sure how I'm going to be with her gone. I've just got to keep on keeping on, like Bob Dylan said."

Bailey furrowed her brow a moment. "Wait, I know that song. Tangled Up in Blue, right?"

I almost smiled. "That's the one. When it all went bad, I hunkered down with a good friend on a rural farm down in Tennessee. He was an old Vietnam vet who loved that era of music. It's all we ever listened to."

She smiled again. "Same with my parents. My grandfather prefers country music."

I thought of Fred. He liked his country music as well. The old stuff. He and the General would probably get along pretty good.

We sat in silence now. When she finished her cup, she set it down gently and stood.

"I'm going to wake up my grandfather and head back home. I'm sorry for your loss, Zach. When you're able, you should come visit." She then gently squeezed my shoulder and walked out.

It was a nice gesture for someone who hardly knew me. A part of me wondered if there was something more to it, but I dismissed it, poured myself a second cup, and walked out. I guess I spent the next hour aimlessly wandering around. Normally, I'd be inspecting, surveying, making mental notes of what needed to be repaired or maintained. This morning, all I did was wonder how life was going to be without Kelly.

CHAPTER 57 – SAMMY & NIKKI

"Are you two sure about this?" Rachel asked.

Sammy swapped a glance with Nikki before speaking. "As sure as I've ever been about anything."

"But what about your child?" Rachel asked.

"She's not my child. Serena admitted it last night," he said. "Oh, and she's pregnant again."

"Oh, my God, really?" Rachel asked. Sammy nodded. "Oh, honey, I'm so sorry."

Rachel wanted to say more. She wanted to ask Sammy if he was sure he could so easily break off the bond he'd formed with the little girl he thought was his but opted to remain quiet. She was reminded of an aunt who was always a busybody, causing strife at every opportunity. Rachel didn't want to be known as that type of person.

Sammy stared at the floor a moment before making eye contact. "Thanks. Anyway, I don't want to dwell on it. I'm moving on."

Rachel nodded and impulsively gave him a tight hug. She then hugged Nikki before walking the two of them to the door.

They found Fred in the barn. He'd already put their horses in the trailer and hooked it up to Nikki's truck.

"Thanks, Fred," Nikki said. Sammy nodded in agreement.

"That item is in a bag on the front seat," Fred said. "I had a chat with Grace. She took a look at the weather satellite and said there's a low-pressure system moving up from the delta. It'll probably be here in about four days. That'll give you two plenty of time to do your little payback before we have a few days of heavy rain."

"Good, we'll make it work," Sammy said.

Fred appraised them in silence. After a moment, he decided that these two needed to do it themselves, without his assistance or intervention.

"So, where to then?" he asked.

"Oak Ridge first, and then we thought we might travel along the east coast. We'll probably be back before Christmas," Sammy said.

"We don't have a set schedule," Nikki added.

"Alright, I guess this is it then," Fred said and held out his fist. Sammy gave him a fist bump but then couldn't help himself. He grabbed up Fred and gave him a tight hug. Nikki immediately joined in. After a long moment and a few slaps on the back, they separated.

"I guess you two should get going then," Fred said.

The two of them jumped in the truck and headed out. It only took them forty minutes to reach their first destination and another hour to set up the contraption that Fred had rigged up for them. After, they went back to the truck and tended to the horses before putting them back in the trailer for the evening.

"What time do you think we should be set up?" Sammy asked.

"He's an early riser, so, at least an hour before sunup," Nikki replied.

They killed the fire after dinner and crawled into the camper. There was no lovemaking tonight. That was last night. Tonight, they were taking turns between sleeping and keeping watch. At zero-four hundred hours, they got up and ate a cold breakfast before saddling up and heading to their prearranged location.

BC and Collin came into view on the old logging road riding a wagon hitched to two mules named Buffy and Molly. The weatherworn and rickety wagon could've been a prop in a Western movie. The mules were almost as old as the wagon, but Nikki knew they were stalwarts. They were the only reason BC and Collin were going to live. At least, for now.

As they passed by the posts which once held a gate, the world around them exploded. It wasn't C4 or some other lethal explosive, it was a glitter bomb, one that Fred had rigged up. Sammy, who was hiding behind a tree fifty meters behind them, stifled a laugh. Their backs were to him, so their facial expressions were hidden, but he definitely heard Collin shriek like a little girl.

BC had dived off of the wagon and came up with a pistol in hand. Collin sat on the wagon seat, stunned. Something was in BC's eyes. He dabbed at his face with his free hand and came away with it bloody. Looking down, he saw where his head had smacked against a rock. He straightened and looked over at his son.

"Are you okay?"

Collin, who was still sitting on the wagon, looked down and then looked at his father.

"I've pissed myself," he said.

BC stared at him with disgust. "Get off the damn wagon and check on the damn mules."

He grabbed a soiled rag out of the back of the wagon and held it up to his head while he walked over to the origin of the explosion. It only took him a couple of seconds to recognize what it was, and the manner in which it had been rigged meant it was specifically rigged up for them.

He held the rag against his head and continued staring at the remains of the booby trap when he saw a rider on horseback walking up. BC narrowed his eyes and soon he recognized the rider.

"Nikki?"

After a minute, Nikki stopped Leeroy a dozen feet away and stared at BC.

"You two never saw it until it exploded. Is that how you expected it to go with me?" she asked.

BC stared with incredulity. "Did you do this?"

"You totally missed the monofilament line. I didn't miss it when you strung it out and attached it to the hand grenade."

"What are you talking about?" BC demanded. He gestured around. "And why the hell did you do this?"

Nikki stared at BC for a couple of seconds. "You're a good liar, but not good enough."

BC's expression slowly changed from incredulity to acceptance. He glanced at his son. "Look at this bitch, would you? She actually thinks she can kill Colton and then call us out like we're nothing."

"Well, Barnabas, you have a gun in your hand. We're the only ones out here. Nobody will ever know what happened to me, except for you and your idiot son. What are you waiting for?" she asked.

BC's jaw dropped open when he realized she was challenging him to a gunfight. He lowered his free hand and dropped the rag.

"Do you really think you're scaring me?" he asked.

"The only thing that scares you is that you've been caught trying to commit murder. You failed at it, but I'm giving you a second chance."

BC gave her a cold smile through his thick beard. "I've got to admit, you're tougher than most people give you credit for. I could easily shoot you off that horse, you know."

"Maybe. Or maybe before you're able to do it, I can draw my gun and put a bullet in that black heart of yours," Nikki replied.

BC continued giving her a baleful stare for several seconds before looking around.

"No, something isn't right," he said. He looked around again. "You've got someone watching over you. I'm betting I'm in someone's crosshairs right now."

Nikki wanted a confrontation so she could kill the man. Collin too, if he tried anything. But it didn't look like it was going to happen. BC stared down at his handgun before slowly putting it back in his holster. He gave her a baleful stare before turning his back to her and got back on the wagon. Motioning for his son to do the same, he snapped the reins. The mules took off at a slow pace.

Nikki continued watching them long after they'd ridden out of sight. Eventually, she nudged Leeroy and walked him over to where Sammy was hidden.

"I'm kind of surprised you didn't kill him outright," he said.

"Yeah, I thought about it, Lord knows I thought about it, but this way he knows I'm not a murderer," Nikki said and then smirked. "Besides, now he'll have to live with the fact that I made him back down. With his ego, that's going to drive him nuts."

Sammy chuckled. "What do you say we head back to the truck and get out of here?"

"Yeah, lets. Hop on."

JOURNAL ENTRY: SEPTEMBER 1ST, 10 A.Z.

It has been a long summer. Hotter than normal. We've had many significant events happen over the past three months. I'll try to summarize them.

- On July 4th, we had our customary party. Everyone enjoyed themselves. Not a care in the world. Everyone seemed happy.
- On July 6th, the South Mountain survivor settlement was attacked by zeds. Our QRF responded and rescued them, but only a dozen of them survived. These zeds showed some evidence of muscle regeneration. Some of them fled. That's not usual behavior for a zed. It's believed they realized the QRF soldiers were wiping them out. Fred tracked them back to Fort Detrick. We later went to Fort Detrick, but it had been abandoned by the zeds. More on that in a moment.
- We have created a new waystation in Stephens City, which is about 30 miles from Mount Weather. It's designed to be a safe stopover for weary travelers. We have more planned, but it's a slow process.
- Project Asphalt has been completed. We now have two lanes of Interstate 70 free of potholes and washouts. It's not pristinely smooth, only a complete resurfacing would make it like new, but it's good enough for a fully loaded truck to travel at forty miles per hour.
- Project Tire has been completed, with mixed results. We were able to manufacture five hundred tires. However, we were only able to produce one size and have depleted some of the materials needed for production. Even so, we are counting it as a success. Our next project is to possibly go to a tire manufacturing plant that produced truck tires. It will be a huge undertaking, but Dimitri believes he can accomplish it.
- On July 23rd, we launched an attack on the zeds in DC. We called it Operation Eradicate DC. We killed over four thousand zeds. Where did they all come from, why were they still alive, and how were they surviving? We're still examining and analyzing, but honestly, my heart's not into

finding those answers. It simply is. There are zeds. We kill them and kill them and yet we can't seem to eliminate all of them. How many of them are up in Canada? How many of them are in the rest of the U.S.? How many of them are on other continents? I don't know the answer and at the moment I don't think the answer matters. What matters is if we can't find a way to manufacture new ammo, we're going to be fighting them with swords, spears, bows, arrows, rocks, and sticks.

- We thought we had a gang of marauders operating in our bailiwick, but it turned out to be one man who called himself King Rat. He lived in the Shenandoah community, and it seemed nobody was aware of his actions. He'd committed a few crimes, including rape and murder. The O'Malley brothers attempted to arrest him. He resisted and was killed. I say good riddance, but the only negative to this is we were unable to properly interrogate him and learn of any other evil things he'd done.
- In more bad news, during the second week of August, the satellites picked up a wildfire raging across the southern half of Nebraska. It was massive, and the air hung with hazy smoke for several weeks. As a result, we're not going to have a bumper crop this year. Also, there was a survivor settlement near North Platte. We've had regular radio contact with them, but since the wildfires, there's been nothing but radio static.
- And now, there is one more thing I'd like to enter into this, my personal journal. In two months, it will be eleven years since the world as we knew it ended. In the preceding years, I've had three wonderful children. Two of them, Frederick and Macie, were from Julie. My third child, Hardy, is the son of Kelly. I lost Julie in the second year of the apocalypse and Kelly had been with me ever since. And now, she's gone. Murdered by a despicable piece of trash by the name of Parmelee Jones. I was the target of his attack, but she intervened, saving my life, and losing her own. Our unborn child died with her. I cannot put into words the sense of loss I'm feeling and how depressed I am.

EPILOGUE

I couldn't sleep. Looking back, I always complained how much space Kelly seemed to take up when we were in bed. She liked to either snuggle up to me as closely as possible or assume her second favorite sleeping position which I called the starfish. Now, the bed seemed empty.

I got up and checked on the kids. They were in their own beds, sleeping soundly. Seeing them gave me a small amount of comfort. It took over a week before they were emotionally able to sleep in their own beds after Kelly's death.

Getting my laptop, I fluffed the pillows up, got myself comfortable, and logged in. I checked emails, looked at a few files, and then remembered the video that was recorded of Operation Eradicate DC. I should have viewed it weeks ago, but like I said, I've not been myself lately. Everybody noticed, but if anyone tried to talk to me about it, I shut them down. It was something only I could work through.

I hit the play button and watched with only a modicum of interest. The video started with the assault team leaving the main gate and making the journey to DC. I watched halfheartedly as they traveled along the roads. Eventually they turned onto Dulles Access Road, the road where Team Joker got stranded and surrounded. As they began engaging with and killing zeds, something caught my eye.

I froze the video and slowly jogged the recording backwards. It took me a moment to spot it, and perhaps another moment before I realized what I was seeing. There, standing on the top of a retaining wall on the westbound side of Dulles Access Road was Eve. She appeared to be dressed in clean clothing, and she was staring directly at the camera as the vehicle it was mounted on drove by. It wasn't accidental. I played the video multiple times and there was no mistake. She was staring directly at the camera. She knew it was there, she knew what it was, and she knew that I would eventually see the recording.

"Everyone thinks we've killed all of you, right? They don't know the truth, do they?" I murmured.

The End

CHECK OUT OTHER GREAT ZOMBIE NOVELS

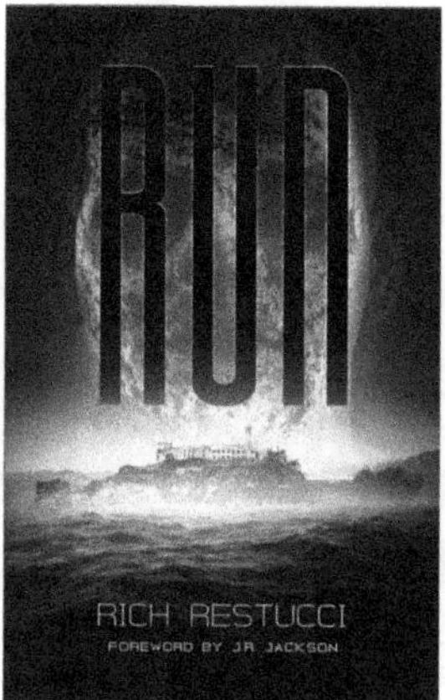

RUN
by Rich Restucci

The dead have risen, and they are hungry.

Slow and plodding, they are Legion. The undead hunt the living. Stop and they will catch you. Hide and they will find you. If you have a heartbeat you do the only thing you can: You run.

Survivors escape to an island stronghold: A cop and his daughter, a computer nerd, a garbage man with a piece of rebar, and an escapee from a mental hospital with a life-saving secret. After reaching Alcatraz, the ever expanding group of survivors realize that the infected are not the only threat.

Caught between the viciousness of the undead, and the heartlessness of the living, what choice is there? Run.

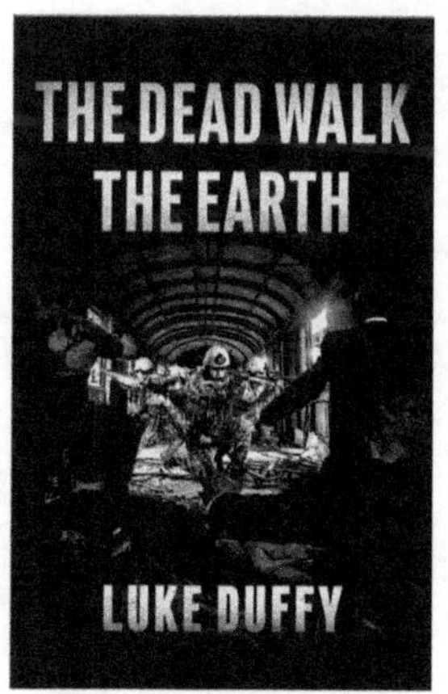

THE DEAD WALK THE EARTH
by Luke Duffy

As the flames of war threaten to engulf the globe, a new threat emerges.

A 'deadly flu', the like of which no one has ever seen or imagined, relentlessly spreads, gripping the world by the throat and slowly squeezing the life from humanity.

Eight soldiers, accustomed to operating below the radar, carrying out the dirty work of a modern democracy, become trapped within the carnage of a new and terrifying world.

Deniable and completely expendable. That is how their government considers them, and as the dead begin to walk, Stan and his men must fight to survive.

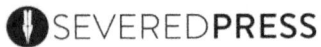

CHECK OUT OTHER GREAT ZOMBIE NOVELS

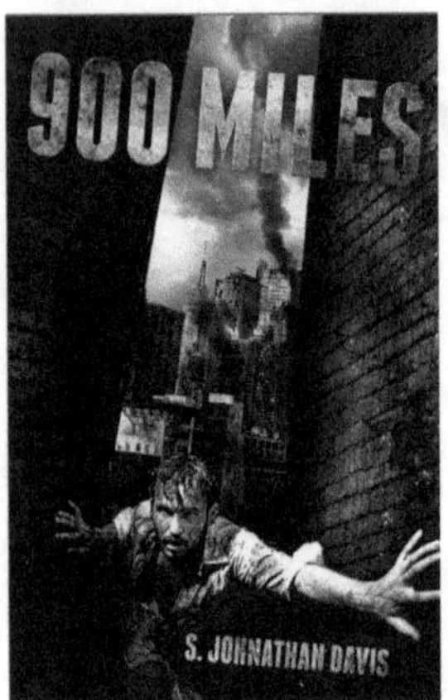

900 MILES
by S. Johnathan Davis

John is a killer, but that wasn't his day job before the Apocalypse.

In a harrowing 900 mile race against time to get to his wife just as the dead begin to rise, John, a business man trapped in New York, soon learns that the zombies are the least of his worries, as he sees first-hand the horror of what man is capable of with no rules, no consequences and death at every turn.

Teaming up with an ex-army pilot named Kyle, they escape New York only to stumble across a man who says that he has the key to a rumored underground stronghold called Avalon..... Will they find safety? Will they make it to Johns wife before it's too late?

Get ready to follow John and Kyle in this fast paced thriller that mixes zombie horror with gladiator style arena action!

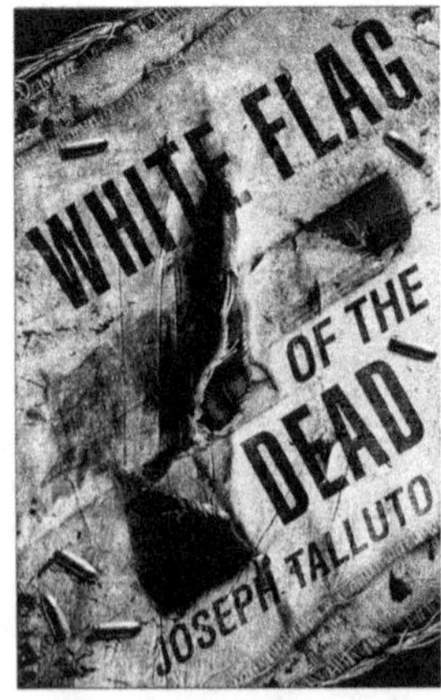

WHITE FLAG OF THE DEAD
by Joseph Talluto

Millions died when the Enillo Virus swept the earth. Millions more were lost when the victims of the plague refused to stay dead, instead rising to slaughter and feed on those left alive. For survivors like John Talon and his son Jake, they are faced with a choice: Do they submit to the dead, raising the white flag of surrender? Or do they find the will to fight, to try and hang on to the last shreds or humanity?

facebook.com/severedpress
twitter.com/severedpress

CHECK OUT OTHER GREAT ZOMBIE NOVELS

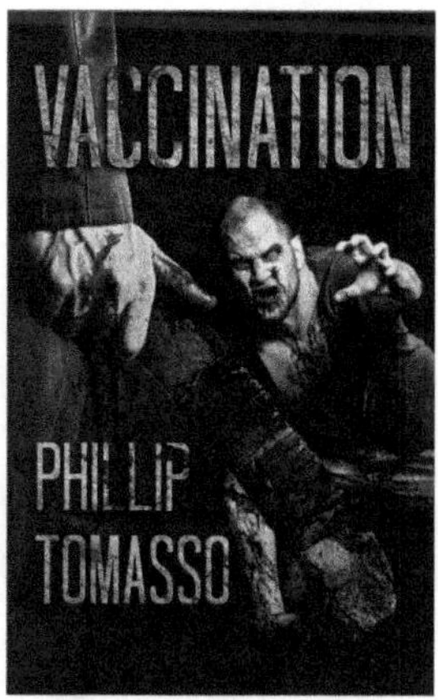

VACCINATION
by Phillip Tomasso

What if the H7N9 vaccination wasn't just a preventative measure against swine flu?
It seemed like the flu came out of nowhere and yet, in no time at all the government manufactured a vaccination. Were lab workers diligent, or could the virus itself have been man-made?
Chase McKinney works as a dispatcher at 9-1-1. Taking emergency calls, it becomes immediately obvious that the entire city is infected with the walking dead. His first goal is to reach and save his two children.
Could the walls built by the U.S.A. to keep out illegal aliens, and the fact the Mexican government could not afford to vaccinate their citizens against the flu, make the southern border the only plausible destination for safety?

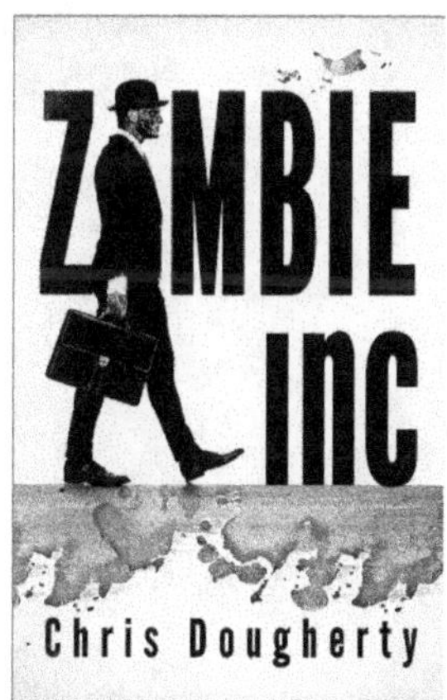

ZOMBIE, INC
by Chris Dougherty

"WELCOME! To Zombie, Inc. The United Five State Republic's leading manufacturer of zombie defense systems! In business since 2027, Zombie, Inc. puts YOU first. YOUR safety is our MAIN GOAL! Our many home defense options - from Ze Fence® to Ze Popper® to Ze Shed® - fit every need and every budget. Use Scan Code "TELL ME MORE!" for your FREE, in-home*, no obligation consultation! *Schedule your appointment with the confidence that you will NEVER HAVE TO LEAVE YOUR HOME! It isn't safe out there and we know it better than most! Our sales staff is FULLY TRAINED to handle any and all adversarial encounters with the living and the undead". Twenty-five years after the deadly plague, the United Five State Republic's most successful company, Zombie, Inc., is in trouble. Will a simple case of dwindling supply and lessening demand be the end of them or will Zombie, Inc. find a way, however unpalatable, to survive?

www.ingramcontent.com/pod-product-compliance
Lightning Source LLC
Chambersburg PA
CBHW071131200626
46817CB00018B/2677

* 9 7 8 1 9 2 3 1 6 5 2 8 1 *